INFERNO

A DCI JAMES HARDY THRILLER

JAY GILL

DCI James Hardy series

Knife & Death

Walk in the Park
(A short thriller)

Angels

Hard Truth

Inferno

A free bonus chapter is available for each book. For more information visit, www.jaygill.net

CHAPTER ONE

Friday, 14 August 2015

Helena Hardy scooped up her handbag and house keys and pressed the phone to her ear with her shoulder as she shut the front door and locked it. She waited for the number she'd called to go to voicemail.

"It's me, again. That crazy-hot woman you share a bed with. This is a reminder, Detective Chief Inspector James Hardy, that it's date night tonight. I haven't booked a table because I know you're busy, so you'll probably be late, and I don't want to sit in a restaurant alone looking embarrassed. That's not a dig about our last date, I promise." Helena chuckled. "Anyway, Alice and Faith will be at your parents' house, and I'll be cooking your favourite. I also have something very special planned for dessert, if you know what I mean. James, I promise – you won't want to miss it." She chuckled again. "Text me, darling, when you get a chance. Let me know you got this message and what time you'll be home. I'll be waiting."

Helena's face was full of smiles as she tucked her

phone into her handbag. She thought how funny it would be if James played the voicemail back on loudspeaker in the office. She could imagine him fumbling around, frantically trying to mute it.

Right now, though, Helena needed to get a few ingredients for their romantic meal. It was a short distance to the shops, and for the first time in a couple of days it wasn't raining. She looked at her car and was tempted to drive but decided it would be good to walk, get some exercise. She glanced over the roof of the car and noticed a man across the street. He was wearing a dark-blue or black hoodie and pretending not to watch her. As she watched him, he looked away and started walking. He was talking to himself and scratching his right arm.

Helena watched as the man fleetingly glanced back at her before he picked up his pace. She sighed. It would take longer, but she decided to turn around and walk the other way around the block to the shops. She shouldered her handbag and set off. Before turning the corner at the end of the road she looked back over her shoulder. The man was gone.

She had just rounded the corner when she realised she'd forgotten the list of ingredients for her special meal with James. "You idiot, Helena Hardy," she muttered to herself as she searched pointlessly through her handbag. She could picture exactly where she'd left it – right on the worktop beside her pen. For a moment she considered carrying on without it; she felt sure she could remember most of it. But after running through the list in her mind and knowing she'd come up short, she decided to go back. After all, she was only a few hundred yards from home.

As she approached the house, she unzipped her handbag and reached inside for her house keys. She rooted around for the keys and looked down into the bag.

"Gotcha," she murmured. As she looked up, she sensed someone approaching from behind. Out of the corner of her eye she saw a figure moving between the parked cars at the side of the road.

Helena spun around and, in an instant, the man in the hoodie was in front of her. Her hand shot into her handbag for her pepper spray, but she felt the bag being pulled away. She tugged back, then thought better of it.

"Take the bag," said Helena. She shrugged the strap off her shoulder and released the bag from her grip. He snatched it away from her.

"Helena Hardy?" said the man.

"How do you know my name?" Helena edged away, moving carefully along the pavement and closer to the house. He looked in a bad way. Sores on his face and sunken eyes suggested he was on something. She spoke slowly and clearly. "Just take the bag and go. I don't care about the bag. There's money in it. It's yours. Okay?"

The man matched her step for step. "You're the copper's wife, aren't you?"

"Yes. My husband is a policeman. That doesn't matter. There's money in the bag. I'm not worried about the money – take it," repeated Helena. She glanced over her shoulder; she wasn't far from the house. She felt the house keys in her hand. She wanted to run and hoped he'd turn and run in the opposite direction, but, instead, he kept coming.

Helena inched backward, and the man reached into the pocket of his hoodie. Her heart, which was already pounding in her chest, went up a gear as she saw the dull metal blade of a knife appear in his hand. She had to act first. This was no time for self-doubt.

Helena screamed and yelled at the top of her lungs. As the hooded man turned to look around, Helena took two strides forward and hit him in the face with a palm strike, just the way she'd been taught by James and at her self-defence classes. As he staggered back, stunned, she reached in and clawed at his face and eyes before following through with a kick. She'd hoped to hit between his legs, but he blocked her by twisting his body. Even so, his leg buckled and he crumpled to his knees.

Helena took her chance to run. As she ran, she fumbled with the keys, desperately trying to find the one for the front door. Just as she found it, the bunch of keys slipped from her hand and fell to the pavement. She looked over her shoulder and could see that the hooded man was back on his feet and bearing down on her. With a sob of frustration and fear, Helena made a grab for the keys but missed them. Then her hair was yanked up and back, bringing her face to face with him.

Helena gasped as he plunged the knife into her stomach. She stared at him wide-eyed and open-mouthed as he pulled the knife out partway and then plunged it once again deep into her belly. Then he did it again and again and again.

Finally, he pulled out the blade and released his grip on her hair. Her legs buckled, and she collapsed onto the pavement.

He knelt beside her and looked at her. "That's a message for your copper husband, bitch. He needs to back off. Got it? *Back off.*"

He looked up, startled, at the sound of shouts from across the street. He stuffed the knife back in his pocket, leapt to his feet and ran, grabbing Helena's handbag as he went.

A woman appeared beside her, breathless, she crouched down. "Helena, it's me, Karen, from next door.

Don't worry, love. An ambulance is on its way. The police too. Don't try to move."

"Call James," said Helena. "Karen, please, call him. You have his number."

Pointing to an elderly male neighbour, Karen said, "Keep talking to her. I'm going to call her husband." Karen took off her jumper and placed it under Helena's head. "I'll be right back. I promise. You just stay strong. Don't close your eyes. He'll be here before you know it."

"Thank you," said Helena. The elderly man knelt beside her and she closed her eyes. She could picture Karen phoning James's mobile, the call going to voicemail the way it had done for her. She hoped Karen didn't waste time leaving a message but instead dialled the landline number she had for him. *It's my turn to ruin date night,* thought Helena. She lifted a hand from the wound and looked at the blood. *I'm not going to be able to do the school run and nursery run.* Her mind ran through a list of standby mums. Then she remembered that James's mum, Nana Hardy, was picking them up. *That's good. I don't want Alice and little Faith worrying.*

Helena focused on waiting for James, her soulmate, her best friend. She knew he'd come. He'd help her; he'd sort this out.

Over the hum of the gathered crowd, she finally heard James's voice. At first she thought she'd imagined it, then she saw his face. *My handsome husband,* she thought. *James looks scared. Don't worry, my love. It'll all be okay. I just need to close my eyes for a bit. I'm tired. I just need to rest.*

CHAPTER TWO

Monday, 29 July 2019

Governor Lloyd Trent stepped into the cell and looked down at the prisoner, who lay on his side clutching his stomach and moaning. Staff had informed him that the bouts of pain had become more frequent, and Trent knew he was duty-bound to ensure the prisoner received proper medical attention. That said, he intended to postpone that decision for as long as he could.

Trent knew all there was to know about the piece of shit in front of him. His name was Edward Fischer, though at the time of his arrest he'd been going by the last name Richter, his mother's maiden name. Seems he thought it had a nice ironic ring to it, what with Richter meaning *judge* in German. His parents were both from Hamburg, Germany, and the family had moved to England when he was four years old; his parents had divorced when he was eight. He had grown up with his mother, Christa, on the poor estates of London. She had never remarried. Died from lung cancer when Edward was nineteen.

The path that had led Fischer to end up residing in Trent's maximum-security prison had started with petty crime at the age of eleven. Over the years, Fischer had moved up the criminal ladder, progressing to high-end burglary in the more affluent areas of London. And when that thrill had become too routine, it appeared he had turned his hand to serial murder.

Prison Officer Terry Farley filled the cell doorway, his eyes moving between Fischer and his boss.

"Give us a minute, will you, Farley," said Governor Trent. It wasn't a question.

Farley hesitated. "Sir? I …"

"I want a moment with the prisoner. Fischer knows better than to do anything stupid. We have an understanding, don't we, Fischer?"

Fischer slowly moved his legs around and sat up with his back against the cell wall. His face contorted with pain, his hands gripping his emaciated stomach. "Yes, sir."

"I'll be right outside, sir," said Farley.

Governor Trent turned to the chair by the desk and sat down opposite Fischer. The usually toned and muscular body of the prisoner had been replaced by a bony figure whose clothes hung off him. Unkempt and unshaven, he looked like he'd aged a good ten years. Trent displayed no concern.

"Why am I here, Fischer?"

Fischer tried to sit up straighter before speaking, the movement causing him to wince with pain. "I'm not right. I've been telling you lot for over a week now. I've got no appetite. When I do manage to eat something, I can't keep it down. And my stomach is getting worse. When I move, it feels like I've swallowed a bag of nails. It's excruciating."

"The doctor says he can't find anything wrong with you."

"I know. But look at me. Does it look like there's nothing wrong?" Fischer held out a skinny, tattooed arm.

Trent sucked his teeth and tilted his head, then leaned forward and spoke in a low, clear voice. "You're in my prison because you're a sick bastard who sliced up young women to the point where they had to be identified through dental records. Forensic evidence put you at the scene with two of the victims, yet you won't give the families of those poor young women the closure they deserve by admitting to the crimes. You still maintain your innocence."

"I *am* innocent. I was framed—"

"Let me finish," growled Trent. "You come into my prison and immediately kill three of my inmates. At great expense and inconvenience, I'm now forced to keep you away from the general population. My point is, if it was up to me, I'd leave you to die a slow, agonising death here in this cell. And while you were writhing around on the floor, I'd invite the families of your victims to come and watch while I piss on you. Do you understand?"

"I need tests. Proper hospital tests."

Trent got to his feet. He lifted his leg and put his foot on the hand Fischer held over his stomach. He pressed down. Fischer gritted his teeth and stifled the cry of pain, not wanting to give Trent the satisfaction.

Officer Farley appeared at the door. "Everything all right, sir?"

Trent removed his foot. His eyes fixed on Fischer, he said, "Yes. Yes. I'm trying to establish the extent of the problem."

Farley watched as Fischer doubled over. "Shall I get the doctor?"

"Yes. Get the doctor. Tell him to increase Fischer's

8

painkillers. If he's no better in a week, I'll review the situation and decide whether he should get an outside evaluation. We're not sending this piece of shit to hospital any sooner than need be. Understood?"

CHAPTER THREE

Afternoon walks across clifftops with Sandy – who spends most of her time nose down, tail in the air, searching for rabbits – are one of the great joys of our having moved to the coast. There's far more open space out here than in the city, and the opportunity to go outside and find time to reflect, while surrounded by incredible natural landscapes, is a real incentive to get out and about.

The car park, which was bare chalkstone where the grass had been worn away, was empty except for my car and a sports car, which was parked close to mine. *You've got the whole empty car park and you had to park so close?* I thought.

I opened the back of my car and Sandy knew what was next. She looked around, probably wondering if she could make a break for it. "Come on. Up you jump." She wasn't ready to leave; never is. "Come on, girl." Sandy looked at me then reluctantly did as requested. "Good, girl." I rubbed her over with her towel. She tried to lick my face. "Sorry to break it to you, but you stink. Time for another bath, I think." Sandy put her paw on my arm and tilted her head. "Sorry, no debating it."

As I rounded the car to get to the driver's side, the door of the sports car opened and prevented me opening mine. I stepped back to let the person out. Nobody got out.

I walked up to the open door and peered inside. A young woman in a cashmere sweater and short skirt smiled at me. She pointed a manicured finger towards the cliff edge.

"James!" came a voice ahead of me. "James, darling."

In front of the two cars, beside a fence separating the well-worn grassy path and the cliff edge, stood a woman. Her shoulder-length brown hair blew in the sea breeze. She pulled up the collar of her three-quarter-length camel coat against the chill breeze. She wore black jeans, low heels and sunglasses. She waved, then turned her back on me to look out to sea. I knew immediately who it was. I slammed the young woman's car door closed, almost catching her hand, and yanked open my own car door. I looked around for something I could use as protection. The only thing I could find was a ball-point pen. I tucked it in my pocket, told Sandy to sit tight, shut the door and strode over to the woman on the cliff.

"Kelly Lyle," I said. "Psychopath, sadist, narcissist, millionaire, and deceased."

Lyle chuckled. "You can be so cutting at times, James. You know I prefer to be called a *multi*-millionaire."

"What's to stop me arresting you right here and now, Lyle?"

"If you arrest me, I'll tell the world about our deal. Your glittering career will go up in flames – *poof!*" She made a flicking motion with one hand. "And every investigation you've ever worked on will be brought into question. More importantly, it means we won't be friends anymore, and I've got big things planned for us. It's all very exciting."

"Oh, cut the bullshit," I snapped. "Kelly Lyle, I'm taking you in. I am arresting you on suspicion of murder. You do not have to say anything, but it may harm your defence if you…"

Lyle put out her wrists. I grabbed her right arm and put it up behind her back.

"Do you have cuffs back at your car, James?" she said coquettishly. "If you're going to put cuffs on me, you kinky boy, we'd better have a safe word." Lyle pretended to think. "What about *Alice*? Yes, Alice is the perfect safe word. Don't you think?"

I stopped. I released her arm.

Lyle lifted her sunglasses and rested them on the top of her head, letting me see her eyes now. She looked at me sympathetically. "Please call me Kelly. A lady doesn't like to be called by her surname; it's unbecoming. I'm not one of your little subordinates back at New Scotland Yard. And anyway, I'd so hoped we could be friends. I've decided we simply got off on the wrong foot, and I'm here to make amends." Lyle pouted. "What's up, James? You look sad. Don't be sad."

Lyle looked me up and down, then stepped close. Her hand hovered close to my cheek, poised to stroke it. I grabbed her wrist and held it.

"Please, don't touch me," I said.

Before I could stop her, Lyle grabbed me and kissed me. She gripped me tightly and pressed herself against me.

I pushed her away. "What the hell are you doing?"

"I've been wanting to know how it felt. You don't disappoint. You're a good kisser, James. A little stiff, maybe, but that's to be expected. Given time, though, I know we'd make incredible lovers. I've given it a lot of thought." Lyle watched my anger rise. "From the very first day we met, in that little cottage, when we sat under the stars together and you held me – do you remember? I've only ever been trying to help you."

"Help me? How have you ever helped me?"

"You really are a tease, James. For a start, without me, you wouldn't know who killed your wife. Please don't tell me you're not immeasurably happier now that you know Richter – or Fischer, to call him by his proper name – is the man behind the murder of your beloved Helena?"

"You nearly killed my daughter. You kidnapped her, drugged her and put her in a water tank, where you left her to die. Is that what you call helping? Christ, why are we even having this conversation? It's insane. You're insane."

"Sticks and stones… You know what your problem is, James? You're so overly dramatic, serious, blinkered, inconsiderate and a little pig-headed. A typical man. You need to lighten up. I was never going to let Alice die. She and I became friends during our time together. She's like the daughter I never had. She's just like you, you know. Strong-willed little thing. A chip off the old block."

"What do you want?"

"Is that our foreplay over already, James? You're going to have to work on that if we're to be lovers."

Lyle put a finger to her face and made out she was thinking. "Tick-tock, tick-tock. What do I want? What do I want?… You know what I want. We made a deal. We've been thrust together, bound by a union of body, mind and spirit. This is the culmination. Can you feel it, James? It's very stimulating. My whole body tingles at the thought of our climax. What a thrill." Lyle tossed her head back and softly moaned. "Oh, James, James." She took my hand and placed it on her chest. "Our connection. We're locked together and it feels so… natural."

I pulled my hand away.

Lyle put on a face of disappointment.

"I'm leaving," I said.

"No, you're not," said Lyle.

"You're not capable of empathy, so all this about helping me is bullshit. You care about no one. You know that. I know that. You have no sense of compassion. So why all the theatrics?"

"I don't know. Fun? Excitement? Exhilaration? Creativity? Challenging myself? Challenging others? Take your pick. But don't be like that – I do care about you. I treasure our relationship. It's special. You're special to me."

"So why threaten me and my family?"

"Leverage. Killing is easy. I want Fischer dead. It's more fun for me these days if I can encourage someone whose moral code prevents them taking such action to do it for me. That someone is you. We're scratching each other's backs, that's all, James. Fischer's an itch. Let's scratch him out together."

"And if I don't follow through, Kelly? What? You'll kill me?"

"You already told me I lack empathy. So yes, reluctantly. I'll kill Alice and little Faith, Monica and unborn baby Hardy, and you. Probably Nana Hardy too. You I'll kill last because you get to watch the others die. Boo-hoo. But a deal is a deal. I gave you back Alice; you get to save your family in exchange for killing the man who sent that nasty little drug addict Tony Horn to murder the mother of your two beautiful daughters. Don't forget – Fischer also killed someone I loved dearly. Two birds, one stone. To me that sounds like the deal of a lifetime. Ta-dah! I give you the opportunity to kill him guilt-free."

"Guilt-free?" I asked.

"It's guilt-free because you have no choice. I'm gifting that to you because we're friends, soon to be lovers. We are friends, aren't we, James?"

"The answer is no. We're not friends, and I'm not killing him. Even if I wanted to kill him, which I don't, he's locked away in a maximum-security prison. Be satisfied with that." I turned and walked away.

Lyle called after me. "Don't worry about little details like prison. I'll make sure he's put in your crosshairs."

I kept walking and didn't look back.

"Bye, James. Nice butt. Love you, James. Don't test me. I will slaughter your family in a blink of an eye. Oh, and my sexy assistant in the car there took photos of our passionate clifftop embrace. I'm sure Monica would love to see how amazing we look together. Don't make me send them. You know how insecure pregnant women can be."

I looked inside the parked car and the young woman held up a camera with a telephoto lens. She was all smiles.

"Kill him, James," Lyle shouted. "Save your family. For both our sakes, I want him dead. You hear me? Dead."

CHAPTER FOUR

Father Somerset held out his trembling hand. He took a deep breath and stepped forward. Terry Farley looked him up and down. "Are you okay, Father?"

"Yes, thank you. A little nervous, I suppose." He tried to smile.

"Sorry to hear Father Jones is unwell. Is it anything serious?"

"No, no, he's just a little under the weather. Touch of the flu. It came on very suddenly. Occupational hazard. There's a lot of it about – flu, I mean. He has a large parish to cover, a large congregation. He will have picked it up on his rounds."

"Send him my regards."

"I'll be sure to do that. Thank you."

Farley started to walk and Father Somerset followed. The prison officer took long, purposeful strides, and Father Somerset had to work hard to keep up. "So, you're here to see Fischer today, Father. You sure you're ready for that?"

Father Somerset nodded and said, "Yes. I believe so." He swallowed hard and his stomach turned.

Farley looked around and appraised Father Somerset for a moment, then smiled. "I'm just kidding with you. You'll do fine. Don't let him get inside your head with his bullshit. Don't give him any personal details; given the chance, he'll use them against you. Personal and head. Remember that and you'll be all right."

Farley stopped at a set of doors and looked up at a security camera. The door buzzed open and while Farley held the door, Father Somerset shuffled past. "Wait there, please," said Farley, waving to a guard at the end of a long corridor. The guard waved back and Farley turned to look at Father Somerset. "Fischer gets very few visitors. Occasionally a lawyer, a reporter; sometimes a police detective. More recently, as you're likely aware, every two weeks he meets Father Jones. Fischer claims he's found God." Farley scoffed at the last part.

Father Somerset, who had been looking at the ground in contemplation, lifted his head and met Farley's eyes. "Every man should be offered the opportunity to save his soul. Even a man like Edward Fischer. The Lord will judge him."

Farley raised his eyebrows. "Tell that to his victims and their families. They want justice in this lifetime, not the next. Why you'd want to help save the soul of a man like him is beyond me. In my opinion, Fischer and men like him deserve to go straight to hell. No second chance. He's beyond saving."

"No one is beyond saving. We all sin, each one of us. Sometimes, what causes us to sin is beyond our comprehension. Those touched by the Devil's hand are unable to control the evil that resides within."

"Well, I guess you know what you're talking about. Sounds a little like a pardon for those that do evil, but if you want to try and save him from eternal damnation, good luck to you; I won't stand in your way."

"In God's eyes, everyone's worth saving. There are sins both large and small. It's simply the magnitude of the sin that must be atoned for."

Farley smiled unconvincingly. "I'm just playing with you, Father. I couldn't do this job and sleep at night if I didn't think there are some men in here that might change. I've seen plenty change their ways, and most found God at some point." He pointed to the end of the corridor where the other guard stood facing Fischer's cell. "Go down to the end, Father. Officer Nessie's waiting for you. You'll be fine."

The cells on the wing lined the left side of the corridor. Father Somerset took a deep breath and began the short walk to the last cell. He kept his head down as he walked past the cells, his eyes fixed on the ground. A wolf whistle from the one of the cells caused him to pick up the pace. When he reached Fischer's cell, a tall, skinny prison officer, a Scot whom everyone called Nessie, introduced himself. The Scot had an extraordinarily long, narrow head with a messy patch of greying hair perched on top, like a stork's nest atop a telephone pole.

Nessie pointed to the chair he'd placed just inside the door. He took Father Somerset's arm and spoke quietly to him. "Don't take any chances. If for any reason you feel uncomfortable, threatened or harassed, end the meeting. Remember everything you've been told. Nothing personal, and never let a prisoner get inside your head. You'll be fine." Nessie walked Father Somerset into the cell. He looked to Fischer and said, "Behave, Fischer. You know what happens if you don't."

"I'll be good. I promise. I don't want no trouble," said Fischer, putting on a cockney accent. He had been sitting on his bed reading *Hamlet*, but as soon as the priest entered, he put down the book and got to his feet, holding out a hand to Father Somerset to shake. But as he did, he buckled over, clawing at his stomach and wincing from pain. "Look at me, Nessie, I'm sick," he said through gritted teeth. "I'm dying in front of your eyes and you fuckers are doing nothing. The governor knows how much pain I'm in and he's doing nothing. This is inhumane. I need proper tests."

"I'm working on it," said Nessie.

Fischer managed to straighten up. "Well, hurry." He turned his attention to Father Somerset and said, "In the absence of professional medical care, I need some spiritual healing, which means, Nessie, I'll be good."

Father Somerset jumped nervously as the prison officer put a hand on his shoulder. "I'll be down the end of the corridor," he said. "You just holler if you need anything. I'll give you men some privacy."

Fischer bent over again, holding his stomach and grimacing. He gave Nessie a middle-finger salute as he departed.

Father Somerset sat down on the chair just inside the door, watching Fischer like a mouse might observe a snake.

Once Nessie was out of sight, Fischer straightened up and turned his attention to Father Somerset, who was perspiring profusely. The lack of eye contact, trembling hands, pale skin, bad haircut, unfashionable jacket and comfy shoes – it was all just as Fischer had pictured him.

Father Somerset stole a look up the corridor. Then, leaning forward in his chair, he whispered, "Please tell me my nephew is safe. You must promise me Josh is okay. He's just a boy."

CHAPTER FIVE

Rayner looked adoringly at his wife, Jenny.

She nodded. "Go on, you tell them."

They both had big grins on their faces, like schoolchildren with a big secret. Monica and I looked at each other suspiciously. *What's going on?* I thought.

The four of us were gathered in the kitchen of my new home. The room was filled with the smell of homemade curry, the table was set, and we were getting ready to sit down.

Having requested early retirement from the New Scotland Yard, I was starting over, building a new life with Monica and my two daughters, Alice and Faith, on the south coast. Even though the past had a way of dragging me back, I was fighting for a different future. A future free of maniacs and serial killers.

My new life was looking rosy. I stood with my arm around the waist of my gorgeous partner, Monica. Her hand rested lovingly on her belly, caressing our unborn child. I was in love again, in a way I'd never expected to be. Life had been hard for several years after losing my wife Helena in a knife attack. The man who had orchestrated Helena's murder, Edward Richter, real name Edward Fischer, was now behind bars for the murder of several women. I learned he had arranged for Helena to be murdered to distract me from investigating his crimes. Helena's loss, and the whole truth about what really happened, still haunts me to this day, but life moves on whether we're ready for it or not. Right now, I held the remarkable woman who had stood beside me and my children through all the dark times and shown me how to love again. I honestly didn't know how my life would have turned out without her fortitude and unwavering support. I felt like the luckiest man alive to once again be able to laugh and enjoy life surrounded by love and friendship.

My old Met partner and lifelong friend, the "Man Mountain," Detective Inspector Gabriel Rayner, and Jenny were staying with us for a few days. I loved seeing them together. Rayner is the toughest guy I know. Honest, a brilliant detective inspector, and a man I'd trust with my life, which I'd done on more than one occasion.

Rayner doted on Jenny, and she was perfect for him. When he was with her, he was all smiles and even more jokey than I knew him to be. Around her he was like a big ol' grizzly bear who gently handles a precious kitten.

Rayner was taking a long overdue holiday from the Met and one of the toughest cases of his career. He'd been working flat out on an investigation involving a young family who had been murdered while they slept. It was the third such family to be targeted in a little over two years. The only similarity linking each case was the disturbing fact that the children in each family were twins. After months on a case full of long, gruelling days, Rayner was still no closer to cracking it, and it was getting to him. Chief Webster, his boss and my old boss, had decided he needed to take a break and come back fresh. Time and distance might give him a new perspective.

Monica wriggled impatiently in my grasp now, giddy with excitement. "Okay, you two," she said. "Don't keep us in suspense any longer. What's going on?"

Rayner put one thick, muscular arm around Jenny's shoulders and placed his other hand on her stomach. Jenny placed her hands on top of his.

"You tell them," said Jenny.

"It'll be better coming from you," said Rayner.

"We have some news," said Jenny. Her eyes sparkled and her cheeks flushed. "We're going to be three. I'm pregnant! We're going to have a baby!"

Monica and Jenny squealed and rushed together to hug each other.

"How long?" said Monica breathlessly.

"Four months," said Jenny. "I'm sorry. I wanted to tell you sooner."

I put out my hand to Rayner in congratulations, but he wasn't having any of it. He grabbed me, wrapped his arms around me, and nearly squeezed the life out of me with one of his bear-like hugs.

"Okay, okay. Put me down, you big softie," I managed.

"Look, guys," said Rayner. "We're not trying to steal your thunder here. We realise you've only just announced your own fantastic baby news. We've been trying for a while, and it's purely coincidence."

"Get out of it!" I said.

"You've got to be kidding," said Monica. "This is amazing news. The best news." Monica gave Rayner a kiss and hug, while I congratulated Jenny.

"The only downside," said Jenny, "is the morning sickness. There are some days it seems to last all day."

"I'm so sorry," said Monica, her brow furrowing. "You poor thing."

"I thought I should warn you," said Jenny.

"If it gets too bad, just kick us out," said Rayner. "Jen and I can stay at a hotel."

"You suggest anything like that again and *you'll* be staying in a bloody hotel," I joked. "Jenny's not going anywhere."

"I have an idea," I said. I put the cork back in the bottle of red wine and got out another bottle of fizzy apple drink. "If the women aren't drinking alcohol, then neither are we."

"No," said Jenny. "Not on my account."

"Don't be silly," said Monica. "Rayner's on holiday."

"That's right," joked Rayner.

"That's a really sweet gesture," said Jenny. "You boys don't need to do that."

"I'm with Hardy," insisted Rayner. He winked at me. "Not every meal though, right?"

Jenny gave Rayner a playful punch in the arm. We were all high on excitement and laughed loudly.

"Are you sure this big fella is ready to be a father? I mean, he's barely house-trained," I said.

Jenny reached up and wrapped her arms around Rayner's neck and gave him a kiss. It was wonderful to see them so into each other.

"I'm getting there," said Jenny. "After nearly seven years of marriage, he puts the toilet seat down and has also learned how to cook a roast dinner."

"Ha ha, very funny," said Rayner, giving Jenny a squeeze. "I've also mastered a first-class cheesy beans on toast."

I poured us all a glass of fizzy apple juice and we

toasted Jenny and Rayner's fabulous news. "To Jenny and Rayner, and to Little Bump."

"To Little Bump!" everyone repeated.

It could have been a trick of the light, but I was sure Rayner had tears in his eyes. "Did someone say something about food?" he boomed. "This baby-making machine is famished."

"Oh, my," said Jenny in mock dismay. "Perhaps you're right. Is there any chance this beast in man's clothing will learn etiquette?"

CHAPTER SIX

Fischer looked up at the clear blue sky and basked in the late spring sun as it caressed his skin. A smile spread across his face like a river bursting its banks. In that moment, he remembered what freedom felt like.

Fischer waited in the yard with Prison Officer Farley. Their hands were cuffed together, meaning that each time Fischer winced and doubled over in pain, Farley's arm was suddenly yanked sideways.

Farley gave him a sideways glance and said, "Are you sure you're going to be all right? I don't want you throwing your guts up in the back of the car. It'll be muggins here who has to clean it up. I can call an ambulance."

"Nah. An ambulance is a glorified hearse with lights. Anyway, I don't feel sick anymore. It's the shooting pains again. Deep down in my guts."

Eventually, the unmarked car, a white Renault, appeared and pulled up in front of them. Nessie, got out and opened the back door.

Fischer got in first. He groaned as he slowly moved across the back seat to make room for Farley. Once they were inside, Nessie slammed the door and jumped into the front seat.

The journey to the hospital would take no more than twenty-five minutes. Nessie was hoping there wouldn't be too much mid-morning traffic and they'd get there in under twenty. He put the car in gear, waved to the officer on the gate and inched the Renault out into the road.

"You look like shit, if you don't mind me saying," said Nessie, glancing at Fischer in the rear-view mirror. "You don't sound much better, either. If you're going to vomit, use this bowl." He passed a plastic bowl into the back. Farley took it and put it on Fischer's lap.

Fischer nodded, then continued staring out the window.

Nessie started picking at his back teeth with his finger. He dug out a piece of breakfast, examined it and ate it. He glanced in the rear-view mirror to look at Fischer again. "You know, you've lost a ton of weight. Skinny as hell. I remember when you first arrived, all brawn and no sense. Spitting hellfire day and night. Now look at you – you probably weigh less than the dump I took this morning." Nessie slapped the steering wheel and chuckled at his joke.

Fischer wasn't listening. He was focused on the streets and shops and the people going about their morning.

"Nobody loses that much weight, and that quickly too, unless it's serious. You should have seen a doctor sooner," added Nessie.

"Give it a rest, will ya?" said Farley. "Leave him alone."

"I'm just saying. What if it's, you know..." Nessie mouthed the word *cancer*.

Farley looked across at Fischer, whose prison clothes were hanging off his skinny frame. "Just keep your eyes on the road and your mouth shut. Let's get to the hospital and get this over with. The sooner these tests are done the better."

Nessie didn't appreciate being dressed down in front of a prisoner. For the rest of the journey nobody spoke, which suited Farley down to the ground.

Fischer continued to stare out at the people going about their lives. He felt lightheaded, tired and puny. He hated feeling weak. Despite feeling like crap, though, he was excited. He couldn't let the guards see his pleasure, but this was a rare opportunity, and after more than four years behind bars, being out lifted his spirits.

As they approached the hospital Fischer leaned over and looked between the two front seats, scanning the hospital car park through the front windscreen. It was nearly full, and the prison had pre-arranged for them to park in a 'disabled only' parking bay at the front of the hospital.

"This'll do," said Nessie. "I'll get the doors." He jumped out and opened the back door for Farley and Fischer. Farley went first, and the still-cuffed Fischer inched along the back seat behind him, groaning as he moved. He put his feet on the pavement and straightened up, and as he did, he immediately grabbed at his stomach with his free hand. He doubled over and moaned loudly as he retched repeatedly. Nessie and Farley took a step back, worried he'd vomit over their shoes.

Fischer slowly straightened himself up. He wiped his mouth on his sleeve. "Sorry, guys. I'm fine. Thought I was going to vomit, but I'm okay. False alarm."

"Let's get inside, quick," said a worried-looking Nessie.

Fischer saw the car, but Nessie and Farley had been distracted and didn't notice the white BMW M3 pull up behind them. By the time they saw the two figures wearing ski masks and carrying sawn-off shotguns, it was too late.

The first ski-masked figure ran around to the front of the white Renault and on to the pavement, where he immediately raised the gun over his shoulder and brought the butt down hard on Nessie's nose. *Crack*. He then turned the gun and, pointing it at Nessie's long face, said, "Do as I say, and you'll live. Do something stupid and I'll blow a hole the size of Piccadilly Circus straight through that ugly face of yours. Hear me?"

Nessie held his bloody nose and nodded.

Farley put both hands in the air, bringing Fischer's arm up with his own. The second, smaller figure stood in front of him and pointed its sawn-off shotgun at his chest. A feminine voice said, "Uncuff him. Do it now. Quick."

Farley dug around in his pocket and pulled out the keys. His hand shook as he released Fischer from the handcuffs.

As soon as his wrist was free, Fischer ran to the white BMW and jumped in the back. Farley's eyes followed Fischer before returning to the barrel of the gun. He felt sure his time was up.

"Down on your knees. Do it," said the woman's voice.

Farley reluctantly did as he was told; his breathing was rapid. He closed his eyes, fully expecting the worst. "I've got kids," he said.

"Look at me. Open your eyes and look at me," the woman demanded. Farley did as he was told.

The woman then nodded to her accomplice. "Ready?"

"Uh-huh."

The woman lowered the shotgun and sprayed Farley's eyes with pepper spray. The man did the same thing to Nessie. As the two prison officers furiously rubbed their eyes, the masked pair ran back to the BMW, got in and, with tyres screeching, exited the hospital car park and disappeared into traffic.

CHAPTER SEVEN

Timothy Spicer and Faye Moon took off their ski masks. Spicer was driving. He headed out of town, keeping off the main roads, preferring quieter roads instead. He had the route all planned out. He'd driven it several times, on different days and at different times of day. Now, he punched the car roof and yelled.

"We did it, guys! We bloody well did it."

Faye Moon unbuckled her seatbelt and climbed between the front seats into the back, where she straddled Fischer. "Of course we did it. No one could stop me getting my man back." Moon wrapped her arms around Fischer's neck and gave him a long, hard kiss. Fischer's hands worked his way up Moon's shirt. Timothy snatched a look in the rear-view mirror then got his eyes back on the road to focus on the job in hand.

Moon got off Fischer's lap and sat beside him with her head on his shoulder. "I booked us into a nice little guest house. It's a place I know. We'll be fine there; it's quiet. The landlady, Fiona Crabb, is on our side. I gave her a little extra to keep her mouth shut. She'll be fine; she knows the score. Her old man is doing time for fraud."

"You're a clever girl," said Fischer.

"Timmy's going his own way when we get there. He's going to dump the car for us. Isn't that right, Timmy?" Moon slapped Spicer on the shoulder.

"Damn right. I got a mate who is getting me out of the country. Short trip across the channel, and I'll be screwing French tarts before you can say *Vive la France*." The three of them howled with laughter.

"I owe you, man. I mean, big time." Fischer put his hand on Timothy's shoulder. "Soon as I'm straight, I'm gonna make it up to you. I promise you that."

"I know you will, mate. Damn, it's so good to see you. It's just like old times."

"How's your mother?" Fischer asked.

"Still a cranky old bitch. I've been looking after her. Make sure she's got everything she needs. You know how it is."

"Good man. Nothing more important than family. Send the old cow my love."

Spicer looked in the rear-view mirror at his friend. "I will do. She'll be stoked to hear you're out." He didn't want to tell Fischer the truth. For his mother, the end was close. The drugs she was on meant she spent most every day sleeping. He planned on going to France but couldn't leave his mother right now.

"So how are you going to celebrate, now you're out?" asked Spicer.

Moon jumped in before Fischer had a chance to answer. "Well, we've got a lot of catching up to do." Moon put her hand between Fischer's legs and gently squeezed. "I'm going to have to feed him up. He's going to need all the energy he can muster." Moon ran her fingers up his body to his tattooed chest. "Look at my poor baby. He's all skin and bone."

"Yeah, but it was worth it," said Fischer. "It worked like a dream. Starving myself and complaining of chronic stomach pain got me to the hospital. Then boom! You two show up, and here I am." He leaned forward to answer Timothy's earlier question. "How will I celcbrate? Well, apart from my Moonbeam here, do you know what else I've been fancying?"

"Oh, Fischer," Moon cooed. She kissed two fingers and planted the kiss on the back of Fischer's neck. He reached back, took her hand, and cradled it.

"Soon as I knew I was getting out I've been dreaming about it," said Fischer. "I've been fancying a Colonel's bargain bucket with all the sides. Crispy coated chicken. Pepsi. Corn on the cob on a stick, all covered in butter. Gravy for the French fries. Beans and coleslaw. And those hot wings they do. A ton of hot wings."

"That sounds great. Hot wings sound really good right now. You've got me feeling hungry," grinned Spicer. "And what else?"

Fischer leaned back and put his free hand behind his head. "There are one or two scores to settle. But also, I've been thinking that maybe it's time to, you know, settle down. I'm not going back inside, that's for sure, and the only way to make sure that happens is to go straight. I need to put my affairs in order, then me and Moon here, we're going to disappear somewhere tropical."

"Amen to that," said Moon. "You just know I'll look hot in a tiny bikini, baby."

"Sounds like you've got it all planned out. Good for you, man," said Spicer.

"I've had a lot of time to think," said Fischer. "And nothing else makes sense anymore. It's time to do things differently."

Moon started bouncing excitedly up and down in her seat. "But first, we're going to have some fun. Then we're going to settle some scores. Isn't that right, baby?"

Fischer put both his hands around Moon's face and pulled her to him. He looked into her eyes then kissed her passionately. He released her, looked at her and smiled. "Yes, we are."

"Am I still your Moonbeam?"

"Yes, you are."

Spicer drove the three of them through the night to the guest house he and Moon had pre-booked for her and Fischer.

At the guest house, they said their farewells and wished each other luck before Spicer went on alone.

Before going inside, Moon showed Fischer the car, a black Ford Galaxy. She opened the Ford's back, then lifted a tartan blanket to reveal two black canvas bags.

"Our getaway money," said Moon. "One hundred thousand pounds. I counted it. It's all there. Less the twenty grand we agreed for Timothy. He didn't want to take it, but I insisted. Said he didn't want it because he owed you a favour, a big favour."

"He's a good man. Reliable," stated Fischer.

"Yeah, he is." Fischer and Moon looked up as a pair of circling seagulls squawked and cawed. "We're near the coast," added Moon. "Southampton docks aren't far from here."

"That means we're near the home of Inspector James Hardy." Fischer closed the back of the Ford. "We'll give it a day or so and then we'll pay him a visit."

"But right now…" said Moon. She put her arms around his neck and kissed him. She started giggling and pulling him towards the front of the guest house. "I've booked us the honeymoon suite. Let's go and test it out."

CHAPTER EIGHT

It was a couple hours before opening at Moriarty's cocktail bar in Edinburgh. At the owner's insistence, the head barman and chief mixologist, Shane Flanders, had handed over the bar's keys to two women for reasons he was told were best left unsaid. Shane would normally be at the bar prepping at this time, but instead he was two streets away eating a bagel and drinking espresso.

At the bar a meeting was taking place. The cocktail bar's low lighting gave it a theatrical look. Bottles sat in a row front of a bar-to-ceiling mirror and were lit from beneath; the coloured bottles glowed like the chemicals of a mad scientist's laboratory.

A young woman sat at the bar. Her long coat lay over the barstool next to her. She scrolled through the news on her phone as she sipped a gin and tonic. She knew what her role was and the importance of the meeting taking place behind her. From time to time she glanced in the mirror at the reflection of the table behind her, where the meeting would shortly reconvene.

Barton ran his fingers through his dyed black hair

before resting his elbow on the arm of the low-backed black leather armchair. He slouched down in the chair and rested his head in his hand, legs outstretched in front of him, his burnished caiman cowboy boots protruding from beneath his tight pale-blue jeans. The woman at the table with him was Kelly Lyle. He'd heard stories about her being a psycho rich bitch businesswoman. He guessed the stories must be bullshit. *She didn't look much like a killer,* he thought. *She's too damn hot – fantastic legs and great tits.*

The real prize, though, was the pretty young brunette perched on the bar stool behind Lyle. He guessed she and Lyle must be together, as in together-together. Oh, boy – now that would be something to watch. He'd love to be in the middle of the pair of them. His eyes, one brown, one blue, traced their way from the brunette's blue-painted python-skin pointed-toe ankle boots up her legs, around her hips, up over her body until they reached her plunging V-neckline and rested on her soft white bosom. He sighed and swallowed.

Behind him, the door to the men's room slammed shut. Snapping out of his trance, he looked up to see Lyle watching him. Realising his mouth was open, he snapped it shut and smiled awkwardly. He sat up in his chair.

Lyle watched as Donny Dodd, the man coming from the men's room, flapped his hands back and forth on his jeans to dry them. He was complaining to himself in the high-pitched whiney way he did when he was annoyed. His skinny frame and long limbs made him resemble a six-foot-tall stick insect. Reaching the table, he pulled out a chair. Tilting it up, he brushed the seat with his hand. Inspected it. Sat down.

Donny Dodd smelled one hand and then the other. "Christ, I smell like pot-fucking-pourri. Soap doesn't smell like soap anymore. Smell that." Donny stuck out his hand

and Barton backed away. "When I was a kid, soap smelled like soap. You remember? These days, after you wash your hands, you smell like a florist's apron. I like flowers and fruit. They're good for nature and all that. Bees and butterflies – where would we be without them? Yeah, I like flowers. I just don't want to smell like one. I want to smell clean, but that's not the same as smelling like a hyacinth or like that rhubarb-and-raspberry-scented handwash like I saw on a supermarket shelf the other day." He looked at Lyle and then at the hot brunette perched on the barstool and threw up his hands in dismay. "It's fine for ladies. I mean, it makes sense. I think women smelling fragrant is a beautiful thing. But for men it's different. They should have a masculine smell. To my mind it doesn't seem natural for a man to smell of wild fig and iris. Wouldn't you agree?" He didn't wait for an answer. Conspiratorially, he leaned forward in his chair. He looked first to Barton and then to Lyle. "I blame the whole liquid-soap revolution. Now we have liquid soap. Every time I use the bathroom, I end up dispensing liquid fucking perfume into my hands: jasmine, magnolia, eucalyptus, honeysuckle, lavender, grapefruit, even pomegranate. Do I look like the type of man who wants to smell like summer meadows or cherry blossom?"

Barton wanted to say he did, that he whined like a bitch, but he wasn't quick enough to interrupt Donny's flow.

"I kid you not. I was in a pub recently – I'm talking about a traditional British pub. I'd finished my local ale. It was very nice, as I recall. I'd gone to the little boy's room. I'd taken a leak. So far, so good. Naturally, I wanted to wash my hands – after all, cleanliness is next to godliness – but there, beside the sink, was liquid soap. Mandarin and grapefruit. Why would I want to smell like mandarin and grapefruit? Like a fruit flippin' salad?"

"Have you finished?" said Barton.

"It's all right for you. You're an animal," said Donny. "You don't wash your hands. Don't think I didn't notice last night at the hotel."

Barton glared at Donny. He nodded towards Lyle.

Donny shrugged and turned his bug-eyes to Lyle. "Hygiene. It's important. I'm sorry. Please carry on, Ms Lyle. You were saying you have a job."

Lyle pushed two envelopes across the table. "Twenty-five thousand each now; the remainder once it's done."

Barton picked up his envelope and looked inside. He flicked through the notes and was about to tuck the envelope in his inside jacket pocket when Donny put out a hand to stop him. "Whoa there, cowboy."

Donny looked at Lyle and said, "Please don't take this the wrong way. I don't mean any disrespect – I'm very appreciative of the opportunity. I say opportunity, but in truth, I'm not entirely clear what the job is. I mean, I know you probably want somebody dealt with. That's a given. Who that person is – that, I don't know. I don't like working in the dark. I don't agree to a deal until I'm aware of all the facts and at the very least who the intended is." He put out a hand and gestured towards Barton. "Also, no offence to the rhinestone cowboy here, but I work best alone."

Barton looked himself up and down.

Donny continued. "I'm not saying I don't want the job. I'm not saying that at all. What I am saying, however, is I'd rather do this thing alone. Whatever this thing is. No offence to Wild Bill here, as I said, but I'd work better without the complications of an unquantified partner, such as the cowboy to my left."

Barton rubbed behind his ear with his knuckle as he tried to digest everything the weird-looking fella had just said. He'd spoken so fast he was unsure whether he'd been insulted. He thought he might have been, but breaking the bug-man's neck in the middle of a meeting wouldn't be a smart move. He'd do it later. Once the job was done. He wanted the money.

"You either work together and do the job," Lyle said, "or I find two others to do it. I want to be sure it's done and done properly, which is why I want the two of you. It doubles the chances of success. I need a man found and I might want him dealt with, in a permanent way." She looked at the two men and waited for agreement.

"Hey, I'm fine with it," said Barton. "I got no better plans." He and Lyle looked at Donny.

Donny's head moved in a figure of eight while he thought about it. "Crap. Okay. One condition. I run the show. I can't have the Cisco Kid here wrecking my reputation. I'm a professional."

Barton shrugged.

"Is that a yes?" asked Donny. "You know, that hole in your face is for communicating. Words and like. Jesus!"

"Yes," said Barton. He slipped the money inside his jacket.

The brunette at the bar slid off the stool and came to stand beside Lyle. She placed a report file in the middle of the table before returning to her seat at the bar.

Barton watched her. *I'd love to swap places with that stool,* he thought.

"No mistakes," said Lyle to Barton and Donny. "Find him and call me. Here's a phone with my number. Bring it back to me when the job's complete. I don't want you to touch him until you've spoken to me. Is that understood?"

Barton nodded. "Yep."

Donny opened the file and pulled out the mugshot. The photo was of a man named Edward Fischer, also known as Edward Richter. He showed it to Barton and began to read the two-page report.

"Uh-huh. Why do you want him dead?" asked Donny when he had finished. When no reply came and he sensed the chilly silence, he looked up. Lyle's unblinking eyes were stone cold. He cleared his throat. "You know what? That doesn't matter." He closed the file. "Consider it done. My new partner and I will call you as soon as we find him."

"Inside, you'll find details of his last known location," said Lyle. "I'm in touch with Fischer's girlfriend, Faye Moon. She's been keeping me abreast of their movements, but she's proving to be unreliable."

"Don't worry, we've got this," insisted Donny.

"For your sake, I hope so. Don't fuck this up," said Lyle.

Barton got up and walked around behind the bar. He grabbed a bottle of tequila and poured two shots. He passed one to the brunette. When she ignored him and continued reading the news on her phone, he took the shot back and drank it, then drank his own.

Donny got to his feet. "Lovely to meet you, Ms Lyle. We'll be in touch." Passing the brunette on his way out, he gave his best smile. "Miss."

Barton followed Donny to the exit, carrying the bottle of tequila he'd opened and a second unopened bottle under his arm. He saluted and bowed and backed out of the bar.

Donny reached into his pocket and pulled out the keys to his rented silver-grey Toyota Avensis. "Stop screwing around. Let's get the fuck out of here. You're going to get us both killed, behaving like a prick, showing no respect. You clearly have no idea who she is. I can't believe I'm saddled with you. I'm going to wind up dead or worse. That bitch in there is psycho. You know that, right?"

Barton shrugged. "She seemed pleasant enough. You worry too much. I sense that about you: you're a worrier. I'm sure anything you think you've heard is bullshit."

"That might be so. But even bullshit is founded in truth. Let's be smart and err on the side of caution. Let's do this job and go our separate ways."

"I'll drive," said Barton.

"'Christ's sake! Get in. I rented it. I drive it."

CHAPTER NINE

I woke with a jolt. I felt like I was suffocating. My heart was pounding, and my body was covered in sweat.

Monica sat up and switched on the bedside light. She squinted at me through heavy eyes. "Are you okay? Is it another nightmare?"

"Yeah. Sorry. I didn't mean to wake you."

"Can I do anything?"

I reached out and held her soft hand. "I'm fine. Thank you. You go back to sleep. I'm going downstairs to get a glass of water."

"They're becoming more frequent," said Monica.

"Perhaps." I climbed out of bed and put on my dressing gown and slippers. Not wishing to wake the rest of the house, I crept downstairs. I filled a glass with water and went to my study.

I sat behind my desk and looked at the wall where I pinned photos, notes, leads and ideas. Everything faded into the background except the photo of Edward Fischer, the man behind the murder of Helena. The man whom the psychopath, Kelly Lyle, wanted me to kill. Fischer and Lyle were the cause of my recurring nightmares.

"You okay, buddy?"

"Christ 'n' Jesus! You scared me." I whirled around and took a deep breath. It was Rayner.

"Awfully jumpy, mate." Rayner sat his mountain-sized body down in my favourite well-worn comfy chair. "What's going on?"

"Nothing," I said, unconvincingly.

"Doesn't sound like nothing. Doesn't look like nothing either. Want to talk?"

"What time is it?" I looked at the clock on the wall. "Why don't you go back to bed? You're on holiday. Besides, you don't want to get into this now."

Rayner looked at his watch. "It's just before six. Now is the perfect time to get into whatever's going on with you."

I looked again at the photo on the wall and my heart sank.

Rayner followed my eyes. "In the last few weeks you've had to deal with the sudden loss of your father. You're just getting over the shock of rescuing your daughter from that psycho bitch, Kelly Lyle, and learning that the man who really killed Helena has escaped prison. Dealing with just one of those things is going to take its toll. Yet, you're trying to process all of it without talking. Bottling it all up isn't going to do you any good. We've both had enough Met counselling over the years to know that." He turned back to me. "Talk to me. I know there's something more. I know you as well as anybody. Whatever it is, James, it has something to do with him." Rayner pointed to the photo of Fischer on the wall.

"Fischer," I said. "Edward Fischer." I wanted to tell Rayner the truth. I've known him since we were children; he's like a brother. He and I joined the Met together.

The trouble was, he was still a serving detective inspector and I was retired, or at least I was supposed to be. The truth would put him in a moral predicament. How could I tell him that, in exchange for getting my daughter back, Kelly Lyle's price was that I kill Edward Fischer? How could I tell him that a part of me wanted Fischer dead and that I wanted to be the one to do it? That I wanted to squeeze the life out of him for leaving my children without their mother?

At the time of her kidnapping, I could see no other way of getting Alice back and so I'd made the deal. Kelly Lyle swore that if I reneged on our agreement, she'd rain hell down upon my family, promising she'd murder every single one of them. And I didn't doubt she'd try.

I had to move our conversation away from my agreement with Lyle. "There's nothing more. I've been having nightmares. They're incredibly vivid. They're flashbacks to when I was searching for Alice. In the nightmares, I find my little girl drugged and half-dead in a water-butt behind the farmhouse Lyle was hiding at when I tracked her down. What if I hadn't reached her in time? What if I hadn't been able to get the lid off the water-butt and she'd drowned right in front of my eyes?" I choked on the words.

"You saved her. That's all that matters."

"And what effect might an experience like that have on her? She's a child."

"She's doing great. She's still the Alice I've known since she was a baby: super-smart, full of fun and the spitting image of her mother. Helena would be proud."

I tried to smile. "I suppose. She does look like Helena, doesn't she?"

"Yes, she does," said Rayner. "There's nothing more?" He studied me. He was like a bloodhound that had picked up a scent and was in pursuit. I could feel him looking for signs of what I was hiding. I got up and walked over to the corner of the office, took the milk from the small fridge, smelled it, and made us both coffees. I handed my friend a steaming cup.

A half-truth might throw him off the scent. "There are a few loose ends I'm trying to process, that's all."

"Let me help."

"No," I said a little too sharply. Too many sleepless nights were catching up with me. "Thank you. I'm working with Emma Cotton," I lied, again. I hadn't spoken to Detective Inspector Emma Cotton for a few weeks. She'd checked in with us a couple of times after we got Alice back, but since then, she was giving us space.

Once again changing the subject, I said, "You're on holiday. Let's figure out what we're going to do today. Monica and I were wondering whether you and Jenny would like to go to Lyme Regis beach and do some fossil hunting with the children. We can take a picnic. You can practise your parenting skills. If Jenny's not up to it, we could do something closer to home. What do you fancy?" I looked out the office window. "It's still early, but it's going to be another sunny day."

The big man eyed me while sipping his coffee. "Fossil hunting sounds great. I'll see how Jenny's feeling." Rayner got up and walked to the office door. "When you're ready to talk, I'm here for you."

"I know you are, mate. Like I said, there's nothing. Thank you." Inside, I was crying out for help. I needed to answer the question of what the hell I was going to do when Lyle demanded I make good on our deal.

I hated myself for repeatedly lying to my best friend, but the fewer people I involved the better. For the time being, I just had to hope Lyle would move on and leave us alone.

CHAPTER TEN

Moon and Fischer were in what the guest house described as the Lavender Honeymoon Suite. A four-poster bed, white bed linen with lavender-coloured silk edging, and a couple of heart-shaped red satin cushions were all meant to suggest the room was tailored to newlyweds. Water stains on the bathroom ceiling from a recent leak, a carpet long past its best, mismatching furniture, chipped paintwork and an inharmonious colour scheme would disappoint even the most ardent couple.

Plates and empty beer bottles were on the floor in the corner of the room after a large steak dinner, delivered to the room by the amiable landlady.

Fischer was sprawled out on the bed in just his boxer shorts, cigarette in one hand, beer in the other. His lap held a teacup, which he used as an ashtray. He stared into space while blowing large clouds of smoke into the 'non-smoking' room.

Moon wrapped her hair in a towel as she came out of the en-suite bathroom. She finished tapping out a message on her phone.

"Who's that?" asked Fischer.

"No one," said Moon. "It's nothing."

"Doesn't look like nothing."

Moon perched on the bed beside Fischer. Her eyes wandered over his lean, inked body. "What's next?" asked Moon.

Fischer passed Moon the packet of cigarettes and lighter from the bedside table. He enjoyed watching her deftly light a cigarette. "First thing tomorrow," said Fischer, "we get out of here. It's not safe to stay in one place for too long."

"Okay. Then what?" Moon reached over and took the bottle of beer from Fischer, took a swig and handed it back.

Fischer knew what Moon was getting at. He'd promised her that as soon as he was free, they'd vanish. Go somewhere tropical and start over. "There hasn't been a single day that's passed where I haven't thought about three things."

Moon flicked ash from her cigarette into the cup ashtray. She enjoyed listening to him speak. He was the smartest man she knew. She'd missed the sound of his deep, rich voice while he'd been locked up. Moon sucked hard on her cigarette and pressed it out in the teacup. The certainty in the way he spoke made her feel secure; the rhythm and tone comforted her.

Fischer rubbed out his cigarette and continued, "One: you. Every day, before I even opened my eyes, I thought of you. Every single day. And not just that sweet body of yours. *You*. Being away from you was the hardest part of doing time."

"Aw! Eddie. That's so sweet." Moon scooted down the bed, put her head on his chest and wrapped an arm around him. Fischer finished his beer and let the empty bottle drop down the side of the bed. He put his arm around Moon and squeezed her and kissed her shoulder. He ran the fingers of his other hand over her soft skin as he spoke. "Two: getting free and as far away from this godforsaken island as is humanly possible."

"Now you're talking," said Moon.

"Three: Detective Chief Inspector Hardy."

Moon lifted her head and looked at him.

Fischer pushed her fringe aside with his fingers so he could look into her eyes. He added, "I want compensation for time served. That bastard put me away. I won't be able to live with myself if I don't deal with that." He shook his head. "Before I go anywhere, I want to make sure I hurt him in a way that he'll remember forever."

"That sounds like fun," said Moon. She was up for a bit of excitement before skipping the country for good.

There were actually four things he'd spent most days thinking about, but he couldn't tell Moon the last one. It didn't feel right. How could he explain to Moon he had the urge to see his daughter? He figured she must be about sixteen years old by now. A young woman. She was in first school the last time he'd seen her. He'd driven past and watched her mother kissing her and sending her in through the school gates.

"Listen, baby," said Fischer. "You've done so much for me. I'm not sure what I'd do without you. I understand if you want to sit this one out. What I'm saying is, you could go ahead to wherever we decide to go while I finish up here."

Moon sat up on the bed and crossed her arms, her face like thunder. "Are you saying you've had enough of me already? I do all this for you – kidnap a fucking kid, blackmail his bitch mother – so you could drop me at the first fucking chance you get? Are you fucking joking?" She punched him hard in the chest.

Fischer cracked up and brought up his knee to protect himself from her fist. The teacup spilled ash over his boxer shorts and the white bed linen. He loved it when Moon threw a tantrum in that little-girl way she did. "Ouch! Not a chance," insisted Fischer. "I'm just saying, I understand if you want to bow out of this one. Hardy and me is personal."

"Screw you."

"Yes, please."

"You're such an idiot."

Fischer pulled Moon to him and tried to kiss her. She brushed him off.

"I'm not going anywhere without you. I've been twiddling my thumbs all the time you've been inside. If you're going after Hardy, I'm coming too. He didn't just screw up your life, he screwed up mine as well. I want to make him pay as much as you do."

Fischer grabbed Moon and pulled her to him. She laid her head back on his chest and listened to his heartbeat.

"Do you think they've found the boy yet?" asked Moon. "He was a real crybaby."

"I promised the priest they'd have him back by now."

"You should have let me kill him. He might ID Spicer or me," said Moon.

Fischer grinned. "It won't matter soon. We do Hardy, and we're gone forever."

CHAPTER ELEVEN

The windscreen wipers thrashed from side to side as the silver-grey Toyota Avensis made steady progress along the M6 motorway.

Donny leaned forward, peering through the windscreen with his bulging, buggy eyes. "Can you believe this weather? The last time I saw weather like this I was in Manchester. I'd just topped some fool who'd run up debts with the wrong fella and I was heading out to see my then girlfriend. Boy, she was a pain in the arse. She had a nice arse, don't get me wrong, but she was very demanding, and not in a good way, you know? Not demanding in the bedroom sort of way."

Donny scoffed and raised his eyebrows as the memories came flooding back. "More in the 'Buy me this, take me here, take me there, do this, do that' sort of way. Anyway, I'm heading out of Manchester, and this almighty storm hits. The sky's lighting up with forked lightning, like a New Year's firework display. I decide to pull into a service station and rent a room for the night, Holiday Inn I think it was. The room was okay, nothing special. Sometimes you get lucky; this time I didn't. Anyway, I take a shower and decide that before heading downstairs to grab a bite to eat, I should call Linda. Linda's the pain-in-the-arse girlfriend I mentioned a moment ago. I call and get no answer. I give it a minute and call again, figuring she might have left her phone out of reach and missed the call. You know how it is. Anyway, she picks up this time and we're chatting away. I tell her I'll be back, not that evening because of the rain, but in the morning. That's when I hear the voice of someone else. 'Where do you keep the shampoo?' That's what I heard. She denies anyone's there. Says it was the TV. Of course, I know immediately the bitch is screwing around while I'm out of town. There I am, working my nuts off to make a future for the both of us while she's on her knees for some stud I later discover she picked up at the supermarket checkout.

"I pretend I believe her. I even joke about how silly I was being and apologise for my paranoia. I tell her, 'It's only because I love you so much.' But I know the truth. I skip dinner. I check out. I get right back in the car and drive through that fucking storm. With the rain hammering down and the thunder booming and the lightning striking all around, it's like God himself is trying to hold me back – you know what I mean? Anyway, there's no way on this earth I'm stopping.

"It's the middle of the night by the time I arrive back. I let myself in. I creep upstairs. I push open the bedroom door. Voila! There, in my bed, is Linda and Mr Supermarket Checkout Guy. His crappy supermarket shirt and tie resting on *my* chair, where I put my clothes. I kicked the bed. 'Checkout guy. Time to check out,' I said. And check out he did. Right there in my bed, with a bullet between his fucking eyes. Followed shortly thereafter by my Linda."

Barton lifted his head and opened an eye.

"Were you even listening?" Donny asked. "Some company you are. You don't converse. It's like you've bypassed ever having a complete conversation in your life. You don't like me putting the car radio on. You say you want to drive, but then decide you don't want to drive because you don't like automatics. The least you could do is stay awake and listen when I'm talking."

Barton took out a packet of cigarettes.

"What the hell are you doing?" asked Donny. "You can't smoke in here – the car's a rental. See?" Donny pointed to a No Smoking sticker stuck to the dashboard in front of Barton.

Barton lit his cigarette, sucked on it, then exhaled in Donny's direction. He ran his fingers through his hair and watched the bug-man get all flappy.

"F' Christ's sake," said Donny, his eyes bulging more than usual. He pressed the button and the car window opened. "You know, you're not that sociable. In fact, I'd go as far as to state you're unsociable. Uncongenial. That's the word. Arsehole is another." Donny flicked the indicator and started changing lanes. "I need a break. Stuck in this car with you is too much. I need some air. You're a waste of space, you know that? A waste of space."

Barton smiled and looked out the window at the passing traffic. *The stick-insect man is funny,* he thought.

CHAPTER TWELVE

Fischer arose early. He collected up their belongings and dropped them in one of the two bags by the door. He went through the black canvas bag containing the eighty grand, took out a thousand, tucked it into his jacket and zipped the pocket. He put another ten thousand in the bag he'd give to Moon, in case the pair of them should become separated at some point.

He stood at the foot of the bed and watched Moon as she slept. It would be easier to do what he had to do without her, but it wouldn't be as much fun. He also knew she'd never forgive him if he simply left her a note and went on ahead. She looked like an angel. She could do that, but Faye Moon was the product of her upbringing, or lack of. Her soul was tainted by her sickening childhood experiences. When she unleashed her dark side, she was like the fury of a winter storm, raging and unpredictable.

Fischer kicked the bed. Moon mumbled. He kicked it harder. "Wake up. Moon, wake up. It's time to go." He walked around to the other side of the bed and shook her.

"Now. Come on. Get your pretty arse up. How can you sleep so much?"

Without opening her eyes, Moon said, "You didn't let me get much sleep last night, remember? I was dreaming about us. We were on a sunny beach together. Drinking cocktails. Whiskey sours. Think it was the Caribbean. Somewhere hot with a gorgeous beach and handsome waiters." Moon opened one eye and squinted at Fischer, who was standing over her. "That's where we need to go. After this, we should go to the Caribbean. With eighty grand, we could live like royalty."

"Maybe. But right now, you need to get your butt out of bed. Come on, now!"

Moon opened her other eye and pouted. "Maybe? That means no. You said maybe. That means you're not taking me. You promised."

"You sound like a child," said Fischer. "Get your clothes on. It's time to go. If you're not up in one minute, I'm going without you and I'll do Hardy alone."

"Screw you. I want something nice to look forward to. I was stuck with that kid for days. Before that, I was sofa surfing. I've been running around for you, you ungrateful bastard. I've spent weeks getting all your shit together to break you out. And now you're barking orders at me, like I'm nothing." Moon pulled the sheets over her head and curled up in the foetal position.

Fischer bit his tongue. You couldn't force Moon to do anything she didn't want to do. When she got like this, he had to try a gentler approach. He placed his hand on the sheet where her shoulder was. "I'm sorry, Moon. It's just we need to get going. Right now, I'm a bit jittery and want to keep moving." He spoke softly now. "The last thing I want is to be separated from you again. Equally, it's important we avoid detection."

54

Moon lowered the sheet and peeked out. She looked up at him. He nodded encouragingly and Moon smiled. Fischer bent over and gave her a kiss on the forehead. "Come on, Moonbeam. Let's get on the road. We need to find someplace else to stay. Time to check out Inspector Hardy. Then we can do whatever you want. Go wherever you decide."

"Promise?"

"Of course."

"Okay, then. Give me five minutes. I need to shower." Moon rolled across the bed and jumped off. She skipped to the bathroom. While turning on the shower, she called out. "Get the landlady to make us some bacon rolls to go. We need to get some food. I'm starving. You definitely need to get some food; you need to get some muscle back on that body of yours. Looking at you now, I reckon I could take you down with one hand tied behind my back."

"I'd like to see you try."

Fischer sat on the end of the bed and listened to Moon giggle. She was hard work at times, but she was good company.

"Are we really going to kill him? The cop, I mean."

"I haven't decided yet. That wasn't my intention, but we'll see how things pan out."

"Where are we going to stay when we get there?"

"I have an idea about that."

CHAPTER THIRTEEN

Donny zipped up his trousers and stepped carefully back along the edge of the field towards the car. He took out an antibacterial gel cleaner from his pocket, squirted it into his hands and rubbed them together. He looked up at the sky, which was finally clear and blue.

Edging his way through a gap in the hedgerow, he heard grunting and gasping and the scraping of gravel. His long arms out to steady himself, he sidled through the thorny gap, twisting and unpicking his way through. Having examined his clothes for tears and his arms for scratches, he straightened up and was confronted with Barton and a policeman. Barton was sitting with his back to the car, legs splayed, his arm clamped tight around the police officer's neck. The policeman's face was red, his eyes staring. *He looks young,* thought Donny. *Maybe only in his twenties?*

Donny glanced down the road to the garish-looking squad car. "What the fuck?" said Donny. "What the hell are you doing? Are you nuts?"

The police officer stopped struggling. Barton kept

squeezing until he was sure there was no life left. He shoved the officer's body aside and got up, then doubled over and held his knees as he got his breath back. "I thought he was never gonna croak," he panted. He looked up at Donny. "Help me get him into the squad car. Grab his legs."

"What?"

"Grab his legs."

"Look, let's think about this for a minute. I mean, I didn't hear Lyle say anything about killing fresh-faced police officers. He's just a kid, for Christ's sake. I don't know that I want any part of this."

Barton straightened up. "Maybe I should kill you too."

"What? Why would you say that? Are you insane? You and I are partners, remember?"

"A partner would help. If you're not a partner, then it's best for me that I kill you. It'll look like you two struggled and killed each other."

"Genius. You're a real Einstein. That would be your plan? That we strangled each other to death? You see, that doesn't work. I'm pretty sure even Inspector Clouseau would see through that."

Barton stared at Donny.

Donny sighed. "Okay, I'll help. But when we next speak to Lyle, you let me do the talking, all right?" He looked down at the dead police officer and shook his head in dismay, then turned and looked up and down the country road. On either side of it were hedgerows and open fields. He reached down and grabbed the officer's ankles. Lifting the body together, the pair heaved the body towards the squad car.

"I'm still trying to understand how we ended up with a dead cop. We pull off the motorway into a country lane so I can answer a call of nature. I'm gone five minutes, at most. In that time, you manage to kill a man. What happened – did you get bored? Did you think, 'I know what'll do to alleviate my boredom: I'll kill the next person I see. Better still, I'll strangle a bobby'?"

"He wanted see my driving licence."

"And? So what?"

Barton pulled a face that suggested the problem was obvious.

"Oh, I see. You're wanted. Outstanding conviction? That's great. I'm working with the Outlaw Josey Wales. You're on the 'Wanted' list. Terrific, bloody terrific."

"I couldn't have him digging around," said Barton. Using his knee and leaning against the side of the squad car, he balanced his end of the body. At the same time, he reached out to open the car door.

Donny adjusted his grip. "This guy weighs a ton. He's a small-looking fella, but by God, he's heavy. Will you keep it steady? I nearly dropped him."

Barton threw the door open and slung his end of the body behind the steering wheel, leaving Donny holding the legs. "Would it be too much for you to give me a hand here? My back is prone to herniated disc problems. You wouldn't believe the pain when…"

Barton showed no interest, and Donny looked around to see what had caught his attention. He followed Barton's gaze. At the top of the road, coming towards them from the direction of the motorway, was a figure on a pale-blue and white moped. Wearing an open-faced red, white and blue crash helmet, a black leather jacket, a shirt and tie and tan chinos, the rider was eyeballing them, clearly trying to make out what was going on.

Donny began frantically heaving and shoving the body into the car, but on his own the body wasn't going anywhere. Turning, he saw Barton walk behind the squad car, lift the hatchback and duck down.

As the rider slowed to pass, Donny nodded and smiled as though nothing was amiss. "Afternoon," he said.

The rider, a man in his late sixties with large grey eyebrows and a matching grey moustache, suddenly comprehended what he was seeing, and his eyes widened.

From behind the squad car stepped Barton, swinging a bright orange traffic cone. He hit the rider in the centre of his chest, knocking him off his bike. The moped continued forward, lurching wildly from side to side like a drunk, before finally ending up in the hedgerow. Barton loomed over the rider with the plastic cone and rained down blow after sickening blow.

Still holding the police officer's legs, Donny grimaced as the rider's face deteriorated into a bloody pulp. "I think he's dead, Barton. *Barton!* You can stop now. You're getting blood and brain all over your cowboy boots, and I don't want blood in the rental. I'll lose my deposit."

Barton, panting heavily, dropped the orange plastic traffic cone. He rubbed his boots on Moped Man's chinos. "I love these boots."

"I'm sure he'd be mortified to know his brains went on your boots. Now, if you don't mind…" Donny looked at the dead police officer he was still holding and then back to Barton. "A hand? So we can get the hell out of Dodge."

CHAPTER FOURTEEN

Fischer took a final bite of his second Big Mac. Eyes closed, he sank back in his booth, letting the juicy flavours of the burger caress his tongue.

From beside him, a woman in a McDonald's uniform said, "You look like you enjoyed that."

Fischer looked up in surprise. Wiping his mouth with a napkin, he replied, "You're right. It was terrific. I've been looking forward to a burger, fries and Coke for very long time." He looked at the name on the badge pinned to her chest. "If you don't mind my saying, you have a very pretty smile, Judy."

Her greying golden-brown hair was tied back and tucked under a McDonald's baseball cap. Fischer guessed she was in her late forties. She had a good figure, full around the hips the way he liked, and she looked after her appearance. He watched her hands as she collected the packaging from his meal and placed it on a tray. She wore several rings, but no wedding ring. "Thank you, Judy," said Fischer.

Judy gave the table a brisk wipe.

"It's just a shame I ate it alone," Fischer went on. "The sad truth is, a meal might taste good, but sharing it with someone is what makes a meal truly memorable. Eating alone is no fun. The meals we remember are the meals we share with someone special. Sometimes, I look around and it seems everyone has someone." He dabbed his mouth with the napkin. "Listen to me rattling on to a complete stranger," said Fischer apologetically. "I'm sorry – I'm keeping you. I'm sure you have no idea what I'm talking about."

For a moment Judy was unsure how to respond. She held the tray out in front of her and leaned against the table. "I do know what you mean," she said at length, smiling politely. "'Happiness quite unshared can scarcely be called happiness; it has no taste.' Charlotte Bronte said that."

"That is so true," said Fischer. "'The trouble is not that I am single and likely to stay single, but that I am lonely and likely to stay lonely.'"

Judy tilted her head, her brow furrowed. She put the tray down and leaned on the table. "You know Charlotte Bronte? You are a surprise."

Fischer leaned forward and looked deep into Judy's eyes. "Finding myself alone for many years has given me time to broaden my mind. Literature is the purest form of escapism. Don't let this rough exterior fool you, Judy. I have many hidden depths. My name's Fischer." His strong hand, with a scar two inches long from thumb to wrist, reached out, and a finger teasingly touched the back of her hand.

Judy's face blushed faintly. Fischer saw it. He relaxed into the seat, twisting around in his booth and bringing his knee up on the seat. He put his elbow on the table and took a long look at Judy. "What sort of crazy world are we living in when a fine, educated and extremely attractive woman such as yourself finds herself lonely? It's just that you look, to me, like a woman no man would ever let out of his sight. Not for a second."

"You do speak your mind. I'm not used to that. Most people talk around what they mean. They never just come straight out with it."

"Was I being too personal? Forgive me."

"I like it. It's refreshing." Judy touched behind her ear. No strand of hair was straying, but her fingers checked. "My husband, ex-husband, hit fifty and traded me in for a younger model: long legs, tight arse, tits that give men whiplash."

"Great tits can do that," joked Fischer.

Judy laughed along. She then said soberly, "He took my son with him. I got the house and lots of memories. I live alone. I say alone – I have a cat called Darcy. Even he rarely visits these days."

"I'm sorry. Your ex-husband is a fool. He'll come to see that, eventually."

Judy placed her clasped hands on the table. She leaned close so she got his full attention. "That might be so, but I think you're being less than honest with me. I want you to know, I saw you in here earlier with your lady friend. I'm guessing that was your wife or girlfriend. I noticed the way she was with you. I'm not being fooled and let down by a man ever again."

Fischer widened his eyes as though he was innocent of all charges.

Judy stood up straight and swept imaginary crumbs off the table onto the tray.

Fischer put his hands up in playful surrender.

Judy moved to the next table and started cleaning it.

Fischer turned in his seat and spoke softly. "She isn't

my wife or girlfriend. She's my younger sister. Her name's Faye. She had to get home to put her kids to bed. I was hoping she would stay so I'd have somebody to share my meal with, but she took a cab home. She has her life and commitments. Also, her husband doesn't like me. She fits me in where she can. And that's fine. I understand. I've made a few mistakes in the past. All that's behind me, but not everyone is as forgiving as my little sister. She has a generous heart."

Judy stopped and looked his way again. "In that case, I'm sorry. I didn't mean to be rude. Thank you for the compliments. I'm not used to them."

"Not enough people do it. A small kindness, especially when true, can brighten someone's day. I like to do it. I see no harm. And I mean it – your husband was a fool." Fischer drained his drink.

Judy watched out of the corner of her eye as Fischer stood and walked towards the exit. He dropped his empty cup in a bin next to the door. She felt her chest tighten and her neck prickle as he turned and walked back towards her.

"What time do you finish here? I'd like to buy you a drink, or a meal. I'd like to see you again."

Judy stopped what she was doing. She looked into his warm, dark eyes and wanted to say yes. She couldn't figure him out; he was full of contradictions. He was assertive, almost to the point of arrogance. Yet there was also something soothing, kind and reassuring in the language he used and in his manner. The stark-looking tattoos, his scarred hand and lack of dress sense didn't reflect a man who could quote Charlotte Bronte. She was finding it hard to work out whether he was trouble in a good way or trouble in a bad way. Unsure how to respond, she picked up the tray and started clearing another table. Then, sensing him turn to walk away, Judy said, "My shift finished ten minutes ago. If you'd like, we could go somewhere and get a coffee. I just need to get rid of this." She held up the tray full of empty packaging. "Do you have a car? I walked to work this morning. Left my car at home."

Fischer beamed "Yes, I do. I'll wait for you outside."

Judy gave a shy smile. She felt like a teenage girl getting a wink from the school heartthrob. She cleared off the tray and, with a spring in her step, headed to the back of the restaurant to gather her belongings.

CHAPTER FIFTEEN

Fischer leaned against the bonnet of the black Ford Galaxy as Judy approached. Her head was tilted down slightly as she tried to contain her excitement, but she couldn't disguise the big smile on her face. Fischer opened the passenger door.

"Milady," he said with a flourish and a sweeping arm gesture. Once she was comfortable, he gently closed the door.

As he walked around the car, Judy watched him and smiled.

Fischer climbed in behind the wheel and fastened his seatbelt. "We can go wherever you like," he said. "I don't know the area well, so it's best you choose."

"Fischer, I was thinking. Would it be okay to drop by my place first? Just so I can get changed and freshen up? I can put some food out for Darcy too. It won't take long."

"Sure thing. I must say, you do look fetching in that McDonald's uniform, but I understand if you'd like to change."

Judy turned in her seat to avoid the eyes of her

colleagues who had also finished their shifts and were outside gossiping. "Take a left out of here and then go up to the roundabout and straight over." As they drove, they chatted, and for some reason she felt the need to explain once again the breakdown of her marriage. "The hardest part of all was when, after being given the choice, my son decided to live with his father. I never imagined in a million years he'd do that." Judy pointed to a pretty red-brick bungalow about halfway up the road. "It's that one there on the left."

Fischer parked the car and turned off the ignition. "I'm sorry to hear that. I understand the hurt. I have a daughter I haven't seen since she was a baby. She's a teenager now. It hurts to think of the time I've missed."

The pair sat in silence for a moment, unsure what to say next. Judy pulled on the door handle. "I won't be a moment."

"I'll be right here waiting. Take as long as you need."

"Okay. I won't be long."

Fischer waited as Judy opened the front door and went in. In the driveway was Judy's car, a pale-blue Volkswagen Polo. He waited five minutes, then got out. He looked up and down the road. It was quiet. He'd not seen a single car the whole time he'd been waiting. He put the keys in his pocket and walked up the drive to the front door. He rang the doorbell. Judy opened the door and peered out. Her face showed a mixture of surprise and pleasure.

"I'm really sorry," said Fischer. "That Coke went straight through me. Would you mind if I used the bathroom?"

Judy hesitated for a second and then opened the door. "Of course. Come in." She stepped aside to let Fischer in and pointed to a door. "Down the hall. It's that first door on the left."

Fischer went to the bathroom while Judy went to the kitchen to open a tin of food for Darcy. Once in the bathroom, Fischer started looking round. He went through a mirrored cabinet on the wall and found it stocked with the usual items: mouthwash, toothbrush, Colgate, plasters, nail clippers, cotton buds and so on. He took the lid off a wicker wash basket. He pulled out a few items of clothing until he came to some cotton tights. He rolled them up and put them in his front pocket. He looked around the room again and noticed a bathrobe hanging on the back of the bathroom door. He pulled out the belt, rolled it up small and stuffed it in his back pocket. He then flushed the toilet before going to the sink and running the tap to suggest he was washing his hands.

In the kitchen he found Judy. She'd changed her clothes, applied a little makeup and, having fed the cat, was now tidying up. He leaned casually up against the worktop beside the door. The kitchen was very orderly. A small oak kitchen table with four matching chairs took up one side, while the other side had white gloss cupboards with silver handles above and a black granite worktop below.

"I think we're done here," said Judy. "Shall we get going?"

"That sounds like a good idea." Fischer waited until Judy was just in front of him. He reached out and put a gentle hand on her shoulder. She turned and looked at him. "You look beautiful," he said.

Judy gave a coy smile. Her face reddened like it had done earlier in the restaurant.

"I don't want to hurt you, Judy. You seem like a nice person. I'm genuinely fond of you."

Judy's smile vanished, replaced by a look of confusion. Somewhere, deep down, a spark of panic ignited and spread through her body like a wildfire. She pushed it away and spoke as if ignoring it would mean it didn't exist. "Hurt me? It'll be fine. We're just going for coffee. It'll be nice." She kept walking towards the door.

Fischer moved to fill the space between her and the kitchen door. Judy almost bumped into him and looked up at his face. He didn't look the same. Where had those kind, warm brown eyes gone? They looked stormy, almost black.

Instinctively, she turned away and considered the back door. She knew it was locked. She could picture the key in the lock. Her legs felt leaden. Her body lurched towards the door and as it did, she felt Fischer's strong arm around her neck.

He reached out and grabbed her. Taking a fistful of hair, he yanked her head back while sliding his other arm around her neck and squeezing just enough to let her know he meant business.

With a firm hold around her neck, he let go of her hair and placed his hand over her mouth. He whispered in her ear. "If you scream, I'll break your neck. Believe me, it'll snap like a twig."

He felt her body go heavy as fear overwhelmed her. He could smell her perfume; it reminded him of his grandmother's rose garden when he was a boy. Her hair felt silky on the side of his face. "I don't want to hurt you, but I need a place to stay for a short while. If you do as I say, and don't do anything stupid, I give you my word you will not be harmed. Nod if you understand."

Judy nodded.

"I'm going to take my hand away. If you scream, I'll crush your neck."

Even if she had wanted to, Judy was too scared to make any kind of sound.

Fischer moved his hand away from her mouth. "Good girl."

Judy was trembling. Her body shook and she couldn't stop it. She thought she might pee herself. She found the strength to say, "I've got money. Take my money and leave me. I won't tell anyone you were here. Not even the police. No one."

"We can talk about money another time. Right now, I just need a place to crash."

"You could let me go and stay here. I'll stay with a friend. I won't say a word. I swear."

"You seem like a very sweet and honest person, and I'm sure you'd keep your word, but I can't take the risk. I'm sorry, you need to stay here."

Fischer sat Judy in a chair. Using the tights he'd found in the bathroom wash basket, he gagged her. He used the belt from the dressing gown to tie her wrists together behind her back and then to the chair. Cutting the flex from a reading lamp, he used it to tie her ankles to the legs of the chair. He then got clingfilm from the cupboard and wrapped the clear plastic around her body and the chair.

Satisfied she couldn't call for help or move, he crouched down in front of her. "Open your eyes, Judy. Look at me. Everything's gonna be okay. I give you my word. Nod for me if you understand."

Judy nodded.

"I've got to go out for a little while and pick up a few things. I should only need to stay in your house a few days. Then, I'll be gone and out of your life for good. So please, be smart. Don't do anything silly, and very soon this will be over and you can carry on with your life. Do you understand?"

Judy nodded her head once more.

Fischer got up and, with his fingers, moved her hair out of her eyes. Judy recoiled.

"About my sister Faye. She likes to be called Moon. You

69

remember we spoke about her in McDonald's? Back in the restaurant I told a little white lie. You were right. She isn't really my sister. Now, the thing about Moon is that she can be a little… how can I put it? Unpredictable. Volatile. Moon can be a little excitable. She's also the jealous type. The thing is, she'll be joining us. I'll do my best to keep her away from you. Don't worry, I feel sure it'll all work out. Sit tight. I won't be long."

Fischer picked up Judy's house keys from the kitchen worktop and walked out without looking back.

Judy shuddered. Hearing the front door close made her feel more alone than she'd ever felt before. Fat, warm tears rolled down her cheeks. Her body shook as she sobbed. She desperately needed to pee. Her throat ached as she moaned behind the gag.

The silence of the house tore through her body like a million screaming sorrows. Her mind raced as she processed all the mistakes that had led up to her being tied to a chair by a madman. She was the victim. Once again, she'd allowed a man to take advantage of her. Why her? How could she have behaved differently? Her instincts had warned her. Why hadn't she listened to them? Why had she been so eager to trust him? She had little doubt that unless she could escape, her need to feel warmth and human contact would have just cost her her life.

CHAPTER SIXTEEN

Fischer and Moon sat in the car watching the home of Inspector Hardy. Moon had her bare feet on the dashboard and was painting her toenails sparkly pink. The radio played a modern song Moon didn't recognise. It didn't stop her singing along.

"For Christ's sake, Moon, can you focus? And do you have to do that now? Your nail polish stinks." Fischer opened the window a little.

Moon wriggled her body to the rhythm of the music. She answered by singing her own words to the song: "Uh-huh. Uh-huh. I need to do my tinkly toe-oe-oe-oes. I want to look hot for my man. For my ma-a-a-a-n!"

Fischer shook his head in frustration.

"What's Judy like? Is she pretty? Is her house nice?"

"She's normal. Just an average, normal person. What can I say?"

"Do you fancy her?"

"No. That's enough. Don't start down that road."

"What road?"

"You know exactly what road. I chose her because she

lives alone. She got unlucky. We're using her house for a day or two. Then we're out of there. We don't need to harm her. We're going far enough away that it's not necessary to hurt her, but she doesn't know that." Turning his attention back to the house, he shifted his weight and leaned against the car door. As he did, a dark-blue Honda CR-V reversed out the driveway. He could make out two women and two girls inside. One of the women he guessed must be Hardy's girlfriend or wife, and the girls were definitely his daughters; they had his look about them. Fischer nudged Moon and nodded towards the car.

Moon looked up and saw the back of the Honda as it turned in the road and accelerated away from them. "About time." She was fanning her toenails with her hand and blowing on them. "We can't go just yet. My toes aren't dry." Moon fanned her feet furiously. "I'll know if you're lying."

"I don't fancy her. Drop it."

"Okay," said Moon, unconvinced.

They waited ten minutes before approaching the house. Fischer carried a black canvas bag containing tools.

Moon peered through the front window. Fischer went around the back. Feeling exposed and unable to see much at the front, Moon followed Fischer to the rear of the house. Fischer looked up at her as she approached. "There's a dog in there."

"Well, it's a shit guard dog. What's it doing? Sleeping?" said Moon, sarcastically.

"I don't think it's noticed us."

"What are we going to do now? I don't want to get bitten by a dog," said Moon as she leaned against the glass and peered inside.

"I've got an idea. We should leave Hardy a surprise."

Thinking whatever it was sounded like fun, Moon

smiled. "I'll go back around the front and distract the dog."

Fischer took a crowbar and a screwdriver from the black canvas bag and started examining the edges of the patio doors. "I'll get these patio doors open, while you call the dog through the letterbox. Just mind your fingers."

Moon skipped as she made her way to the front of the house. Fischer took off his jacket and, leaving his fingers free, wrapped it around his forearm, tying the sleeves in a knot over his wrist to keep the jacket in place.

The dog, a golden Labrador, was barking now. It came running up to the patio doors and watched him as he jammed the crowbar into the gap beside the lock. He waited for Moon to call the dog through the letterbox before forcing the door open.

Moon started calling. "Here, doggy-dog. Come here, doggy-dog-dog."

The dog stopped barking and turned its head. It didn't move; instead, it turned back and barked again at Fischer.

Moon rang the doorbell, knocked on the door and called. "Doggy! Come on, doggy. Good doggy! Look what I've got for you. What's this?"

The dog calmed down at the sound of Moon's soothing voice and trotted across the kitchen and up the hall to the front door, where it stood sniffing and looking back and forth between Moon and Fischer.

Fischer worked quickly. He moved the crowbar back and forth while pressing his weight onto it. He moved the crowbar to the hinges, both top and bottom, and did the same before moving it back to the middle. The patio door creaked and sprang open. He stepped into the kitchen of DCI James Hardy.

Seeing Fischer enter the house, the dog began barking again. It bounded down the hallway and back into the kitchen. Fischer moved around the kitchen table and kept it between him and the dog.

"Hello, girl," said Fischer. "Who's a good girl?" The dog stopped barking and watched him. "Are you hungry?" The dog wagged its tail. "Yeah. You're hungry. Shall I see what there is?" Carefully and slowly, with the arm wrapped in his jacket out towards the dog for protection, he made his way over to the fridge.

Fischer opened it and pulled out some cooked chicken and sandwich ham slices. He unwrapped the meat and threw it down on the floor. Carefully, he stepped forward and stroked the dog. The dog sniffed the meat, looked at Fischer then wolfed it down.

The dog lifted its head when Moon appeared at the patio doors. She stepped into the kitchen and watched. "What are you doing? You look like you're going to adopt it."

Fischer crouched down beside the dog, and it started licking his face. Its whole body swayed from side to side as it enthusiastically wagged its tail. "Have you ever wondered why dogs are so trusting and obedient?" he mused. "The shit and abuse some dogs must take from their owners, and yet they are unquestioningly loyal. Centuries ago, dogs worked out that if they hang around humans, they get fed. We worked out that dogs are great for protection. Perfect partnership."

Moon walked over to the worktop where a block of knives sat. She pulled the large cook's knife from the block. Fischer took some more food from the fridge and tossed it to the dog to underline his point.

Moon's eyes fixed on the dog's neck. She walked around the table to get a better view and raised the knife.

Fischer jumped up and grabbed her wrist. "What the

hell are you doing? We can't kill the bloody dog. It's a dog. It's like killing one of his kids. Are you crazy?"

Moon struggled and yanked her wrist away. She slammed the knife down on the worktop. "What the hell are we here for, then?" She began to walk in circles.

"I don't believe you sometimes. Let's just go through the house. Learn the lay of the land and get out of here. I can't believe you wanted to kill the man's dog!"

Moon continued to pace up and down and around.

Fischer had seen her like this before. "Why don't you wait for me in the car? I'll take a quick look around, and you can beep the horn if you see someone coming."

Moon looked at Fischer and down at the dog. "Okay. I'll do that."

Fischer reached into the fridge and pulled out the tomato-sauce bottle. "Moon, before you go."

"Yeah?"

He handed her the bottle. "Squirt the dog."

Moon laughed. She took the bottle and squirted the red sauce all over the top of the dog's head and down its back and over the floor and table and chairs and cupboards. With her arm, she swept the items on the kitchen table onto the floor, then did the same to the worktops. She went to the sink and swept the plates from the draining board into the sink. Finally, she kicked over the kitchen bin.

CHAPTER SEVENTEEN

While Fischer struggled to open the door to Judy's bungalow, Moon wrapped her arms around his neck and chewed on his ear. The pair of them nearly fell into the hallway as the door opened.

Fischer had wondered whether Moon was using again and, seeing her behaviour now, he was sure of it. She was more restless, excited and agitated than usual. Before his arrest, she'd given up the drugs. It had been tough, but she'd done it; he was proud of how hard she'd fought. But without him looking out for her, both her cravings and the bastard dealers had got their claws into her again.

"That stupid dog – we should have killed it. Bam!" Moon ran around waving and thrusting her hand like she held a knife. "Slash! Slash! Slash! I'd have loved to see the look on Hardy's face when he got home and found his pooch with its throat cut. Why didn't you let me kill the dog?" Moon made a whining noise like a dying dog as she unbuttoned his shirt and unfastened his trouser belt.

Moon led the way, pulling him through the house by

his waistband, looking for the bedroom. Her left eye was twitching, and she kept touching her face and hair.

Turning on the hall light, Fischer took Moon's chin and tilted her head to look into her eyes. They were red and bloodshot. Her skin was sweaty, but she was cold to the touch.

"Come on, Eddie," said Moon. She stood in front of him in the hallway and kicked off her shoes. She unbuttoned her jeans, rolled them down with a wriggle and kicked them behind her. She then took off her sweater and threw it over her shoulder. She unfasted her bra and let it fall to the floor, then began dancing provocatively in just her knickers. "I need you. I want you. Come and get me." Seeing the door to the lounge open, she ran into the room and jumped on the armchair.

Fischer followed. "Are you high?"

"I'm buzzing, that's all. We just broke into Inspector Hardy's house. Now get over here. I'm horny as hell." Moon sat down and leaned back on the armchair, then spread her legs over the arms of the chair. She reached out and repeatedly called to him. "Get your arse over here now," she demanded. "Fischer? Now!"

Fischer remained by the door. He could see it now; she was definitely high. "You know what I mean. You're high. Don't you lie to me."

"Yeah, okay, so I did a little coke. So what? Who doesn't? It's no big deal. What are you, my dad?"

"Do you remember how hard it was to get off all that shit? Do you remember what it was like? It starts with a little coke, and then what? Uppers to keep you even when you crash and downers to help you sleep?"

"Fuck you! Don't get all high and mighty. If it wasn't for me, you'd still be rotting in a cell. You want to know something? You've been a real pain in the butt since you got out. I don't know what's been going on in that head of yours, but I don't like it. Whatever it is, you need to get over it. You're at serious risk of becoming a bore."

"What the hell are you talking about?"

"You came out and you were spouting all this stuff about making Hardy's life a living hell, and now you're all 'Don't kill the dog! What are you doing, Moon? We can't kill the man's dog!' I don't get it. What's with you?"

Moon got up and started examining the room. She picked up ornaments and pictures in frames. Finally, she said, "I'm going to take a shower. You missed your chance to screw me. Which way is the bathroom?"

She tried to push past Fischer, but he grabbed her by the arm. Moon shrugged and pulled away, but Fischer didn't let go. "I didn't mean to upset you. I'm sorry. I just don't want you going back down that rabbit hole. Putting that shit into your body... Neither of us wants that. Promise me you'll stop, before it's too late."

Moon couldn't look at him.

"Please, Moon. It's the real Moonbeam I want."

"Okay. I'll stop. But you've got to lighten up. At least tell me what's going on. It's more than just Hardy, I know that much. I'm not stupid."

"You're right. There's something else I have to do before we leave the country. But I don't want to say anything right now."

Moon lifted her head and looked at him. "Fine," she said. "You don't want to tell me, that's fine."

"I do and I will. Just not right now," said Fischer.

"Mind if I take a shower?"

Fischer let go of her arm. "It's down there on the right."

Fischer sat down on the sofa. He listened to the shower come on, Moon stomping about, and the shower curtain being thrashed along the rail. He could feel her anger resonating from down the hall.

Fischer pulled his wallet from his trouser pocket. He opened it and took out a dog-eared and faded photo of a child. The infant was sat on a low wall. She wore a white dress with embroidered yellow daisies. Her white, soft shoes had silver buckles. Her brown hair, which reached her shoulders, was fine and had a slight wave in it. She was smiling and holding out an ice cream to the camera. He remembered the moment like it was yesterday.

Fischer tucked the photo back into his wallet. He got up and walked down the hall to the bathroom. He opened the door and stood in the doorway watching Moon through the shower curtain. She was motionless, head down, letting the water cascade over her hair.

"So, what's next?" asked Moon. "You know we've left prints all over his house. He'll know soon enough it was us that broke in."

"I want Hardy to know it's me. Otherwise, there's no point in me doing any of this. I want him worried."

"What do you have in mind? I assume you want to do more than cover his dog in ketchup," scoffed Moon.

"We give it a few days and then we go back. We're going to seriously heat things up." Fischer was feeling the joy of freedom again. Even having an argument felt good. Arguing was what normal couples did. He also had purpose. For him, the greatest hardship of life in prison had been a lack of purpose. "I don't want to be looking over my shoulder the rest of my life. We go back and we give Hardy a message he'll never forget. It needs to be big and direct. We send him a message that demonstrates in no uncertain terms that any time I choose, I can rain down fire and brimstone. It's not something I relish, but it's the only way to guarantee he doesn't come after me."

CHAPTER EIGHTEEN

It was a warm day, so Rayner and Jenny had gone for a spin in his new toy. Just before he'd learned he was going to be a father, Rayner had treated himself to a sporty Mercedes convertible. He now joked he'd better make the most of the car before needing to trade it in for a more sedate family saloon, with space for a buggy and all the paraphernalia that goes with transporting a child. Plus, child-proof fabrics that wouldn't show dropped and ground-in food and spilled drinks or vomit.

While they were out, we'd taken the opportunity to get some food shopping done. I opened the front door of our home and stepped aside to let Alice, Faith and Monica go in first. When Sandy didn't come bounding up the hallway, I assumed she'd managed to get herself stuck in one of the rooms. She has a habit of entering a room and knocking a door shut with her backside.

Barking came from the kitchen. "Sandy! Where are you?" called Faith. She ran towards the barking while Alice went to the sitting room to charge her phone. Monica, with a shopping bag in each hand, followed Faith to the kitchen.

I put my bags in the hallway and went back out to grab the last bag and lock the car.

"James!" called Monica. "James! Come see this."

I grabbed the shopping bag and shut the back of the car.

"Daddy!" called Faith with alarm in her voice.

I ran into the house, almost knocking over Alice, who had come out of the sitting room to see what the commotion was about. Monica and Faith stepped aside and let me through the kitchen door. Alice followed me.

Sandy was barking at us and furiously wagging her tail, wondering why nobody was making a fuss of her.

"Who did it, Daddy?" said Alice.

Faith was clinging to Monica. "Is Sandy okay? Who did that to her?"

"I don't know," I said. "She's fine." It had looked at first glance as though Sandy were covered in blood, but the smell told me it was ketchup. Her coat was matted with it. There was red fluid on the floor around her feet and up the side of the white refrigerator that she had been tied to with her lead. The kitchen looked a wreck. Somebody had gone to town on trashing it.

"Who tied her to the fridge?" asked Faith.

"I don't know," I repeated.

"Have you seen the back door?" asked Alice.

"Yes. I've seen it." I looked at Monica. She understood the look.

"Okay, girls. Let's go," said Monica. "Let's give Daddy some space." Monica led the girls away despite a barrage of complaints.

I untied Sandy and led her out to the front of the house, where I asked if the girls would like to hose her down. They jumped at the chance, while Sandy, who quickly worked out what was coming, looked less enamoured.

Back in the kitchen, I examined the back door. It had been forced. I phoned the local police. While I waited for them to arrive, I checked around the house to see what had been stolen. It quickly became apparent nothing was missing. Perhaps we'd disturbed them as we arrived home. Maybe some kids just wanted to let off steam and thought it would be funny to vandalise a home. I sighed and leaned against the worktop. What a bloody mess.

CHAPTER NINETEEN

At the driveway of the house, I took the lead off a freshly scrubbed Sandy and let her run up to the house. Across the street was a familiar face. Detective Inspector Emma Cotton got out of her car and crossed the road.

My dog-walking buddy, Faith, spotted her and waved. "Hi, Emma," she called. "Did you hear we got burgled, kinda? Nothing was stolen, but Sandy got slimed with ketchup."

"Hi, sweetheart," said Emma. "Yes, I heard about that. I'm sorry.

"Daddy said she looked like a hot dog."

"Your daddy's funny, isn't he?"

"Sometimes," said Faith. "Usually, his jokes are rubbish." She looked at me with a cheeky smile, then back at Emma. "Your hair looks nice. I'd like mine short like yours. I bet Monica won't let me."

"Your hair is perfect just the way it is. I love seeing yours in plaits. If you have it short like this, you won't be able to do that." Cotton flicked her new haircut to demonstrate how short it was.

"Suppose you're right. I'm going to ask anyway. Are you staying for dinner? You can sit next to me. We're having tuna pasta and garlic bread. Monica said we'll probably have to have fruit for dessert because that's all we've got and it's good for me. I do have some jelly snakes in my school bag we can share."

"I can't tonight, honey. Maybe next time."

"Are you doing anything nice instead?"

"I have a date."

"What's his name?"

"Alex. He's a dentist."

"Make sure you brush your teeth before your date then. He's bound to check."

Emma laughed. "I will. I'll brush them good and proper, even the back ones."

"Why don't you run in and wash your hands ready for dinner?" I said to Faith, who looked disappointed. She gave Cotton a hug and ran inside. "You know she says she want to be an inspector like you when she grows up," I told Emma. "Not like me – like you."

We both laughed.

"A date? That sounds nice," I said, encouragingly.

"It's more of a drink with a friend who happens to be male and recently single. I'm not sure I'm ready for anything serious, to be honest. David was a big part of my life for so long."

The image of Cotton discovering David's mutilated body flashed across my mind. "It must be tough to move on," I said. "But somehow we must."

I watched as her expression changed, and I knew her visit wasn't the social kind. She looked down at the ground as she gathered her thoughts.

"What's on your mind, Cotton?" I leaned against the garden wall and held my breath. "Is it the break-in?"

"No." I watched as she chose her words carefully. "There's been a prison escape. I was worried you might have seen it on the news before I got here."

"No. We've been out all day. I've not heard the news yet."

Cotton looked me in the eye. "It was Edward Fischer."

"What?" My mind exploded with a million questions and even more concerns.

"I'm sorry. I've only just heard, myself. At first it was kept quiet in the hope he could be recaptured quickly. That was five days ago. Now, news outlets are free to broadcast details."

"This can't be happening. You're telling me that almost exactly one month after Kelly Lyle informs me Edward Fischer murdered my wife, he miraculously escapes a maximum-security prison? That's no coincidence, Cotton." Suddenly a horrible thought struck me. "Is that why you're here? Do you think this break-in is connected?"

"I don't know, Hardy. It could be. What we do know is that Fischer was being moved between Larkstone Prison and hospital. The prison officers were held at gunpoint. There's good reason to believe he had inside help."

"No kidding. Of course he had help." I wasn't angry at Cotton; she was just the messenger used to soften the blow.

"Word is he's planning to get out of the country. The chances are he'll be picked up at a port or airport or train station. As soon as I know more, I'll be in touch."

My mind was doing somersaults. I needed time to think. "I might have some questions. If I do, can I call you later or tomorrow? I need to take this news in."

"You have my number. I'm going to be busy. If I don't pick up, leave a message and I'll call you back. I was one of the last people to interview Fischer, so it's considered important I'm added to the task force tracking him down. I've also been questioned. You know how it is."

"Yeah, I do." I looked over my shoulder at the house. I could hear laughter coming from inside. "Can we keep this between us for the time being? Rayner's here with his wife, and we've been celebrating their good news. They're going to be parents."

"That's wonderful." Cotton beamed. "Please pass on my congratulations. And of course I won't say a word."

"Are you sure you won't come in for a few minutes?"

"No. Thank you. I'd better get going." Cotton checked the time on her phone. "I'll pop by again soon. It'll be good to catch up."

"Thank you, Cotton." I stayed leaning against the wall as I watched her drive away. I felt physically sick. I didn't want to go inside the house. I knew what this was. This was Lyle's first move in her sick game of chess. She'd just moved her pawn. Edward Fischer was free. Now, I felt sure she was waiting to see what my move would be.

CHAPTER TWENTY

From their candlelit table, Cotton could see the shimmer of the full moon on the sea beneath the clear night sky and twinkling stars. Lights sparkled along the quayside and from boats moored in the marina.

"I've had a lovely evening, Alex. Thank you," said Cotton.

"Me too," said Alex. "I'd like to do it again… if you'd like that."

"A third date," Cotton said. "Are you sure you can put up with me a third time?"

Alex smiled and said, "Why do you do that?"

"What?"

"Put yourself down. Why wouldn't I want a third date? You're intelligent, funny and beautiful." Alex took Cotton's hand. "I definitely want to know you better, Emma."

Cotton blushed. "My last relationship ended badly. He betrayed me. I suppose I thought it was my fault the relationship had gone off the rails. My job sometimes takes over. Truth is, I know it was at least partly my fault. I let it happen. It was easier to ignore the problems than to deal with the truth that we'd drifted apart."

"I'm sorry," said Alex. He squeezed Cotton's hand. "It's better you broke up than had a lifetime of unhappiness. Hopefully, he's found someone now who's right for him."

"He died."

"Oh, I'm sorry. How did he die? Was it an illness?" He paused and reddened. "That's personal – you don't need to answer that."

"He was murdered. Let's leave it there. I don't want to put a downer on the evening."

"Of course. Unlike my life as a dentist, I suppose I'll have to get used to some questions about work being out of bounds if my girlfriend is a detective inspector."

Cotton's heart fluttered. "Girlfriend? Is that what I am?"

Alex sat a little straighter. He took a hand away and nervously fiddled with his cuff link. "I'd like that, if you would."

"I would," said Cotton. "I have an early start tomorrow, but if you'd like to, you're welcome to finish the evening with a nightcap at my place."

"That's a lovely idea, Emma. Next time, maybe?"

Cotton suddenly wanted the ground to open up and swallow her whole. "No, no, that's fine. I understand. That's not a good idea." She could feel her face glowing like a furnace. *What was I thinking? Idiot.*

"It's a beautiful idea. You have no idea how much I want to. I'm in agony – believe me, there's nothing I want more. I just want to take things slowly. I have a good feeling about us. Let's take it slow. We've got all the time in the world." Alex took Emma's hand again and kissed it. "Thank you."

CHAPTER TWENTY-ONE

"Is that you, Timmy?"

"Yes, it is, Mum."

"I can always tell, you know."

"I know you can. It's time you get some sleep, Mum."

"You'll turn the light out, won't you? I can hear it crackling if you don't."

Spicer kissed his mother's forehead. Despite the room being hot, she felt like ice. He pulled the blanket and duvet up over her shoulders. "I'll turn it out, Mum."

Before leaving the room, he checked around the bed one last time that she was tucked in and comfortable. He switched off the light and closed the door behind him. "Night, Mum," he said softly. "Love you."

"Night, sweetheart," said the old woman. "Love you too."

Spicer went down the stairs to the kitchen. He looked in the fridge and took out half a cold pizza and a can of fizzy orange. He bit off a chunk from the pizza. The rest he flopped on a plate and nuked in the microwave until the cheese bubbled.

"Timothy Spicer?" said Donny.

Spicer spun around to find two men stood in his mother's kitchen. He could see immediately they weren't police. One was dressed like some sort of cowboy but without the Stetson. His right boot had some nasty-looking stains. The other man was skinny and funny looking; his eyes bulged out and he was stick thin, like a praying mantis.

"How'd you get in here?" barked Spicer.

"Don't be alarmed," said Donny. "My associate and I would like to ask you a couple of questions."

The cowboy let the skinny fella talk. The cowboy's slick, dyed-black hair glistened under the kitchen's strip lamp. While occasionally keeping an eye on proceedings, he picked at his teeth with his fingernail and at the same time looked through cabinets and drawers.

Spicer had a bad feeling about his unwelcome guests. Deciding his best option was to get out of the house, he looked around for a weapon to defend himself with. He picked up the silver pedal bin and threw it at the two men, then made a bolt for the back door.

Barton stopped looking through the cereal cupboard. Having anticipated the move, he grabbed an empty saucepan from off the worktop and hurled it at the back of Spicer's head. Spicer lurched sideways and smacked his forehead on the corner of a wall-mounted glass cabinet. The glass door of the cabinet shook and the pudding bowls and side plates inside rattled. Spicer fell backwards and was out cold.

"Christ! What did we talk about in the car? What did I say?" said Donny.

Barton began sorting through the cereals.

"So that's it? You're just going to ignore me? If we have a plan, we both need to stick to it. You agreed I'm in

90

charge. That means I come up with the plan and you follow it. Simple. That's how plans work. That's how me being in charge works. Did I or did I not say we'll present ourselves, act friendly and appeal to his sense of right and wrong before possibly, I repeat possibly, progressing to any less civil activities? Are you even listening?"

Barton didn't answer. Having chosen his preferred breakfast cereal, he put the rest back in the cupboard. He then walked across the kitchen and lifted Spicer onto the yellow-and-white-checked Formica table. The sides of the drop-leaf table were down, making it narrow. He rolled Spicer onto his front; his head flopped over one end of the table and his legs sprawled over the other end while his arms hung down the sides. With Sellotape from the kitchen drawer, he taped each limb to a table leg, wrapping the tape round and round to make Spicer was secure. He then picked up the saucepan he'd thrown and filled it with cold water.

"Oh, Jesus! What are you going to do?" asked Donny.

Barton held up the saucepan and slowly poured water over Spicer's head.

Regaining consciousness, Spicer spluttered and struggled as the cold water soaked him.

Donny stepped back as the water splashed over the floor. He didn't say anything; he simply nodded in appreciation. The cowboy might be infuriating, but he certainly had a way of getting things done.

With Spicer conscious and cursing, Barton went back to his breakfast cereal. He read the ingredients on the side of a packet of honey nut puffs before filling a bowl, adding milk from the fridge and choosing a spoon from the drawer.

"What, you're hungry? Now?" asked Donny.

"Uh-huh. Low blood sugar," said Barton.

"What about *him*?" Donny pointed at Spicer.

"What *about* him?" Barton took a mouthful of cereal and ate it noisily. Slurping and chewing loudly. Topped off with a loud, satisfied sniff.

"What do you mean, 'What about him?'" said Donny.

"I dunno. Get on and ask him your questions. You're in charge, remember?" Barton scraped a chair to the corner of the kitchen, sat down and continued to get stuck into his bowl of sugary cereal.

Donny turned and looked down at Spicer, who was writhing furiously. He crouched down, so that their eyes were level, and smiled sympathetically, then turned and scowled at Barton. "Would you mind keeping it down? You're eating really noisily. The slurping is off-putting. I'm trying to think."

Barton raised his eyebrows and muttered under his breath. He put the spoon down on the worktop, held the bowl to his lips and slurped deliberately loudly as he drained it.

Oh, for fuck's sake. Donny turned back to the matter at hand. "Mr Spicer," he started. "Timothy. I'd like to assure you, we're not the police."

"Are you for real? Of course you're not the police," said Spicer.

Barton chuckled.

Donny turned and gave him a look that asked, *Whose side are you on?* He turned back to Spicer and continued in a calm, almost apologetic manner. "Before I get into the why of why *we're* here, can I ask why *you're* here? Why, after breaking Edward Fischer out of prison, with the help of Faye Moon, you didn't vanish. Disappear. *Poof!* Fade away?" He smiled. "Yes, we know all about your exploits."

Spicer raised his head. "Edward who? Edward

92

Flintoff? Edward Bishop? May Spoon? Who did you say? My ears are still ringing from the saucepan to the head."

"Fischer, Edward Fischer. Let's not do this the hard way. We know you helped Fischer escape. We know you planned on leaving the country after you left them. I just wondered why you didn't leave the country."

"My mum," said Spicer. His eyes turned towards the upstairs. "She's terminally ill. She doesn't have long. I can't just leave her."

"Okay, I'm sorry about your mother, but this is good. So you care for your mother. We're getting somewhere." Donny looked proudly over his shoulder at Barton.

Barton shook his head in disbelief.

"My next question," continued Donny, "and please think before you answer: where did you take Fischer? Where is he? We'd very much like to speak with him."

"You have the wrong guy," insisted Spicer. "I don't know any Fischer. You're barking up the wrong tree, mate."

Speaking in a soothing tone, Donny pressed on. "You're not the wrong guy. I'm certainly not your mate. Think about it. Do we look like amateurs to you?"

"No. You look like a couple of rejects from some second-rate circus freak show."

Donny raised his voice. "Jeez! Why are you making this difficult? I'm trying to be a gentleman. I'm being civil. I'm asking you politely. Yet you're rude and uncooperative. I don't get it."

The chair behind Donny scraped as Barton got to his feet. He slammed his cereal bowl on to the worktop and grabbed the packet of honey nut puffs. He lifted the inner clear packet containing the cereal from the box and set it aside. He then flattened the box with his fist on the worktop.

Marching up to the table, he pushed Donny aside. Standing so Spicer could see, Barton rolled the empty cereal box into a tube. He then grabbed a large clump of Spicer's hair and wrenched his head back as far as he could. He put the rolled-up cereal packet to Spicer's mouth, which was clenched tight.

"Pinch his nose," growled Barton. "Donny! Snap out of it. Pinch his nose."

Donny jolted. He pinched Spicer's nose with his thumb and forefinger.

Spicer held on as long as he could, but as soon as he gave up and his mouth sprang open to gasp for breath, Barton jammed the end of the packet into Spicer's mouth and down his throat.

"Oh, Christ," said Donny, yanking his hand away. His face screwed up in discomfort at the sight of what looked like Spicer being skewered alive.

Spicer choked and gagged and groaned. His body bucked and shook. The table rocked like a wooden horse as Barton put his weight behind the rolled-up cereal box, forcing the rolled cereal packet deep into Spicer's mouth and throat. Barton bent over and whispered into Spicer's ear. "Are you gonna answer his questions?"

Barton took some of his weight off the cereal packet, and Spicer sobbed and nodded furiously. Barton removed the rolled-up cereal box and put it on Spicer's back. "I'll leave this here in case you change your mind." He returned to his chair, where he poured more cereal into his bowl and continued noisily eating his sugary snack.

Donny stared at the blood and spit dripping from Spicer's mouth. "I was hoping the cowboy wouldn't need to get all… you know… brutal," he said, shaking his head. "If you just answer the questions, we'll be on our way. Shall we try again?" said Donny.

With tears from the pain streaming down his face, Spicer nodded. "Fischer's got the money. It's in a black canvas bag with a few clothes an' shit. They gave me a few grand, that's all. My money's gone. I spent it on nursing care for my mother. She's dying."

Barton stopped mid-slurp and listened in on the conversation.

"What the hell are you talking about?" said Donny. "We're here about Fischer. Where's Edward Fischer?"

"I took him to a guest house."

"Where?"

"Southampton," croaked Spicer. "My throat's swelling up. I need some water."

"In a minute. What was the name of the guest house?"

Spicer whispered the name.

"What? What did you say? Speak up."

Spicer whispered again. Quieter.

Donny knelt beneath Spicer's lolling head. Spicer's voice was now barely audible. "Whaddaya say?" Donny put his ear close to Spicer's mouth… too close.

"Fuck! Ah, shit! This fucker's… he's biting my ear!" screamed Donny. "Fucking fucker!"

Dropping his cereal bowl, Barton jumped to his feet. He grabbed a cook's knife from the knife block that sat on a window ledge over the sink. In seconds, he was over Spicer with the knife raised. He brought it down at the base of Spicer's skull. The blade entered one side and came out through the other, where it carved a groove in the edge of the table. The penetrating knife caused a reflex that made Spicer's jaw clamp down and bite off a large part of Donny's right ear.

Blood spilled from Spicer's throat. His body convulsed and urine spilled over the edges of the table. He made gurgling and spluttering sounds while his body trembled and eventually shut down.

Donny fell back onto the floor. He held his hand where his ear had been. Blood streamed down his neck and wrist. "My ear. It's gone. That fucker… Where's my ear?"

Barton threw Donny a tea towel. "Use it. You're making a mess. I think your ear's in his mouth."

"Get it. Get my ear."

"No way. I might lose a finger."

Donny looked at Barton pleadingly. "He's not moving. He's dead."

"You want your ear? Then what? Hospital?"

"Yes, I want the hospital. I want my ear sewn back on."

"We can't go to a hospital. We just killed a man."

"You killed a man."

"Only because you were getting your ear bitten off." Barton cracked up at the thought. "You should have seen your face. 'He's biting my ear! Help me! Help me!' You crack me up." Barton leaned against the kitchen door to steady himself as he doubled over with laughter. "Why'd you get so close? Hoping he might tongue your ear? If you need a woman, I'll get you a woman."

Still laughing, Barton tiptoed over to Spicer. He pulled the knife out. Spicer's mouth sprang open, and the piece of ear dropped out like a Snickers bar from a vending machine.

Donny picked up the piece of ear.

"You might want to wash it," snorted Barton. He went to the freezer and grabbed a tub of ice cream. "Here you go. Keep it cold." He dropped the knife in the sink and washed it. Using another tea towel, he dried it and, careful not to leave prints, placed it back in the block.

Donny picked up the piece of ear and carefully wrapped it in some kitchen towel, then placed it inside the half-eaten tub of ice cream. "Let's get out of here. You're taking me to the hospital whether you like it or not. I don't care what we tell them happened, but they're going to sew this back on."

"Whatever."

"What about the old woman?" said Donny.

"You want her to tongue your other ear? You're a sick man."

"No. I mean, do we just leave her?"

"Yeah. You want to kill her, be my guest. I'm out of here."

Donny trotted to keep up as they left through the back door and stepped into the darkness of the back garden. "Why would you say something like that?" asked Donny as they crossed the lawn. "About the sick old lady tonguing my ear. You know I like regular babes, right? You know, pin-ups, like most guys."

Barton shrugged. He opened the back gate at the end of the garden and let Donny go first. He wasn't done teasing. "What you're into is none of my business."

Donny could hear Barton laughing. "I'm not into anything. Regular, hot, beautiful women – that's it. Okay? I have a reputation. You know how gossip spreads. I don't want you spreading rumours."

"We just killed a guy," said Barton. "You have your ear bitten off, and you're worried I might think you're into kinky fetish sex stuff with terminally ill old ladies. You're weird. All right, let's get to an A&E. If we don't, I know you're gonna be whining for the rest of this job. More importantly, I don't want to be looking at your messed-up ear. It's ugly."

CHAPTER TWENTY-TWO

Moonlight sparkled on the water. Wave after wave crashed on the shore, sweeping shells, sand and pebbles back beneath the retreating tide. On the beach a fire crackled and popped as driftwood heaved and splintered amidst the flames.

Moon sat hunched beside the fire. With her arms wrapped around her knees, she stared at her toes as she wriggled them beneath the cold sand. She turned and looked at Fischer as she flicked her cigarette ash into the flames.

Fischer lay on his back, cigarette in hand, blowing smoke and staring up at the night sky. "I can't remember the last time I just stopped and looked up at the stars," he said.

Moon gazed up. "They're beautiful. So bright. You don't see them so bright in the city."

"When I was little," said Fischer, "my mum told me the stars were angels. 'The sky is full of billions of angels. Don't ever be scared of death or of being alone. When you die, you join them. During the day all those souls are playing and having a good time. You only see them at night, because at night they're resting and looking down on us and keeping us safe.'"

"Aw! That's so sweet. Your mum sounds amazing," said Moon.

"Yeah. She told me that right before she took an overdose and opened her wrists. Shortly after, I was taken into care. I was ten years old."

"I'm sorry, babe."

"I guess she was trying to tell me something. I didn't know it at the time. I just felt lost, confused and guilty and angry."

"She was definitely telling you something. Just because she couldn't cope with the world doesn't mean she wasn't looking out for you. You were her little man."

"I guess she's up there now. I wonder which one she is."

Moon looked up at the stars. She pointed at the brightest one. "That one," said Moon.

Fischer twisted his head to look. "Yeah. That's a good one."

"You can introduce me, when we both join her. I'd like to meet your mum."

"You bet. She'll have a lot of explaining to do when I see her," said Fischer.

"You will too, baby."

Fischer grinned. "You're right. Still, I can blame her for my life getting screwed up."

Moon dragged her bag close and unzipped it. "You cold? How about a drink?"

"Uh-huh."

Moon took out a bottle of vodka, unscrewed the cap, took a sip and passed Fischer the bottle. "Can I ask you something?"

"Depends what it is." Fischer zipped up his jacket then flipped up the collar against the cold.

"Hardy's wife? We never got a chance to talk about what really happened."

"What do you want to know?"

"Why was she killed? I never did understand."

Fischer sat up and took a long swig from the bottle. He flicked his cigarette butt into the flames and watched it burn. "It's complicated. I don't suppose it matters anymore whether you know or not."

"I know you don't start things. Though I do know that when necessary you finish them."

Fischer sighed deeply and gathered his thoughts. "I did this job with a couple of fellas called Berg and Zippy. I hardly knew them. I didn't want to do the job, but I owed Stan Wires. Do you know Stan Wires?"

"I've heard the name. Is Wires the one who put his cousin's hand in a deep fat fryer when he found out he'd been dating his virgin daughter? What was his cousin's name?"

"Picky. But that story isn't true. His cousin, Picky – they call him Picky because he won't leave his nose alone. Anyway, he burned his hand when his Rolex slipped off his wrist into a pan of boiling pasta at his brother-in-law's restaurant. Without thinking, he stuck his hand in to get it. But the deep-fat-fryer story became legend when Stan Wires retold it. A story like that one will make anyone think twice before going near your daughter. Not many people know the truth. And everyone except Wires knows his daughter is no virgin.

"Anyway, Stan Wires is a man short for this big job he has lined up. He knows I'm good at breaking and entering but that I prefer to work alone. The trouble is, I owe him. And he's not interested in my preferred working arrangements. He tells me it's a quick in and out. Nobody gets hurt, he says, and he reminds me what happens to people who refuse a gig when they owe him. So, I agree to help.

"Wires had been given a tip-off about a rare green diamond called Green Star owned by a private collector. Green diamonds, and coloured gems in general, are increasing in popularity and their value is rising, and Wires wanted to get his hands on it. Naturally, the private collector, an international businesswoman who owned the house, was loaded. I mean filthy rich.

"Wires had it on good authority she was going to be away, and the house would be empty. As Wires predicted, we got into the house easy enough.

"Berg had been part of the team that installed the house security, including the safe containing the diamond. Once we're inside we start going room to room. It was like winning the lottery. There were paintings on every wall. They looked like they belonged in a museum. They just had that look, you know, like they were worth a fortune. I know a bit about art, and I could tell. There were vases and ornaments in glass cases. But we were there for what was in the safe. The safe had the gem in it. I figured we'd do the gem, then I'd come back another time and rob the place again.

"I found out later, when Wire was found shot dead in his car, that he owed some Greeks, and it was them who insisted he get the Green Star diamond.

"Anyway, I'm following Berg and Zippy, going room to room. Remember, the place is supposed to be empty. So, we get upstairs to the master bedroom and surprise, surprise, we find a woman asleep in the bed. Just like Goldilocks, says Berg, and we're the three bears. Zippy assumes she's the owner of the house and the Green

Star. He puts two and two together and comes up with three.

"I'm thinking we're going to back up and get out of there. Instead, Zippy drags her out of bed and insists she opens the safe. She refuses, says she doesn't know the combination.

"While Berg attempts to get into the safe, Zippy gets handy with Goldilocks, slapping her about, trying to get the combination. Berg is trying to concentrate on the safe. I'm in the background trying to intervene on Goldilocks's behalf. I insist she knows nothing and tell Zippy to go easy on her. Zippy's not listening; he even threatens me. I can see his blood's up, and he keeps slapping her. Eventually, he gives her one slap too many and she goes down hard. I'm hoping she's unconscious: if she's unconscious, Zippy will leave her alone. But she's not. The idiot killed her."

"Christ! What a cock-up," said Moon.

"You said it. The whole thing's a fiasco, and it gets worse. Somehow, while trying to open the safe, Berg sets off an alarm. A separate alarm he claims he knows nothing about. We have no choice; we have to get out of there without the Green Star diamond."

"How does Hardy's wife fit into all this?" asked Moon.

"I'm getting to that. Turns out Goldilocks was the girlfriend of the businesswoman who owned the house and the Green Star diamond. A real piece of work called Kelly Lyle. One thing Wires neglected to tell us, or simply didn't know, is that Lyle's a complete psychopath. I mean she's nuts. She makes Jack the Ripper look like an amateur. And we killed Goldilocks, real name Leanne Dupres. She and Kelly Lyle were really into each other. I mean deep affection.

"With her money and connections, it didn't take Lyle long to discover who was behind her lover's death and who we were. She tracked down Zippy and Berg and literally took them apart piece by piece. I was told she kept them alive for days to prolong their suffering. From what I heard, the forensics team used a scoop to collect the pieces.

"Somehow, I managed to stay one step ahead of her. Or at least that's what I thought. The next thing I know, I'm in the frame for a string of murders because my DNA is found at each of the scenes. The women all have a similar look to Lyle's dead girlfriend. Lyle set me up to flush me out. I find myself not only on the run from Lyle but also being pursued by two Scotland Yard murder detectives, DI Rayner and DCI Hardy. I'm their prime suspect.

"You must understand, by this point I wasn't thinking straight. My head's spinning. One minute I'm helping out at a break-in, the next I'm standing over the dead girlfriend of a psychopath. Then, before I know it, I'm being framed as a serial killer. And the two fellas I did the job with are carpaccio.

"I'm hiding out wherever I can. Stan Wires is nowhere to be seen. As I said, the Greeks killed him when he didn't deliver the Green Star diamond. He got lucky. He could have been turned into chunks like Berg and Zippy.

"At the time, of course, I'm thinking Lyle got to him and I'm next. I also get word Inspector Hardy thinks it's me that killed Stan Wires, Berg and Zippy as well as the women. Next thing I know my face is all over the TV and I'm top of Britain's Most Wanted list.

"About this time, I'm staying with our mutual friend, DJ, party animal, pimp and small-time drug-dealing gangster, China Frizzell.

"Now China says he knows a fella who knows a fella who can stop Inspector Hardy. China explains to me that Inspector Hardy is like a bloodhound. He's Scotland Yard's number one manhunter. He's the Yard's top man when it comes to tracking down killers, especially serial killers. He tells me Hardy spent time with the FBI learning their techniques. At the time I couldn't see a way out. I had Lyle closing in on one side and Hardy on the other. And most likely the Greeks were gunning for me too. China convinced me that if I could get a break, I could somehow get out of the country and disappear.

"I couldn't see any other option. It's all a bit of a blur, if I'm honest, but I agree China should arrange for me to meet a fella called Tony Horn who would scare Hardy's wife enough for Hardy to take his eye off the ball so I could slip away.

"Here I am in the middle a storm, hanging on by my fingernails, and I think things can't get any worse. What I didn't know is that Horn is one of China's junkie customers. Horn was paying off part of what he owed China by scaring Mrs Hardy. So, I agree.

"Next thing I hear is that Hardy's wife is murdered. Horn stabbed her. In broad daylight, in the middle of a busy London street."

"You didn't kill her?" said Moon. Fischer shook his head. He lit another cigarette, tossed the packet to Moon and continued.

"Do you think any jury is going to think me innocent? I wasn't holding the knife, but I as good as killed Hardy's wife. Indirectly, Horn was working for me. Hardy has no idea I was behind it. When Horn was sent down for the murder, China made sure he was looked after and wouldn't talk. He also made it abundantly clear to Horn that if he ever mentioned my name or China's name it would be the last thing he ever did."

Moon lit herself a cigarette. She brought her knees up under her chin and listened. "What happened next?"

"That's the ironic thing. It didn't slow Hardy down at all. I thought the death of his wife would destroy his willpower, but it didn't. It simply made him more determined. You've got to admire the guy's tenacity. The guy's a machine. He's so distraught he throws himself into his work. Hardy redoubles his efforts, working day and night. Then, he gets a tip-off, and I get picked up."

"Who tipped him off?"

"Kelly Lyle. She visited me in prison and told me so herself. It must also have been her or one of her lackey followers who killed all the women I was framed for. She must have hoped the police would flush me out so she could pick me off. In the end she settled for seeing me behind bars until the time came that she could treat me to the same fate as Berg and Zippy. I was like a treat you set aside for a rainy day."

"You've been through hell, baby. That's all behind you now."

"I pray you're right. In a day or so, we'll send Hardy a message for the years I lost behind bars. Then we're out of here. We'll go somewhere no one will ever find us."

CHAPTER TWENTY-THREE

Cotton picked up her shopping bag. She was kicking herself that she'd had to buy one; her understairs cupboard was full of them. She took her keys from her handbag and walked to her car.

"Emma, isn't it? Emma Cotton?"

Cotton turned and looked blankly at the woman in front of her. "Yes. Do we know each other? I'm usually excellent with faces."

"No, we don't know each other. Do you have a minute? Do you think we might talk in your car? I need to discuss something private."

The woman was about her own height and build, her hair brown and shoulder length and not quite tidy. She wore no makeup, and her lips looked dry. Cotton noticed her clenched hands trembling.

"Follow me," Cotton told her. "I'm parked just here. I didn't catch your name."

"Louise Greenslade. I'm sorry to bother you like this. It's important we talk."

Cotton opened the car. She dumped her shopping in

the back while Louise got in the passenger seat. As Cotton closed the back door, she looked through the car and noticed Louise looking around nervously.

"There," said Cotton, climbing into her seat, closing her car door and turning to face Louise. "How can I help?"

Louise closed her eyes as she gathered her thoughts. "Difficult to know where to start. It's about Alex. Alex Nash. He's the dentist you've been seeing."

Suddenly Cotton felt a tsunami of emotions sweep through her body. Feelings she had never known were there: jealousy, annoyance, anger, curiosity. Cotton gripped those feelings and held them tightly; she smiled pleasantly. "You know Alex?"

"It's not what you think," Louise said. "It was, but it's not now. This is embarrassing. I'm not sure I should say anything."

"You're here now, so why not tell me what's on your mind."

"You're annoyed. Forget it – I'm sorry. I shouldn't interfere. Only, I'm worried for you." Louise was trembling all over now. Even her voice shook. "Alex is not what you think. He's charming, educated, wealthy and handsome."

Cotton felt her heart skip a beat as Louise spoke about the man she was falling for.

Louise's breathing quickened. She looked around outside the car before leaning closer to Cotton. "He's very controlling."

"What does that mean? Who are you?"

"I was with Alex for several years. Everything was lovely at the beginning. I couldn't believe my luck. I'd met the perfect man and he wanted me. Then, slowly, things began to change. I didn't see it immediately. Bit by bit Alex dictated who I could see, when and for how long. Later, as his control tightened, he would fly into jealous rages over the smallest thing. He's manipulative, threatening and violent. By the end I was like a robot. I became depressed. I even tried to commit suicide. I've been in and out of hospital ever since."

"Did you report any of this to the police?"

"I tried, but he'd always find a way to make it look like it was me. He'd tell them I was on medication or depressed or clumsy or even violent myself and that he was the victim. He'd convince them he was the long-suffering husband who was standing by me and doing all he could to help me."

"These are very serious allegations, Louise. You realise that. If they're true, I can help you. We can put a case together."

Louise suddenly looked very pale. "No. Definitely not. I'm trying to get my life back together. I don't want anything to do with him. I'm only here to warn you. Stay away from him." She grabbed the door handle and got out, then leaned back inside the car. "Whatever you do, don't tell him we spoke. I'm afraid of what he might do." Then she was gone.

Cotton got out of the car to stop her – she had more questions – but Louise was running, head down, out of the car park.

CHAPTER TWENTY-FOUR

Sunday morning and the street was quiet. Fischer and Moon sat in the black Ford Galaxy watching the house. Moon was turned in her seat; her shoes were off and her feet were across Fischer's lap. She chewed gum as she scrolled through YouTube on her mobile phone. Without looking up, she asked, "Why are we just sitting here? I'm bored. Can we go now?"

Fischer flicked his cigarette stub out the car window and ignored her. He shook his packet of Marlboros, took out the last cigarette, crushed the packet and tossed it over his shoulder onto the back seat.

"My phone is low on charge. If we're just going to sit in the car for hours on end, we need to get a car charger for my phone. How much longer?"

"You sound like a little kid. You ask the same question every five minutes. Just give it rest."

"I could've just stayed back at the house."

"I told you. I don't trust you," said Fischer.

"And I told you, no more coke or weed. I'm going to be a saint from now on." Moon traced a halo above her head.

"Saint Faye. The good Catholic girl you always wanted. I guess that's what turns you on these days."

"I also don't want to leave you with Judy."

"What do you take me for? I wouldn't touch Judy. She's sweet. A bit moody, though."

Fischer raised his eyebrows and gave Moon a look that implied he didn't believe her. "She has a right to be moody. She's tied up and gagged in the middle of her own kitchen."

Moon gave a little giggle and said, "I wouldn't touch her. Unless I got really, really, really bored."

Fischer sat up straight. Moon looked up from her phone. "What is it?" She twisted around in her seat, slipped her feet back into her shoes and followed Fischer's eyes as he studied the house.

The front door opened and a teenage girl came storming out. Slung over her shoulder was a black leather shoulder bag. She was wearing tight navy-blue jeans, black ankle boots and a cropped black sweater. Her straight blonde hair covered her ears. It was down to her jawline on one side and down to her shoulder on the other.

She was arguing with a woman who followed her onto the front step. They were really going at it. A man came to the door as well, pushed past the woman and started yelling and pointing at the teenage girl.

"Who are these people? Why are we here?" asked Moon. "Why aren't you telling me what's going on?"

"Just hush for a minute."

The teenage girl threw her arms up in the air, yelled at her parents, then stormed down the front path and away from the house. She marched at speed for a few metres and then slowed, took out her mobile phone and put it to her ear.

Moon looked at Fischer; his eyes followed the girl.

"Put your seatbelt on," said Fischer. He waited for the man and woman to go back inside the house and close the door, then he started the car.

"Where are we going, baby? She's a little young, don't you think?"

"Sit back and shut up. Just for ten minutes, please, be quiet. I'm trying to think."

"Moody git," she muttered as she clicked her seatbelt into place. Curiosity quickly took over, and she wasn't mad at Fischer for long.

Fischer followed the girl, staying well back and out of sight. She walked to a children's play park. Fischer parked the car. He reached into the glovebox and took out a new pack of Marlboros. He lit one up and passed the pack to Moon. Fischer wound down his window to release the smoke and watched as the teenage girl crossed the green to the children's play area. She waved to a fitful toddler as she passed. The toddler's father had lifted his little girl off the roundabout and now fought to get her into a pushchair. The child arched her back and resisted with all her might.

The teenage girl headed towards the larger children's swings. She perched on the middle one and gently rocked herself back and forth with her heels while making another phone call. She spoke briefly then hung up. She then continued rocking back and forth while staring at her phone.

Moon's attention switched back and forth between the teenager and Fischer. She'd not seen him this way before. He was anxious; his breathing was rapid. He smoked furiously.

After watching the teenage girl for a few minutes, Fischer said, "Wait here. Don't get out of the car. You hear me?"

Moon took off her seatbelt, slumped down in her seat and grunted.

Fischer got out of the car and headed across the green towards the teenager. He looked back at the car to make sure Moon wasn't following. Moon was now kneeling on her seat with her elbows on the dashboard, watching. She gave Fischer the finger and smiled mockingly. She watched in disbelief as he tidied his hair and straightened his clothes.

The teenager looked up as Fischer approached. She stopped rocking back and forth, then got off the swing and stood behind it, putting the seat between her and the man.

"If you're some sick perv or rapist, back off!" said the teenager. "You come near me and I'll cut your balls off and feed 'em to you." To back up her threat, the girl reached down into her shoulder bag, which was on the ground beside the swing, and produced a knife with a six-inch blade. "I saw you and your girlfriend following me. Whatever your sick game is, I'm not into it, so fuck off." The teenager tossed her hair back and thrust the knife towards him.

Fischer smiled with pride. His little girl had grown up and knew how to take care of herself. He looked back at Moon and smiled. She was now outside the car and leaning against the bonnet. Moon put up her hands to say, *What the hell is going on?*

Fischer's mouth was dry. He was mesmerised. He'd forgotten everything he wanted to say. He just stared at the girl. She was amazing. There she was, right in front of him, all grown up. She was beautiful.

"I saw you arguing back there at the house. I want to make sure you're okay," said Fischer.

"I know what you want. You sicko. And it isn't to make sure I'm okay."

"It's not like that at all. I've come to see you. To make sure you're okay."

"What? What are you, some sort of stalker? My boyfriend will be here in a minute. You better fuck off."

"Jessica. Would you mind not swearing?" Fischer stepped closer.

"What? How do you know my name? You kiddin' me? Whoever you are, you better seriously, seriously… just go. Back away. If you come near me, I will stick you with this. Don't think I won't." The teenager continued to point the knife. Using her thumb, she swiped her phone.

"Please don't do that," said Fischer. "I'm not here to cause trouble. I'd like to talk. If you give me a moment, I can explain."

"I'm not interested." Jessica tapped in a number and put the phone to her ear. "Where are you? Well, hurry up. Some rapist perv's been stalking me. He knows my name and everything… What sort of question is that? What do rapist pervs usually want? Just get here now… What?" Jessica looked Fischer up and down. "He's real skinny and looks like he needs a bath. He's got loads of tattoos. Checked shirt, black t-shirt and jeans." She hung up. "Idiot!"

Fischer stepped forward and held the chain of the swing. He moved around the swing and sat down.

"Will you please stay where you are?" Jessica said and brandished the knife again.

Fischer put up his hands and chuckled. "Whoa. Careful with that thing. If you just let me speak…" He unbuttoned the sleeve on his right arm and rolled up his shirt. He turned over his forearm. Amongst the montage of tattoos, the name 'Jessica' ran along the inside of his arm.

Jessica looked confused. "I don't know who you are, but

my boyfriend will be here any second. If I were you, I would just go. Why won't you just go? Please."

"You know who I am. I'm not going anywhere. I want to talk."

"No, I don't know who you are. I'm calling the police."

Jessica looked down at her phone. Fischer jumped up and grabbed it from her hand. "I can't have you doing that."

Jessica swiped the knife wildly towards him but was too slow. She held the knife in both hands and stood in a defensive position. "Give me my phone back."

"No."

"Give it."

"No." Fischer started scrolling through the photos on the phone.

"They're private. Stop it."

"Only if you listen to me." Fischer looked up at his daughter. "Bloody hell, Jessica. Will you calm down and hear me out? This isn't supposed to go like this. I have something important to tell you." Fischer took a step towards her.

"Stay back. I've warned you." Jessica glanced over Fischer's shoulder at the sound of a car screeching to a halt beside Fischer's black Ford. Fischer looked around to see a young man who appeared to be about five years older than his daughter – too old – jump out brandishing what looked like a short sword. He was dressed in a combat-green t-shirt that looked two sizes too small for his large, muscular body.

Seeing her boyfriend running towards them, Jessica relaxed.

Fischer sighed. This whole situation had turned into an unnecessary mess. He now needed to take control of the situation. Moving swiftly, he grabbed Jessica's wrist and twisted the knife out of her hand. She yelped. He let her go and scooped up the knife and tucked it in his pocket.

Jessica rubbed her sore wrist. She swung her foot and tried to kick him in the balls. She missed, again. "You creep – you're dead."

"No. I'm *Dad*." He raised his eyebrows and smiled. "It's me. Daddy."

Jessica stood open-mouthed.

The boyfriend was bounding towards them now with the sword over his head. He looked like a charging cavalry officer who'd forgotten his horse.

"This isn't working. We need to go somewhere and talk. Somewhere away from here." Fischer grabbed Jessica by the arm and started dragging her towards his car.

The boyfriend came to a halt in front of them. "Let her go, or I'll cut you to pieces."

"Christ. What is it with you two and knives and stabbing and cutting?"

"I'm serious. Let her go." His eyes blazed; he meant business. He gestured with the sword. "Let her go and step away."

Fischer released his grip slightly, but not entirely, and the girl stepped to one side. She looked up at Fischer when she realised he hadn't let go completely. The boyfriend was incensed; he stepped forward and raised the sword above his head. "I said—"

Moon swung the eighteen-inch crowbar and brought it crashing into the side of the young man's knee. His leg crunched and buckled. He collapsed onto his back, screaming in agony. He dropped the sword and grabbed his knee. Moon came around and held the crowbar over his ankle. The boyfriend sobbed uncontrollably, like a toddler who'd fallen and grazed his hands and knees for the first time.

Jessica started wailing. "Don't hurt him. He wouldn't hurt a fly. It's not a real sword. It's fake. It's blunt."

Moon looked to Fischer, then at the girl, then down at the boyfriend. She pointed the crowbar at the boyfriend as she spoke. "The only reason you're not dead is I have no idea what the hell is going on."

"Leave him," said Fischer. "Take her. We're bringing her with us." Fischer passed Jessica to Moon. He crouched down beside the boyfriend. "What's your name, son?"

"Ryan," he said between sobs.

"Okay, Ryan. I'm Jessica's father. Her real father. I want to talk with her. She's safe with me. When we've talked, I'm taking her back home to her mother. My point is, you don't need to call the police. As I said, I'm her father. If you call the police, my friend Moon here will come back and do your other knee." Ryan looked up at Moon. "Do we have an understanding?"

Ryan nodded enthusiastically. "Yes, sir."

"Good, lad." Fischer got up and looked back down at Ryan, who was still clutching his knee. "Do you need a hand back to your car?"

"No, sir. I'm okay. Thank you."

"Are you sure? It's no bother."

"Yeah. Sure. I'm fine."

"Okay." Fischer was about to walk away when he turned back. "One other thing."

Ryan flinched.

"Aren't you a little old for my daughter?" Behind him Jessica sighed.

"I'm only a year older. I'm just big for my age," explained Ryan.

"Oh, okay. See you around, Ryan."

Fischer, Moon and Jessica headed to the car, leaving Ryan in the middle of the playground clasping his knee.

CHAPTER TWENTY-FIVE

Faye Moon sat cross-legged on the floor. She was watching Judy, who was now tied to a radiator in the kitchen. Judy was gagged and blindfolded, and as an extra measure a pillowcase had been placed over her head.

Moon poked Judy on the arm with a finger to watch her jump. "Judy, don't be scared. It's only me." Moon poked her in the ribs. Then again on the thigh. Bored, she lay back on the kitchen floor and stared at the stipples of the Artex ceiling.

Fischer appeared at the door and silently mouthed and pointed down the hall to indicate he was going to look in on Jessica. Moon nodded. When Fischer turned his back, Moon, who still lay on her back, lifted her head and slowly stretched out her leg and waved her bare foot close to Judy. Pointing her toes, she inched her foot closer and closer until her big toe touched where she imagined Judy's nose might be beneath the pillowcase. Moon smiled when Judy flinched and complained. She rested her foot on Judy's lap and reached out for her cigarettes and lighter, which were on the linoleum floor beside her.

"Do you want to play a game, Jude? I'll touch you with my toe and you have to try not to flinch. I'll count to ten and then we'll start." Moon lit a cigarette while she counted. She scooted around and looked down the hall. She watched as Fischer stood outside the bathroom door gently knocking. "Judy, we'll play later. I want to see something."

Moon got up and flicked her cigarette into the sink. She made her way down the hall to the bathroom.

Fischer stood at the bathroom door listening. He looked back at Moon, who nodded encouragingly. "Go on," she mouthed silently.

Fischer turned the handle and peered around the bathroom door. "Can I come in? We need to talk."

"Suppose so. This should be good." Jessica, the daughter he'd waited years to see, sat curled up on the floor with her back to the bath.

"Promise you won't get annoyed?"

Jessica shrugged and rubbed her wrist. "You really hurt my wrist, you know."

"I'm sorry, Jess." Fischer stepped into the bathroom. He put the lid of the toilet seat down and sat on it. "I need to explain."

"Which bit? Kidnapping me or never being around, ever? I'm seventeen. You're too late. I'm all grown up."

"Not being around wasn't my choice. I wanted to be. Believe me, I did."

Moon, who had been listening outside, couldn't contain her curiosity and poked her head around the door.

"Your dad didn't kill all those girls," she blurted. "Someone else did it and framed him. Your dad's a good man. He's done some crazy shit in the past, some of it pretty shady, but that's all behind him now."

Jessica looked up at the two of them in horror.

Fischer spun around to look at Moon. He put his finger up to silence her. "You know what, Moon? You're not helping. I don't want her thinking we're psychopaths. This is one of those moments when you try to make a good impression. Why don't you knock up some food? And while you're at it, check on Judy. We don't want her getting loose."

"Oh, yeah, like that makes us sound like regular people."

Fischer glared at her and turned his attention back to Jessica. Moon shut the door behind her and stomped off.

"I haven't kidnapped Judy. She's just letting us stay in her house a while; she'll be fine. I'll leave her some money for her trouble. I haven't kidnapped you, either. You can leave whenever you want. I just hope you'll hear me out. I'm sorry about your boyfriend. I'm sure his leg will be fine in a few weeks. He might walk like a one-legged pirate for a while, but that'll give him character."

Jessica didn't laugh.

"I got you this," said Fischer. He passed her a fluffy black-and-white panda on a keyring. "I thought you could hang it on your bag?"

Jessica stared at him. Fischer leaned forward and tossed the panda keyring towards her. "I am your father."

Jessica tutted. "You think I don't know that?"

"Nah. You didn't, not really. I also wanted to say it out loud."

"I did know. Mum said you are an arsehole, and only arseholes would kidnap a teenage girl in broad daylight from a public park in front of her boyfriend. Plus, we've got the same big ugly ears." Jessica pulled back her blonde hair to show him. "The difference is, I can cover mine with my hair. Yours must send you in circles, like a spinning top, any time the wind picks up."

Fischer laughed. "You really are a piece of work."

"I'm your daughter. I don't know what you expect from me. You turn up out of the blue, probably with a load of preconceived ideas of how it'll be between us. I mean, where the fuck've you been my whole life?"

"It's a long story. Don't swear."

"Well, you've obviously got stuff you want to get off your chest. And just like you, I'm all ears." Jessica broke into a smile at her impromptu joke.

Fischer looked uncomfortable. None of this had gone the way he'd imagined it.

"If you don't want to tell me where you've been, then tell me who the woman is. Moon. Is she your wife? She looks like a junkie hooker."

"She's a friend. She's had a tough life. She does a little coke from time to time. She thinks it keeps her even, but all it really does is keep her crazy."

"Will you stop staring at me? It's creeping me out."

"I'm sorry. I've been waiting for this your whole life. Your mother wouldn't let me see you. The only thing I have is this photo." Fischer took his wallet from his back pocket and passed Jessica the photo.

"Is this me?"

"Yep, I took you out for the day. We went to a farm where they had lots of animals. Sheep, pigs, little goats, guinea pigs, rabbits, ponies. A petting zoo, I think that's what they called it. You wanted an ice cream, and when I got you one, you wanted to share it with me. You kept smiling and asking me to come closer and lick it. Though I really think your plan was for me to get close so you could stick your ice cream on the lens of the camera."

Jessica was smiling, and Fischer felt pleased.

"It was one of the best days of my life. A few weeks after that, your mother told me she'd met someone else. Someone who could give her and you a better life. We argued a lot. I did love her, but I knew she was right to leave me."

"She said you raped her, and I was the result."

"Why would she say that?"

"Well, is it true?"

"Your mother was just like Moon when I first met her. She got herself clean, and I guess I reminded her of what she used to be like. She wanted a fresh start. I was a constant reminder of her past. I never raped your mother. Why she told you that, I don't know. All I can think is she wanted to protect you from me. It's a hateful thing to say, but maybe she was desperate to keep you away from me. She was protecting you, that's all."

"You seem pretty mellow about it."

"What can I say? She was right. My life is a mess. I can't bring you into it. At least, not right now. I… I just wanted you to know me a little bit."

"Brilliant. Your dumb kidnapping means you'll have every copper in the country looking for you."

"They already are. It's why I wanted to see you. I'm leaving the country."

"What? When?"

"Moon helped me break out of prison. It's another long story."

"You were in prison? You broke out?" She gaped at him. "You show up, say hi, and then leave? What is that? It helps you, perhaps, but where does it leave me? You're so—"

The bathroom door swung open, and Moon stuck her

head around. "I've done beans on toast. With grated cheese on top."

"Let me properly introduce you," said Fischer. "Moon, meet Jessica. Jessica, meet Moon. Jessica is my daughter."

"Hi, Jess," said Moon. "I knew he had a secret, and I guessed it was a daughter. He's been really, like, weird for days. I think he was scared. Look at him – the tough guy, scared by a little girl."

"No, I wasn't scared. And you didn't know I had a daughter," said Fischer.

"Yes, I did. She's got your ears as well. Soon as I saw her, I knew."

"Why does everyone say that?" Fischer got up and looked at his ears in the mirror. "They don't stick out. Not really. You couldn't have seen Jess's ears anyway. Not under her hair." Fischer started pushing his ears back and mumbling to himself.

"Sorry about your boyfriend," said Moon. "I hope he'll be okay. If Fischer had told me you were his kid, like any normal person would, I would have gone easy on him. Instead, he wanted to keep you a secret."

"Are you saying, in a roundabout way, it was my fault?" asked Fischer.

Moon shrugged in a way that suggested it was.

Jessica laughed at the pair of them. "I was going to dump him soon anyway. He's not the sharpest tool in the box. I'm not ready for anything serious yet, anyway."

"I was thinking the same thing," said Fischer. "He definitely looks too old for you."

Jessica and Moon laughed. "I think Fischer's going for Father of the Year," said Moon.

"I'm not sure he'll win. He'd be disqualified for kidnapping his daughter."

"I suddenly feel very ganged up on. Why don't we see

what Moon has cooked up? Her beans on toast really take some beating." Fischer winked at Jessica and ducked as Moon gave him a playful punch.

Fischer put out his hand and helped his daughter to her feet.

CHAPTER TWENTY-SIX

"Will you be okay walking from here?" said Fischer. "There will likely be police all over the place by now, so I don't want to get too close to the house."

Jessica rolled her eyes. "Of course. I'm not suddenly helpless because you showed up."

Moon sniggered from the back seat of the car. Jessica unfastened her seatbelt and twisted around to look at Moon. "Nice to meet you, Moon."

"You too, Jess. I hope we meet again soon."

Jessica looked at Fischer. "Bye. It's been… I'm not sure what you call it. Memorable."

"One of the best days of my life," said Fischer.

"Let's swap numbers," said Jessica. She took out her mobile phone.

"Here's my phone. You'll have to do it. I have no idea what my number is."

Using her thumb, Jessica exchanged numbers. "I'm putting you in my phone as Rihanna. Just in case the police decide to go through my contacts.

"Smart girl," said Moon.

"There we go. All done." Jessica handed Fischer his phone back. "Okay. I'd better go." Jessica lifted her bag and gripped the handle of the door.

Fischer couldn't stop himself. He reached out and held Jessica's hand. She turned and looked at him in surprise. He wanted to memorise the feeling of her small, soft hand in his. After a few awkward moments, he let go. She smiled fondly and got out. He watched as she strode away, pride welling up inside him.

Halfway across the road, Jessica turned and walked back to the car. Fischer lowered the window and Jessica stuck her head in. "You're probably busy, but I'm singing a week on Sunday. It's kind of a big deal. I'm doing a gig. I've got quite a following and it'll be the biggest event I've done. Anyway, as long as you're still around, you can come. If you want?"

Fischer opened and closed his mouth like a fish. "Yeah. You sing?"

"Uh-huh. I sing and play guitar."

"Sounds amazing. What sort of music?"

"Stuff I wrote myself and a few covers: Joni Mitchell, Joan Baez, Janis Joplin, Florence Welch influence. If it's not your thing, that's cool."

"We'd love to," said Moon and Fischer together.

"Wouldn't miss it for the world," said Fischer.

"Cool. I'll text you the time and address."

Jessica turned and walked away.

"Thank you, Moon," Fischer said, turning to her. "I know you want to get away, but…"

"Don't sweat it," said Moon. "She's a nice girl."

"Yeah. She is," said Fischer. He puffed out his chest then felt an overwhelming sadness. "Look at her. She's amazing. Beautiful, so beautiful. Look at what you took away from me, DCI James Hardy. I'll never get those years back. I missed so much."

Fischer started the car. "It's time," he said. "Time to get my payback."

CHAPTER TWENTY-SEVEN

Seeing the car pull into the guest house car park, Mrs Fiona Crabb twisted the end of the packet of chocolate Hobnobs, put a peg on it, and put the packet back in the drawer. She swiped the crumbs off the desk into her hand and dropped them in the bin beside her desk. She straightened her hair bun and adjusted her mustard-coloured cardigan. Her fluffy slippers flip-flopped on the hardwood floor as she hurried to the front desk. Standing to attention, she waited behind the reception desk for the two men to come through the front door.

Since the Sterling Inn, part of a national chain, had been built a mile and half away, closer to the motorway and the docks than her little guest house, bookings had dwindled. Regulars, who had been the lifeblood of the guest house's income, hadn't rebooked. She could only assume their employers, who made the bookings, had been seduced by the benefits of Wi-Fi in every room, modern en-suite bathrooms, the vast and cheap international restaurant menu, and beds that come with a 'comfortable night's sleep or your money back' guarantee.

With Ian gone, every day she felt more and more isolated and lonely. The guest house had been Ian's idea and was now an albatross around her neck. While he did time for fraud, life was grim. Her idiot husband had somehow thought the building firm he did the bookkeeping for wouldn't miss a few thousand pounds here and there. Their lawyers had thought otherwise.

I love you. I did it for you, he'd mouthed from the back of the police car. Oddly, all she could think as he was being taken away was how large the bald spot on the top of his head had grown. He used to have lovely, thick hair.

The only benefit to come from Ian's incarceration was an introduction to Faye Moon. The cash from Moon to put up escapee Edward Fischer for a night or two – she felt sure she could deny knowing he was on the run – would mean she could make a fresh start. With her life turned to shit, helping Moon was a risk worth taking. What other choices did she have? The cash meant she'd be able to pay off her debts and start over. Life was suddenly feeling less bleak. At last there was light at the end of the long, dark and joyless tunnel.

"Are you looking for a room, gentlemen?" asked Mrs Crabb. Her large, round, rosy cheeks bulged more than usual as she smiled. She tried not to stare at the large padded bandage over the skinny man's ear; it must be sore, she thought, given the way he repeatedly touched it and winced.

"No. A new car," said Donny, sarcastically. "Jeez. What do you think we're here for?"

"Yes, please. A room," said Barton. He winked and smiled at her before returning his attention to the leaflets for local attractions beside the front door. He pulled out one on vintage cars and then came and stood beside the skinny rude man.

Nice teeth and twinkly eyes, thought Mrs Crabb. *Ooh, differently coloured eyes like David Bowie. Don't see that very often.* Before she could stop herself, she was looking him up and down. He was a little taller than the skinny one and looked strong. Thick forearms and big hands. She liked his unusual dress sense. A fancy black shirt, pearly buttons and a red rambling rose across his broad shoulders. He reminded her of a seventies movie star she'd seen on TV, but she couldn't think of the actor's name. The word 'heterochromia' popped into her head as she looked in his eyes; one blue eye and one brown eye. The hours of watching quiz shows and doing crosswords were paying off.

"Certainly, gentlemen. How many nights?"

"One night," said Donny.

The strong one was leaning on the desk and watching her. She could feel herself getting warm. Embarrassingly, her face went red when she was excited. She tried to concentrate.

"Depends how warm the welcome is," said the cowboy. He reached across the reception desk and touched her hand.

Oh my God, thought Mrs Crabb. She pulled her hand away. She felt her heart galloping like a race horse. Her hand trembled as she picked up the pen to enter the details in the guest book. He was smiling at her; she could feel it. She placed a laminated card in front of them that showed the room prices.

"Would you like a double room or two singles?"

"Double." "Singles." The two men spoke at the same time.

"A double room," said Skinny.

"Names?" said Mrs Crabb.

"Paul McCartney," said Skinny.

"Knights, with a K," said the cowboy. He held her gaze. "Randy Knights."

"Good grief," muttered Donny with a sigh.

"Don't mind him," said Barton. "He's been a bit grumpy lately. Cut his ear while shaving." Barton leaned close and spoke in a low, deep, gravelly voice. "Some men are better with their hands than others. Know what I mean?"

"I'm right here," said Donny. "I can hear what you're saying."

Mrs Crabb could feel her face was red hot. She passed Barton the key to the room and a breakfast menu. "If you'd like breakfast, just mark your choices on the card and drop it back here before ten p.m. Your room is at the top of the stairs, first on the left. Anything you need, just let me know."

"Where will you be if I need you?" asked Barton.

"I have a small private room in the back there. Just ask for Fiona – that's me. Just press this button on the desk and I'll come."

Barton gave a cheeky grin. "I bet you do."

"For crying out loud," said Donny. "Excuse Lothario here. He thinks decorum was a general in the Roman army." He snatched the room key out of Barton's hand. "When you're done, please go get the bags from the car."

CHAPTER TWENTY-EIGHT

While Fischer slept, Moon watched the house. They'd spent the morning in the car, parked a short distance from the house with a direct view. She hummed softly to herself, some piece of classical music that was lodged in her head from who knows when.

Her phone beeped. A message. She knew who it was. She glanced over at Fischer, checked he was asleep before answering, then went back to watching the house.

To pass the time, she pressed a finger against Fischer's cheek and giggled as he sleepily swatted it away. She gently put a finger in his ear and grinned as he once again waved the sensation away. Slowly she ran a finger around his nostril and nearly split her sides as he wriggled his nose and sneezed.

Her phone beeped again. Once again, she checked Fischer was still sleeping before replying with a curt message.

Moon leaned over and kissed Fischer's arm and ran her fingers through his hair. She opened her packet of cigarettes, lit one, then took out two more and tried to balance them end to end on top of the packet.

Finally, the front door of the house opened and out came a man. She compared him to the photo they'd found of Hardy on the internet. It was definitely him. She watched as he opened the back of a Honda CR-V then opened the rear doors for the children. Hardy was joined by a big, muscular man who went over to a sporty-looking white Mercedes convertible also parked in the driveway. Two girls came running from the house with the Labrador on a lead.

Moon squeezed Fischer's thigh then gave his chest a nudge to wake him. She watched as Hardy hurried the girls. He was asking them to get into the car, and they seemed to be ignoring him by doing handstands on the front lawn. This Moon found funny.

Moon knelt on her seat and leaned on the dashboard as Hardy and the big man laughed together. After he'd called and called the girls and they did eventually come, they passed the dog's lead to Hardy and, instead of jumping into the family car, got into the big man's Mercedes.

A middle-aged woman, who Moon assumed to be Hardy's girlfriend, came out. She was followed by an older woman who Moon guessed was Hardy's mother. There was lots of toing and froing until finally the front door was locked.

Moon gave Fischer a shake. "Wake up." When he didn't respond, she gave him a prod. "Wake up," she said again. Then a firmer punch and shake. "Wake up. They're leaving. This could be it," said Moon.

Fischer sat up and stretched. "At last. I thought they'd never leave. Why didn't you wake me?"

Moon and Fischer watched as the two vehicles reversed

out of the driveway, turned and headed away. The pair of them smiled at each other.

"This is it," said Fischer. "We do this, watch Jess's gig and then we're out of here for good."

Moon gave him an excited kiss and squeeze.

They waited a few minutes then got out and went to the back of the Ford Galaxy. Fischer lifted the back, where two petrol cans sat. He looked at Moon. "Before we do this, go knock on the door and ring the doorbell, just to be sure the house is empty."

"C'mon, we just saw them leave not ten minutes ago," said Moon. Knowing Fischer wouldn't back down, Moon quick-stepped over to the house. She knocked on the door and looked through the letterbox. The house was quiet. She shrugged and raised her hands. *See? Told ya!*

Fischer mimed the pressing of a doorbell with his finger. Moon pressed the doorbell to satisfy Fischer. When nobody came to the door, she turned and ran back to the car.

"Happy now? Let's do this," said Moon.

Fischer and Moon crossed the road and casually walked up the driveway. "You put yours through the letterbox and I'll go around the back of the house. I'm going to need to break a window and pour it in. Let's do this quick and get out of here."

Moon undid the lid on the petrol can and unscrewed the spout. Resting her knee against the door and placing the heavy can on it, she poured most of the petrol through the letterbox. She then poured the remainder over the front door and the doormat and splashed the last few drops over a flowerbed under the bay window.

Fischer made his way along the side of the house. Around the back, he could see that the patio door had been repaired since their earlier visit. He moved to the far side of kitchen window and peered in. The house looked empty. He looked around for something heavy to break the window. Seeing nothing obvious, he put down the fuel can and set to work kicking off a brick from a low retaining wall beside the patio. A few blows with his heel of his boot and a couple of bricks came away.

He covered his eyes with the crook of his arm and, with his other hand, smashed a small window with the brick. Lifting the can to shoulder height, he poured the petrol through the window. It spilled over the kitchen worktop and onto the kitchen floor.

He set the can aside, took a sharp breath, lit a match and tossed it in. The flames caught immediately. He watched as they ran over the worktop, raced up to the kitchen cabinets and engulfed the dark pine kitchen table.

Fischer ran to the front of the house, where he met Moon. "Light it up."

Moon took the box of matches, lit one and flicked it at the doormat. The petrol-soaked mat and surrounding area immediately exploded into flame. Fischer and Moon stood back as the heat warmed their skin. "Woohoo!" yelled Moon. "Burn, baby, burn."

"Now, just like me, Hardy is going to have to start his life all over again. Just like me, he's got nothing but the clothes on his back and a few quid in his pocket."

Fischer took the can from Moon and the pair made their way to car.

Moon looked back at the house and could see the fire had spread inside and the curtains at the front windows had caught light. She cast her eyes upstairs to one of the windows, where she thought she saw movement. In a brief moment of panic, she wondered if she'd actually heard the doorbell ring. She'd pressed the button for sure, but what if it wasn't working? What if it didn't make a sound? She looked again at the upstairs window. Nothing. She was mistaken; there was no movement.

From the car, Moon watched thick, black smoke billowing from the house.

"Shall we go?" said Fischer. "I'd love to stick around and watch the show, especially later when he returns. It's only bricks and mortar, but a man's home is his castle, and we just hurt Hardy in a way that is hard to imagine. That's what I call payback."

"Let's go," said Moon. She was checking her phone. More messages. She deleted them.

"Are you okay? You seem a little quiet."

Moon put on her seatbelt. "I'm fine. Let's move."

"Okay, Moonbeam. We'll celebrate tonight and pack up our stuff in the morning," said Fischer. "We lie low from now on. Catch Jess's gig, then it's goodbye Blighty. We're outta here!"

"Hasta la vista, baby!" Moon said.

CHAPTER TWENTY-NINE

Bartholomew Hall is a picturesque seventeenth-century country house in Dorset with surrounding gardens and a yew tree maze. It's a favourite with Alice and Faith, who were excited to spend the afternoon racing their way around the maze with Rayner.

Unfortunately, Jenny's pregnancy sickness was leaving her debilitated. She'd insisted we all go and that she'd be just fine on her own at the house.

Part of the day's excitement for Alice and Faith was to take a spin in Rayner's Mercedes cabriolet with the top down. Rayner being Rayner, and not wanting to disappoint, had gone a short part of the journey with the girls in the car. Then we all pulled over at a petrol garage for the girls to get into my car and Rayner to turn around and head back to be with Jenny.

Alice and Faith climbed out of the Mercedes.

"Can we go out in the car again tomorrow? I like it with the roof down," said Faith, patting her hair. "My hair's gone all over the place."

Alice rolled her eyes at her sister. "Rayner needs to look

after Jenny. Just be grateful he took us out today. He didn't need to."

"Mind your own business. You're always trying to be so grown up. Rayner doesn't mind. Do you?"

"Well… let's see how we get on, shall we? I don't want to make a promise I can't keep." Rayner crouched down, put out his huge arms and hugged the two girls close to him. "Bear hug! We'll go out again as soon as possible, but the last thing I want to do is disappoint my two favourite girls."

Alice put her head on Rayner's shoulder. "I wish I could've stayed behind with you to look after Jenny. Tell her to try eating ginger biscuits, and I'm going to look online to see what else I can find to make her better."

"I will. You're a star. We might need to hire you to be our nurse." Rayner straightened up then picked up Faith and held her over his head. "And as for you… You're nothing but trouble."

Faith giggled and said, "I'm going to make Jenny a get-well card. Do you think we could go in the car later? What about when we get home?"

I rescued Rayner before Faith's negotiations went into overdrive. "Faith," I said sternly. "Stop hustling Rayner. He's an amateur against you, and you know it."

Alice and Faith said a last round of goodbyes and hopped into the back of my car alongside Mum, aka Nana Hardy, who was holding onto Sandy's collar. Monica was in the front seat, and she turned to listen to the girls' excited chatter.

"We'll be out most of the day," I said to Rayner. "We'll eat out this evening, which will give you and Jenny some space. Help yourself to whatever you want in the house. The fridge is well stocked. Call me if you need anything. I hope Jenny feels better soon. She really is going through it, poor thing."

"Hopefully, it'll pass. Usually, the sickness and vomiting lessen in the afternoon. If it does, I'll try to get her out for some fresh air."

"Is that your phone?" I asked.

Rayner touched his pockets and then realised he'd left his phone in the car. He leaned into the car and checked who the caller was. He said over his shoulder. "Speak of the devil, it's Jen."

Wanting to make sure everything was okay, I waited for Rayner to answer the call. He turned and looked at me with a cheeky schoolboy grin as he answered. He spoke in a sexy Sean Connery voice. "Your amazing one-in-a-million husband here."

Then his demeanour changed. He straightened up and looked at me with fear in his eyes. All the colour drained from his face and his eyes narrowed. "Open the windows. Every window. If you can't get out, stay close to the window and as low to the ground as you can. Call the fire brigade. I'm coming now. I'm on my way, sweetheart."

"What is it? What's going on?" I couldn't fathom what could be so wrong.

"The house. Your house. It's on fire. Jen's trapped upstairs. She can't get out. I've got to go."

I didn't believe what I was hearing. How could this be? "You go. I'm right behind you."

Rayner didn't need to be told. He leapt into the car, threw it in gear and accelerated away like a Formula 1 racing car driver out of the starting grid.

I ran to my car and jumped into the driver's seat, slinging my seatbelt around me. All eyes were on me as I turned the car around. "Seatbelts," I insisted. "Get your seatbelts on, and make sure the dog is secure."

"James, you're frightening us," said Monica.

"What on earth's got into you, Jamie?" asked Mum, leaning urgently forward. "What's going on?"

I checked everyone had their belts on before screeching out of the garage forecourt. My breathing was rapid as I spoke. I really didn't want to say it in front of Alice and Faith, but I had no choice. "Our house is burning. It's on fire."

I could hear Faith begin to cry. She and Alice held tight to Nana Hardy.

Monica mouthed as quietly as possible, "Jenny?"

I shook my head and widened my eyes. I half-whispered, half-mouthed, "Inside. She's trapped."

Mum, who was sat in the middle of the back seat, saw what I had mouthed. She gasped, "Oh, dear God. No!"

CHAPTER THIRTY

I raced through the traffic, all of us hoping the fire was some kind of terrible mistake. Apart from Faith, who was sobbing, everyone in the car was silent, lost in their own fearful thoughts.

As we got closer, the knot in the pit of my stomach grew. I could see thick grey smoke rising high into the sky. I could only pray Jenny had been able to flee the inferno in time. I turned into our road and saw neighbours standing in the street, helplessly watching as the fire raged. Rayner's abandoned car was on the pavement next to the house, the engine still running. Rayner himself was nowhere to be seen.

Nothing could have prepared me for the true horror of seeing up close our home engulfed by fierce flames. Raging flames that were fanned by a midday breeze.

I parked a good distance from the house and opened the door to get out. "If you decide to get out of the car, stay well back," I told Monica. As I spoke, a booming explosion inside the house made us all jump. Faith began sobbing louder. Everyone's eyes fixed on the billowing smoke. In the background, the sound of sirens from approaching fire trucks caught my attention.

I got out of the car and sprinted across the street towards the front of our house. The downstairs windows, broken from the heat, glowed as flames consumed everything inside. Flames licked what had once been the front door, leaping and dancing around the doorframe. I needed to find Rayner and Jenny. I looked to the upstairs windows for any sign of Jenny. Nothing. The windows were open. Smoke poured out.

Behind me, the first fire truck pulled up and blocked off the street.

I ran to the side of the house, raising my arm to protect my face as the heat of the flames fought to push me back. "Rayner!" I yelled. I got no reply. I moved along the side of the house. "Jenny!"

As I rounded the side of the house, I found Rayner hosing himself down with water from our garden hosepipe. He was blackened from smoke, coughing and wheezing, barely able to stand. He'd already been in the house and the heat had driven him back. He was readying himself for another attempt.

"Jenny's in there. I heard her," he shouted. He let the water run over his head.

I looked up at the top windows.

"She's stopped calling. I'm going back in." He dropped the hosepipe, pulled his jacket over his head and turned to run back through the shattered patio doors and into the inferno.

"No!" I yelled. "It's suicide. The fire brigade is here." I reached out to grab him, but Rayner's big arm swept me aside like I wasn't even there. I fell hard on my back. As I got back up, I could only watch helplessly as he charged forward and disappeared into the smoke and flames.

I looked up at the windows again. I needed to get up there.

From down the side of the house appeared two of the fire crew. The first crew member looked at me while the second spoke into her radio.

"Are you okay, sir? Are you hurt?" asked the first crew member.

"I'm fine."

"Do you know if anyone is inside?"

"There's a woman trapped inside. Her name is Jenny Rayner. She's upstairs, I think. Her husband just ran in through there." I pointed at the doors, which were charred and framed by flames.

The fireman turned to his partner. "It's true. Only it's two people inside. Husband and wife." The pair got themselves ready, putting on their breathing gear. I then watched with amazement as each of them stepped into the burning house after Rayner.

Two more fire crew arrived, carrying a ladder that they leaned against the back wall beneath the window. I wanted to climb the ladder with them. I felt completely helpless. In seconds, one of the fire crew had scaled the ladder and climbed in through the second-storey window. I watched with eyes watering and stinging, my face sore from the heat and my throat raw from the acrid smoke.

At the top window the fireman remerged. He was holding the motionless body of Jenny. His partner was already waiting at the top of the ladder. I watched with my heart in my mouth as Jenny was passed, legs first, through the window. With her legs over the shoulders of the fireman on the ladder, her back resting on the ladder, the fireman moved slowly, rung by rung, down the ladder, Jenny sliding down with him. Reaching the bottom, the fireman laid Jenny down and checked her vitals.

"Is she going to be okay? Is she alive?" I couldn't help myself.

"Stand back, please, sir. For your own safety. Get right back."

"I'm a police officer, a detective chief inspector," I blurted.

"I don't care who you are. Get back to a safe distance."

I did as I was told. I watched as the second fireman joined the first and they both worked on reviving Jenny. I couldn't tell if she was breathing. Her bare feet and legs were blackened, raw and burned. From as far back as I was, and with the firemen attending to her blocking my view, I had no idea how badly she was injured.

Through the patio doors came the other two crew members who'd gone inside searching for Rayner. They'd found him and were half-carrying him out, his arms slung over their shoulders. He was barely able to walk, his legs giving way beneath him. He stumbled and had to be half-dragged to safety. Getting clear of the house, they laid Rayner down beside Jenny. An oxygen mask was put over his blackened, swollen, tear-stained face.

Rayner lay on his back, eyes shut, gasping for air. The only movement came from his hand as he slowly reached out for Jenny, his fingers searching for her, not resting until they found her hand and held it.

CHAPTER THIRTY-ONE

Waiting for news at the hospital was unbearable.

"Sit down," said Monica. "Your pacing is driving me mad."

"Why haven't we heard anything?" I fumed.

Monica's phone bleeped. "It's your mum. She says the girls are fine. She's asking if we have any news." She started tapping out a reply. Alice and Faith were being looked after by their Nana at her home, and I was grateful once again that the girls had this relatively peaceful port in what seemed to be a gathering storm.

"I'm going to go and find someone. This is ridiculous." I stormed out into the hall where I ran straight into Dr Jakub Kowalski, the plastic surgery and burns consultant who'd been assigned to Jenny. I backed up into the waiting room.

Kowalski took off his round spectacles and cleaned them on his shirt "You are friends of Mr and Mrs Rayner, yes?"

"We are," said Monica, who was now standing beside

me. I could feel her trembling. She took my hand and squeezed it. "How are they?"

"Have you heard from their family?" asked Kowalski. "I really need to speak to the immediate family first."

"I've spoken to the parents. They're on their way. They'll be here in the next two to three hours. Jenny's mother, a little later. Listen, Jenny and Gabriel Rayner are our family, maybe not by blood, but they are family. I'm a detective chief inspector, and Detective Inspector Rayner is my partner. I need to know if they are going to be okay." Kowalski didn't need to know I was retired. "Gabriel Rayner is also my best friend. They were in my house when this happened. So, please, tell us how they are. Please."

Kowalski put his glasses back on and looked at the two of us. "I suppose, under the circumstances." He gestured to the seats, and we all sat down. "Mr Rayner is being treated for smoke inhalation and minor burns. He's on an IV for dehydration. We're also giving him antibiotics for possible lung damage."

"Lung damage?" I asked. My mouth suddenly felt dry.

"It is precautionary. Nothing serious. I would expect Mr Rayner to be back to his normal self in a few days. He's been very lucky."

"Thank goodness," said Monica. She sighed with relief. "And Jenny?"

"Mrs Rayner..." Kowalski unnecessarily straightened his glasses. "Her situation is more serious. She remains unconscious and heavily sedated in intensive care. Due to swelling in her throat, we are assisting her breathing. Aside from the smoke inhalation, I'm sorry to say, she has extensive burns to her legs, feet and back. They cover at least twenty percent of her body."

"No. Oh my God," said Monica, putting her hands to

her mouth. Tears streamed down her cheeks. She took a tissue from her pocket and wiped them away, determined to be strong. "She's pregnant. You know that, right?"

"Yes. We were made aware of that. Though we can't be certain…" He chose his words carefully. "There are no guarantees as to how Mrs Rayner's body will react after such trauma, but I see no reason why the baby should have been harmed. Unfortunately, at this stage, it's all a bit of a waiting game. Only time will tell."

"When can we see Jenny and Rayner?" My voice crumbled as I spoke.

"You can see Mr Rayner right now. Mrs Rayner is still being treated and assessed. In all likelihood she'll require skin grafts. My team are currently working to prevent infection and are doing what they can to reduce scarring and ensure she regains as much function as possible to joints where burns have occurred. It's going to be a long recovery. After all her treatment, which will take many months, she'll require physical therapy exercises and emotional support and follow-up care, but we will discuss that with her at a later date. I'm sorry I don't have better news. In some respects, she's lucky. Here in Bournemouth we have one of the leading plastic surgery and burns units in the country. My team are highly specialised experts and incredibly experienced in treating this sort of trauma. Right now, they're both in safe hands." A nurse came to the door. "I'll leave you for now. We can talk again, if you wish. Speak to one of the nurses and they'll take you to Mr Rayner's room."

It was all too much to comprehend. The consultant's words were swimming around in my head, yet none of what I'd heard seemed real. My emotions felt like they'd travelled the world's most terrifying rollercoaster. We'd been swept up in the joy and celebration of hearing that

Jenny and Gabriel would soon be parents and had been sent crashing down into the devastating prospect of Jenny's life being altered forever. I looked helplessly at Monica. She couldn't contain her emotions any longer and burst into wrenching sobs. She buried her face in my shoulder, and we held onto each other.

"I need to stay strong. For Jenny. For Rayner," said Monica after a few moments. She sniffed and impatiently wiped her eyes and nose. "Jenny especially will need us to stay strong." She cleared her throat and adjusted her hair. "Right. No more tears. At least not in front of them. Let's go and see Rayner."

CHAPTER THIRTY-TWO

Rayner was sat up in bed when Monica and I walked into his hospital room. He was negotiating with a nurse.

"Nurse Chukwu, if you won't remove this IV, I'm going to do it myself. I'm not staying in this bed while my wife is fighting for her life somewhere in this hospital. I need to be with her. She needs me."

"Hello, buddy," I said. "You causing trouble?" I tried my best to be upbeat, but my words sounded flat. Rayner's hospital gown stretched tight across his broad chest and muscular arms. His hair was scorched off in places; there were white padded dressings on the right side of his jaw. His hands were wrapped, and his right forearm was encased in crepe bandaging. I was shocked. To steady my nerves, I reached out and placed my hand on the small of Monica's back.

"Mr Rayner," began Nurse Chukwu, sounding exasperated

"Stop acting like you know what's best for me," interrupted Rayner.

"I do know what's best for you. So do the doctors."

"I just want to see my wife."

"She's in intensive care right now."

"You said that. That's why I need to see her," said Rayner. "I'm taking out the IV and then, if I have to, I'll search this entire hospital until I find her."

"It's important you keep the IV in for at least twenty-four hours. You've been badly injured. Your body needs fluids, antibiotics and time to heal. When the doctor says it's okay to see your wife, we'll arrange for you to visit her in a wheelchair. The IV stays in."

"Bloody wheelchair. Not a chance." Rayner lifted the bedsheet and swung his legs around to get out of the bed. His gown flapped open and Monica averted her eyes. "Where is she? I want to see Jenny now. There is no way on earth you're stopping me."

Nurse Chukwu moved like lightning around the bed. Monica and I jumped forward too.

"Whoa! Hang on. Listen to the nurse," I said. If the big man stumbled, I didn't fancy our chances of catching him. Rayner put his feet down, attempted to stand and fortunately thought better of it. He reached out and grabbed a cardboard sick bowl. "I'm fine, I'm fine," said Rayner in between vomiting. "Ah, my head's splitting."

Finally, he submitted and lay back on the bed. Monica poured him a glass of water.

"This is bullshit," said Rayner. "What have they given me?"

"You're in shock," said Nurse Chukwu. "Dizziness and nausea are common. I'll see what I can find out about your wife. Rest, Mr Rayner. I'll be right back."

"Thank you, nurse," said Rayner. He flapped his hand in a feeble attempt to wave.

Nurse Chukwu wrote some notes on Rayner's chart and left us alone.

Rayner put down the sick bowl and looked at us with a fear in his eyes like I'd never seen before. His voice sounded scared and small, like a child's. He said one word. "Jenny?"

"We don't know any more than you. She's in intensive care," I said. I was searching for the right words. I was trained to handle situations like this, I'd done it far too many times, but this was different: this was Rayner and Jenny and...

"What about the baby? Nobody will tell me about our baby," said Rayner.

Monica stepped forward. She placed a hand tenderly on Rayner's shoulder. She spoke softly, confidently and reassuringly. "Jenny does have serious injuries, but the doctor we spoke to said she and the baby are going to be okay. He sounded very optimistic. They're both receiving the very best care." Monica looked at me as if to say that was all the truth Rayner needed to hear right now.

"I tried to get to her," said Rayner. Tears filled his eyes; he swiped them away bitterly. "I couldn't see anything because of the smoke. I couldn't get through the fire. The heat was so intense. Fire everywhere I looked. I couldn't get through. I should have done more. I should have driven faster back to the house. I shouldn't have left her this morning. If…"

"You can't blame yourself," said Monica. "You did all you could, and more."

"You risked your life," I said. "You ran into a burning house. Even the fireman, in all their gear, struggled. It was an inferno. I don't know how you did it."

We were all silent for a moment.

Rayner stared out of the window, lost in his thoughts. "What caused it? The fire, I mean. The house burned so quickly. How could the fire have spread so fast? I remember your front door being ablaze. It was burning on the *outside*. I've seen a few house fires and I remember thinking that was odd. House fires usually start inside, and in the early stages they're contained within the building."

"I have no idea," I said. "The fire service will investigate. Don't you worry about that. All that matters right now is that you, Jenny and the baby focus on recovery."

Voices behind us made me turn. It was Rayner's parents, Keith and Winnie. "Oh, my boy!" said Winnie. Monica and I stepped aside to give them some room.

"James," said Keith. I shook his hand.

"This is Monica," I said.

"Nice to meet you," said Keith. He stood beside us.

We watched as Winnie fussed over the injured giant. She was in floods of tears as she checked him over, touching his dressings and inspecting his cuts and scratches and singed hair, all the while asking him questions.

"We're going to go," I said to Keith. "Give you some time alone."

"Good lad," said Keith. "Speak later, perhaps."

Quietly, Monica and I waved our goodbyes and left the Rayner family alone to comfort one another.

"We should get back," said Monica once we were in the corridor. "Check the girls are okay. I don't think we're going to hear any real news about Jenny for a while. We can come back later. It'll give the families some time together."

Neither of us wanted to leave, but Monica was right. We let the nurse at the ward desk know we were leaving.

In the car on the way home, my mind kept coming back to what Rayner had said about the fire, '…your front door being on fire. It was burning on the *outside* … the *outside … outside*.' If the fire had been started deliberately, then I needed to know, especially with Fischer at large. But surely Fischer wouldn't risk coming at me like this? He'd be crazy to do that. I now wondered whether keeping his escape to myself was a mistake; I should've told Rayner.

"I'll make sure the girls and Mum are okay, and then I'll nip out," I said. "I'm going to speak with the fire brigade. They might be able to shed some light on what happened."

Monica nodded. "I want to get back to the hospital later if possible. Don't be too long. I'll phone your mum and ask if she and the girls need us to pick up any dinner."

"Okay. Great idea." I was suddenly overcome with guilt about not thinking about my children and my mother. I hadn't even considered whether Mum had enough food in the house. Let alone dog food for Sandy.

Since Dad had died, only a few weeks ago, she'd lived alone and with little appetite. She wouldn't have a freezer stocked with pizza or a cupboard stocked with tuna and pasta. Not like we do… or did.

But instead, my mind circled back to what had just happened, to theories on how the fire started, who might have started it, and for what reason. I needed answers, and I needed them quick.

CHAPTER THIRTY-THREE

Fischer opened the front door, and Moon went straight to the bedroom and closed the door without a word. Fischer guessed her bad attitude was down to cutting out the coke and pills.

He went to the kitchen and got himself a glass of water. Leaning against the worktop, he watched Judy. She was trussed up, wrists and ankles bound. The rope from her wrists was fastened to a door leading from the kitchen to the dining area. Her head was flopped forward, and she was sleeping. She must have sensed him watching. She opened one eye and then the other.

Fischer held up the glass of water and Judy nodded. He filled a glass, got down on his knees in front of her and removed the strip of tea towel being used as a gag.

"Will you let me go? I promise I won't tell anyone. I swear," pleaded Judy.

"Drink." Fischer held the glass to her mouth and Judy gulped down the water. He dabbed her mouth with the gag and sat on the floor next to her.

"I know you're not a bad man," said Judy. "I sense it."

"You don't know anything about me."

Fischer stared at the glass of water he was holding, and Judy watched him.

"I have a daughter, you know," said Fischer. A smile flickered across his face as he thought of Jess. "I never saw her grow up, and I regret that. Decisions I made, bad luck and circumstance mean I don't know her. I'd like to know her – properly, I mean. She's incredible. She's the only good thing I'll leave behind when I'm gone." He reached up and put the glass of water on the worktop. He folded his arms and looked at Judy.

"It's not too late," she said.

"Yeah, it is. I know that. For a little while I thought I might be able to have something good and precious but…" Fischer held out his hands and looked at them. "I'd just taint it. It's better for her if I stay away. It was selfish of me to want more."

"I'm sure she'd want to know you better."

Fischer got up, went to the sink, turned on the tap and held his hands under the water. He was mesmerised by the cool liquid cascading over his skin. "We'll be leaving in a day or two. As soon as we're safe, we'll make a call and inform the police of your whereabouts. You have my word. I'm sorry to have put you through this."

"You could let me go now."

"In a day or two."

"I think your girlfriend has other plans."

"How's that?"

"She wants to kill me."

"No, she doesn't."

"She does. She said so."

"Don't listen to her. She's just trying to scare you."

"It worked."

Fischer stopped staring at his hands and turned off the tap. "She wants me to go to a gig. She's singing. Playing the guitar too."

"Who? Your daughter?"

Fischer nodded. "Do you think I should go?"

"Why are you asking me?"

"I need someone to ask. Moon is in a bad mood about something, so I can't talk to her about it."

Judy tried to sit up straighter. Her bound wrists were sore, and her left buttock felt numb. "If you have time, you should go. If she wants you there, then definitely, you should go."

"You think so?"

"Yep. What could be more important than seeing her perform?"

"Thank you, Judy. I think I will. I'd better fix us some dinner. Can I leave the gag off for a while? Can I trust you?"

Judy nodded. "My wrists hurt."

"I'll think about it. Perhaps we can untie you at dinner."

Fischer turned the oven on and got some fish fingers from the freezer. "You okay with fish finger sandwiches?"

"I'm not hungry."

"You haven't been eating while we were out, have you?"

Judy looked at him quizzically.

"Sorry. Bad joke." Fischer poured the box of fish fingers onto a baking tray. "I'm going to need you to call in sick again. Tell them you'll be off for the rest of the week. I'll get the dinner underway, then I'll get the phone."

Judy's head dropped. She looked defeated. "Okay. You'll keep me safe from Moon, won't you?"

"You're not in any danger, unless you do something

stupid. You have my word." Fischer opened the oven door and slid the tray of fish fingers onto the rack. "Unless my cooking gets you. If it does, then we're all doomed."

CHAPTER THIRTY-FOUR

I stood in the driveway and looked at what had once been our home. I stepped towards the shattered front window and peered inside. Everything was blackened and charred and sodden. Water dripped and pooled from the hundreds of gallons used to put out the fire. My home was unrecognisable. Everything was gone. Memories that could never be replaced were now destroyed. Early photographs of Helena with Alice and Faith as babies. Soft toys and baby clothes, the girls' locks of hair, pregnancy scans Helena and I had kept. Lost were all the drawings and paintings Alice and Faith had created as birthday cards and on Mother's Day and Father's Day and Christmas. Gone too were Alice and Faith's favourite toys, clothes and keepsakes, items precious to them in personal ways, many of which were a last connection they had with their birth mother. The fire hadn't just destroyed a house; it had stolen emotional connections and the feeling of security and safety that everyone strives to feel within the four walls they call their home. It would take us all time to comprehend and process the full extent of the physical, personal and emotional loss.

"Hardy… Hardy?"

I jumped as someone called my name.

"Hardy?"

I turned to discover Detective Inspector Cotton standing behind me. "I'm so sorry."

"Yeah. Me too," I said. Cotton was with a man I didn't recognise.

"I was on my way to the hospital to speak to you when I spotted your car. This is Fire Investigation Officer Paul Teal."

Teal didn't smile. He had a serious look about him, and his dark-brown eyes meant business. He put out his hand and I shook it. He was in his mid-forties and, judging by his grip, he worked out. "As I've explained to Detective Inspector Cotton, we're investigating arson. The fire appears to have been started maliciously."

"There will be a full criminal investigation," said Cotton. "I've asked to lead it."

I could tell from Teal's cautious manner that even I hadn't been ruled out as a possible suspect. "What makes you think it was arson?"

"I've sent samples away to the lab for forensic analysis, but I'm already convinced an accelerant was used to start the fire. The lab will determine what that chemical was." Teal became more animated as he explained his work and the process involved. He clearly enjoyed his job. "Typically, there is a point of origin, the place where the fire starts. We establish this by looking at the burn patterns."

Cotton and I followed Teal as he walked the perimeter of the house. "What's unusual about this blaze is that there are two points of origin." Teal stopped and looked at me, his eyes unblinking. "The front of the property and the back were doused with an accelerant."

"What kind of accelerant?" I said.

"If I had to guess. I'd say petrol."

"Officers have spoken to neighbours," said Cotton. "A man and a woman were seen approaching the property right before the fire started."

"Do you have a description?" I asked.

Cotton looked at Teal. "Not at this time."

Teal took his cue. "I'll leave you two to it." Speaking to Cotton, he said, "As soon as I get the results back, I'll be in touch."

Teal and I shook hands again, and he left us alone.

"What is it? What didn't you want to say?" I asked.

"The description of the male we received matches that of Edward Fischer. The woman is also a close match to a known associate, Faye Moon. The witness believes the car was a black Ford Galaxy. She has a friend with a blue version of the same style of car."

Edward Fischer, the man Kelly Lyle wanted me to kill. The man I put away for a string of murders, and who I was told by Kelly Lyle was the man behind the killing of my wife, Helena. He'd escaped prison and decided he wanted to burn my house to the ground.

"Do you have any leads on where he is now?" I asked, keeping my voice steady.

"It's better if you take a back seat," said Cotton. "Emotionally, it would be wise. Even if you weren't retired, I don't think the chief would agree to have you involved."

I checked my jacket pocket and pulled out my warrant card. I held it up. "See this? All I have left are the clothes I'm standing in, that car behind me, my phone, my wallet, and this warrant card. You gave me this warrant card when you needed my help. It still has a few months until it expires. I intend to bring in Edward Fischer. My best friend's wife is close to death because of what that man did. I'm going to find him and put him back where he belongs. Being emotionally invested is what makes me perfect for stopping him. I'm asking for your help. Please don't stand in my way."

"You've already made the call, haven't you?" said Cotton.

"Yes. It's nothing personal. I just had to make sure I'm part of the investigation. I made several calls. I can pull a lot of strings when I need to."

Cotton had no choice, and she knew it. She knew trying to stop me would be fruitless. "We'll do it together."

"I was hoping you'd say that. I really didn't want to go around you. I'm going to text you an address. It's my mother's home, where I'll be living for the foreseeable future. We need to work out what we do next."

"Actually, how about I pick you up in the morning? I'm going to visit a crime scene. Edward Fischer's alleged getaway driver was found dead. I guess he's covering his tracks."

CHAPTER THIRTY-FIVE

Fischer woke to the sound of banging coming from the kitchen. He looked across the bed for Moon. Her side of the bed was empty. He looked at the bedside clock: 08:07. He swung his legs off the bed and walked barefoot to the kitchen. He scratched and tugged up his boxers and straightened his t-shirt.

Judy looked up with anger in her eyes. She stopped banging her feet against the kitchen cabinet and mumbled furiously from behind the gag. Fischer removed the gag.

"I need to pee," blurted Judy. "Quickly! If you don't hurry, I'm going to literally pee my pants. How can you sleep so deeply? Did you not hear me?"

Fischer untied Judy and walked her to the toilet. He kept the door open and stood sideways on, so he wasn't looking directly. "Where's Moon?"

"I don't know. She went out early. I need to, you know, go properly. Can I please have some privacy…"

Fischer looked at her perched on the toilet.

"…and pull the light switch. It starts the extractor fan."

Fischer stepped out and closed the door.

"Thank you."

Fischer spoke louder, through the door. "Did she say anything? Like where she was going?"

"No. She was on the phone to someone."

"Who?"

"I don't know."

"Man or woman?"

"How would I know that? A woman, I think."

"Are you sure?"

"I don't want to burst your bubble, Fischer, but you and her are keeping me hostage. Moon and I don't have heart-to-hearts. Girl chats. She doesn't tell me anything. Christ's sake!"

"You all right?"

"Yeah. Can you get me some paper? This roll is empty. There is a new pack in the tall cupboard just behind the kitchen door. Middle shelf."

"I wish you wouldn't keep calling it that. You're not a hostage."

"What would you call it? You're keeping me here against my will."

Fischer thought about it. "'Hostage' implies demands need to be met before you're released. It's not like that."

Fischer found the toilet paper. On the way back to the toilet he picked up his pack of cigarettes, lighter and mobile phone. He threw a couple of rolls in to Judy, then lit a cigarette and called Moon. The phone rang and rang but Moon didn't pick up. He hung up and tried again. Nothing.

Judy came to the door.

"You done?" asked Fischer.

"Yes. Better. Shame I had to have an audience," Judy said sarcastically.

Fischer went to tie her wrists.

"How about I make us some breakfast?" said Judy. "I noticed you bought stuff for a full English."

"Okay. Don't do anything stupid."

"Like what? Overpower you with a rasher of bacon or beat you unconscious with a string of sausages? Then make my escape? Yeah, that sounds like a plan."

Fischer laughed. He noticed Judy eyeing the cigarettes. "Want one?"

"I stopped seven years ago. Not a week goes by…"

"I think under the current circumstances you can be forgiven for having one." He passed Judy a cigarette. Holding out the lighter, he pressed down his thumb and up popped the little flame.

Judy closed her eyes and inhaled deeply. She slowly let out a long, satisfying plume of smoke. She sighed. They walked to the kitchen and Judy started preparing breakfast. Fischer sat at the table watching her. Judy placed the frying pan on the hob and poured in a little oil, then went to the fridge and took out sausages, mushrooms and tomatoes, bacon and eggs. She placed the cutting board on the worktop and put the mushrooms and tomatoes beside it. She gestured towards the knife block for Fischer to see. He nodded and Judy picked out a knife and began to slice the mushrooms and tomatoes into quarters.

"You know, you could have just asked to stay here. You didn't have to force your way in," said Judy. "Cup of tea?"

"Tea would be nice."

Judy filled up the kettle and dropped teabags into two daisy-patterned mugs.

"I don't think that would have worked out. Do you? 'Hello, Judy. I know we just met, but can my crazy girlfriend and I stay indefinitely at your house?'"

"Milk and sugar? So, you broke out of prison?"

"Milk and two, please." Fischer held up two fingers. "You don't miss much."

"You and Moon are very chatty after… you know… sex. Hard not to overhear in a bungalow."

Fischer thought about Moon. He picked up his mobile phone and sent her a text message. *U okay? Where r u?*

Judy placed a cup of tea down in front of Fischer. "She took a bag with her. Black canvas. I thought maybe she was leaving."

Fischer jumped to his feet and ran to the bedroom. He went around in circles looking for the bag of money; he opened the wardrobes and looked under the bed. "Shit!" He lifted his jacket, which hung from a wardrobe door. The jacket's pocket was unzipped. His emergency thousand pounds was gone. "Bitch!"

From the kitchen came a crashing sound. Fischer tossed the jacket aside and ran to the sound. The kitchen blinds were pulled; they swung gently from side to side. The window was wide open and Judy was gone.

Fischer stood in the middle of the kitchen and laughed hysterically. *Two women run out on me in one day,* he thought. *That's got to be a record for anyone.*

Fischer hunted around for the keys to Judy's Volkswagen Polo. Finding them on a hook by the front door, he went to the bedroom and collected his jacket. He scooped up his cigarettes and mobile phone from the kitchen table on his way out of the house. He closed the front door behind him and headed for Judy's car.

CHAPTER THIRTY-SIX

I let myself in to Mum's house. It was quiet. Everyone had gone emergency shopping for clothes and shoes. They stayed until the last of the shops shut then called me to tell me they'd be eating out.

I pulled the handles tight on the rubbish bag and yanked it from the kitchen's silver pedal bin. I unlocked the back door and stepped out into the cool, dark night. Lifting the lid of the wheelie bin, I dropped the rubbish bag inside. I tipped the wheelie bin and dragged it to the front of the house. Collection day tomorrow.

Across the street a car's interior light came on. I looked left and right before crossing the street to the car. As I approached, Kelly Lyle lowered the window.

"Evening, James, my darling. Get in, please."

I looked up and down the street then back at the house.

"Oh, come on, James. Where's your sense of adventure? I won't bite. Unless you want me to."

I opened the door and got in. Lyle was wearing a cropped navy jacket with a pale-blue silk scarf. Her hairstyle and colour had changed to a short choppy blonde.

"Have you and Sienna been formally introduced?" asked Lyle. "Sienna, say hello to James."

Sitting in the back seat of the car was the woman I'd seen in the sports car on the clifftop when I'd last met Lyle.

"Hello, James," said Sienna. "It's lovely to meet you."

"I told you he's even more dishy up close, didn't I?" said Lyle. "And so domesticated. See how he takes the bins out?"

"Uh-huh," said Sienna, turning her attention to her phone.

"Sienna is a little bit jealous. She thinks I'm obsessed with you," Lyle whispered. "I suppose I might be, just a little."

"I heard that," said Sienna without looking up from her phone.

"You were supposed to, Sienna, my love. I'm teasing." Lyle winked at me.

"Well, ladies, this is all very cosy and it's a delight to take a peek inside your relationship, but what do you want?"

"Can a girl not just pay her man a visit without there being a reason?" Lyle looked at me incredulously then broke into a laugh. "I want to make sure you're still on message, that's all. I hear Fischer has miraculously escaped prison. Whoops! How did that ever happen? And suddenly the word on the street is that you and the little firecracker, DI Emma Cotton, have teamed up again. Does that mean you're investigating Fischer?"

"I can't discuss any possible investigation with you. You know that."

"But I wanted to wish you luck in your endeavours. And find out what your plan is."

"I'm investigating the attack on my home. We will be pursuing all lines of inquiry."

"Such a stickler for the rules, James. I imagine one line of inquiry would be to look at Edward Fischer. I mean, why wouldn't you? He's such a bad boy. It can't be pure coincidence that only days after his escape, your home is razed to the ground, can it? It looks to me, and I'm only speculating, that he might want some sort of recompense for time served. Remind me who put him away?"

"You know it was me."

Lyle looked across the street at Mum's house. "How is Mummy Hardy? It must be lovely for her having you all under one roof. One big happy family. Good night, John Boy; good night, Mary Ellen; good night, Jim-Bob…" Lyle looked over her shoulder at Sienna. "She's too young to—"

"The Waltons," said Sienna.

Lyle raised her eyebrows in surprise then turned her attention back to me. She rested her hand on my arm. "More importantly, how's Detective Inspector Rayner and his gorgeous wife, Jenny? I heard she might be a tad crispy."

"That's enough," I barked. "You don't get to talk like that. Not about my family and friends. You hear me?"

"So sensitive, James. I love how protective you are. It's a real turn-on. I sent Jenny flowers and a card. I'm not completely heartless."

I grabbed the door handle to leave. I'd had enough for one day.

Lyle touched my arm. "James, a couple of things before you go. First, Fischer wants to leave the country. He has the money to do so. I've put pressure on his girlfriend, Moon, to delay that happening. In other words, you need to step up the pace of your investigations. If he's arrested before you get to him, you'll lose your chance to…" Lyle dragged a finger across her throat, tilted her head, stuck her tongue out the corner of her mouth and made a croaking noise.

"I'm leaving," I said. "I told you, I won't do it." I started to open the door.

"Second," said Lyle. "I have something for you." She turned in her seat. "Sienna, my little sex-pot, could you pass me our gift for James, please?"

Sienna put down her phone and reached into the footwell behind my seat. She passed me a gift-wrapped box with a pink silk bow. "It's more for Monica and the baby," said Sienna. "I chose it myself."

"She did," said Lyle excitedly. "Open it. Please open it, James."

The two women looked at each other and seemed genuinely excited as I tentatively untied the ribbon and unwrapped the parcel.

"It's not a bomb. Just look inside," Lyle said impatiently.

I lifted the lid slowly.

"It's Versace," said Sienna. "It's a playsuit with a bib and hat. It'll be a bit big at first, but we thought he or she can grow into it. Look – there's another gift underneath. It's a Versace hoodie. I just love the Italian Baroque gold print."

I put the gifts back in the box and closed the lid. "I can't take these," I said.

"He doesn't like them," said Sienna. Her face dropped and she sat back in her seat and looked out the window.

Lyle looked disappointed.

"It's thoughtful. Thank you, Sienna," I said. "I love them. They're not necessarily something I would have chosen myself, but that's possibly because I don't frequent

Versace stores. I'm grateful, nonetheless. I just can't take them. I'm the law and you're, well…"

"Criminals," said Lyle.

"You really do like them?" Sienna asked.

I nodded. "Thank you."

Sienna smiled, satisfied.

Lyle took the box from me and passed it to Sienna. She started the car, indicating our time was up. "I've extended your window of opportunity. Kill Fischer. I don't care how you do it, I just want him dead."

I got out of the car and walked back to the house. As I watched them drive away, I wondered what the hell I was going to do about Fischer and how life had ever got this crazy. My watch informed me it was nine thirty. I decided to call my old boss, Chief Webster.

CHAPTER THIRTY-SEVEN

"This is nice," said Alex. "I can't remember the last time I went out for breakfast on a weekday." He reached out and took Emma's hand but immediately sensed a distance between them. "What is it, Emma? You're not yourself. Is it something I said?"

"No. It's not you," said Cotton. She stirred her coffee absentmindedly.

"Talk to me. Whatever it is, it can't be that bad. A problem shared is a problem halved," said Alex lightly. "Come on, I want to hear what's worrying my girlfriend."

A smile crept across Cotton's face. "It's stupid, really."

"It's not stupid if it's worrying you. Tell me."

"I bumped into someone you used to know. She told me some things and warned me to stay away from you."

"I don't believe it." Alex leaned back in his chair and squeezed the bridge of his nose. "I'd hoped that was all over. I'm really sorry, Emma. This is why I'd all but given up on relationships. Whenever I get close to someone, that woman destroys it. I won't let that happen this time. I've never met anyone like you before. I won't let her come between us. I can't stop thinking about you. I'm crazy about you."

"Who is she? She worried me; I won't lie."

Alex moved his chair close to Cotton and put his arm around her. "I was in a relationship with Louise Greenslade for four years. I tried to make it work, I really did. We simply grew apart. She drove me away with her jealousy and questions and the way she belittled and berated me. We'd go to parties and she'd flirt with other men in front of me. Taunt me. Tell me she wanted a real man. A man that could satisfy her. She bullied me, and – this is embarrassing for a man to say – she threatened me. Told me she'd kill me in my sleep if I so much as looked at another woman." Alex started perspiring. He loosened his tie. "This is hard to talk about. I'm sorry. I get upset thinking about it."

For a moment or two Cotton stared at Alex, unsure what to say. "She told me it was the other way around. That you were violent towards her."

"You're a police officer. Check up on me. I don't have a criminal record. I've never hurt anyone. She's lying. You have to believe me. She's scheming and manipulative. A compulsive liar."

Cotton couldn't very well tell him she had already checked; the only thing she could find on Alex was a speeding fine. "You're saying everything she told me is fabricated. She looked pretty shaken up. She looked scared."

"Believe me, she's a bloody terrific actress when she needs to be. She could win an Academy Award for her performances. You can't trust a word that comes out of her mouth."

"Why did you never go to the police, press charges?"

"You saw her. Who would believe me? I'm almost twice her size. I'm a man. How seriously do you think I'd be taken if I had reported her? At the end of the day, I just wanted to get away. Which I managed, eventually. But now she's back. And she won't stop."

Alex looked ashamed. He ran his finger over the handle of his coffee cup and around the saucer. "I'd hoped that by now she'd have moved on. Forgotten about me. I really don't want to lose you, but I'd understand if you want to run a mile. I'm sorry I got you mixed up in this. The truth is, she will come between us, and she'll not only make my life a misery, but yours too."

He got to his feet, then took his jacket from the back of the seat and put it on. "I'd better go. I'm sorry. You mean too much to me to put you through this." He leaned over and kissed her softly on the cheek. His eyes glistened. "Goodbye, Emma."

Cotton grabbed Alex's wrist as he began to walk away. "I'm a kick-ass detective inspector. I think I can handle myself." She pulled Alex to her. "Don't go." Placing her hand on his face, she gave him a long, passionate kiss. She could feel Alex smiling. "What's funny?"

He crouched down beside Cotton's seat. "We're in the middle of a busy coffee shop. People are having their breakfast."

Cotton looked around. At the next table a middle-aged woman with a half-eaten bagel was looking on disapprovingly. Cotton mouthed an apology. Then both Cotton and Alex burst into laughter.

"Come on. We'd better go before we're thrown out," Alex said.

Cotton checked her watch. "We'll talk more later.

Right now, I'm supposed to be picking someone up. I've got a packed day today, but I'll call you tonight."

"Deal," said Alex. "And thank you. Thank you for not giving up on me."

CHAPTER THIRTY-EIGHT

My late-night conversation with Chief Webster went well. We talked over the Edward Fischer case, chewing over the old investigation before speculating on how he might have escaped prison. After the business of the call was over, we discussed Rayner and Jenny's condition, then spent a good hour reminiscing and chatting over old times. I felt better for having talked. I didn't consider Webster just my boss; he was also a friend, and as such, he was also interested in my plans for the future. It didn't take him long to suggest my return to full-time duties within the police force. He ventured various ideas and roles that I had the feeling he'd been mulling over for some time.

Meanwhile, I still had time left on my temporary warrant card from my previous case with Cotton, and I planned to make the most of it.

I watched as Police Constable Polly Hoyle wriggled the key in the lock and opened the front door. "The lock's a bit sticky," she said with an apologetic grimace. Hoyle's dark hair was tied back and wrapped in a bun below her hat. She had big eyes and a broad nose that was covered in light freckles. She gave the door a kick and rattled the key in the lock. "Here we go. I just need to…" The door sprang open.

Hoyle picked up the letters and free papers and leaflets inside the door and placed them on the telephone table. She then pointed the way. "The victim's mother has been moved to a care home. Dementia and cancer," she said as we moved along the hallway. "It seems Timothy Spicer was caring for her before he… well… you've seen the pictures. It was a grim way to go." Hoyle showed us through to the kitchen.

"Of course, I know you've seen far worse, Chief Inspector." She looked at me as if she'd said something she regretted. She blushed. "I mean, it's just, they were talking at the station about you and your cases. When you were at New Scotland Yard, I mean."

I didn't need to see Cotton's face; I could feel her laughter as she walked behind me.

Hoyle continued. Her eyes widened even more. "You're kinda famous. I heard you're writing a book about investigating serial killers?"

I heard Cotton snort. I turned and saw her put her hand to her mouth to hide her giggles.

"The book's on hold for the time being." I turned back to Hoyle and smiled at her politely. "Where was the body found, Constable?"

We entered the kitchen, and she pointed to a Formica table. "That's where he was. The arms of the table were folded down, just like they are now. Mr Spicer was laid over it, like he was hugging it." Pointing at the floor, she added, "There was blood and water and… urine on the floor. It was gruesome.

"District nurse called it in. She called to check on the mother and when she didn't get any response from Mr

Spicer, she called us. I was first on scene. I assumed the old lady had croaked it, and that was why there was no response at the house. Happens all too often, of course. Thought it was just a routine call-out. What I didn't expect to find was something out of a Martin Scorsese movie. I'd just finished a vegetarian sausage roll from Greggs. Only just kept it down. Thought the district nurse was going to have a heart attack... She'd attended one those recently – poor old sod on a bus, the number 11 into town."

"This must be where the knife exited the body." Cotton examined a groove in the edge of the table.

"Yep, he was that way round. His head was there. He looked like a carcass on the butcher's block."

"What about the weapon?" Cotton asked.

"The knife had been removed. It wasn't in the body, if that's what you're asking. Forensics confirmed it was very likely washed in the sink and placed back in the knife block. They found DNA in the sink and on one of the knives in the block."

I walked over to the sink.

Hoyle came and stood next to me and we looked in the sink together. "It makes sense, doesn't it? The killer broke in, probably wanted to rob the old lady – easy target. Was interrupted by Timothy Spicer. The killer then restrained him on the table, tried to extract the information with threats of torture and mutilation, and when he wasn't forthcoming..." Hoyle raised her arm over her head as though she were holding a knife. She then brought it down sharply. "The killer lost his temper and struck the fatal blow. Spicer choked to death on his own blood."

"You might be right. That's certainly a possibility," I said. "Good work."

Hoyle added, "I'm also pretty sure that if I'm wrong

and the motive wasn't robbery, then we can rule out Spicer's mother as a suspect."

"Why's that?" asked Cotton.

"She's ninety-two and blind. Fifty years blind, so the district nurse says. Not saying it's impossible she killed her own son. Just unlikely, in my opinion. And it's only my opinion. Mind you, probably worth checking she really is blind, don't you think?" Hoyle rubbed her wide nose and looked at us both eagerly.

Cotton tried to hide another smile. She nodded appreciatively.

"Thank you, Constable. Would you mind if we look around?" I said. "Just Cotton and I. It's just so we can examine the scene with fresh eyes. It's a technique I like to use."

"Oh. Uh, no. Not at all. Yes, good idea. I'll be just outside, if you have any questions. I'll be, you know, out here."

Hoyle watched us for a moment before slowly backing out of the room. I heard the front door close.

"You're so diplomatic. You've got a fan there," said Cotton. "She'll be wanting an autograph and a selfie."

"Certainly enthusiastic," I agreed. "Detective material, perhaps?"

"Quite a vivid imagination," laughed Cotton. "She'll fit right in."

"I bet you were just like that not so long ago. All bright-eyed and eager to please."

"How did you know?" chuckled Cotton.

I crouched down beside the table. There wasn't much to see; the crime scene cleaning team had already been. Forensics had their samples. The scene had been photographed and catalogued by local detectives. We were just there to learn what we could.

Discoloration showed where blood had stained the linoleum flooring. "The report says there were two types of blood?"

"Yes. The first being Spicer's, the other unknown. It'll be a few days before we find out whether it's Edward Fischer's."

"Some sort of struggle," I said to myself out loud. I went over to the back door at the end of the kitchen to check the lock. "It was forced."

"Yes." Cotton looked at the report she carried courtesy of the local detectives.

I examined the back door: all the edges, the handle and the hinges. The lock had been replaced for security, but I could still see where the door had been forced. "Why would Edward Fischer need to force the lock? Surely Spicer would just let him in? They know each other. They're supposedly friends."

"Maybe they had a disagreement? Or Fischer didn't want any loose ends? He might have been worried Spicer had a big mouth."

"Mm. Perhaps," I said. "If it was loose ends, he'd just kill him. Why tie him to a table?" In my mind, I was thinking this was more like the work of Kelly Lyle. Though her killings were more staged and flamboyant. Her style leaned more towards the dramatic. "What else do we know?"

Cotton was examining the window ledge where the knife block had sat before Forensics took it away. "Spicer was face down on the table, head pointing this way, towards me. The weapon was driven through the back of his neck. It went right the way through."

I watched Cotton stand on a chair and check on the tops of cupboards. "Lazy detectives don't look here."

I grinned. "Supposing it wasn't Fischer. That would

mean this murder was spontaneous. Had it been premeditated, the killer would very likely have brought their own weapon."

"What do you want to do next?" asked Cotton.

"I'd like to speak the witness who saw Fischer and Moon outside my house on the day of the fire. I have doubts about whether it was them. This killing doesn't make sense. Why kill Spicer days after successfully escaping prison?"

"Maybe it's what we first suggested: Fischer didn't want to leave anyone who could point to his current whereabouts."

I checked inside the cupboards and the fridge. "If they were all hiding out here, there would be more food in these cupboards, and I see no evidence of that. These are almost empty, and so is the fridge. I don't get it. It makes no sense for Fischer to rely on Spicer to get him out of prison and then to kill him days later."

Hoyle peered into the kitchen. "How are you getting on?"

"We're almost done here," I said.

"Hoyle, the report says there are multiple footprints. Someone walked in the blood." Cotton passed me the police report on the page of the footprint photos.

"Footprints. Yes. A partial handprint, too," said Hoyle. "One of the men put his hand in the blood on the floor. I heard the forensic guy get really excited about that."

"Why did you say 'one of the men'?" asked Cotton.

"Don't know. From what I heard, I just assumed it was two men. Certainly, more than one person walked in the blood. Suppose it could be women with big feet? Ignore me. I probably put two and two together and got three." Hoyle smiled to hide her embarrassment.

"Maybe. Maybe not. We need the forensic report as

soon as possible," I said. "Thank you, Hoyle." We followed Hoyle out of the empty house. As she climbed into her squad car I said, "Hoyle, will you do me a favour?"

"Sure. If I can." Her face lit up with excitement.

I handed her a card. "Here's my mobile number. If any developments come to light that you think might interest us – anything at all, like a theory or a suspect – would you call me?"

"Definitely. I can do that," said Hoyle. She gave a thumbs-up and a wave as she drove away.

"Mr Smooth," said Cotton. "You've definitely got a fan there. She might even have a bit of a Hardy crush."

"Enough of that," I said with a sideways grin. "Who better to help keep an ear to the ground than an ambitious young officer?" I tutted. "'Hardy crush.'"

Cotton chuckled to herself and opened the car.

"Pass me the keys. My turn to drive," I said. "By the time we get back, there might still be time to visit my neighbour, the one who claims to have identified Fischer and Moon. Are you okay for time? No big date tonight?"

"I've got no plans. You know me. Work comes first."

"What about your date from the other night. Did it go okay?"

Cotton smiled. "He's nice. We're taking it slow."

"Sounds serious."

Cotton threw me the car keys. "Complicated might be a better word."

CHAPTER THIRTY-NINE

Nurse Chukwu stood at the door to Jenny's room, her hand poised over the handle. It was important Rayner was prepared for Jenny's condition.

"I spoke to the critical care team," she told him, "and Jenny will need to remain in the intensive care unit for at least a week. She'll be drowsy and unresponsive because of the sedatives. It's important her airways remain unobstructed, so she'll remain intubated for a while yet. The burns are mainly to the lower part of her body and are severe."

Rayner nodded that he understood. "I want to see her." He looked at Nurse Chukwu pleadingly. "I need to be at her side."

Nurse Chukwu pushed open the door and held it as Rayner entered the room. "Would you like me to leave you alone together? I can pop back in a little while."

"Thank you, nurse," said Rayner. He waited for the door to close behind him before anxiously edging towards the bed.

A curtain partially obscured his view. As he

approached, he saw only Jenny's wrapped and bandaged legs and torso. As he moved closer, her arms and shoulders became visible and then, finally, her face came into view. Her eyes were closed in a way he'd seen a thousand times when watching her peacefully sleep beside him. Only now, tubes fed into her nose and wires monitored her body; her face was swollen, and her body was bandaged to protect life-changing injuries. A sob from deep inside forced its way up through his body, immediately followed by an uncontrollable flood of tears. His body trembled as he spoke.

"Oh, Jen, I'm so sorry. Oh, sweetheart. I should have been there for you. I swear, if I could swap places with you, I would. You don't deserve this. How can this be right?"

Rayner kissed Jen's forehead. Tenderly, he moved her hair from her face with a finger. He pulled a chair alongside the bed and sat beside her, watching her breathe. Occasionally, her eyes flickered. He felt sure they flickered when he spoke. He spent the next few hours talking to her. Telling her everything would be okay, how she and the baby were the most precious part of his life. He talked about the time they'd first met. How foolish and clumsy and tongue-tied he'd felt around her as he fell hopelessly in love. About holidays they'd had. Jokes and funny situations they'd shared that had made them both laugh. He vowed he would protect her; he'd never again leave her side… ever.

CHAPTER FORTY

Donny adjusted the pillows so he could sit upright on the bed. His ear felt like it was on fire and his head pounded. He drank down a couple of paracetamols with water. Eyes closed, he soaked up the quiet. He steadied his breathing, slowly in and slowly out. He let his body relax and go heavy. A wave of calm washed over him. He let his mind rest. Long slow breaths in and out, in and out. Peaceful. Soothing.

KNOCK! KNOCK!

KNOCK! KNOCK! KNOCK!

"Damn it." Donny climbed off the bed and plodded over to the door. He opened it and walked back to the bed.

Barton dropped the bags next to the bed. "You look like shit," said Barton.

"What do you expect? Because of you, I got my ear bitten off. I now just need to hope the stitches work. The hospital was a dump. I probably caught some incurable flesh-eating disease while sitting around waiting to be seen."

"You should get private medical insurance."

"You have private medical insurance?"

"Of course. In our line of work, it's important to have a comprehensive healthcare plan. I have the Titanium package. It can be used anywhere in the world."

"Well, you really are full of surprises. And speaking of which, what's with you and Mrs Crabb? We're here to find out about Edward Fischer, not explore your libidinous desires for fleshy suburban housewives."

"I thought you'd appreciate a gentler approach." He bit his bottom lip, put a hand behind his head and thrust his hips back and forth.

"Jeez. Enough. Your plan is to seduce her and hope she'll tell you all during pillow talk?"

"Why not?" Barton checked his hair in the mirror, adjusting strands that were out of place. He shined his boots with the duvet hanging over the edge of the bed. "You take a nap. Leave it to me." Barton lifted his collar and checked his cuffs. Before leaving, he took out his roots-touch-up pen concealer and went to the bathroom, where he began examining his hair more closely.

Donny closed his eyes and tried to regain his moment of composure.

The sound of humming came from the bathroom.

Donny groaned. He recognised the song as "Take Me Home, Country Roads." His mother had been a John Denver fan. "Would you mind closing the door? I'm trying to meditate. Still my mind. A little consideration would be appreciated."

The bathroom door slammed shut.

"Thank you," called Donny, his eyes still closed. He'd be glad when this job was over and he could be rid of the animal in the next room.

Long slow breath in, long slow breath out. In and out.

CHAPTER FORTY-ONE

Barton found Mrs Crabb sitting in her office doing the crossword.

"Knock, knock, Fiona," said Barton, a big friendly smile on his face. He knew he looked good.

"You startled me; I was miles away. I'm stuck on four down. Stewed vegetable rat." She pointed to the crossword. "You're not supposed to come back here." Mrs Crabb leaned back in her leather office chair. "How can I help? Is the room comfortable?"

Barton gently closed the door behind him. He strutted over and perched on the desk beside her. "My late wife loved crosswords," said Barton. "Sudoku too. Any sort of conundrum."

"You were married?"

"I was. Best years of my life. She passed away twenty-seven years ago. Twenty-seven long, lonely years." Barton stroked Mrs Crabb's hand. She blushed and moved it away. "I've found being alone very difficult. Being a passionate, tactile man, the lack of physical contact is hard. The intimacy of a partner to share *everything* with. I think it's in our nature to seek human contact. Wouldn't you say?"

"I suppose I would. Since my husband left, I will admit I've felt isolated. There are certainly times when I miss Ian's companionship. We used to do a jigsaw puzzle on a Thursday afternoon. Sometimes afterwards we'd get a little carried away, and we'd…"

"Yes?"

"We'd do some baking. Cakes. Carrot cake was his favourite. It was our special time together, an opportunity to be close."

"And what about *real* intimacy, Fiona?" Barton inched closer; he leaned forward and gazed into her eyes. "You look like a woman full of dark, dormant, untapped desires. You may have been forced to suppress your sexuality, but I can feel you're a passionate woman waiting to be unleashed. In my opinion, there is nothing more arousing than a beautiful, mature woman needing to express and explore and exult in her erotic appetite."

"I don't know about that." Mrs Crabb nervously moved her favourite crossword pen from the desk to the orange plastic stationery organiser. Her cheeks reddened; she suddenly felt very warm. "Ian wasn't very physical, if you know what I mean. He was never very active in the bedroom department."

"That's unforgiveable, Fiona. A crime." Barton appeared mortified. "A woman like you should be savoured. Every pleasurable inch examined and probed."

"Goodness, you almost make it sound normal and proper." Mrs Crabb suddenly felt restricted in her mustard M&S cardigan. "Yet, I'm here all alone. Where would I find a man to take someone like me and shine a light on something so elusive? Feelings padlocked and buried for so long."

Barton turned Fiona so she was facing him. He moved along the desk and placed a leg either side of her chair, his tight blue jeans front and centre. "I can help you, Fiona. It would be an honour."

Mrs Crabb looked at her hands, which she clasped in her lap. She got up and walked to the door. She put a hand on the handle.

"You're right," said Barton. "I should leave. I've offended you."

Mrs Crabb didn't turn the handle. Instead, she took a key from off a heavy-duty four-drawer filing cabinet and locked the door. She leaned against the door and looked at Barton. Reaching up, she removed the pins from her bun and shook her hair loose; it fell over her shoulders. She kicked off her fluffy slippers, rolled down her tights and unbuttoned her mustard cardigan. She walked back to the desk and pressed herself against Barton. "You're not going anywhere, cowboy. This woman needs to be wrangled."

"Happy to oblige, ma'am."

Mrs Crabb grabbed Barton by the shirt, pulled him to her and kissed him. She ran her fingers through his dark, thick hair. She twisted them both around so she exchanged places with him. She swept a hand across the desk; her crossword and orange stationery organiser tumbled to the floor. Mrs Crabb lay back on the desk. "Take me," she demanded.

Barton knelt between her legs and began kissing her softly, his fingers caressing her body like ten tiny Casanovas.

Ratatouille, she suddenly thought. *Clue: Stewed vegetable rat. Four Down. Eleven letters. Of course!*

187

CHAPTER FORTY-TWO

Watson sat beside Cotton and stared at her. "What?" said Cotton. He rolled onto his back and looked at her. When she didn't stroke him immediately, he reached out with a paw and meowed. "Typical man," said Cotton. "Wanting attention all the time."

The sound of the doorbell made them both look around. Watson got up and ran to the armchair and climbed up on the back, where he liked to sit and watch visitors.

"You just wait there. I'll get the door." Watson curled up and stared at her.

Cotton peered through the spyhole. She felt her body tense. *What's she doing here?* thought Cotton.

"I'm sorry to bother you at home. I got a sudden urge to check you are okay. I hope you don't mind. He's not here, is he?"

"Hello, Louise. No, Alex isn't here, if that's who you mean. How did you find out where I live?"

"I followed you. I know that sounds crazy, but I haven't been able to sleep. I kept going over our conversation, and

188

I've been worried I didn't stress enough how concerned I am for you. How dangerous Alex is. Can I come in?"

"I'd rather you didn't."

"Oh? Okay." Louise looked surprised, a little hurt. "Are you all right?" She tried to peer around the door into the house.

Cotton put the door on the latch and stepped out onto the doorstep, closing the door behind her. "Why are you really here?"

"I told you, I'm worried about you." Louise reached into her pocket and pulled out a folded piece of paper. "My telephone number, in case you need to reach me. Don't tell him I gave it to you. I'll be going. Sorry to have bothered you."

"You know I'm a police officer, right?"

"No. I don't know anything about you. Except you're seeing Alex."

"I'm a detective inspector. Serious crimes. When I looked, I couldn't find any record of Alex having been charged with any offence, only a speeding ticket. He has a clean record. You, on the other hand…"

Louise's face dropped. She wrapped her arms around herself and appeared to shrink in stature.

Cotton stepped forward. "I found you were once charged with assault, though the charges were later dropped. The victim of the assault was Alex. He refused to press charges. How would you explain that?"

Louise's body started shaking. "I can't do this. I'm trying to help you, don't you see? It's him, not me. He twists the truth. He twists it so you become unsure of what is right and what is wrong. He gets inside your head." Louise wrapped her arms around her head. "You must stop seeing him. You must."

"I'll tell you what," said Cotton. "I'll decide who I see

and who I don't see, not you. I don't want you coming here again. I don't want to see you again. I don't want you contacting me or Alex. If I think you're watching me, or Alex, I will assist him in getting a restraining order against you. Do you understand?"

Louise began to cry. She nodded.

"Now, I suggest you leave." Cotton watched Louise walk to her car. She never looked back. Cotton went inside and closed the door.

"What?" said Cotton, looking at Watson. "That woman's trouble. All I did was set out some rules as politely and firmly as possible."

Watson jumped off the back of the armchair and disappeared through his cat-flap.

"Okay, so you disagree. There's no need to be rude. Christ, I need a drink." Cotton opened the fridge and poured herself a glass of ice-cold Chardonnay. "At least with a glass of wine in my hand I don't appear completely crazy when losing an argument to a cat."

CHAPTER FORTY-THREE

"I'll have the peppered steak and spicy wedges, please, Cheri," said Barton. "I need to keep my strength up." The waitress made a note and took his menu and tucked it under her arm. She looked at Donny expectantly.

"How hot is the vegetable curry?" asked Donny.

"It's a medium."

"Is that mild-medium, medium, or medium-hot? Medium varies a lot. I have trouble digesting anything too spicy. My digestive system is very sensitive."

Cheri did her best to look patient. "How would you like it? I can ask the chef to prepare it to your taste."

"Really? I wouldn't want you to go to any trouble."

"No trouble at all, sir," said Cheri.

"That would be great."

"So, you'd like the curry?"

"Mm. You know, I think I'll have the deluxe cheeseburger. No onion. Or relish. Or pickle. Or mustard."

"Christ's sake," said Barton. "Why don't you just have the bun?"

Cheri put her hand over her mouth to hide her giggle.

"Also, just regular fries," said Donny. "Not spicy fries. If you have tomato, then that would be great on the burger."

"I'm sure we can do that for you, sir. Will that be all?" said Cheri.

"For now, sweetheart. But don't go too far. I'll miss that beautiful smile of yours."

Cheri smiled politely. "I'll be right back with your drinks." She took Donny's menu and headed to the back of the restaurant to go over the order with the chef.

Barton leaned out of the booth and watched Cheri walk away. "Oh boy, look at the wiggle. Women really are God's greatest creation. Wow."

"Why do you have to that?" asked Donny.

"Do what?"

"Humiliate people."

"What are you talking about?"

"What am I talking about? First you humiliate the waitress…"

"How did I do that?"

"The way you talked to her. She's doing a job. A hard job. A job she gets paid minimum wage to do. She's doesn't need you speaking to her like she's some bimbo. If that was your daughter, how would you feel about some lecherous old man ogling her? Staring at her backside."

"'Bimbo'? There's a word I haven't heard in a decade or two."

"You know what I mean. You're talking to her in a way that's, like, I dunno… It's like you're groping her with words."

"I'm being friendly. I'm complimenting her."

"Try being polite, or civil, instead. You also keep belittling me in front of people. That's humiliating for me, and them too. It's embarrassing."

"Like who?"

"You just did it then, in front of our waitress. And in front of the owner of the guest house."

"Fiona?"

"Yes, Fiona. Mrs Crabb."

"Don't take it personally. It was all part of the act."

"Banging her over the desk was part of the act too, I suppose."

"Fiona is a passionate woman. A woman like that can only be truly fulfilled by an alpha male."

"You're full of shit."

Barton took a piece of paper from his top pocket and passed it to Donny.

"What's this?" asked Donny.

"It's our next stop. Fiona – Mrs Crabb to you – overheard Fischer and his girlfriend, Faye Moon, talking. Fischer wanted to pay a visit to the detective who put him behind bars. I say we do the same."

Cheri arrived back at the table with the drinks. "Your meals won't be long."

Donny waited for the waitress to be out of earshot. "Mrs Crabb told you that?"

"Of course. I just had to promise her another rodeo in the very near future." Barton winked.

"Jeez! You're revolting." Donny took a sip of his drink and rested the cold glass against his bandaged ear. The cold offered a little relief against the constant hot, throbbing pain. "Where did the address come from?"

"Just like you, I have connections."

Donny tutted and sipped his Pepsi.

"What are you really pissed about?" asked Barton "You're always angry."

"What are you, my counsellor now?"

"You have a counsellor?"

"It's a figure of speech. Just, you know… let's change the subject."

"Fine," said Barton. He leaned back and surveyed the room.

Donny checked that nobody was in earshot and then leaned forward. "Look, here it is. You know nothing about me, and I prefer to keep it that way. I was quite happy before you came along. I like working alone. Now, I'm driving around with the world's most vulgar wannabe cowboy. I'll be lucky if I don't lose half my ear. And, I'm probably wanted in connection with the murders of a cop and some fella returning home on his moped. All because you decided they should be killed – no planning, just killed in broad daylight. It's amateur, man."

"It was necessary."

"Necessary? Let me explain something to you." Donny spoke slowly. "You're not a cowboy. This isn't the Wild West. You're not Clint Eastwood, and you don't reside on the High Chaparral."

"I know that."

"I don't think you do. Where are you from? Originally?"

"Billericay, Essex."

"There you go. Billericay. Quite a way from the American frontier. Not many buffalo, Sioux or prairies in Essex."

"You don't like my style, that's fine. At least I have style. You, on the other hand—"

Cheri returned with the meals. "There you go, gentlemen. Can I get you anything else?"

"No, thank you," said Donny.

"Just one of those smiles, princess," said Barton. "There it is. Beautiful. Thank you, sweetheart. And please tell the chef for me, the food looks great."

Cheri went to assist another table, where a toddler had spilled her squash over herself and onto the floor.

Barton cut into his steak. "You, on the other hand, have nothing but complaints, opinions and mood swings. You also think you're a better driver than me. I'm glad he bit your ear off. He did me a favour. You know why? You don't talk as much. Before it was blah, blah, blah, all the time."

Barton and Donny ate their meal in silence. They split the cheque and Barton left a large a tip for Cheri. They walked to the car in silence.

Next to the car, Barton said, "I shouldn't have said I was glad he bit your ear off."

"It was a bit harsh."

"Yeah, you didn't deserve that."

Donny leaned against the car. "I actually quite like your boots. Not so much the shirts."

"Fair enough. You want to drive?"

"Up to you."

Barton spoke in a western accent. "How 'bout I drive the wagon first? Halfway, we find a watering hole, rest the horses, then you take the reins."

Donny laughed. "Okay. I'll take a couple of painkillers and get some shut-eye."

The two men got into the car.

Barton sat behind the wheel and looked across at Donny, who had reclined his seat and was attempting to sleep. Barton smiled to himself. What he hadn't told Donny was that Fiona had also told him about Fischer's money. According to Fiona, Fischer was in possession of nearly a hundred grand.

That sort of money would top up his retirement fund nicely.

CHAPTER FORTY-FOUR

I opened the fridge door and closed it. Folded the tea towels and emptied the dishwasher. I held my breath for a moment before speaking and gathered my thoughts.

"While Alice and Faith are on a play date," I began at last, "there's something I need to talk about. With both of you."

Mum was at the kitchen table; she looked up from her newspaper. Monica was at the breakfast bar. She stopped scrolling through her phone and looked at me, puzzled. I felt myself tighten up; this wasn't going to be easy, but I needed to get it out in the open. I couldn't allow it to continue chewing me up.

"What's going on?" asked Monica.

I sat down at the table opposite Mum. "Why don't you join us," I said to Monica. "This is important."

"What is it, James? You're worrying me," said Mum. She put down her newspaper and folded it. She gave me one of her looks that told me I needed to spit it out. All of it. No matter how hard. And it had better be the truth. So help me, it had better be the truth. It was a look I'd been seeing since my brother and I were children and getting into all sorts of mischief.

Monica pulled out a chair, her hand resting on our unborn baby as she sat, a look of concern on her face. "What is it, honey?"

My voice trembled. "You were right, Mon, there's been something on my mind. The nightmares. There's a reason for them."

"Whatever it is, you can tell us," said Monica.

"Of course you can. We're family," agreed Mum.

I decided to dive right in. "It's about when Kelly Lyle took Alice. Something I didn't tell you. A secret. I didn't know how to…" I swallowed hard. My head started spinning. I'd rehearsed what I was going to say, but now that the time had come it was harder than I'd ever imagined it would be. "I can't carry on without the two of you knowing."

Monica moved her chair closer and put an arm around me. Mum reached out and placed a hand on me. I didn't feel like I deserved their comfort right now. I got up and moved to the corner of the kitchen. I could feel my hands trembling. I shoved them behind me and squeezed the worktop with the tips of my fingers to get control.

"I'm afraid I might be responsible for the house fire and why Rayner and Jenny are in hospital. It might all be my fault. If Jenny dies…"

"You listen here," said Mum. "I know you. Monica knows you. When your little girl was snatched, we knew that come hell or high water you would get your daughter back. There is nothing, and I mean nothing, on this earth that matters more than keeping the babies safe. Whatever it is you've done, or think you've done, you tell us. You understand me?"

I was silent for a moment as I tried to put the jumble of

words and thoughts in order. "When I found Alice, I'd tracked Kelly Lyle down to a remote farmhouse; there was nothing else for miles around. It was night-time, cold and raining heavily. Lyle insisted I come alone. When I first saw her, I wanted to kill her. I could have, and she knew it. She told me if I did, Alice would die. Her body would never be found. So, I sat across a table from Kelly Lyle, just like you two are now with me. All the while, every fibre in me was wanting to hurt her. I wanted to make her tell me where she was hiding Alice. Lyle told me Alice was running out of time, that she'd soon die, and that the only way I could save her was to make a deal.

"I tried to find another way, but I could see no other option. She gave me no choice but to make the deal. Lyle also told me if I reneged on it, she'd find us and kill the girls, and you two as well. We all know what she is. I have no doubt she meant it. You have to understand – I was running out of time. As far as I knew, Alice had only minutes to live. I had to be quick. I had to let Lyle go. Once she felt safe, she'd tell me Alice's location."

Both women were silent for a moment, absorbing what I'd just said. Finally, Monica spoke.

"You had no choice," she said softly. "You had to let Lyle go."

"She left you no other option," agreed Mum. She narrowed her eyes at me. "But there's more, isn't there?"

"Yes. I also had to promise…" I took a deep breath. *Now or never, Hardy*. "…I'd kill the man who murdered Helena."

"Edward Richter?" said Monica, her eyes widening.

"Yes. His real name is Edward Fischer. It's the same man. Fischer has escaped prison. I wouldn't be surprised if Lyle is behind his escape and the house fire was a warning from her to make good on our deal. Don't you see? It means I'm responsible for Jenny's injuries."

Tears filled my eyes. "How can I ever look Jenny in the eye, or Rayner for that matter? What if Jenny dies? What if they lose the baby?" My body began to shake uncontrollably; my legs gave way and I sank to the floor. All the pain and hurt and fear erupted to the surface. "I've failed," I whispered, my voice raw.

Monica got up and came to me. She knelt beside me and cradled me to her. "You haven't failed…"

"Of course I have. I've failed you and the children," I insisted. "On top of that, I gave up the security of my job for a dream. I've lost our home. Gone forever are things precious to you and the children, things that can never be replaced. All my papers and reports and presentations, and the book I was writing. Everything has gone. Why did I think I could escape my past? What have I done?"

I buried my head in my hands and howled like a child.

CHAPTER FORTY-FIVE

Finally, spent, I dragged myself up and sat at the table and tried to sort out what I was feeling. Shame – I'd made a deal with Lyle to get my daughter back. Despair – my actions had caused harm to people I love. Uncertainty – how would I support my family with no income and all my work, reports and writing lost in the blaze? Concern – where was my family going to live now that our home was in ruin? Fear – what would our future look like, and would anyone ever forgive me? And how could I ever forgive myself, for that matter? I'd been drowning in a tide of intense emotions, and now they'd overflowed like a river bursting its banks.

"This isn't a burden you need to carry alone, James," said Monica. "None of us knows what's around the corner. What is certain, though, is that we'll get through this together." Mum nodded and Monica continued. "You were put in an impossible position and did what any parent would have done to get their child back. You, more than anyone, know you can't blame yourself for the insane actions of Kelly Lyle. Screw her and her goddamn deal." Monica hit her fist on the table. "The woman's crazy. You can't reason with a psychopath. If she comes near my family, I swear, I'll rip her fucking heart out."

"Not if I get there first," said Mum.

Like sun after a rainstorm, a tentative smile rose from somewhere inside me, and I looked adoringly at the two supremely maternal women beside me. There's nothing more fearsome than a mother protecting her child.

"And what happened to Jenny is not on you," insisted Monica. "Never was and never will be. Jenny and Rayner will not for one second blame you. You're taking on a burden of blame that is simply not yours to bear, and you're doing it because you love them like family."

I nodded. I could feel the weight easing a little from my shoulders.

"As for money, I'll get more hours teaching. While you go back to doing what you're best at. You speak to whomever you need to and get back on the force. It doesn't have to be Scotland Yard. Down here is just fine. Cotton has been trying to persuade you to join her department since the day we moved down. You just need a desk, and Dorset police is just fine. You'll be inundated with cases from up and down the country as soon as word gets out DCI James Hardy is back working serious crimes." I opened my mouth, and she put up a palm to stop me. "Don't pretend it's not what you want. Your mother and I both know you miss it. So, you get your arse back in the inspector's seat where it belongs."

Mum agreed, and she repeatedly pressed a finger down on the table as she spelled out her thoughts. "It *is* where you belong, James. Much as we might like to think of you safe and sound in an office or giving presentations, it's not what makes you happy. There are some things we cannot change. The sad truth is, you need to go back full time to investigating serious crimes. We all know it. Your father, God rest his soul, knew it too."

"Thank you," I said, looking at both of them in turn. "You don't know how much it means to me to know you're behind me. This is more than I could've imagined."

"As for where you're going to live. Well, I have more than enough room," said Mum. "You father's passing has left a huge hole in my heart and my home and my life." Her voice broke as she thought of Dad. "You're welcome to stay here for as long as you want. If that turns out to be permanently, you'd be making this old lady very happy."

"We couldn't do that," I said. "It's unfair to you."

"That's utter tosh. This is a huge house, far too big for just me. I've been considering downsizing, but maybe I don't need to. I told your father it was too big when we bought it. Did he listen? No. Well, maybe this is why. It was fate. Your father had in his mind that his granddaughters would be sleeping over regularly, and we needed the space. I also know that a couple need their space – I'm not stupid. With the baby on the way, it could work out well. I'd be an extra pair of hands. I'm sure we could make it work. Nothing would make me happier than to be useful again. I don't want to spend the rest of my years alone and without purpose. We could easily convert part of the house to an annex for me. Promise me you'll think about it. I have only one stipulation, and that is I reserve one night a month."

"Why's that?" asked Monica.

"The first Tuesday of each month is poker night," said Mum with a sly smile. "The girls come around, and on occasion we've been known to get a bit squiffy. We're trying a new gin each month. It's been quite an education."

"Your offer is incredibly generous," I said. "We'll certainly think it over."

"Yes, we will," said Monica. "I won't deny the thought of an extra pair of hands when the baby comes is quite appealing. I'm not a young mum."

"I don't want to railroad you into anything," said Mum, "but you have so much going on right now, let's say this is now your home. I know it's a few months until the baby arrives, but that time will fly past, and that infant isn't going to wait. So, until such time as you decide it isn't, this is now your home. That way we all know where we stand. I'll sort out my living area. Alice and Faith can relax and decorate their room; I'll help them. Jamie, you can convert the garage to your study. Monica, you and I will prepare the nursery."

"Oh, that's amazing," said Monica, beaming. "What would we do without you?"

"Nonsense," said Mum. "It's logical."

"Mum, you're a godsend. Thank you. Thank you, both of you." I got to my feet and came around the table. The two women got to their feet and we all held each other. "I feel like an impossible weight has been lifted from my shoulders. My mind feels clearer already."

"Good. That's settled," said Mum.

"I can't wait to tell Alice and Faith," said Monica. "They're going to be so excited."

Within the hour Monica and Mum were busy organising and planning the new living spaces. I was in the garage moving things around and figuring out how my office space would be arranged.

I thought about the call I needed to make to get myself back on the force. I took out my mobile and called Chief Webster. It felt like the right thing to do. I was keen to get the wheels in motion and find out what my options looked like. I couldn't return full-time as a Met DCI, but I wanted his blessing to start again as an inspector down here in Dorset. I felt sure he'd put in a good word for me.

What I hadn't anticipated was that Webster might have an exciting opportunity of his own for me.

CHAPTER FORTY-SIX

A sharp tapping sound woke Fischer. Startled, he looked up to see a face peering in through the window of the pale-blue Volkswagen Polo. He lowered the window and looked around to check whether anyone else was about. He'd parked up during the night when it was dark and needed to get his bearings.

"You wanna move, buddy? You're blocking the bloody gate." Directly ahead was an idling tractor. The young farmer, in his thirties, pale-faced with copper-red hair, strode back to the tractor shaking his head.

Fischer threw off the jacket he'd used to keep warm overnight and started the car. He reversed back out of the field and pulled up at the side of the road. As the tractor came out, the young farmer glanced down at the small car. Fischer mouthed, "Sorry."

Stern-faced, the farmer acknowledged his apology with a nod.

Fischer needed to decide his next move. He turned off the car and pulled the jacket back over him. As he lifted the jacket, he noticed a piece of white paper sticking out of a pocket. He took it out and unfolded it. It was a note from Moon.

Eddie, I hope you read this in time. I'm not supposed to tell you anything. I swear I never wanted to leave you. I had no choice. Kelly Lyle made me give you up. She's nuts. She knew all about my sister and the boys. She said she'd kill them. She made me take all the money. I'm sorry. She wants you dead. She helped me get you out. I didn't know who she really was until it was too late. Run, baby, run.

Your ever-loving Moonbeam XXX

Fischer read the note over and over.

What to do? Moon had his money. He needed that money to get out of the country. There was no doubt that by now the police were looking for him in Judy's stolen car. There was also little doubt Hardy was coming for him. He now knew Lyle had eased his escape; she'd probably bribed the screws, Nessie and Farley. Then there was Jessica. He was desperate to see her perform but didn't want to put her in harm's way. His future looked bleak. He was either going to spend the rest of his life behind bars or wind up dead at the hands of Lyle. Best-case scenario was he'd live out the rest of his days looking over his shoulder in some Third World backwater.

He set his jaw. No; whatever happened, he had to see Jessica perform. That meant he had five days to stay ahead of whatever was coming for him and to find Moon and get back his money.

An hour later Fischer was heading away from the coast. Away from Hardy's hometown and away from Jessica. He'd return for the gig once he'd dealt with Moon.

Then he'd be gone, forever.

He was pretty sure he knew where Moon would go. Whenever she was in trouble, she returned to her roots. He needed to get to that place before she outstayed her welcome and moved on. In all the time they'd been together, there were only two people Moon ever talked about with fondness: her sister and her godmother.

CHAPTER FORTY-SEVEN

The house was cordoned off. The front door and windows were charred and blackened, and the walls were streaked with smoke. An acrid odour hung in the air. Water from the fire service's attempt at saving the house dripped, pooled and trickled. There was a gaping hole in the roof where heat and fire had burned through, causing it to collapse.

"I hope the inspector had house insurance; otherwise, he's screwed," said Barton. Flowers from well-wishers had been placed along a low wall at the front of the property. Barton picked up a small teddy bear that had fallen over. He brushed it off and sat it back down.

Donny held a handkerchief over his nose and mouth. He lifted it off briefly to speak. "I guess we can safely assume Fischer was here; there's no mistaking this message. Fischer's clearly a man who harbours a grudge."

"Agreed. So, now what? Fischer will be long gone after a stunt like this."

Donny looked around at the neighbouring houses. In the front garden of the house opposite, Donny noticed a woman tending her flowerbed and watching them. She looked away when Donny caught her eye.

"Where are you going?" asked Barton.

"Neighbourhood watch. Every street has a nosy neighbour. They're a fount of information." Donny put on his most friendly smile and crossed the street. Barton followed him. "Hello," he called over the fence. "Excuse me."

The lady got to her feet. She clapped her hands together; excess soil fell from her gardening gloves. She rubbed her nose with the back of her wrist and put on a surprised and helpful face, as though she had been unaware of their presence. She took off her gloves and brushed off her light-grey trousers before adjusting her bright flowery blouse. She stepped up to the garden gate. "Yes? Can I help?"

"I hope so, Mrs—?" said Donny.

"Ms Montgomery."

"Sorry to bother you, Ms Montgomery. The thing is, we're friends of the occupants across the street. Inspector Hardy and I go way back."

"You're not the press, are you? I don't talk to journalists." She eyed Donny, showing particular interest in his bandaged ear. Barton she was clearly unimpressed with. It was unclear whether it was his appearance or just the look in his eye, but her face puckered as she examined him. She turned her attention back to Donny. "So, what are you? I don't for a minute believe you're police officers, retired or otherwise."

Barton almost growled.

"Very astute," said Donny. "No, no. I can see I need to be straight with you." Looking over her shoulder, he said, "Are those dahlias you're putting in? I'd recognise those tubers anywhere. You know, my father won prizes for his dahlias. He always told me the secret to big, bold, beautiful dahlias is to ensure they get at least eight hours of direct sun each day." Donny could see Ms Montgomery soften.

"He's right," she said. "Deadheading daily is also essential for prolonged flowering. They also prefer a rich, well-drained soil, slightly acidic. My soil isn't ideal, but I make do. I have devised my own formula to enrich the beds."

"You clearly know your *Bora Bora* from your *Clearview Daniel*."

Ms Montgomery smiled at his apparent knowledge of dahlia varieties.

"Now, I don't want to keep you," continued Donny. "Those giant and spectacular *Boogie Nights* won't plant themselves. So, back to your question. We're private investigators. We're trying to trace the man who started the fire. He's a dangerous man, and—"

"It was a man and a woman started the fire. I saw them."

Donny looked at Barton. "You did? What did you see?"

"I told the police exactly what I'll tell you." Ms Montgomery pointed down the road. "The car was parked just down there, on the corner. I saw the woman cross the street. She went over to the house on her own and came back to the car. Then, they both walked over, bold as brass, and set light to the house. Broad daylight it was. It wasn't until the fire was well underway that I realised what they'd done; otherwise I would have stopped them. Of course, the poor woman who was in the house is in critical condition in hospital. I heard she'll probably die. Serious and extensive burns. Smoke inhalation. It's not usually the flames that get you; it's the smoke, of course. I thank the Lord the inspector's two girls weren't in the house. Such sweet children. They always wave whenever they see me.

Smile and wave, they do. So polite. Well brought up, you see. Lovely family."

"Yes, yes," said Donny. "About the man who started the fire – our role is to complement the police effort and bring him to justice as swiftly as possible. We can't have people like him roaming the streets. Putting fear into hardworking, decent folk."

"A man like that doesn't scare me. He's a coward. Burning down a house the way he did is cowardly. He should be ashamed. Those poor, poor children. I've cried every night since it happened." Ms Montgomery took out a large embroidered cotton handkerchief and dabbed her eyes before loudly blowing her nose. "I think about those children, Alice and little Faith, and all they've lost, and I can't help myself. They must have been so scared. It's all so terrible. I know they weren't a married couple, James and Monica, and I know they have a baby on the way, but I like to think of myself as forward thinking. We have to move with the times, don't we?"

Barton jumped in. "Any of your gossipy friends tell you where he might have gone? The man we're looking for?"

Donny put up a hand to stop Barton continuing. "What he's trying to say is, with this no doubt being a close-knit, neighbourly community, we wondered whether any rumours might be circulating. Often, we find, rumours are based to some extent on fact."

Ms Montgomery gave Barton a look that could have withered a cactus. "No. Nothing. Now, I must get back to my tubers. I'd like to get them in before the sun goes down." She turned her back, dismissing them, and returned to her flowerbed.

It was Donny's turn to give Barton a hard stare. "Mr Tactful. Had to open your big fat mouth."

"She's nothing but a busybody. She was just droning on

and on. She probably knew nothing. Just likes the sound of her own up-herself voice. Self-important old hag."

"Thanks to your flapping brainless mouth, we'll never know whether she knew anything, will we?"

The two men stood at the edge of the pavement and waited for a single car to pass. A voice from behind them made them turn. It was Ms Montgomery; she was standing by the gate again, trowel in hand.

"I do apologise – I missed that," said Donny.

"I said, you know about the kidnapping, I suppose?"

"Kidnapping?" They trotted back over to the fence.

"It was in the paper. They believe the same man kidnapped a woman from McDonald's. That fast-food restaurant. I've never been to one myself; I'm not a big fan of cheeseburgers and those French fries. Myself, I prefer the more traditional thick-cut chip. Generational thing, I suppose. Anyway, from what I heard at the bowls club – I bowl on a Tuesday and Thursday; that's lawn bowls, not that American-style bowling-alley bowls – he held her hostage in her own home, then he and his lady friend did all sorts of perverted things to her, so I've heard. Ghastly. I feel sure the poor woman is going to need therapy to get over an ordeal like that." Ms Montgomery pulled the top of her blouse tight and shook her head in disgust. "Could happen to anyone. You just never know."

"I think you're safe from any interference of that nature," mumbled Barton.

Donny gave Barton a discreet kick with his heel. "You wouldn't happen to know who this woman is or where she lives?"

Ms Montgomery frowned as she thought about it. "Hold on. I'll get the article. I might still have the paper."

Donny and Barton held their breath while Ms Montgomery disappeared inside the house. A few minutes later she returned, victorious. "Here it is. You're welcome to it. Take it with you. It says here her name is Judy Primmer." She pointed to the article and handed the paper over the gate.

"Thank you, Ms Montgomery. You've been most helpful. I have no doubt that, with your assistance, we're one step closer to ensuring this man is brought to justice."

"He needs to pay for what he did. Scaring those poor girls. All their toys destroyed. How a child gets over something like this I don't know." Ms Montgomery teared up again.

"Thank you," said Barton, trying desperately to sound sincere.

Ms Montgomery scowled at him.

Barton smiled anyway. For amusement, he pictured beating her over the head with her spade before burying her lifeless body beneath the bed of dahlias.

CHAPTER FORTY-EIGHT

Fischer sat outside the house of Moon's sister, Sandra. He was waiting for her to return from doing the school pickup. The last thing he wanted was a scene, especially in front of her kids, but he was pressed for time.

He and Moon had once pressed Sandra for cash, back when he had become the prime suspect in the hunt for the UK's most-wanted serial killer. He felt sure that if Moon was in trouble, this is where she'd come.

Fischer sank down in his seat as, in his wing mirror, he spotted Sandra's metallic-red Land Rover swinging into the driveway. Fischer didn't waste a second. As Sandra got out of the car, he was across the road and walking up the driveway. On seeing him, Sandra looked at her boys, Philip and Max, in the back of the car. She attempted to get back inside the Land Rover, but Fischer grabbed her arm and pulled her away from the car.

"Tell the boys to stay in the car," he barked.

"Boys, stay where you are. Listen to Mummy. Do not get out of the car. Do you hear me?"

The boys nodded then clambered across the car seat and pressed their faces against the glass to get a better look.

"You have to leave," insisted Sandra. "I don't know where she is."

"You see, Sandra, that tells me a great deal." Fischer waved to the boys. "How old are they now? They must be seven and nine?" The boys were fighting over whether or not they should disobey their mother and open the car door to get a better look at the tattooed stranger worrying their mother.

"What do you want?"

"She has my money. I want it back. Leave the boys in the car and let's go inside for a chat."

"I'm not going anywhere."

Fischer squeezed her arm. "I'm not asking."

Sandra considered her options. "Philip, Max, stay in the car," she said again. "If you get out, you'll be punished. Mummy's going inside. I'll be back in a few minutes."

"After you," said Fischer. He smiled and winked at the boys. Max, the youngest boy, started crying.

Fischer held Sandra's arm as they marched up to the house.

Sandra's hand trembled as she struggled to unlock the front door. "My husband will be home any minute. He finishes work early today."

"Let's hope he doesn't get here before I have what I need."

Inside the house, Sandra started acting breezy, even though she knew Fischer couldn't be reasoned with. Full of smiles, she opened her purse and took out some notes. "Forty, sixty, eighty-five pounds. It's all I've got. Take it and go. I don't know where she is. I swear."

Fischer took the money and tucked it into his back pocket. "Why are you making this more difficult than it needs to be? I love Moon; you know that. I just want my money back."

"If you loved her, you'd leave her alone."

"What do you care? In your fancy house, with your fancy clothes and perfect life. You've never cared about Moon. It was me that helped her, not you. Even though I was dealing with a ton of my own shit, it was me that got her straight. You didn't want to dirty your hands. She'd be dead from an overdose by now if it wasn't for me."

"That's crap and you know it. I tried to help her, more than once. But I couldn't have her around the boys. I got her into rehab. She wouldn't stay. She was volatile. Unpredictable. I guess you just found that out the hard way."

Fischer moved close, and Sandra found herself pressed against the tall fridge freezer. A child's Iron Man fridge magnet slipped, causing a crayon drawing to fall to the floor.

"I'm losing patience, Sandra," he said. His hand whipped up to grasp Sandra's throat.

"She was here," gasped Sandra. "Only a few hours. She didn't tell me where she was going, I swear."

Fischer sniffed Sandra's hair. He continued to smell her neck and shoulder. With his knee, Fischer forced Sandra's thighs apart. "Why are you going to make me hurt you?"

"I'm telling the truth."

"I don't believe you. I need to find her. She's in danger." Fischer's hand went under her sweater, where he cupped her breast. "You know, Sandra, you're a very beautiful woman." He moved his hand down over her body. He unfastened the button of her jeans and slipped his hand inside. "I've often wondered, during those long days in my prison cell, what similarities you and your sister share."

Sandra turned her face away and gritted her teeth. "Fuck you. You're an animal."

Fischer forced down the zip of the jeans to give his hand more freedom. "Where's Moon? This is nothing. I can really hurt you if you make me. Right here on the kitchen floor. Feels to me like you'd like that."

"You try it and I'll cut your balls off," spat Sandra. She hit him and tried to push him away, but he was too strong. She groped around on the worktop for something she could use against him, but Fischer grabbed her wrist.

He changed tack. "It would be a terrible shame if your boys should meet with an accident. Kids get hit by cars every day. They wander off and fall into lakes. Drown in canals. So many accidents a child could have."

"You bastard – you stay away from them. You promise me you won't hurt my boys?"

"I promise. I just want my money and to know Moon is safe. She doesn't know what she's got herself into. That's all. Then, I'll be gone. Forever."

"Okay."

Fischer removed his hand and once more gripped her throat. "Where?"

"She was here overnight. One night. She wanted my passport. She thought she and I looked similar enough that she could use it. I told her she couldn't have it. There was big argument and she left. That's it."

"Did she take the passport?"

"No. I checked once she'd gone."

"Where is she going?"

Sandra hesitated.

"Where?" Fischer tightened his grip.

"Aunt Patti. She'll go to Aunt Patti. I'll give you the address."

Fischer released his grip and Sandra took a deep

breath. He watched as she wrote the address down on the back of an old envelope. "If this is bogus, I'm coming back. You understand me? And next time I won't be so nice."

Sandra nodded. "Yes."

The youngest boy, Max, appeared at the door behind Fischer. Sandra looked panicked.

Fischer crouched down in front of him. "Hello, mister. What's your name?" Max ran past him and clung to his mother, like a koala hugging a tree. Philip, the older boy, now appeared and ran straight to his mother.

Sandra passed Fischer the address and held her boys close to her.

"Okay, well, it was lovely to see you again, Sandra. Sorry, I can't stay. Sorry I didn't get more time to meet you boys." Fischer waved the envelope and said to Sandra, "Thank you for this. Don't call the police and don't call ahead. My visit to Aunt Patti's needs to be a surprise." Fischer stepped forward and pinched the youngest boy's cheek. "Perhaps, if things don't work out when I get to Aunt Patti's, I'll come back. How does that sound?" He looked up at Sandra. "Best for us both if that doesn't happen. Wouldn't you say?"

Sandra stepped in front of her boys, holding them behind her. "Go. Get the hell out of here. I never want to see you or my sister ever again."

Fischer winked at the boys. "Take care of your mother, boys. You only get one. And this one's real special." He turned and walked away.

CHAPTER FORTY-NINE

My neighbour, Ms Montgomery, took me by surprise when she reached out and hugged me. I introduced DI Cotton, and Ms Montgomery showed us both through to her reception room.

Cotton and I sat at a table with carved legs and ornate edging in front of a large window with fancy net curtains. On the window ledge sat a narrow trough filled with flowering cacti. In the corner of the room, a canary enthusiastically trilled and sang. Cotton watched the bird jump back and forth from perch to perch.

After making some tea and bringing it through on a tray with biscuits, Ms Montgomery sat and joined us.

"Never mind him," she said, indicating the canary. "That's Bublé. I named him after Michael Bublé. He's singing like that because he's excited." She went up to the cage and made kissing noises. "Are you showing off for the pretty lady? Are you? It's time for a little nap. Beddy-byes, Bublé." She took a cover from off the top of a low cabinet, unfolded it and placed it over the cage. "He'll quieten down now."

She pulled absently on a broken fingernail as she spoke. "How are the girls, Alice and Faith? Monica? And that poor, dear woman friend of yours. Her husband must be beside himself with worry. I'm so sorry. I sent a card and flowers to the hospital. I hope she got them?"

"That was very kind. Thank you. The flowers are a lovely thought. She's not out of the woods yet, but she's stable. Monica and the girls are okay. They're with my mother."

"Send them my love. They are dear, sweet girls, a credit to you. So how can I help? Does this mean you're back out of retirement?"

"For the time being, yes," I admitted.

"Well, I'll do whatever I can to help you catch the scoundrels who did this to your family. Shame on them. I've hardly slept a wink since it happened. I know I'll rest easier knowing you're out looking for them yourself."

Cotton produced some photographs. They included Fischer himself, as well as pictures of men similar in appearance. She laid them out on the table side by side. "We were wondering whether you'd be able to identify the man you saw on the day of the fire. We're aware you've already made a statement, but it would be very helpful if you would spend just a moment to look at the photographs again."

Ms Montgomery reached behind her and picked up a pair of reading glasses. She then lifted each picture one at a time. She immediately separated one and placed it down in front of Cotton. "Him," she said. She pressed the photo with her finger. "He was skinnier, but it was definitely him. I have no doubt. None whatsoever."

Ms Montgomery had identified Edward Fischer. Cotton then repeated the process with photographs of women. Just as quickly, Ms Montgomery identified Faye Moon.

"That's her," said Ms Montgomery, once again tapping the photograph with her finger. She removed her reading glasses. "I got an even better look at her. She went back and forth across the road once or twice before the blaze. The way she was dressed, she didn't look like much of a lady, if you know what I mean. Slutty, I call it." Ms Montgomery curled her lip. "Right little tramp."

I had hoped Ms Montgomery would be unable to identify Edward Fischer and Faye Moon. This would have supported my personal theory that it wasn't them who had destroyed my home, that it had in fact been two as-yet-unidentified men. The same men who had left fingerprints and footprints at the scene of Timothy Spicer's murder. However, her positive identification now meant we were looking for Edward Fischer and Faye Moon as well as Spicer's killers. I should have known better. Investigations rarely come gift-wrapped.

"Well, thank you for your time," said Cotton.

"One moment," said Ms Montgomery. "Before you go, I have a gift for Alice and Faith." She disappeared for a moment and returned with two knitted dolls. "They're only silly, but I thought the girls might enjoy them. I made one slightly taller than the other, like your daughters."

"Oh, they're lovely," I said, genuinely touched. "The girls will be over the moon with them. Thank you."

"You're welcome." We all got to our feet, and Ms Montgomery walked down the hall with us and opened the front door. She followed us to the front gate, where we all looked across the road at the ruin that was once my home.

"I'm sure you'll catch them soon," she said reassuringly. "With all the people I've spoken to – police, private investigators and journalists. At any rate, with so many eyes looking, those two in the pictures have nowhere to hide."

"I hope you're right," said Cotton.

We climbed into Cotton's car. I tried not to look at my home again; it was depressing. "I'd better get back," I said. "Monica and I are visiting Rayner and Jenny this evening."

"Send them my love."

I put the keys in the ignition and started the car. I put it in gear and was about to release the handbrake when Ms Montgomery's words fluttered through my mind again. I stared straight ahead as my brain processed the last part of our conversation.

"Are you okay?" asked Cotton.

I look around her at Ms Montgomery, who was still standing at the gate waiting to wave us off. I turned off the car and got out and walked back to Ms Montgomery. Cotton joined me.

Ms Montgomery had a look of concern and confusion on her face. "Everything all right?"

"You said you'd seen a few people about the house fire?"

"Did I?" Ms Montgomery frowned as she recalled our conversation. "Obviously, local police, a couple of times. A couple of private detectives, working alongside the police. A young man from the local paper, *Daily Echo* – pleasant young man. Looked about sixteen years old, of course."

I looked at Cotton as Ms Montgomery repeated what I thought I'd heard her say earlier.

"And I've spoken to you. I did get a phone call from BBC South. They wanted to clear up a couple of points. I watched the evening news, but there was very little coverage."

"About these two private investigators," I said. "What sort of questions did they ask you?"

"They wanted to know about the couple who burned your house. One of them was very impolite. Said they were working alongside the police to investigate the escape from prison."

"Did they show you any identification?" I asked.

"I didn't think to ask," admitted Ms Montgomery. "How foolish of me. You don't think they were journalists, do you?" She put a hand to her chest. "Do you think I've been hoodwinked?"

"Can you describe them?"

"Goodness gracious, yes," said Ms Montgomery. "One was pipe-cleaner thin and funny looking. Had a bandage on his ear. The other reminded me of the Marlboro Man, but mean looking, and not wearing the Stetson hat. He had different-coloured eyes: the left eye was blue and the right eye brown."

"Why don't we go back inside for a moment?" said Cotton. "It'll be more private and I can take down a proper description."

"Of course, of course. Anything to help," said Ms Montgomery. "I'll put the kettle on again, make a fresh brew. What a lot of excitement."

CHAPTER FIFTY

Moon rang the doorbell a second time. Trying to see inside, she peered through the colourful stained-glass panel in the front door. The chain rattled and the door opened as far as the security chain would allow.

Moon was shocked at how old Aunt Patti had gotten. She'd pictured seeing the sprightly old lady she'd stolen from all those years ago. "Hello, Aunt Patti. It's me, Moon."

Aunt Patti peered at Moon through the gap in the door, then without saying a word she closed it. Moon kicked the doorstep in frustration. She was about to curse the old bitch when she heard the chain rattle again and the door opened once more.

"Don't just stand there, girl. If you're coming in, come in. Wipe your feet on the mat. No smoking in the house. We no longer have a smoking room." Aunt Patti moved slowly and with the aid of a cane. "If you steal from me again, I'll cut your hands off." She put out an arm and Moon helped her to her armchair. Aunt Patti settled herself by brushing out the creases in her skirt and making sure her *Times* newspaper and magnifying glass were within reach. "Put the kettle on, girl. You know where everything is. Then we can talk."

Moon turned towards the kitchen.

"And there's no need to slam the cupboard doors. I remember you always slam the cupboard doors."

Moon returned a few minutes later with the china tea service on a silver tray, everything laid out the way she had been taught as a child.

Aunt Patti leaned forward and examined the tray. "Mmm. Good. Did you warm the pot?"

"Yes, Aunt Patti."

"Good girl. I hope you used the Earl Grey. Nothing else will do in the afternoon."

Moon nodded. "I remembered." She looked around the room. It hadn't changed since her childhood. The familiarity was somehow comforting. For the first time, she wished she could stay and never leave.

"Sit there and let me look at you."

Moon perched on the edge of the two-seater sofa. She straightened her t-shirt and tidied her hair with her fingers. She tried to smile.

"Mm, not much of you," said Aunt Patti. "You always were a little flat-chested. You're still prettier than your sister, though. Always were." Aunt Patti took off her glasses and sat back. "I cannot abide strong tea, so pour mine, if you will. I don't want to hear the teaspoon touch the sides of the cup. Remember, when you remove the teaspoon, to place it on the saucer behind the cup. I want to see the handle of the spoon and the handle of the cup pointing in the same direction."

As Moon poured the tea, she could feel the old lady's penetrating x-ray vision. She handed the cup to Aunt Patti, who took a sip and placed it on the antique French rosewood and mahogany table beside her.

Aunt Patti's steely grey eyes looked Moon up and down. "You were always brighter than your sister, but I should have known your wilfulness would lead to trouble. I blame myself for what you have become."

"Don't sugarcoat what you're thinking on my account. Say what you mean."

"There it is. The backchat, lippy as ever. An unwillingness to listen to sense. What do you need this time? Money, is it? Don't give me that look. You wouldn't be here unless you wanted *something*."

"I don't need your money. I just need a place to stay for the night. Maybe two nights."

"Are you still doing the drugs? I won't have it my house."

"No, I'm not on drugs. I kicked all that."

"If I find anything missing after you've gone, like last time, I won't hesitate to phone the police. Do you hear me?"

"You have my word."

"Lot of good that'll do me. But it'll have to do."

The pair sat in silence for a while, the grandfather clock ticking in the corner of the room like a time bomb.

Moon realised she was holding her breath. She needed a cigarette and a beer.

"You can stay; of course you can. The guest room is ready, as always. You know where it is. You can stay as long as you like."

Moon let out a silent sigh of relief. "I have a bag in the car…"

"Let's drink our tea. You can fetch your bag later; there's no hurry. Tell me what you've been up to these past few years."

CHAPTER FIFTY-ONE

Fischer drove back along the road they'd travelled after escaping prison. He didn't like the idea of deviating from his initial plan, but he needed to catch up with Moon. He didn't just want his money back; he also needed to understand how Lyle had forced Moon to betray him. He knew Moon was scared, but he hoped he could persuade her she'd be safer with him than alone.

Seeing a pub up ahead, Fischer decided to pull over. He needed some hot food and a bathroom break. He parked the car in the far corner of the car park and went inside. He found a small table close to a window and ordered steak and chips. While he waited for his order to arrive, he called Jessica. He wanted to hear her voice again.

Fischer watched people at other tables while the phone rang. A businessman on his laptop, a retired couple holding hands and chatting, young parents watching their son playing with his action figures on the floor beside the table while also feeding a toddler in a high-chair. The toddler was more interested in watching her big brother than in the roast-chicken paste being spooned to her from a jar.

Jessica answered in a whisper. "I can't talk right now. The police are here. They're saying you burned a house down. An inspector's house. The one who put you in prison. Is it true? They have witnesses who saw you at the scene. Both you and Moon. Are you crazy?"

"It's complicated." Prickles of shame ran over his scalp and down his back.

"They're saying I could be an accessory to attempted murder. If I know where you are, I must tell them."

"Attempted murder?" His voice was a squeak.

"Yes. The woman nearly died."

"What woman?" Fischer's head dropped onto the table. His throat tightened and his breathing felt laboured. "What are you talking about?"

"There was a woman in the house."

"There couldn't have been. I watched the whole lot of them leave the house. The whole family. Is she okay?"

Jessica stopped talking to him for a moment. Fischer could hear mumbles as she told someone she was talking to a girlfriend. That she wanted to be left alone.

"No! They're saying she might die," said Jessica when she came back on the line.

"My God. What about the children?" asked Fischer.

"Apart from having their house burned down, you mean? How do you think they are? What kind of person does something like that?"

Fischer couldn't answer that question. Hearing Jessica's disappointment and disgust was breaking his heart. He had never planned for her to know about any of this. It was between him and Inspector Hardy. "Who was the woman?" was all he could think to say.

"She was the wife of another detective. Rayner, I think

his name is. She was trapped inside while the house burned around her."

"Moon rang the doorbell," he said, almost to himself. "I saw her do it. She was supposed to check nobody was inside."

Jessica was crying now, her voice breaking. "You're blaming Moon? Mum was right – you're an arsehole. I can't have anything to do with you. Stay away from me. I never want to see you again. Never." She hung up.

Fischer's head was spinning. Jessica's words felt like electric shocks through his body; they tore at his heart. How could everything have gone so wrong? He got up to leave.

The waitress arrived with his food. She placed it down on the table and looked at him.

"Change of plans, sweetheart. I won't be eating." Fischer threw a twenty-pound note down on the table.

"What about your food, sir?"

"Not hungry."

Cursing and full of fury, Fischer stormed out of the pub. As he rounded the corner on his way to the car park, he bumped into a young man who was arm in arm with his girlfriend. The couple were full of laughter and young love. The young man looked up and smiled apologetically. He straightened his suit jacket and brushed the sleeve where Fischer had bumped into him. He looked Fischer up and down and kept walking.

"Watch where you're going," Fischer called after him.

"I'm sorry," said the young man. He turned to look at Fischer and put out his hand in a way that said *No harm done*. The young woman stifled a giggle and pulled her man towards the pub.

Fischer turned and walked at speed towards the couple. Seeing Fischer coming towards them, the young man stopped. He held his girlfriend behind him. "Look, I'm sorry. It was an accident. All right?"

"Is something funny? What's the joke?" said Fischer.

"Nothing. There's no joke. We're just having a good time. We're happy. All right?"

The young man stifled a guffaw, but his girlfriend's laughter increased as she watched the grumpy man in front of them throw a wobbly.

"Then why the hell are you laughing?" yelled Fischer. "If there's no joke, I can only assume you're laughing at me. Are you laughing at me? Am I funny to you? Tell me. Am I some sort of fucking clown?"

The young man looked confused. "Just take it easy. We're not laughing at you."

"Why are you looking at your little slut? It's a simple enough question. Either tell me what the joke is, or I'll assume you're laughing at me."

"Look, mate. We're just here for a drink and a bite to eat. We're not laughing at you. I didn't even notice you until you bumped into me. I think maybe you've had one too many, so go on your way and let's forget it."

Fischer nodded and smiled politely. "I've not had a drink. But you're right – let's forget it." He walked towards the couple and put out his right hand for the young man to shake. "I apologise. Let's shake on it."

Reluctantly, the young man reached for it. "No hard feelings."

Fischer's hand shot out and grabbed the young man's throat, yanking him down. The young man crumpled onto his knees as he choked. Pain seared through his body. His girlfriend screamed and tried to push Fischer away.

"Don't! Leave him. What's wrong with you?"

Fischer brushed her aside. She fell back and toppled into a flowerbed. Fischer spoke into the young man's ear.

"You say you didn't notice me. Do you notice me now, you little fucker?" Fischer's grip hardened. The young man groaned. "You want me to go on my way, do you? Who the fuck do you think you are?"

"Let him go! You're hurting him. He can't breathe." The young woman clambered to her feet and screamed at Fischer. She pounded her fists on Fischer's back, but it had little effect. The young man's eyes bulged, and his lips turned blue.

The young woman took off her shoe and hit Fischer with the heel. He looked up into her face and saw the fear in her eyes. He looked at the young man below him, then at his hand gripping his throat. The young man's hand on his own hand. Fischer released his grip and the young man collapsed onto his back. The young woman wrapped her arms around her man.

"Look what you've done."

Fischer looked at the young man grasping his throat and struggling for breath. "I'm sorry. I…"

Moon caused this, thought Fischer. *Everything is falling apart because Moon screwed up.*

"I'm sorry," he said again. "I've just received some bad news. I don't know what came over me." He reached into his pocket and pulled out a twenty-pound note, which he held out. "Buy yourselves a drink. I'm sorry."

The young woman looked at Fischer with contempt. "I don't know what your problem is, but we don't want your money. Just leave us alone." She helped her boyfriend to his feet.

Fischer watched the couple walk away. What was happening to him? He needed to take back control. If he didn't, he'd end up back behind bars quicker than you could say *Life without parole.*

CHAPTER FIFTY-TWO

Rayner sat in a high-backed chair beside Jenny's bed. His hand rested on hers and he hardly took his eyes off her. He wasn't talkative. Occasionally, he'd repeat things he'd already said. Monica and I sat on two plastic chairs on the other side of the bed.

"Jen opened her eyes this morning." A smile flickered across Rayner's face. It vanished as quickly as it appeared. "They weren't open long. Her eyes turned and looked at me. She saw me. It was before you came. It's a sign. A sign she's getting better." His head nodded lightly. He didn't look at us as he spoke. Instead, he studied Jenny's face.

"It is a sign," agreed Monica.

"Mum and Alice and Faith would like to visit," I said.

"I think it's too soon for Alice and Faith," said Rayner. "I'd rather they didn't see Jen like this. She wouldn't want it. She'll be herself again soon. Then they can visit."

"Whatever you think is best," I said.

Rayner nodded. "Yeah," he whispered. "She'll be herself again very soon."

Over Rayner's shoulder, in the corridor, Cotton

appeared. Monica knew what was about to happen. We'd talked about it and agreed Rayner needed to be kept informed of developments. We decided that if the roles were reversed, it's what any of us would want.

Monica got up and walked around the bed. She put a hand on Rayner's shoulder and kissed him on the cheek. She spoke softly to him. "I'm going to step outside for a minute. I'll be back." As Monica left the room, she was replaced by Cotton.

Cotton stood at the end of the bed. Rayner glanced up at her, then looked at me, then back at Cotton. "What is this? What's going on?"

"We need to talk," I said. "It's about the fire."

"What about it?" said Rayner. He was pale and unshaven, and his eyes were bloodshot with dark circles under them.

Cotton was uneasy talking about the developments in front of Jenny. "I wonder whether we should go to your room. It'll be more…"

"I'm not leaving Jen," insisted Rayner. He shook his head. "She needs me."

"It's important," I said.

Rayner ignored me. I regretted my poor choice of words. To Rayner nothing mattered more than being at Jen's side.

"Come on, mate," I said. "Take a break. We need to talk. You need to hear this. You know I wouldn't ask otherwise. You told me yourself, Jenny can hear what you're saying. Let's not have this conversation here. How about we ask Monica to sit with her?"

Reluctantly, Rayner got to his feet. He leaned over Jen and kissed her. "I won't be long, I promise. Monica's going to sit with you. I'll only be a minute, sweetheart."

Monica was waiting silently by the door as we came

out. She watched as Cotton and I followed Rayner down the hall to his room before she returned to sit with Jenny.

The few belongings we'd brought in for Rayner sat in a packed bag on a chair beside the bed. "They're discharging me. Sometime today."

"That's great news," said Cotton.

"I'm not leaving, though. I'm staying right here," added Rayner. He searched our faces for understanding.

"Of course," I said.

Rayner looked at the pair of us expectantly to remind us we were keeping him from something more important. I took that as my cue.

I decided to come right out with it. "The fire is being treated as arson. Somebody deliberately set fire to the house," I said. "Whether they knew anyone was in the house, we don't know."

Rayner sat himself down on the edge of the bed. It was as though he'd received the final knockout blow and his legs had turned to rubber and given way. "Who?"

"A witness has put Edward Fischer and Faye Moon at the house just before the fire started. Moon is a known associate of Fischer's."

Rayner stared at the floor.

Cotton continued. "Fischer was being transported to a hospital close to the prison when he absconded. Unfortunately, he's still at large."

"I know this isn't news you *want* to hear," I said. "We just thought you *should* hear it."

Rayner looked like a man totally defeated. His head was down, and his shoulders slumped forward. Without saying a word, he got up off the bed and left the room.

Keeping our distance, Cotton and I followed him. We remained in the corridor, watching. He reached Jenny's room and heaved open the door like it weighed a ton.

Monica appeared at the door beside him. She glanced down the corridor at us before putting an arm around Rayner's waist and walking him back to sit beside his beloved Jenny. Seeing Jenny and Rayner like this was breaking my heart. I was ready to make someone pay.

"Let's find this bastard," I said to Cotton. "Whatever it takes."

She nodded. "Next on my list is Faye Moon's sister. Her husband called. It seems he's not a fan of Moon, and he's keen to talk."

"Give me one minute. I'll let Monica know I'm leaving and give her the keys to our car."

CHAPTER FIFTY-THREE

Aunt Patti had gone out early. Wednesday mornings were spent planning fundraising events for Macmillan, a cancer charity. For almost forty years, since her own cancer scare when she was in her late thirties, Aunt Patti had organised events and rallied support. Moon had once asked her how much money she thought she alone had raised. Aunt Patti's blunt reply: *Not enough!*

Aunt Patti's house backed onto greenbelt grassland, meadow that developers were fighting to get their hands on, and government, weakened by the pressure for more affordable housing, would eventually sell to the highest bidder.

Moon gripped a knitted shawl slung over her shoulders. All kinds of birdsong filled the air. She listened as a bird she could not identify, perched on what she thought was a silver birch, repeatedly sang and paused, seemingly waiting for a reply that never came.

Mist hung over the fields, and the crisp morning air made Moon feel alive. She rested on a low wall and took out her cigarettes. The same low wall on which, as a child, she had lined up her dolls for imaginary Miss World competitions. Walking them up and down, giving them names and nationalities and announcing stories of why they were special and deserved to be crowned this year's winner. She guessed the dolls were somewhere in Aunt Patti's house, perhaps in a dusty box labelled Memories.

Moon lit a cigarette. The tip glowed red like a tiny warning beacon.

Fischer would come after her. Her mistake had been to take *all* the money. She'd panicked and not thought things through. Had she left some money, even a few thousand pounds, he could have found a way out of the country using the money for bribes. Leaving him with nothing was stupid. What she didn't know for sure was whether he'd forgive her. She guessed not. Even if it had been for the right reason, she'd still betrayed the only man who had ever treated her well.

She'd met Kelly Lyle at a bar. They'd both been waiting too long to get served, and when Lyle had finally got the barman's attention, she'd offered to order Moon's drink too. They had then spent the rest of the evening drinking together and discussing their misfortunes. Moon had found Lyle easy to talk to and soon told her about Fischer's wrongful arrest and trial and life sentence. Over the next few weeks, they had met up several times, drank lots, talked more. They'd had fun imagining a plan to get Fischer out of prison. That was, until out of the blue, Lyle had suggested the plan was perfectly feasible and she'd be happy to help; after all Fischer was a victim of a miscarriage of justice.

Moon had been unaware who Kelly Lyle was until it was too late. She'd had no idea she was a serial killer with a fortune and seemingly limitless reach, capable of making pretty much anything happen through coercion, extortion and blackmail. It was only when Fischer was out of prison that Lyle had contacted Moon again and explained they weren't friends, that she wanted Fischer dead and why. If Moon had told Fischer anything about her or jeopardised her plan in any way, Lyle said, she would kill her sister's young boys, Philip and Max, while their mother watched, then she'd kill Sandra and finally Moon too.

Having now heard Fischer's side of the story on the beach, she knew everything about Lyle was true and that he really had been there at the murder of Lyle's lover. It was at that moment Moon had decided she had to get as far away from Fischer as possible. Distance herself and not be caught up in whatever Lyle had planned for him. She had done as Lyle asked and taken the money.

Moon had no doubt that if Fischer was coming after her and the money, he'd figure out she would be here. He'd know she always went to her sister when she felt threatened or was in trouble. She knew she was predictable that way. If he went to see Sandra, she knew Sandra would tell him what he needed to know; Sandra was weak. Always was, always would be. She guessed she had forty-eight hours at most before Fischer showed up. It wouldn't be wise to allow Aunt Patti to wind up in the middle of her mess.

Aunt Patti had been something of a surrogate mother while Moon was growing up. With Mother being so unreliable, drinking and hitching up with any man that looked her way, she hadn't been around much. So, with no children of her own, Aunt Patti had stepped in.

Aunt Patti had always wanted more for Moon and Sandra, and she had taken them under her wing. Her rules and insistence on a good education had worked for Sandra. Moon, on the other hand, had pushed back. Resisted. Felt the need to go her own way. She was more like her mother in that regard.

In the early days, finding her own path in life and not following the plan expected of her had led to some great times. After leaving home, Moon had spent a few years travelling. She'd been to more countries than her mother had been to towns in Britain. Moon had pushed the boundaries, lived different lifestyles, met people from many different cultures and backgrounds. Unfortunately, her enthusiasm for exploring drugs and hallucinogens in search of spiritual enlightenment had taken its toll and eventually, having spiralled down into a place she feared she might not return from, she had returned home to save herself.

Returning home had not been the salvation she'd hoped for, however. The leeches and parasites could sense her vulnerability, and she was quickly partying and mixing with a crowd like the one she thought she'd left behind.

China Frizzell, who liked to dress from head to toe in white – white shoes, white silk suit and white panama hat – had been one of those exploiting her. He'd fed her cocaine habit for payment in kind. She'd whored herself for an endless supply of whatever chemical high she could get.

She had been introduced to Fischer at one of Frizzell's invitation-only private parties, a place for Frizzell's friends to talk business and indulge in drugs, drink and sex. All accompanied by a DJ with a thumping soundtrack.

Fischer was a guest of Frizzell's and looked like he'd rather be elsewhere. Moon had made a beeline for him, and they had taken their drinks poolside where the music was less deafening.

Fischer had told her how he and Frizzell went way back. He was open with her about how, through no fault of his own, he was backed into a corner. He didn't go into detail, but she'd encouraged him to keep talking about himself. She had enjoyed listening to him talk. He had a nice voice and attractive eyes. He didn't try it on, either; she'd liked that.

Fischer and Moon had immediately hit it off. Unlike the muscle she'd met in the past, Fischer wasn't full of himself. He was smart, funny, sensitive and confident. He showed a genuine interest in her thoughts and her travels; she liked that he asked questions about her and her opinions. That night, she had gone back to Fischer's place. She'd stayed the night and immediately realised she didn't want to be anywhere else.

In the days and weeks that followed, they would drink, smoke and talk into the early hours. One evening during one of their marathon state-of-the-world debates, he'd broached the subject of her drug use. He told her he found her wild side sexy but assured her she'd have more fun and could still be wild if she got off the drugs. For the first time, with him supporting her, she really thought she might get clean. And it had worked, because for the first time she was ready. She had stayed clean right up until the day Fischer was arrested.

Moon flicked her cigarette butt out onto the neatly mowed lawn and went back in the house. She needed to stay one step ahead of Fischer, and that meant organising her passage out of the UK. It was time to make some calls. She'd made up her mind that she'd like to go back to Poland. She'd spent a month there during her travels and found the cities of Kraków and Gdańsk among the most picturesque places she had visited in Europe. The people were friendly and hospitable; it also helped that her money would go a long way over there.

Moon decided to get dressed and go out before Aunt Patti got home. She didn't need the old lady overhearing her travel plans or talk of forging passports.

CHAPTER FIFTY-FOUR

It was past midnight. The signage of the petrol station shone out in the night, a beacon to weary travellers. Life on an otherwise dead stretch of road.

Governor Lloyd Trent's low-fuel light blinked red, demanding his attention. It had been a long day, and he was more than ready to get home and pour himself a large Cognac before bed.

Since Fischer's escape from Larkstone Prison, Trent had had to deal with more bureaucratic bullshit than usual. He'd been fielding phone calls for days, and it was wearing thin. On top of that, trouble from inmates had escalated exponentially; the men were clearly emboldened by the sheer audacity of Fischer's enterprise. An air of restlessness hung over the prison like a putrid fog. Old scores being settled and petty squabbles rapidly escalated into violent clashes. Staff and inmates alike were on edge, ready for trouble to ignite without notice.

Governor Trent had had to come down hard on the ringleaders. Blood had been spilled and bones broken, a reminder, if any were needed, that he was God. He,

Governor Trent, giveth and taketh away. Under his roof he was the Almighty.

Trent sighed heavily, checked his mirrors, flicked the silver Volvo XC90's indicator and turned off the dual carriageway onto the petrol station forecourt.

As he got out of the car and walked around to the petrol pump, he waved to Parviz. Trent noted he was sat in his usual position behind the cash register, mobile phone in hand. Parv, as he liked to be called, waved and smiled eagerly. Trent filled up the car then walked over to pay. He paid no attention to the car pulling in at the pump in front of his Volvo.

Trent spent a few minutes chatting with Parv, listening to how Parv's daughter was getting ready to start her degree course. Trent made all the right noises, but tonight he was keen to get away. He wished he'd kept going and stopped at the next petrol station where they changed staff regularly and he knew no one on first-name terms. He made a mental note to do that next time. He really didn't give a rat's arse about Parv's daughter and her plans after she graduated. What the fuck was it to him what she did? Just because he'd been polite once or twice, he was now subjected to this man's life story every time he wanted to fill his car up. No. He would definitely continue on to the other petrol station next time.

As he walked back to the car, Trent squeezed the bridge of his nose with his fingers to relieve the tension. He tilted his head from side to side and felt his neck click.

As he reached his Volvo, a noise behind him made him turn. It took a second for his brain to comprehend who stood in front of him, but then he blurted "Fischer?"

"Hello, governor. What a happy coincidence. You look almost as surprised to see me as I am to see you. I was on my way to visit my friend Moon when I spotted your car. What a stroke of luck."

Keeping his eyes on Fischer, Trent reached behind his back and felt around for the car's door handle. "Whatever you're thinking, don't do it. Harming me will do you no favours. Just hand yourself in. You can't run forever. If you hand yourself in, I'll do all I can for you. I give you my word."

"If I go back, I'll never see the outside again. You know that."

"I'm concerned for you. Trying to stay on the run could end very badly for you."

"Bullshit. You're not concerned for me. You think I'm here to kill you."

Trent straightened his neck. "Why would I think that?" He gently lifted the handle on the car door and felt the latch click open.

"I've thought many times about killing you. You must admit, you're a sadistic son of a bitch. I'd be doing every inmate a favour." Fischer got up in Trent's face, toe to toe. He put an arm over Trent's shoulder and rested his hand onto the roof of the Volvo.

Trent could smell stale cigarette smoke on Fischer's clothes and alcohol on his hot breath. Behind them, a car shot past on the otherwise empty road.

"I want you to understand, Trent, you're not beyond reach. The punishment and unnecessary brutality you dish out in that concrete and steel fiefdom of yours can easily come tumbling down. Do you understand?"

"For everyone's sake, I maintain discipline. If I didn't, there would be—"

"Let's not play games," interrupted Fischer. "You're a sadist who enjoys inflicting punishment. I've watched you dole it out with impunity. I bet inside that head of yours you tell yourself we deserve it. And maybe some of it we do. But you *love* dishing it out, don't you? I see it in your greedy little eyes. You get off on it. You're a pitiless bastard, Trent. Don't kid yourself. You're no different to half the men banged up in that hellhole you call a prison. I've been in a lot of prisons and there are proper ways of doing things. There's the right way, and then there's your way." Fischer dusted Trent's shoulder and straightened his tie. "The truth is, I saw your car and I didn't know what I wanted. But now, seeing how pathetic you look on the outside, I simply want to suggest you rethink your methods. I'm not here to harm you. Even though, if I wanted to, I could easily end you right here. No, if I kill you, I might make a martyr of you." Fischer snapped his fingers and Trent jumped. "Dead! Just like that."

Trent held his breath. He closed his eyes. He waited for the bullet to the head or knife to the throat.

None came.

Instead, to his surprise, when he opened his eyes Fischer had turned and walked away. Trent took a deep breath. He opened the door of the Volvo and reached inside to pop open the back. *I've got you now, you bastard,* thought Trent. *Think you're a big man, do you?* He went round to the boot, lifted the mat and opened a metal security box. Inside was a Glock 19 pistol, the weapon of choice for many British plainclothes police officers. He took it out, checked it and pointed it at Fischer. "Stay where you are. Don't move."

Fischer stopped, turned and looked at Trent. He pointed at the petrol pumps as he spoke. "Are you crazy? You fire that around here, you'll blow us all to smithereens."

"Get down on the ground and put your hands behind your head."

Fischer scoffed and walked towards Trent. "You're not going to shoot. If you miss, we both die."

Trent was suddenly unsure of his intentions. "Don't get any closer."

"Or what?" Fischer started dodging from side to side like he was playing a game. Trent had to focus on steadying his shaking hand as he moved the gun from left to right. Fischer kept coming. Ducking and weaving and getting closer.

Hands shaking, Trent fired the pistol.

The bullet passed over Fischer's shoulder and in through the window of the petrol station shop. Parv fell off his chair and disappeared below the window frame. Trent fired again. *CRACK!* This time the bullet went low and wide.

Fischer lurched right and dropped to his stomach. He rolled across the oily forecourt and scuttled to the safety of a steel pillar. "Stop shooting, you idiot!"

Stepping forward, Trent fired again. *CRACK!* The bullet grazed a petrol pump. The two men looked at each other, both relieved there was no mighty explosion.

Fischer took cover behind the pumps. He reached up, grabbed the nearest nozzle and pointed it towards Trent. He squeezed the handle until fuel started flowing.

"Get up!" ordered Trent.

Fischer stood up. "Don't shoot. You'll kill us both." He raised one hand in the air. In the other hand, he held the petrol pump and continued to point it in Trent's direction. Fuel splashed and flowed over the forecourt; the stream gathered momentum and surrounded Trent's feet. "Just back off and I'll leave." Fischer took out his cigarette lighter. "Or I light us both up. I'm not going back to prison."

Trent looked down at the fuel flowing around him and

panicked. Turning on his heels, he stumbled towards the Volvo and ran around the side of it. Putting the vehicle between himself and Fischer, Trent tried to gather his thoughts. He looked down and could see the fuel running under his car.

Peering over the bonnet of the Volvo, Trent looked around for Fischer. *You're not going anywhere, Fischer,* he thought. He looked around for Fischer but couldn't locate him. Where the hell had he gone? Then he spotted the nozzle, which was on the ground with its trigger locked on, still gushing fuel. He looked towards the petrol station shop and was relieved to see Parv through the glass front door, peeking out from the bread and pastries aisle.

"I'm leaving, Trent. Don't shoot," yelled Fischer.

Trent looked wildly around, desperately trying to locate the sound. *There.* Behind the pumps, he saw Fischer scuttling on hands and knees towards a row of bins. Trent raised the pistol and aimed carefully. He told himself that if he managed to hit Fischer, there was no reason to believe the fuel would ignite. He rested the muzzle of the pistol against the car to steady his aim.

Fischer looked out from behind a bin and his eyes widened. "Don't be an idiot, Trent. I'm leaving." He leaned forward, ready to dive in the direction of his own car, which was in the small car park behind the shop.

CRACK! Trent fired and Fischer fell back out of sight.

"Are you crazy? What's wrong with you?" yelled Fischer.

"You're not leaving. You're coming back with me. Dead or alive – I don't care which."

CHAPTER FIFTY-FIVE

Trent peered around the Volvo, searching for Fischer. He dropped to a kneeling position then just as quickly changed to crouching. He looked down at his trousers, which were now soaked with fuel. He decided he wouldn't fire the pistol again unless he had a clean shot; it was too dangerous. *Where was Fischer?* He looked over at the shop.

Trent moved along the side of the Volvo and peered through the windows. *Where had he gone?*

Fischer sprang out from behind the Volvo and landed a foot firmly on the side of Trent's head. Trent went down heavy and hard, sprawling out in front of the car. He could taste blood in his mouth. An intense throbbing gripped his face and the back of his neck. He was cold and wet and he stank of petrol. Suffocating fumes filled his nostrils. Trent pushed himself up to a sitting position and pointed the gun at Fischer. Leaning against the Volvo, he kept Fischer in his sights. "Stay where you are."

Fischer backed away, his tattooed arms high in the air. "You just tried to kill me. That *really* pisses me off. Put the gun down."

Trent staggered to his feet and leaned against the front of the Volvo. "Stay still. Don't you dare move," he said, panting.

"I came here with good intentions. A civilised conversation. That's all I wanted," said Fischer. "And you've turned this into something it didn't need to be." Fischer kept backing away. He watched, half mesmerised, as the fuel continued to pool all around Trent and the Volvo.

Then Fischer and Trent turned, almost as one, as Parv came running out of the shop towards them. Staying a safe distance away, he hollered, "You can't do this, Mr Trent. You must desist immediately. It is very dangerous. Very, very dangerous. Mr Trent, are you okay? You must put the gun down, please. I have called the police. They will be here very shortly. No more shooting, Mr Trent. You'll kill us all."

Fischer could see that the fuel had stopped gushing now; Parv must have shut off the supply.

"Go back inside, Parv," shouted Trent. "This man is an escaped prisoner. A murderer. I'm taking him in, dead or alive."

Fischer waved Parv away. "Get inside," he said, almost conversationally. "Go on. I'll talk some sense into him."

Parv looked at the pistol, then at Fischer, and then at Trent. After a moment's pause to process the situation, he turned and raced back inside to wait for the police.

Trent blinked; his eyes were watering and stinging from the petrol fumes. He decided to call Prison Officer Farley for backup; he knew he lived close by. He felt around in his pocket for his mobile phone. Then, realising he must have left it in the car, he tried the door handle. The car had automatically locked. *Shit!*

Trent rubbed his eyes. Immediately, they started

stinging and watering uncontrollably. *Petrol on my fingers,* he cursed. Unable to see, he started waving the gun around wildly. "Don't you move, Fischer." Tears streamed down his face. The more he rubbed his eyes, the worse they got. Coughing, he put a hand on the car bonnet to steady himself.

Fischer watched him uncertainly for a moment then turned and began to walk away. As he did, he stumbled and kicked over a half-full plastic bucket of water used for cleaning windshields. The bucket overturned and rattled as it rolled on its side.

Trent's body stiffened and his head snapped towards the sound of the rolling bucket. Instinctively, he raised the gun and fired. The bullet narrowly missed Fischer and hit the side of the building. Trent frantically scrubbed at his eyes with his shirt. Everything was blurry, but he could make out shapes.

Fischer got his feet back under him and ran back to the car park behind the petrol station, where he ducked down behind the building's wall.

Seeing movement, Trent fired again. The bullet ricocheted off a steel post between the two petrol pumps and hit the overhead lighting. Glass shattered and sparks streamed down onto the fume-filled forecourt.

With a whoosh, the fuel burst into flame, and a river of fire sped across the forecourt. Trent froze. He watched helplessly as the flames chased across the ground, encircled him and engulfed his feet with a hungry roar. He beat at his legs, which only served to spread the flames to his arms and body. His pitiful screams filled the night air.

Fischer took a tentative step towards Trent but thought better of it. There was petrol on his hands, clothes and shoes; it would be suicide. He whirled towards the door of the office, where Parv stood wide-eyed, hypnotised by the horror.

Flames caressed Trent's body, licking him like the tongues of a thousand greedy demons, melting and consuming his flesh as he staggered and flailed. Arms flapping and hands beating at his body, he screamed as his flesh bubbled and blistered and his skin tightened, cracked and split. He collapsed to his knees, then toppled forward onto his withered, shrunken face. Thrashing from side to side, he clawed and tore at his body. Demonic, guttural, animal-like gasping sounds surfaced from his scorched throat and shrivelled lungs. Eventually, with elbows bent and charred hands clenched like a boxer's, mercifully, Trent's breathing ceased.

Fischer ran to his car on shaking legs. Before getting in, he turned again to look at Parv. Open-mouthed, the man had exited through the back of the shop for safety. He stood now on the grassy embankment beyond the small car park. Hands on his head, he rocked from side to side, moaning.

Fischer shut the car door again and ran to him. "Your clothes," he ordered, snapping his fingers impatiently.

Parv stared at him, bemused.

"Strip down and give me your clothes," repeated Fischer.

Parv nodded mutely. Reluctantly, he kicked off his shoes before removing his uniform shirt and trousers and handing them over. Shivering in his black socks and tight white underpants, Parv made a futile attempt to cover his fleshy body with his hands and arms as Fischer exchanged his own fuel-soaked clothes for Parv's.

"Good man," said Fischer when he was dressed again. He removed the contents of Parv's pockets from his jeans and tossed them aside. "Sorry about all this. And your job." The two men looked at the devasted petrol station. Fischer added, "You'll be okay. You know, sometimes shit happens. It does, but it turns out to be a blessing."

"I don't think my friend Mr Trent would be in agreement with you," said Parv despondently.

Fischer sighed. "You're right. Sometimes shit just happens."

He walked back down the slope to his car and climbed in. Reversing out of the space, he looked in the rear-view mirror. As he did, the pump closest to Trent's Volvo exploded, sending fragments of metal, plastic and glass and a huge ball of flames high into the night sky. Fischer's car shook, and the windows of the petrol station shattered.

As he drove away, he saw a string of blue lights flashing in the distance as the fire brigade sped towards the inferno.

CHAPTER FIFTY-SIX

Moon's eyes wandered over the colourful stained-glass window in the centre of the front door. She rang the doorbell and knocked twice, then waited for the rattle of the security chain. It never came. Instead, a smiling Aunt Patti opened the door. "Come in, sweetheart."

"Is everything okay?" asked Moon. *She's way too happy,* thought Moon. *Perhaps she's been on the brandy.*

"Yes, yes. Come in, child. We've been waiting for you. While you've been off galivanting around as usual, up to goodness knows what, your friend has been keeping me company. He and I have been chatting, drinking tea and eating cake. He's such a charming man. I've haven't laughed so much in years. Such a wicked sense of humour." She leaned forward and dropped her voice to a whisper. "He was just showing me his tattoos. I will admit I blushed a little – he has them all over." She resumed her normal volume. "Don't just stand there gawping, Faye. Come in."

Moon could feel her breathing become rapid and her throat narrow. Over Aunt Patti's shoulder, she could see

Fischer. He'd found her already. His eyes were like wildfires bearing down on her. For a split second she was tempted to turn tail and run, but where would she go? She wouldn't get far. He'd tracked her here and he'd wouldn't stop. She knew he had no choice; he needed his money back and wouldn't stop until he had it. *Perhaps I could do a deal*, she thought wildly. *Yes, I'll strike a deal.*

Aunty Patti took Moon's arm and helped her inside. She took Moon's coat and hung it up. "For goodness' sake, Faye, come in. I sometimes wonder about you. In fact, Mr Fischer – Edward. Such a lovely name. I've always liked that name. It's so masculine, don't you agree, dear?" Moon smiled weakly. "As I was saying, Edward and I were discussing how absent-minded you can be. I told him the story of the time we went out for the day to London, and it wasn't until we were on the train that you realised you were still in your house slippers. The first thing we did when we arrived was catch a black cab to Oxford Street to buy you a pair of shoes. Do you remember? It was so busy." Aunt Patti laughed excitedly.

"Not really," said Moon.

"Yes, you do. We were going to the Natural History Museum."

"I guess I do remember." Moon eyed Fischer.

"Edward here was saying you've done it again, gone off with something precious to him, and he's had to drive nearly one hundred and fifty miles to get it back."

"That's right," said Fischer. "Moon here would forget her head if it wasn't screwed on. Makes me wonder how she's managed to keep her head at all. She can be very silly at times."

Aunt Patti giggled like a schoolgirl.

Moon stared at her. She had never before seen Aunt Patti this way. *Maybe there's life in the old girl yet*, she thought.

Aunt Patti patted Fischer's arm. "I'll leave you two alone for a minute. I'll put the kettle on."

"I'll make the tea," insisted Moon.

"Nonsense. You two sit down. Edward didn't come all this way to see me, more's the pity."

Fischer and Moon each took a seat.

"Now, Edward, can I interest you in more lemon drizzle cake?"

"I shouldn't," he said, putting his hands up in a gesture of mock protest. "You're such a devil. Really you are. Go on, then – just a small slice. How can I resist? I still can't believe you made the cake. No kidding, Patricia; it's the best cake I've ever had. You won't forget the recipe. You did promise."

"I won't forget – how could I? You said you'd murder for it. I can't have that on my conscience." Aunt Patti was beaming from ear to ear. Moon was sure she had more spring in her step than usual. She watched as she practically bounced into the kitchen.

Fischer waited until the kitchen door closed then leaned over and gripped Moon's wrist. Moon winced. "What the hell were you thinking?" asked Fischer. "I ought to break every bone in your body."

"I'm sorry. I got scared. It was stupid."

"Where's the money?"

"It's safe. It's here, in the house. In my room. Are you going to kill me?"

"What? No." Fischer looked at Moon sympathetically. He hated seeing her scared. She looked vulnerable in the way she had the first time he met her. "I just want the money. If you want to go your own way, that's fine. Half the money is yours. You can take it." He let go of her wrist and cupped the side of her face with his hand. "Or, we can stick to our original plan. Go somewhere no one will ever find us, and we can live out the rest of our lives together."

Moon's face lit up. "You mean it? You'd take me back?"

"In a heartbeat, Moonbeam."

Moon knelt in front of Fischer and kissed him. "What have I done to deserve you?" Then her happy face vanished as a thought entered her head. "What about Lyle? That crazy bitch wants you dead. She said she'd kill Sandra and the boys if I told you she was coming for you."

"She'll never know you warned me. Once we've vanished, Lyle will never find us, and eventually she'll forget about me."

"Okay," said Moon. "If you're sure. Let's do it."

"That's my girl." Fischer held Moon and kissed the top of her head. "You've got to promise you'll never do anything like this again."

"I promise, Eddie."

Aunt Patti pushed open the door to the kitchen. Moon jumped back into her chair. The pair of them returned to acting like nothing more than friends.

"Can I help you with that, Patricia?" Fischer got to his feet.

The cups and saucers rattled on the tea tray as Aunt Patti moved unsteadily towards the coffee table. "No, no. I'm fine. Here I come. It takes me a little while these days, that's all. There we go." She placed the tray down. "Would you mind pouring for our guest, Faye?" She pointed at the bowl full of sugar cubes. "Two lumps. That's right, isn't it, Edward?"

"It certainly is. I have a very sweet tooth. Made sweeter in the presence of you two fine ladies."

"Oh, well, I don't know about that," said Aunt Patti. "He's such a tease, isn't he, Faye?"

Moon gave Fischer a friendly kick. "He certainly is. He's a good man. He's had a few tough breaks in life, but he has a heart of pure gold."

"Life can certainly be unfair, I'll give you that." Changing the subject to something lighter, Aunt Patti said, "Tell me more about your daughter, Edward. She sounds like a delightful girl. A talented musician."

"On Sunday, I'm hoping to see her sing. She's not sure she wants me there, but I thought I'd surprise her. I'll be discreet and watch from a distance."

"How exciting. She'll be tickled pink by a surprise like that, I'm sure."

"I hope so. In fact, after I've finished this wonderful cake, I must hit the road. I should be getting back."

"That's such a shame. I so rarely get visitors, and to have you both here is quite a treat." She glanced at her watch. "It's getting late, and it's such a long drive back to Dorset. Must be at least two or three hours. Why don't you take the other spare room? You'd be most welcome."

"I couldn't impose like that."

"Nonsense."

Fischer leaned back in his chair and looked out the window beside him at the dark clouds gathering in the afternoon sky. "Well, it does look like it might rain. I can set off tomorrow morning."

"Good. Then it's settled. We'll have a little dinner later and perhaps a small brandy nightcap. In the morning, we'll take a stroll around my garden. Jack, my gardener, has transformed the walled garden. It's been a labour of love. You really must see it."

Moon tried to hold back her laughter at the thought of Fischer on a tour of Aunt Patti's garden.

Out of the corner of his eye, Fischer could see Moon found the idea funny. "That would be lovely," he said to

Aunt Patti. "With the garden's open aspect, a walled garden must provide a welcome shelter from wind and frost. And as the bricks warm up they act like a radiator, providing the plants with warmth that will extend the growing season." Moon raised her eyebrows with surprise at Fischer's knowledge.

"That's what Jack and I thought," said Aunt Patti. "You've made my day no, my week."

"Thank you. You have such a lovely home. I feel very relaxed here."

"That's very kind," said Aunt Patti. "I hope you won't think me rude, but, if you don't mind, I'll go for a little nap. By all means pour yourself more tea and have another slice of cake. I'll never finish it all." Aunt Patti got up and headed wearily to her room. "You two make yourselves at home."

CHAPTER FIFTY-SEVEN

"Hey. We're here," said Donny. He lifted the handbrake and turned off the car. "We're at the woman's house. The hostage woman, Judy Primmer."

Barton sat up. He yawned and looked out the window. "Good." He stretched and rubbed his nose with his knuckle. Reaching down, he took a bottle of water from the side door, opened it and sipped. "Why don't I go in? If we both go in, it might spook her. I mean, look at you. Your head all bandaged up, you look like a freak."

"I'm not so sure that's such a good idea," said Donny. "No disrespect, but you're not exactly Mr Charming. Tactful you are not."

"I can be tactful. You stay here."

"Hang on, hang on," said Donny. "She's been through an ordeal. She might be skittish."

"Look. You sit tight. I'll do a recce, see how the land lies."

"I dunno..."

"Trust me. I've got this." Barton got out of the car and

walked towards the house. He turned, yanked at his crotch to straighten his jeans out and gave Donny a thumbs-up.

Donny forced a smile and muttered under his breath. "What an idiot. I've got a bad feeling about this, a really bad feeling."

Barton pushed open the front gate and looked down the empty driveway. The back door of the house was open. He watched for a moment then cautiously walked closer and peered into the back garden. A movement on the lawn caught his eye. "Hello," he said softly.

At the end of the lawn, tall conifers shielded the garden from onlookers. To the left stood a greenhouse and beside it a wooden garden shed. To the right of the garden, a six-foot fence and two silver birch trees gave further seclusion.

In the middle of the lawn stood Judy, hanging washing on a three-armed rotary washing line. A basket of washing sat by her feet and a bag of pegs swung from the line; Judy was in a world of her own as she pegged out bedding.

"Hello," Barton said again. He nudged a garden spade alongside the greenhouse. The spade toppled over and knocked against the glass before falling to the ground.

Startled, Judy looked up. She froze.

"Howdy. Sorry to intrude. I knocked at the front door and nobody answered."

Judy frowned. She stepped back and away from the washing line.

"Don't be concerned. I'm part of the team investigating Edward Fischer's escape from Larkstone Prison. I'm the guy the authorities call in when there's a manhunt and the police need a little extra help. I'm like a Texas Ranger but without a horse or spurs." Barton doffed his imaginary cowboy hat and gave a big ol' friendly smile. "I heard about your unfortunate encounter with the fugitive and I wondered if I might ask you a couple of questions. It won't take but a minute."

"I told the police everything I know."

"I know you did, and I'm sorry to inconvenience you further. I read the report cover to cover, and interesting reading it was, too. I just need to go over a couple of points again. I apologise. Perhaps it might be more private inside."

Judy looked around. Curious neighbours on either side might be in their gardens. She nodded, picked up her basket, and led the way.

Barton finished his cup of tea and put the mug down on the kitchen table. He waited while Judy dried her eyes.

"I'm sorry," said Judy. "There were times I thought I was going to die."

"I understand. I'm nearly done. You've been really helpful."

Judy sighed heavily and wiped her nose with a damp tissue.

"You mentioned a moment ago that the woman, Faye Moon, left the house alone. That you believe she took Fischer's money. Do you have any idea where she might have gone?"

"Why are you interested in her? I thought Fischer was who you were interested in."

"I'm just trying to understand what happened. We need to pursue every lead."

"I don't know. I overheard them talking about money. They talked about leaving the UK. Somewhere hot, they said. That's all. It was all whispers. I was in here, tied up, but I could hear them late at night."

"You say Faye Moon took the money. The thing is, if

we can trace the money, we might find Fischer. I don't think he'd walk away from what he would consider rightfully his."

Judy shook her head. "I can't think of anything else."

"Okay," said Barton. "Let's go over it one more time. Did they make any calls? Mention anywhere else they might go? Did they mention any names?"

"No! I told you."

"Okay. I'm sorry to press you."

"I might have heard her talking to a woman one time. Possibly. I don't remember."

"Go on."

"I might have misheard. Moon was on her mobile phone, whispering. She was outside walking back and forth." Judy pointed through the window to the back garden. "Back and forth she went. She was talking to someone. I think they were arguing. Possibly a woman. Moon may have said something about seeing her *nephews*. At least, I think that's what she said. I might have it all wrong, though. She may have said she's going to the *Seychelles*."

"God almighty, woman," blurted Barton.

Surprised by his outburst, Judy sat up a little straighter.

"Sorry. It's just this case. Long days, even longer nights."

"Yeah," said Judy, unconvincingly. "You don't dress like a detective."

"I'm undercover a lot."

"I see." Judy got to her feet. She collected their empty mugs and put them in the sink. "What about ID?"

Barton's eyes followed her as she edged around the kitchen towards the door. "Of course. Though it's not on me. I wouldn't be much of an undercover detective walking around with ID on me." He chuckled and got to his feet. "I'm sorry, I should have shown it to you already. It's in the car. I'll fetch it. You wait here."

"There's no need. I can't help you any further, and I have a doctor's appointment in twenty minutes, so I need to get ready."

"Thank you for your time. I can show myself out," said Barton.

Judy nodded. "Okay."

"Thank you for the tea." Barton turned to leave. He took a few steps before turning back to see Judy touch her front pocket. There was a rectangular bulge in it the size and shape of a mobile phone. *You silly, silly woman,* thought Barton. *Why couldn't you have just believed I was who I said I was?*

Barton stepped out of the back door and strode towards the gate. Once he reached it, he stopped and looked across at the car. Inside it, Donny raised his hands in a manner that said, Well? How'd you get on?

Instead of opening the gate, Barton turned around and looked at the house. Shaking his head, he said to himself, *She's going to phone the law. Stupid bitch.*

Donny saw a look on Barton's face he recognised. He scrambled to get the car door open. "Oh, shit," he said out loud.

Barton turned around and walked back down the driveway. He reached the back door of the house and found it closed. He tried the handle. The door wasn't locked. He stepped inside and listened. Judy was on the phone; he could hear her talking. Barton turned around and went back outside. He walked over to the greenhouse and picked up the spade.

Donny raced through the gate. Not wanting to draw any unwanted attention, he called out in a loud whisper, "Barton. For God's sake, no. Don't you dare. Stop."

Barton picked up his pace. Spade in hand, and with purpose in his stride, he entered the house through the back door.

He found Judy in the hallway.

"Yes. I can do that. No. Umm, I'd appreciate that. How long do you think until the patrol officers get here?"

Judy turned as Barton approached. She screamed into the phone for help. She raised her arms as Barton made his first swing with the spade. Judy collapsed to the floor and Barton kept swinging. Using the edge of the spade like an axe, he kept swinging until Judy stopped moving.

Seconds too late, Donny appeared beside Barton. He watched Barton's shoulders rise and fall as he breathed heavily. "Really? Was that necessary? I mean—"

Barton placed the bloody spade against the wall. "Very necessary." He bent down and picked up Judy's phone. He listened for a moment, then turned it off. He looked at Donny with cold, dark, empty eyes. Blood trickled down his face and neck. He wiped it with his sleeve, examined it, then pushed past Donny. "Let's go. She told me all we need to know."

Donny looked down at Judy's lifeless, blood-soaked body. Her face was no longer recognisable as anything human. He turned back towards Barton. "Jeez. Is there anybody you met you didn't kill?"

"I haven't killed you yet."

"That's comforting."

Barton strode off down the hall and Donny trotted to catch up with him. "So where to?"

"I need to make a call. The woman had a sister. We need to find her."

"Okay. How about we don't kill her? You know, just as an experiment. How does that sound?"

"How about you stop whining? Just as an experiment."

Back at the car, Donny got behind the wheel and Barton climbed in beside him. "You make the call. I'll drive," said Donny. "I'll find us a hotel and somewhere to eat. I'm going to need a stiff drink too. A very stiff drink. Somewhere with girls, too. I need to get laid."

"Whatever you want," said Barton.

"Clearly you're preoccupied. A girl might chill you out. You know, ease some of that tension you carry around with you."

"Do whatever you think best. What's important right now is that we're getting close to Fischer. I can feel it. His woman walked out on him, which means his plans must have changed. He'll go after her. That gives us an opportunity."

Barton figured that was enough information to keep Donny satisfied. He hadn't decided what he'd do if Donny learned of the money. He'd deal with that when the time came.

CHAPTER FIFTY-EIGHT

After getting a call from Cotton, I arrived at the home of Judy Primmer. Judy had recently claimed she'd been held hostage by Fischer and Moon. Cotton and I had planned to interview her, but with the investigation moving along quickly our plan had been to interview her after speaking to Moon's sister.

Cotton took me to the scene in the hallway where Forensics were cataloguing the spade that was considered to be the murder weapon.

Despite looking visibly shaken by the scene, Cotton pressed on. "It seems Judy Primmer was on the phone to officers about a suspicious individual who had just left her home when an intruder attacked her. In all likelihood the suspicious individual and the attacker are one and the same, but that hasn't been confirmed. Officers are going house to house trying to gather more information."

The body was covered, but I could see from the amount of blood spatter on the walls and carpet that the attack had been ferocious. "Could it be Fischer?" I asked Cotton. "Do you think he came back? There will be a shitstorm in the press if he did. I can see the headlines now: 'Kidnapper Returns to Finish Off Hostage.' The press will say we failed her. Which we did." I felt sick. This should never have happened, and I felt responsible for not having seen this scenario as a possibility.

"There's something you need to know," Cotton said. "Before the call ended, Judy described the man as looking like a cowboy."

"You've got to be kidding me," I said. "Whoever this fella is, he's one step ahead of us at every turn. Did she mention whether he was alone?"

"She never talked of seeing anyone else. What do you want to do?"

I looked down at Judy's lifeless body then back at Cotton. "We stick to tracking Fischer. We can't let this cowboy sidetrack us."

"You still want to visit Moon's sister?"

"Yes, that's exactly what we should do. Tell your boss that he should also consider keeping her and her family under discreet surveillance. They might be at risk. Nothing obvious, though. Keep it low key."

CHAPTER FIFTY-NINE

Donny turned off the car's headlights and switched off the engine. He checked the address on the napkin one last time. This was the house.

Once again, Lyle had spoken to Barton and not him. She'd called Barton with the address. That made him feel uneasy. It should have been him she called; he'd made it clear he was leading this job. He was convinced Barton was talking to Lyle about him behind his back. Undermining his credibility. Barton was definitely being secretive, hiding something. Donny always knew. And Barton certainly wasn't being forthcoming about all the details of his conversations with Lyle. There was a lot he was unsure about when it came to Barton.

This job should have been a simple track and hit. Nice and easy. Stress-free. Yet, thanks to Mr Cowboy Boots, they had left in their wake more dead bodies than in a John Wayne western. Barton had overcomplicated everything. He was a liability. Despite all that, Donny felt Barton was the kind of guy who would come out of all this smelling of roses. While he, on the other hand, would have to answer to Lyle. He couldn't leave it any longer; he'd have to confront him soon.

Donny rang the doorbell. He was about to ring again when it opened.

"Hello?"

"I'm looking for Mrs Sandra Palmer."

"I'm John Palmer. Her husband. How can I help?"

"Hi, John. I'm with the parole office. It's about Faye Moon. Sandra's sister."

"My wife's out. She's gone out for a drink with a friend."

"I see. Well, do you know Faye?"

"I know her. Neither of us wants anything to do with her. Whatever she's done, whatever trouble she's in, it's not our problem. Not anymore. My wife has been through enough. She tried to help Faye, we both did, and she threw it back in our face. She's selfish. Only thinks about herself. Never considers the consequences of her actions. Her problems have cost us enough."

John was a short, stocky man with a balding, shaved head and serious brown eyes. His white shirt was tight across his wide chest and around his thick arms. His shirtsleeves were rolled up to reveal forearms with a good covering of thick, dark hair. As he spoke, Donny detected a slight stammer, which seemed to be getting worse the angrier he got.

"I completely understand, and I wouldn't be here unless it was completely necessary."

"If she's violated her parole, then send her back to prison and throw away the key. At least if she's in prison she won't come around here again."

"Has she been here lately?"

"Yes. A week or two ago. Asking for help. Again. Once again, we got suckered into helping. Once again, she metaphorically shat on our doorstep."

"Would you happen to know where she went?"

"Not for certain, but I can make an educated guess."

John reached inside the front door and grabbed a pen and notepad off the telephone table. As he wrote down the address, he said, "If you catch up with her, tell her we never want to see her again. She's not welcome around here ever again." He tore the sheet of paper off and thrust it at Donny, who folded it and shoved it into his pants pocket. "The address is that of Sandra's and Faye's godmother. Moon is probably there right now sponging off her. Bleeding the old lady dry. She has a knack for worming her way in with a sob story."

"That's super. Thank you."

"What happened to your ear?" said John, tilting his head to look at the bandage.

Donny chuckled. "This? It's nothing. Occupational hazard."

John waited for Donny to elaborate and, when he didn't, he said, "Make sure you tell Moon she's not welcome here." With that, he went inside and closed the front door.

Donny looked at the address in his hand with a smug grin on his face. Wanting to make sure things didn't get out of hand, he'd insisted Barton stay back at the hotel. *And that's how you do it,* Donny thought to himself. *Nobody dead. It ain't rocket science.*

He had a spring in his step as he walked back to the car. He could have done this whole job alone; tracking Fischer was a piece of cake. When Lyle had insisted she wanted the two of them to do the job, he should have stood his ground. If he'd done that, she might have backed down, and he could have doubled his money by having Barton's share. Still, very soon they'd have Fischer in their sights, and this job would be over. Maybe next time, once she heard his side of how the job had gone, Lyle would trust him to do a job for her alone.

CHAPTER SIXTY

It was two in the afternoon, but he felt chilly. Donny turned on the car's heater. He figured it was probably down to all the hours of driving and the lack of movement. Poor circulation could do that. He looked over at Barton, who was digging around in his nose with a tissue while staring out of the window.

"Have you ever been to America?" asked Donny.

"What?"

"America. Have you ever been? You know, what with the whole cowboy thing you've got going on, I assumed…"

"That again? I don't mention your shitty taste in clothes, so how about you give it a rest?"

"Hey, man. Jeez. We've been driving for hours. I'm just making conversation. What's wrong with my clothes?"

"Nothin'."

"No, come on. I'm interested."

"I said, nothing is wrong with your clothes."

"You must have meant something. Otherwise, you wouldn't have brought it up."

"I didn't bring it up."

"Yes, you did. I asked if you've been to America. Next thing I know you're talking about my clothes, calling them shitty. So, I ask again. What's wrong with my clothes?"

Barton sighed and looked Donny up and down. "You dress like an old man."

"What? No, I don't."

"You do. You think the shoes are stylish, but I can see they were made for comfort. Your jeans should be Levi's. Your checked shirt has a button-down collar. Your branded sweatshirt looks baggy in the middle and too short in the arms because it doesn't suit your shape. You have a skinny frame."

Donny looked down at himself. "I like this sweater. It was expensive."

Barton shrugged.

"I've been to America," said Donny, changing the subject. "Vegas. Did the whole casino thing. Lost a lot of money but wow, it was out of this world. And the girls!" Donny whistled. "Of course, you'd probably want to go somewhere like Graceland or Nashville."

"Graceland. I plan on going there in the next five years. Everyone should go to Graceland."

"Definitely. You should go. After this job."

"Yeah."

Donny checked the car's satnav. "We must be almost there."

The two men looked to their right at the row of large Tudor-style houses set back from the road with long driveways where expensive cars sat poised. Striped, spacious lawns, tall trees and neat hedgerows separated each house.

Up ahead, a car pulled out of a driveway and into the road. As the car, a black Ford Galaxy, passed them, Donny and Barton looked at the passengers, then at each other. A woman was behind the wheel, and the passenger, a male, looked straight at them. He matched the photograph in the file given to them by Kelly Lyle. His hair was shorter, but it was him.

Donny checked his mirrors for traffic and carefully turned the silver-grey Toyota around in the road. Barton sat up straight and leaned forward, his eyes fixed on the car ahead of them. "Don't lose him."

"I won't," spat Donny.

"Not too close."

"All right, all right. I know how to drive." Donny gripped the wheel tighter than usual. His ear was sore and the side of his head was pounding; he hadn't taken his painkillers for a few hours, but that didn't matter right now. "You want to phone Lyle? Let her know we found him?"

"There's plenty of time for that. Let's see where they go. Get a better look. Make damn sure it's him."

"It's him, all right. You remember what she said? We find him, we call her. We don't kill him unless she says so," said Donny. He looked at Barton to make sure he was listening.

"I remember. Keep your eyes on the road. There's a roundabout up ahead. We can't lose him."

CHAPTER SIXTY-ONE

John Palmer sat beside his wife on their floral sofa in a large, tastefully decorated sitting room. To her right, in a large plush armchair, sat DI Cotton. I sat opposite the couple.

The room had a modern, neutral colour scheme. Tall windows were covered with heavy velvet curtains. Despite the fact that the couple had two young boys, the room looked showroom perfect, without a single toy in sight.

John held his wife's hand until she took it away to wipe her nose with a tissue. John was a short, well-built man who had done well in pet accessories. His business imported and supplied throughout the UK and Ireland.

John was well aware his stammer returned when he got angry. Right now, he didn't care. He ran a hand over his recently shaved balding head. "We've had enough," he insisted. He looked over at the stairs leading to his children's bedrooms. He lowered his voice and continued. "He assaulted Sandra. He's a convicted murderer, for Christ's sake. He might have killed her and our boys. The bastard came into our home and threatened to rape her unless she told him where Faye was… He touched my wife, down there."

Sandra winced. John hadn't stopped ranting about it since she'd told him. She dabbed tears away with the tissue and stuck out her chin.

"All this is new to me. Sandra has only just told me. Faye's boyfriend also threatened to harm our boys, Philip and Max. Said he'd mow them down with his car or drown them in a lake. He's scum – I believe he'd do it. All this because of her bloody sister Faye."

"I'm sorry," said Cotton. She reached out and rested a hand on Sandra's.

"I want to know what the police are doing about it," insisted John. "Why hasn't he been arrested? It seems to me he's able to roam freely and do whatever the hell he wants. A man like that needs arresting, castrating and executing. Bloody prison. It's a joke. Three square meals a day. TV, probably Netflix. No financial worries like the rest of us have. While all of us are wondering whether we're going to have enough to pay our mortgage or the rental charges on the cars, filth like him have none of those pressures. He was found guilty. Guilty of multiple murders. Now he's out, free as you like to kill again or rape my wife. Why don't they just hang him or give him a lethal injection? Better still, electric chair. I'd buy a ticket. I'd sit and eat popcorn while they toasted him. He's a piece of shit."

"John, stop it. That's enough," said Sandra. John's face reddened. He looked at each of us. He crossed his arms and sat back in his chair, his lips pouting slightly. "Fine!"

Sandra leaned forward as she spoke. She smiled at Cotton and took her hand away. "Faye is deeply troubled. Always had a side to her I didn't understand. A darker side. When we were children, she would go to extraordinary lengths to get what she wanted. She can be very calculating. Now I'm an adult I can see the whole person. My parents never really understood her. They just thought she was troublesome. Teachers at school only saw her as a bad child who lacked discipline. I saw close up how she behaved. I saw how she schemed and lied and bullied. Don't get me wrong; there is a part of me that loves her – the good part of her, that is. There is a beautiful, sweet side to Faye." Sandra smiled as she recalled it. "It's like there are two people trapped in one body. The good part of her is being repressed and suffocated. My little Moon is trying to shine, but she can't. The problem is, I simply don't trust her or the choices she makes. I can't have her near those I love."

I understood how hard it must be for Sandra to talk this way about her sibling. For the sake of her family, she was finally letting go. It must have felt like she was throwing her sister to the wolves.

"Wherever Faye is," I said, "we need to find her. If Edward Fischer is looking for her, she's in trouble. Quite likely more trouble than she realises."

"Is it true she helped him break out of prison?" asked Sandra.

"We don't know all the details," I said. I was tempted to tell her about the driver of the getaway car being found dead but thought better of it. "If she was involved, we need to understand the circumstances surrounding that. We'll do all we can for her. Edward Fischer may have put pressure on her to help him. That will be taken into consideration. You have my word."

Sandra looked at her husband and patted his arm. "John and I decided to call you because we're worried. I gave Edward Fischer the address of my godmother, Aunt Patti. I've called a couple of times, but she hasn't answered.

It's where I assumed Faye would go next. Aunt Patti is someone she trusts. Don't ask me why. Growing up, I was always found Aunt Patti stuffy and strict. For some reason, Faye always respected her."

John raised his eyebrow at the thought.

"I had an aunt who never judged me and listened to my point of view," said Cotton. "Growing up, having someone like that, who isn't a parent, can be important."

"You might be right," said Sandra. "At the time, I didn't understand it. As a child I just got jealous. Accused her of wanting Aunt Patti's attention and money."

"We all live with regrets," said Cotton. "It shapes us into who we are."

Sandra produced a slip of paper and held it out. "Aunt Patti's address." I went to take the paper, but before she released it, she added, "Promise me you'll do right by Faye."

"I give you my word. I'll do all I can for her," I said. "My sole focus right now is stopping Edward Fischer. He's destroyed too many lives. Caused too much misery. One way or another, I'm going to stop him, I promise." Out of the corner of my eye I saw Cotton's head spin to look at me. I ignored it. I shouldn't be making promises; I knew that. I'd let down my guard, and my personal feelings had bubbled to the surface. I needed to keep that in check. I tucked the address in my jacket pocket as we got up to leave.

"In reality, Faye will end up serving some sort of prison time, won't she?" said John. "I mean, she helped a man break out of prison, and if her parole officer is concerned enough to come here looking for her, she must be in some sort of violation of her parole, wouldn't you say?"

Puzzled, Cotton and I looked at John. "Her parole officer came here?" asked Cotton.

"What did he look like?" I asked.

"Um, he was tall. Very slim. His eyes were, I don't want to be rude, but I suppose you'd say they were bulgy."

I looked at Cotton. This was a similar description to the private detective who had visited my neighbour, Ms Montgomery. "Was he alone? Was he with another man?"

"No," said John.

"Are you sure?" said Cotton.

"Yes. He also had a bandage. Here." John pointed to his right ear. "He said it was an 'occupational hazard.'"

Cotton and I sat in her car outside Mr and Mrs Palmer's home. My heart was pumping; it felt like we were closing in on Edward Fischer and Moon. "It has to be the same man who visited Ms Montgomery. He tells her he's a private investigator, then he tells the Palmers he's Moon's parole officer."

"Who is he, do you think? Why was he alone when he visited the Palmers?" said Cotton.

"I don't know. I bet you anything you like that the second blood sample found at the murder scene of Timothy Spicer is that of our man with the bandaged ear."

"You think they killed Spicer?"

"I do. I think they're looking for Edward Fischer and Faye Moon, just like we are. They also seem to be one step ahead of us." I pulled Aunt Patti's address from my pocket. "Shall we?"

"Let's go." I passed Cotton the address and she punched it into the satnav. "I'll drive, you navigate. You know that satnav of yours doesn't like me."

Cotton shook her head. "Yeah, yeah. Blame the satnav

for your poor navigational skills. Just don't turn until she tells you to and you'll be fine."

I tried to keep our conversation light to counterbalance how I felt inside. But the closer we got to Edward Fischer, the more I worried about what I was going to do. Kelly Lyle was expecting me to kill him. If I didn't... well, I didn't want to think about the possible consequences.

CHAPTER SIXTY-TWO

Jessica had taken two buses and walked ten minutes to get to Coffee, Cake 'n' Shakes. She'd been angry at him the whole journey, but at the same time felt drawn to seeing him again. She couldn't understand it. Most of her life she'd not thought about him; she'd just got on with the day-to-day. Yet, she realised now, he'd always been there like a mote in her mind. He was an unshakeable question she'd carried with her until now.

And as soon as she saw her dad waiting for her, the anger melted away.

The three of them sat in a booth, Moon stirring her banana chocolate chip milkshake and Fischer nursing a milky coffee while Jessica sipped her whipped-cream-topped hot chocolate. She dabbed the cream with a long spoon as she listened to Fischer repeat himself.

"Is everything okay, guys?" The waitress smiled and tilted her head like it was heavy on one side. "How's your shake? The banana choc chip is my fave."

"Really good. Thank you," said Jess.

"Don't I know you? You play guitar, right? You're a singer?"

"I am, but it's unlikely you've heard of me. I'm still pretty small-time."

"I knew it. I'm Bryony Chase. Bee for short." She pointed to her name badge, which read "Bee."

"We used to go to the same school. I was a couple of years in front of you. I heard you sing at school concerts a couple of times. I've seen your stuff on YouTube – it's amazing. I heard you were doing really well. Got a record deal. Your name's Jessica Walker, right?"

"That's right. I mean about the name. Not the record deal. No record deal. Not yet, anyway."

"I know it's a bit cheesy, but can I get a selfie with you? You know, before you leave. Not now. Don't want to interrupt."

"Of course. Now's fine. If you really want to?" said Jess.

"Yeah, definitely. That'd be great." She leaned in next to Jess, held up her phone and snapped a couple of photos. "Thanks," she said, straightening again. "Anyway, I'd better get back to it. Just holla if you need anything." Bee moved to the next table, where she collected the cups and wiped it over.

"You're famous, Jess," said Moon. "You've got fans and everything. You're going places."

"I'm so proud of you, Jess," said Fischer. "My little girl."

Jessica lowered her head and jabbed at her hot chocolate with the spoon.

"I know what you're thinking, Jess," said Fischer. "I promise I'll be there. I wouldn't miss it for the world."

"I don't care anymore," said Jess. "You burned a man's house down. The woman might die."

"I'm sorry. It was stupid. It's difficult to describe the hatred I feel for that man. I lost everything because of him. When you're in a prison cell twenty-three hours a day, it's easy to lose sight of what's important. I needed someone to pay for the time I lost. I hadn't meant to hurt anyone." Fischer reached out and held his daughter's small hand. "I thought hurting him would help me heal. All it's done is push you further away. I don't want to leave the country without you knowing that not a day goes by that I don't think of you and wish our lives could have been different."

A smile escaped and crept across Jess's face.

"I'm going to be at the gig," insisted Fischer.

"What about the police? I'm sure they've been watching me, expecting you to turn up," said Jess.

"Do you think that's a good idea?" said Moon.

"I'll find a way," said Fischer. "Now, let's order some cake. That carrot cake at the counter looked amazing. Let's get double helpings." Fischer put up his hand to get Bee's attention.

At a small table in the corner next to the door, a stick-like man caught Fischer's eye. The man sat alone nursing his drink. A white bandage was taped over his ear and he looked ill at ease. It was the second time Fischer had looked over at him, causing the man to avert his eyes. It could have been just a coincidence, Fischer thought, but then again, he couldn't take that chance. Not with Jess around. If the lone man was here for him, he needed to find a way to draw him out so Jess was safe.

CHAPTER SIXTY-THREE

From the car park he could see Donny inside Coffee, Cake 'n' Shakes. To look less suspicious, Barton had argued a little when Donny insisted he wanted to go inside alone. It worked; the skinny idiot had thrown his track record of violence and unsocial behaviour back at him. Barton had backed down and watched Donny lollop victoriously over to the restaurant.

Towards the middle of the restaurant, he could see Fischer with the woman he knew to be Moon. He was surprised she was still alive; if any woman of his had even thought about stealing from him, she'd find herself trying to claw her way out of the boot of a burning car. The third person, a teenage girl, he didn't know.

Barton got out of the car and removed the tyre iron from the back of the Toyota. He pushed it up his sleeve and gently closed the boot. To conceal himself, he walked around behind their Toyota and across the car park to the Ford belonging to Fischer. The car had been parked around the side of the building, away from passing vehicles. Barton checked all the doors. The car was locked.

He let the tyre iron drop from his sleeve into his hand. He gave the passenger side window a couple of firm taps and the glass shattered. He reached in and opened the door, then leaned in and checked the footwells and under the seats. Nothing. He moved to the rear of the Ford and opened the boot. He pulled a canvas bag towards him and unzipped it. Clothes. Damn. Barton looked up at the sound of a car pulling off the main road into the car park. He was about to walk away when he decided to lift the boot mat. There, in a storage area under the mat, was another canvas bag. He pulled it to him and unzipped it. Inside, under a couple of shirts, were bundles of fifty-pound notes. *Bingo,* thought Barton. *Easiest money you ever made.* He zipped up the bag before closing the doors and heading back to the Toyota.

He opened its rear hatch; the only things in there were their small travel bags and Donny's coat. Moving them aside, he lifted the mat to reveal the spare wheel. He took it out and stashed the bag. He tossed the tyre iron on top of the money and put the mat back in place. He straightened the travel bags and the coat, then closed the back of the car. Carrying the spare wheel a few car spaces down, he laid it flat and pushed it under one of the parked cars.

Climbing back into driver's seat of the Toyota, he looked over at the restaurant. Fischer had got up and was heading towards the back. Donny was still in his seat and was watching Fischer. He could see Donny was wondering what to do. *What an amateur,* thought Barton.

CHAPTER SIXTY-FOUR

"Moon," said Fischer, "order some cakes for us all. I'll be right back. I need to go to the men's room. Can I borrow your cigarette lighter? I left mine in the car."

"Sure." Moon reached into her jeans pocket and produced a plastic lighter with a picture of a Hawaiian dancer in a grass skirt and flowers in her hair. "Everything all right?"

"Yeah." Fischer looked behind him for the sign to the men's room. "I'll be right back. Carrot cake for me."

"I want my hula dancer lighter back," Moon called after him. "She's my lucky lighter."

Fischer walked to the rear of the restaurant. Passing a vacated table, he picked up a fork and slipped it into his front pocket. He followed the sign for the men's room, pushed through a swing door and entered a short passageway with more two doors. The first door read *Ladies*; the second door read *Gents*. At the end of the passageway was the fire exit. Fischer looked back the way he'd come to see if he was being followed before he entered the men's room.

Just inside the door was a privacy wall, on the other side of which were two sinks, a pair of hand dryers and a row of four urinals. On the opposite side of the room were two stalls. Fischer went over to the stalls, pushed the doors open to be sure he was alone.

Sorry, Jess and Moon. You'd better get your cake to go, thought Fischer. He pulled a large wad of toilet tissue from the dispenser and, moving to the middle of the room, held it to the flame of Moon's cigarette lighter. The hula dancer's face smiled at him as the lighter's flame danced above her head.

Fischer held the burning paper over his head, close to the smoke detector. The restaurant's alarms immediately sounded. Fischer dropped the burning wad into the toilet and flushed it. He then moved out of sight behind the privacy wall beside the hand dryers.

The door to the men's room swung open and Fischer readied himself. His heart was booming to a beat similar to the throb of the smoke alarm shrieking in his ears. He took the fork from his pocket and held it up.

The stick-like figure of the man appeared in front of him. As he bent over to check under the stalls, Fischer jumped out behind him and grabbed him. Wrapping his left arm around his head, he put the fork to the stick man's throat and kicked at the back of his right leg, causing the stick man to go down hard onto his knees.

"Who are you?" spat Fischer. He pressed the fork hard into the man's neck.

"No one."

Fischer used his fork hand to punch the stick man's bandaged right ear. "Try again," insisted Fischer.

The stick man screamed. "Donny. My name's Donny Dodd."

"Why are you following me, Donny?"

"What are you talking about?"

Fischer rapped his ear again.

Donny screeched. "Stop. I'm not following you, man. I came in here to make sure everyone had left the building. I used to be in the fire service."

"Bullshit. You were watching me in the restaurant." Fischer pressed the fork hard into Donny's neck. Spots of blood appeared at the tips of the prongs. "Are you police? This is your last chance. If you don't start talking, your neck is going to leak like a sieve – you hear me?"

"I was paid to find you," said Donny.

"Find me? Paid by who?" Fischer yanked Donny's head back by his hair to expose more of his throat.

"She'll kill me if I tell you," said Donny."

"I'll kill you if you don't."

"Her name's—"

The men's room door opened. The restaurant manager appeared behind Fischer and Donny. "What the—?"

Donny took his chance. He brought his elbow back swiftly, catching Fischer in the groin. Fischer grunted and doubled over. Donny twisted out of Fischer's grasp and crawled away.

Fischer spun around and, one hand on his groin, lunged for the door. He pushed past the restaurant manager, knocking him hard against the hand dryers and sending him awkwardly to the floor.

Exiting the men's room, Fischer turned left and took the emergency exit door to the outside. He ran around the building to the car, where he found Jess and Moon standing and looking at its broken window. "Get in," insisted Fischer. "We have to go. Right now. We have to leave."

"What's going on?" asked Jess.

"I'm taking you home. You can't be around me right now. It's too risky."

Fischer reversed the car out of the space. The tyres screeched as he pulled out of the car park and onto the road.

CHAPTER SIXTY-FIVE

We were only a few miles from the home of Aunt Patti when Cotton got a call. A man matching the description of Edward Fischer was part of a disturbance at a restaurant called Coffee, Cake 'n' Shakes. We changed course and headed straight there.

The restaurant was swarming with police. Inside, the café's manager, Perry Barnes, rested his leg up on a chair. Tea towels filled with ice rested on his ankle. His chubby face shook and his eyebrows bounced around as he spoke breathlessly about the incident. "I swear, they were going to kill each other. It was like something out of a movie. An execution. Right here in the men's room of my restaurant. It happened so quick. *Boom, boom, boom!* I stepped in to break it up. That's when I got slammed. Bam! I was down. Thought I was going to be executed myself. One to the body, one to the head – *phut! phut!* You know, a gun with a silencer, professional hitman style. *Phut! phut!*"

"So, one of them had a gun?" said Cotton.

"Well, no. Not exactly. At least I didn't see one. But they looked the type," said Barnes.

"You've been through a lot, Mr Barnes; I appreciate that. If you can stick to the facts, it would be truly helpful. It's important we find these men quickly, so nobody else goes through what you've endured," said Cotton.

I left Cotton to persevere with our imaginative witness.

Next to the cash register, leaning against the counter, was a waitress who had been serving at the time of the incident. She looked to be in her late teens, wore little makeup and was naturally pretty. Her shoulder-length auburn hair was dyed with a lighter colour at the ends. She had a small, sparkling nose stud that matched a row of three studs in each ear.

As I approached, I looked longingly at the cakes under their glass domes. "These cakes look amazing. Is there any chance at all I could get a piece of that apple cake and a cup of tea?"

The waitress smiled and nodded. "Of course." She picked up the apple cake and took down a clean plate.

"Is that your real name?" I asked.

The waitress touched her name badge. "My name's Bryony. Everyone calls me Bee. Here you go." She passed me a piece of cake and a fork wrapped in a napkin. Bee dropped a teabag in a pot and filled it with boiling water. Placing the pot in front me, along with a cup and a tiny pot of milk, she said, "It's on the house. I'll wrap a piece of cake for your friend." Bee nodded towards Cotton.

"That's very kind. Unfortunately, I have to pay. Them's the rules when you're a police officer," I joked. "How long have you worked here?"

"Nearly six months. It's only temporary. I'm going back to college next year."

"Really? Studying what?" I forked a piece of cake into my mouth.

"Film production and cinematography."

"That sounds interesting. Where are you hoping that'll lead you?"

"The dream is to be a film director. One day. Start at the bottom and work my way up. You know how it is."

"I do. It's the best way to learn." I pointed to the cake with the fork. "This is great cake. I'm not so sure that second slice will make it into the hands of DI Cotton over there." I pretended to hide the cake under a few napkins.

Bee laughed.

"You must have met all the customers at the time of the incident," I said. "How about the two men who got into the altercation? Do you remember them?"

"I didn't see the fight, but Mr Barnes told me which two men it was. They were both in my section. I served them both. One of them was on his own." Bee pointed to the side of her head. "He had a bandage on his ear."

"Anything else?"

"Not really. He was a bit abrupt. Not very talkative. Only ordered coffee."

"Did he have a beard, or was he tall, short, young, old, overweight, muscular?"

"No beard. He was tall. I nearly tripped over his feet a couple of times. Not fat. He was *really* skinny. His shirt collar looked big on him, like he needed a big shirt for the arm length but then the rest of the shirt was too big; does that make sense?"

"Yes. I know exactly what you mean. How about the other man?"

"He was with a girl I knew from school. They were really nice. Even though the smoke alarms went off, they left a big tip."

"That's really nice of them. Can you describe them?"

"The girl from school was Jessica Walker. I've got a selfie with her on my phone." As she scrolled through her phone she added, "Jessica was with a woman and a man. The woman was pretty. I might be wrong, but I think the man was her dad. I heard them talking while I cleared the table behind them. He had lots of tattoos." Bee showed me a photo of herself with Jessica Walker, the two of them smiling. She scrolled some more and then showed me a promotional picture of Jessica with her arms folded over a guitar. "She's a really good singer. Songwriter too. I sent her a message and said I'd love to direct a music video for her one day."

"What makes you think he's her father?"

"He said he'd missed her growing up and regretted it. Wanted to see her perform. It was so sweet."

"Did you hear when she was going to perform?"

"No. Sorry. I think it's probably going to be soon, though, because he said he was leaving soon. Sounded like he was emigrating. He was going to live abroad. At least that's what it sounded like. I shouldn't have been listening, but I was cleaning the next table and couldn't help overhearing."

"Jessica must live quite locally, I suppose?"

"I don't know where, exactly. Though it must be quite local to where we both went to school."

"If I can ask for the name of your school, I can check their records. They'll have her address."

I stepped outside to call the school, trying to figure out the quickest process for getting Jessica Walker's current address.

Cotton sidled up to me and could see the satisfied look on my face. "How did you get on with your witness?" I asked, knowing full well how she'd got on and trying not to laugh.

"Yeah, yeah. Stop looking so smug. It's all right for you. I'm pretty sure Perry Barnes thought he was caught up in an over-the-top action sequence in a *Mission Impossible* movie."

"Well, we got a lead, and it's a belter, so let's go." I unlocked the car and threw Cotton the car keys. "Are you okay to drive? I need to make these calls. You know how it is when a witness delivers a first-class lead," I said with my tongue firmly planted in my cheek.

"Arsehole," retorted Cotton. "Get in the car. Not another word. Not one word. You hear me?"

CHAPTER SIXTY-SIX

Fischer and Moon said goodbye to Jessica two roads away from her house. On the way to their hotel they stopped to buy some booze, a pack of Pepsi and cigarettes at an off-licence. They then bought fish and chips and ate them in the car beside a small pond next to an industrial estate. The pond had two ducks. Mummy and Daddy duck, as Moon called them. A cat sat on the bank watching the birds. While they sipped their drinks and ate chips, Fischer and Moon discussed what the cat might be thinking and what the birds could be saying about the cat. Then Fischer told Moon the story of what had happened at the petrol station and how Trent had got himself killed by being stupid. He tried to make it sound like a lesson on knowing when to stand your ground and when to walk away. "The guy wouldn't back down; he wouldn't listen. If you look at it in context, he killed himself by trying to be a hero. I told him I wasn't going back, but he wouldn't listen."

"You gave him a chance," agreed Moon. "You did all you could, Eddie. The fella didn't listen. That's not your fault." Moon took their empties and threw them out the window.

An hour later they pulled into the hotel car park. Fischer got out, opened the rear hatch, paused, then slammed it down again. He walked around in circles then kicked the car. "Shit, shit, shit." He opened the back of the car again, took another look, then slammed the door down again. "Shit!"

"You've said that," said Moon, as she watched Fischer's outburst. "Was the money definitely in the car?"

Fischer placed both hands on the bonnet and leaned against it. "Yes, it was definitely in the bloody car." He stared at the floor as he thought about what to do next. "Shit!"

Moon didn't like seeing him so upset, especially when she knew she was at least partly to blame. If she hadn't bailed on him, they might be long gone by now. Out of the country, sitting on a beach sipping Bacardi and Coke. "Okay, so we get some more."

"How do you propose we do that? Go to a bank and ask for a loan? That money was supposed to set us up. It was our retirement fund."

"I don't know the best way to get more cash. I do know there are a million ways we could do it. We could rob some pimp or dealer. You could break into some celebrity's pad and pinch their jewellery – it's what you were good at. Or do over a security van. Or rob some rich widow. Shake down or extort some businessman or politician who's screwing their secretary. Kidnap another kid or grab a wife and get a ransom. There are loads of ways. We could even find out who took the money from the car and take it back."

"Hey, that's a good idea," he said acidly. "So who do you think it was that took it?"

"I don't know. We need to look for clues."

"Clues? So, suddenly you're Miss Marple or that woman from *Murder She Wrote* or… or… or Helen Mirren, are you?"

Moon mumbled something Fischer didn't catch.

"What?" said Fischer.

Moon mumbled again.

"What the hell are you muttering about?" barked Fischer.

Moon lifted her head and spoke so Fischer could hear. "Helen Mirren isn't a detective. She's the actress. You probably mean Tennison. Tennison is the detective. Helen Mirren played Jane Tennison in *Prime Suspect*. She was really good."

Fischer stared at Moon open-mouthed. "Are you trying to wind me up?"

"You asked," said Moon. "Look, don't get so testy. You'll figure it out. You always do. You've got Jess's gig coming up. If you're all wound up you won't enjoy it. After the gig we'll work something out. Maybe I could ask Aunt Patti for a loan; she's minted. We could tell her we're getting married and need a deposit for a house. Anything will do; she liked you. You could flash your tattoos again. Horny old bag will love that."

Moon put her arms around Fischer's shoulders and kissed him softly. She pressed her body against his and whispered, "I could tell Aunt Patti thought you were hot. Who'd have thought that uptight, wizened old bitch only ever needed a bit of rough like you to make her smile?"

Moon moved her hips rhythmically against Fischer. "Why don't I see if I can ease some of that tension with some of my sweet Moon-love? What do you say?"

Fischer scratched his head and sighed. He'd never met another woman like Moon; she was infuriating and intoxicating in equal measures. He tried to appear reluctant but knew he wasn't very convincing. He put his hands on her hips. "It's a good idea. I need to clear my head. I can't think right now."

"So romantically put," said Moon with a giggle. She took his hand and led the way.

CHAPTER SIXTY-SEVEN

Jessica Walker answered her front door on the first knock. Cotton and I showed our warrant cards and, reluctantly, she let us in. We followed her into a small study room at the front of the house.

"I'm in the middle of rehearsing. I've got a big show coming up. I don't really have time to talk now. Can we maybe do this another time?" She slumped into her chair; her guitar and notebook lay beside it. A battered guitar case rested on the floor next to her feet.

"My parents are out," said Jessica. "I don't think I should be talking to you." She flicked her cropped blonde hair defiantly and tilted her head.

"You're eighteen, right?" said Cotton.

"Yeah."

"That makes you an adult. Your parents don't need to be here."

Jessica looked seriously pissed off. "If this is about my biological father, then I've told the police I haven't seen him. I have no idea what he looks like. I don't remember him. I was a baby when he and my mum split up. Why would he come here? I mean nothing to him. Why do the police keep bothering us? He's nothing to us. Nothing to *me*."

I let Cotton take the lead while I watched Jessica's reactions. "I'm sorry to say Edward Fischer, your biological father, has escaped prison."

"I don't see how I can help," said Jessica.

"We're pursuing all possible leads. Including everyone he might contact."

"I've told you. He has no interest in me. Never has."

"We understand. It's just, if he did contact you, we'd be concerned for your safety."

"My safety?"

"Yes," said Cotton.

"Surely I'm the last person he would harm?"

"I'm sure you're right. It's just his past would suggest otherwise."

"What if you're wrong about his past?"

"He was tried and convicted."

"Juries get it wrong. It happens all the time."

"We not here to—"

"What if he was set up, or you got the wrong man? Have you thought about that?"

"It's imperative he's apprehended."

"Why? So another innocent man rots in prison?"

"He has a history of violence. Our priority is public safety."

"Having a temper doesn't automatically mean you're a killer."

"That's true. But my job right now is to find him, not consider his conviction."

"Maybe you should. You don't understand him. He's made mistakes, but deep down he's kind and gentle. He just needs a chance to prove it."

"Does that mean he's contacted you? You seem to have taken a keen interest." Cotton leaned closer to her. "Jessica, you must tell us if he has."

Jessica glanced at me uneasily, shifted in her seat, then looked back at Cotton. "I was told by some police officers who came here that he'd set fire to a house. That a woman might die."

"That's correct," answered Cotton. "The woman is in intensive care. She has considerable burns to her body. She's also pregnant."

"I'm sorry," said Jessica. She looked at me. "Was it your house? Your name is Hardy. I read a news article online saying that the house belonged to a DCI called Hardy."

I nodded. "Yes. It was my family's home. I was also the man who led the investigation and eventually arrested your father many years ago."

"Sounds like you pissed him off," said Jessica flatly. She wasn't mocking, just stating a fact. Momentarily, she turned her attention to her guitar. It seemed to me she was a good person who'd found herself in an emotionally difficult situation. No criminal record and most likely very little prior contact with the police; I didn't want to come down hard on her unless it was necessary.

"I have two daughters," I said. "A few years younger than you. My younger is spirited and funny. My elder is a thinker and strong minded. Their mother was murdered when they were just small. They had things in the house that reminded them of her. Those precious links to their mother are gone now. They lost their home and all their favourite possessions. They're having trouble sleeping at night because they're worried that, while they sleep, the man might come again to burn down the house they're staying at now.

"It's a sad truth that some people can't help doing bad things. They just don't consider the consequences of their actions. What separates good people from bad people is that good people are brave enough to do what's right even when they're faced with tough choices.

"Your father was in prison for multiple murders. He was found guilty of killing women who were going about their daily lives. Those women had hopes and dreams and families who cared for them. My children, my friend Jenny, who's fighting for her life, and even you, are all victims of crimes committed by your father. I know it's not what you want to hear, but your father is a dangerous man. He'll continue hurting people. He can't help it. If you were to have met with him and choose not to inform us, you too will have committed a serious criminal offence. I know this puts you in a difficult position, but it's the truth, and now is the time to be brave. If you have any information, you should tell us. I know it feels like a betrayal, but you must think of all the good people who might be harmed all the time he remains on the run."

Cotton nodded encouragingly to Jessica. "It's best you come clean. Before anybody else gets hurt or killed."

Jessica looked at Cotton, and then at me, and then down at her hands. After a moment, she leaned forward and opened the guitar case at her feet. She pulled out a flyer and passed it to Cotton. "He said he'd be there."

"This is tomorrow night?" said Cotton. She passed me the flyer.

"Yeah," said Jessica.

"He took me out for a milkshake with his girlfriend. I wanted him to be the father I dreamed about when I was a child. Don't get me wrong, I love my stepdad, but I always wondered how much I was like my real dad."

"That's only natural," I said.

"It turns out we both have the same sticky-out ears. Great, huh?" Jessica grinned, but the smile didn't reach her eyes. "Thanks, Dad."

"You've done the right thing," said Cotton.

Jessica looked at me. "He says he didn't kill all those women and that he was set up. I believe him. He didn't mean to hurt your friend. I hope she'll be okay. He was just pissed off at you. It was a mistake."

I kept my face carefully neutral. Picturing Jenny in her condition, I had no sympathy for Fischer. Whether he'd meant to cause harm or not was of little consequence. "We'll need you to continue with the performance in the hope he'll show up," I told Jessica. "We'll have plain-clothed officers in the crowd. We'll need your cooperation to make sure he doesn't get wind of the operation. Can you do that?"

Jessica picked at her nail polish. "Yeah."

I wasn't entirely convinced Jessica was being straight with us, but she was our best hope of luring out Fischer so we could finally make an arrest.

CHAPTER SIXTY-EIGHT

Cotton put the shopping bags down at her feet and sorted through the keys to find the front door key. *Why is the one you want always the last one to show itself?* she wondered. She found the key and pushed open the door.

"Hi, Emma. You okay?" She turned to see her neighbour, Declan Carroll, leaning over the fence.

"Oh, hi, Declan. I'm good. You? How was your birthday? Twenty-one, right? That's a big one."

"It was excellent, thank you. I went out for a few drinks with a group of friends. We're also going to Ayia Napa later in the year. There are a few of us turning twenty-one this year so we thought we'd do something special."

"Do it while you're young. How's your new job going?"

"It's great. It's nice to finally put all the college work to use." He made his voice a little deeper to make the information sound important. "My boss is okay. They've got me working on a new backup system in case the main servers go down or get hacked."

"Sounds interesting."

"Not really. I know it sounds boring to everyone else."

He blushed and changed the subject. "I had the day off today. I wanted to be around for Mum. She had a new chest freezer delivered. Did you know I recently joined boxing classes, you know, to get myself in shape?" Declan reddened even further and closed his mouth, looking like he wanted the ground to open up.

"It's good to keep fit," Cotton said encouragingly. "And knowing how to protect yourself, should it become necessary, is no bad thing."

Declan nodded, trying to remember what he'd rehearsed. He desperately wanted to get the conversation back on track.

"How's your mum?" asked Cotton. "Tell her I said hello."

"She's fine. I'll tell her you said hi. Haven't seen you for a few days." Declan tried to look relaxed as he leaned against the fence dividing the two gardens. Then he stood up straight and folded his arms, then unfolded them again and put his hands in his pockets. *Poor Declan,* Emma thought. "Yeah. I, uh, noticed your lawn is getting a bit long. I, uh, I can cut it for you, you know, if you want. I mean, I'm not saying you *need* to cut it. I'm just saying, I know you're busy and I'd be really happy to do it for you. When I cut ours, it would be no bother to cut yours too. I could just pop round and give it the once-over." His hazel eyes shone as he smiled warmly.

"Oh, no. That's really sweet of you, Declan, but I'll do it this weekend. I don't want to put you to any trouble."

"No. Really, it's no trouble. I'd like to do it for you. We've been neighbours for nearly three years. It's just being neighbourly. Not only that, we're friends."

"I'll tell you what – I'll think about it."

"Good. Oh, and I hope you don't mind, but Watson

was meowing this morning, so I gave him some tuna. He's been sleeping on our sofa most of the day."

"I'm sorry, Declan. He'll do that. He's likes the company. I'm sorry if he was a nuisance."

"Not at all. I like him." He folded his arms again and tried to make his arms and chest appear big. His eyes fell on Cotton's rear as she bent over to pick up the shopping. He averted his eyes, then stood up straight, checked the collar of his favourite Ralph Lauren shirt, and tidied his short black hair with the tips of his fingers. His heart was pounding out of his chest. He cleared his throat.

"Emma, I was, uh… I, uh, I was wondering if sometime you'd like to, um, you know, maybe go out and…"

Cotton's phone rang. She dropped the shopping inside the front door and pulled her phone from her jacket pocket. She didn't recognise the number. "Sorry, Declan, I've got to get this. Hello. DI Cotton speaking."

"Okay," said Declan. Out of the corner of her eye, Cotton saw his face fall as she closed the front door. *Poor Declan*, she thought again.

Cotton trapped the phone between her ear and her shoulder as she carried the bags to the kitchen. "When?" she said in alarm. "Where is he now? Bournemouth Hospital. Which ward? Okay. Tell him I'll be right there. Thank you."

Cotton rummaged through the shopping, put the meat and milk in the fridge and the frozen veg in the freezer and ran back out of the house.

At the hospital, she went straight to the ward. Her head and heart were racing with a mixture of feelings that surprised her. She knew she was attracted to Alex but had been unaware until now just how deeply she cared for him.

Half-walking, half-running, she scanned the corridor, looking for the correct room. A nurse stepped out of a room on her right, and Cotton stopped her to ask for Alex's room number. Glancing over the nurse's shoulder, she saw Alex perched on the edge of a bed attempting to put on his sweater. "Thank you, nurse. There he is." She ran in to him. "What happened? They said you were assaulted."

Alex winced as he tried to sit up straight. "I'm okay. It's just a scratch." He lifted his bloody sweater to reveal his bandaged stomach.

"My God. It looks like more than a scratch."

"I suppose."

"How did this happen?"

Alex shook his head. He looked reluctant to say.

"Alex?"

"It was Louise. She attacked me with a kitchen knife. The knife went in and miraculously missed my vital organs. I was lucky. It's nothing. Just a few stitches."

"What the devil are you talking about? 'It's just a few stitches'? This is serious."

"I suppose. The doctor said it could have been serious. Few inches either way and it could have been a different story."

"Where is Louise now?"

"She was taken by officers for questioning. I don't know where she is. I suppose she's at the police station. I really don't know. Look, I'm partly to blame. I went to her home."

"You what?" Cotton stood back and looked at him. *Why would he be seeing her?*

"I'm so sorry. I shouldn't have gone to see her; it was a

mistake. I went to ask her to leave us alone. She wouldn't listen. She flew into a rage. I realised I couldn't talk any sense into her, so I decided to leave. That's when she used the knife."

Alex winced as he attempted to pick up his jacket, which was on a chair.

"Here, let me," said Cotton. She picked up the jacket and his keys fell out. Cotton picked them up and put them back in the pocket. She noticed a second set of keys.

Alex saw her looking. "I still have keys to Louise's flat," said Alex. "I was going to return them to her. With everything that happened, I forgot." Alex got to his feet and held his side. He puffed and blew as he took a step. "I'm going to be sore for a while, I think. But I'm ready to get out of here."

"Louise is not going to get away with this," Cotton said. "You're going to press charges."

"I don't know," said Alex. "Is it really worth it? I don't want my personal life in the newspapers. All the publicity won't be good for my dental practice."

"Look at you. Of course it's worth it." Cotton put her arm around his back. "Lean on me. Has anyone taken your statement?"

"Not yet. I was bleeding too much at the time. Pressing charges – do you *really* think it's the right thing to do? If you think it is, I trust you." He put his arm around Cotton and kissed her tenderly. "Thank you for coming and for standing by me. It means a lot."

CHAPTER SIXTY-NINE

Donny gritted his teeth as he lifted the pad covering his ear. He leaned towards the bathroom mirror to get a closer look. His ear was bleeding again, but he was pleased to see most of the stitches were intact. He replaced the pad. Cupping water from the bathroom tap, he drank down two more painkillers.

The hotel's complimentary hand soap dispenser caught his attention. Squeezing some out, he sniffed it and began washing his hands. *Lemongrass and thyme handwash? Who the hell comes up with this stuff?* thought Donny, shaking his head.

As Donny came out of the bathroom, Barton swiped his phone to off.

"What did she say?" asked Donny.

"I don't think you're going to like it."

"What?"

"She said you're incompetent and I'm in charge. She insisted I make all major decisions going forward," said Barton, his face deadpan.

"What?" Donny started pacing up and down. "We wouldn't have tracked him down if it wasn't for me. Did you tell her that? Did you tell her we know where he is? That we're watching him?" Donny walked to the window and could see Fischer's car at the far side of the hotel car park.

Barton leaned back on the bed and watched Donny's mind do somersaults. "It's not looking good for you, Donny. You told me yourself what she does to people she can't rely on. I didn't believe you, but you convinced me."

"I'd better phone her," said Donny. "Give me the phone."

Barton held the phone up and away from Donny. "She told me it was non-negotiable." He chuckled.

"Give me the bloody phone." Donny moved to grab it and Barton slid across the bed and stood watching Donny, the bed now between them. Donny ran around it. "Stop being an arsehole. We're supposed to be a team."

"A team? Is that what we are?"

"This isn't funny. I need to make this right with her. I need her to understand. Why are you laughing? This is my life we're talking about. I really don't want to be chopped up by that psycho bitch. She cut pieces off a fella once and fed them back to him. He ate his own body. She's crazy."

"Not much meat on you; shouldn't take long. Look at you, all riled up. I'm sorry. I couldn't resist. I was just messing with you. You're still in charge; you're still the big boss. She told us to sit tight. Keep watching Fischer and be ready."

"What?" Donny's eyes bulged incredulously. "You think that's funny? Christ. You're as mad as she is, you know that? Give me that phone."

Barton tossed the phone onto the bed. Donny scooped it up and tucked it into his jacket.

"Keep watching Fischer's car. I'm going to get a bottle

of something to drink. If I don't, I'll end up raiding the minibar."

Donny grabbed the car keys off the bedside table and stormed out of the room. He went to the end of the hall, through the double doors, into the reception area, where he smiled at the attractive Polish receptionist, and out into the car park.

Deciding he was in no hurry to get back and sit in the room with his idiot partner, he went to the car to fetch his coat. He'd walk to the shop. He'd seen a supermarket up the road. It wouldn't take more than twenty minutes. He could probably push it to thirty minutes if he ambled.

Donny opened the car and looked on the back seat. He then remembered he'd left his coat in the back. He opened the rear hatch and spied his coat. Part of the sleeve was under the mat. He yanked it and heard the coat tear. "Crap! I bet that imbecile did this."

Donny yanked up the mat to release the sleeve. *What is that?* he wondered. He put his coat down and now, with both hands, lifted the mat. *What the hell is all this?*

Where the spare tyre should have been was a black canvas bag with a tyre iron on top. Putting the tyre iron to one side, he unzipped the canvas bag. Inside were a couple of shirts and some wads of cash – lots of cash. He flicked through bundles of fifty-pound notes. *There must be at least sixty or seventy grand here, maybe more. What the hell is this?*

Donny looked to the hotel and the window of the room in which he knew Barton was waiting. *That sneaky bastard,* he thought.

CHAPTER SEVENTY

Donny dropped the black canvas bag containing the cash on the corner of the bed. He heard the toilet flush and then the tap running. The door opened and Barton came out tucking his black-and-white-checked cowboy shirt into his blue jeans. He straightened the large oval buffalo-motif belt buckle.

"I didn't hear you come in. Did you get a bottle of something? I could do with a drop of something fiery."

Donny didn't answer. He stepped aside to reveal the bag of money. "I didn't make it to the shop. I thought we could discuss this first."

Barton looked uninterested. "Nothing to discuss. It's mine."

"Oh, it's yours, is it? Where did it come from?"

Barton shrugged. He pushed past Donny and checked out the window. Fischer's car was still in the car park.

"This is Fischer's money, isn't it?" said Donny.

"Would you keep your voice down?" Barton gestured with his hands that Donny should quieten down.

"Spicer mentioned Fischer's money," continued Donny.

"I ignored him because our job is to locate and observe Fischer. Yet, somehow, you found it."

"Let's just say it fell into my lap."

"You mean it fell into both our laps."

Barton stared long and hard at Donny. "It fell into *my* lap. You need to think long and hard before going down this road."

"The way I see it, this money is a bonus. We're doing the job together, so any additional bounty from the job gets split sixty-forty."

"Sixty-forty?" Barton was now perching on a long, low chest of drawers, his arms folded and one leg raised, his cowboy boot propped on the end of the bed. "How do you see that?"

"I'm running this operation—"

"You haven't run anything. In fact, you talk big and act like a pussy. You'd likely be sat in a cell, or more likely dead, if I hadn't stepped in on more than one occasion to save your skinny arse. My advice is that you forget the money. No, I'll tell you what: I'll be generous. Take a grand, as a token of goodwill. After that, we'll talk about it no more. Okay?"

"What? Are you taking the piss? How about I mention this to Lyle? How will she react to you going behind her back?"

Barton opened and closed his mouth. He smiled and stood up. With a chuckle, he said, "You would as well, wouldn't you?" He turned his back on Donny and looked in the mirror. He checked his hair. He could see the grey creeping through at the roots. He hated getting old. "I guess you've got me. Let's be reasonable. I did find the money. Let's split it fifty-fifty."

Donny sighed and looked at the bag on the bed. "You know what? For the sake of maintaining our working relationship and getting this job completed, I accept." He turned his back on Barton and opened the bag. He started pulling out packs of cash and dropping them on the bed. In his head he said, *One for you, one for me. One for you, one for me.*

Donny never noticed Barton ease himself close. Then, in one deadly strike, like the jaws of a croc on a deer stepping too close to the watering hole, Barton's arm clamped around his neck. The arm squeezed and tightened with a terrifying strength. Though Donny struggled, the power of Barton's hold made the end feel inevitable. His legs weakened first; they became empty and light as the strength evaporated from them. In an odd embrace, the pair collapsed onto the bed, Barton's grip never wavering for a second. Donny felt a bizarre intimacy as the stubble of Barton's chin rubbed on the side of his face; his cheek grew damp with the warmth from his foul breath.

Barton's other hand snaked around now and smothered Donny's nose and mouth. *Lemongrass and thyme,* thought Donny as the scent from Barton's fingers reached his nostrils. He punched and kicked as best he could, but it was no use; Barton was too strong. Panic turned to a feeling of sickness and then acceptance.

When it was done, Barton stripped Donny down to his underpants. He tucked him into bed and put his hands over his chest as though he were grabbing at his heart. He gathered the cash and zipped up the canvas bag. Made one last check of the room. Satisfied everything looked normal, besides the skinny dead guy, he exited the room.

Barton hung the Do Not Disturb tag on the door handle and headed to reception. He checked out but extended the stay of his partner another two nights, explaining his friend was feeling unwell. "He's complaining of indigestion; he wants to sleep if off. He'd appreciate it if he could remain undisturbed. I'll be back in a couple of days to pick him up. I'll be taking our car."

"I understand," said the receptionist. Barton watched as her sparkly fingernails tapped away on the computer keyboard. Her name tag read Petra. "A package was left for you and your partner, sir."

Barton watched as Petra crouched down to unlock a cupboard behind the desk and retrieve the package. The neckline of her tight white top was brimming to overflowing. He sighed inwardly. It was sick to think it, but killing Donny had caused a surge of energy in his tight blue jeans that he'd love to share with Petra right now.

Petra stood up again and passed him the package, his receipt, and a ticket for raising the barrier so he could leave the car park. She smiled politely. "I hope you enjoyed your stay. I'll see you in a couple of days."

"You'll make sure my business partner doesn't get disturbed?" said Barton. "He's not a well man."

"I will. I've put a note on the system for you."

"Perfect. Thank you, Petra. Have a sunny day," said Barton with a wink and a smile.

He made his way to the rental car, where he climbed into the driver's seat and discreetly opened the package he knew to be from Kelly Lyle. He instantly recognised the matte-black finish of a Glock pistol. Having decided he'd check the pistol later, he tucked the package under the passenger seat. After some time wondering what he should do next, he moved the car around the car park to better observe Fischer's car.

The quiet from no longer having Donny's perpetually whining voice complaining about the state of the world, boasting about his big plans for the future and speculating on what their next move should be, was a blessed relief.

CHAPTER SEVENTY-ONE

In front of me, the road and the large paved area in front of the shops and restaurants along the quay had been pedestrianised for the weekend's music festival. Gazebos selling food, drink, recordings, musical instruments and souvenirs, from t-shirts to glow sticks, were dotted along the waterfront. Stages and taped-off areas gave musicians ample space to perform. Inside restaurants, cafés and pubs, performers drew crowds and kept the cash registers ringing. It was the first of what the organisers hoped would become an annual event.

Jessica was scheduled to play at 11 p.m. in front of a mix of her growing fan base, ardent music fans and casual onlookers. It promised to be her biggest gig to date. Amongst the revellers were four plain-clothed officers, DI Cotton, and me. Because of the significant police presence such music festivals warranted, it was decided to keep our surveillance unit to a minimum to avoid spooking Fischer and Moon. The large gathering of music fans made it easy for us to blend in. On the flip side, it made the job of locating Fischer and Moon more difficult.

I waded through the sea of music fans, getting bumped and jostled. Each time I got nudged I could feel the Glock pistol concealed beneath my jacket dig into my ribs.

I checked my watch: 10.57 p.m.

I stepped up on a low wall and could see Jessica getting herself comfortable. She was adjusting the height of her microphone and positioning her seat. I climbed down and radioed Cotton. "DCI Hardy. I'm in position."

"DI Cotton. In position."

The four plain-clothed officers all radioed in to state they were in position. We were as ready as we could be. All we could hope now was that the man of the moment appeared.

The audience grew quiet as Jessica began her set, effortlessly singing and strumming and picking her amplified acoustic guitar. Her voice was captivating, and from my vantage point I could see the crowd draw closer to the stage. Fans who knew her lyrics were singing along, and others were swaying or clapping in time to the chorus. It was hard not to be enthralled. Sadly, my job this evening was to identify and arrest her father. I preferred to do that with as little disturbance as possible and preferably out of sight of Jessica.

I scanned the faces of the crowd, working my way along methodically from figure to figure to prevent the sea of people becoming a blur. Two men pushing and shoving caught my attention. From what I could see, it was nothing more than an argument over a pint of spilt lager.

I pressed my finger to my earphone as Cotton's voice came over the radio. "Possible ID. Two suspects approaching the stage from the corner of Mr Gold's Amusement Arcade. I repeat, corner of Mr Gold's Amusement Arcade."

From my position I couldn't see it; my view was

blocked by the roof of a gazebo selling marijuana-themed souvenirs. Everything from cigarette lighters to phone cases and carved wooden fruit bowls had the shape of the marijuana leaf on it.

I stepped back up onto the low wall as Cotton's voice came through again. I lowered my head and pressed the earpiece to better hear over the noise of the crowd. "Negative. I repeat, negative. It is not Fischer."

I looked up and scanned the crowd again. As I did, I made eye contact with Jessica. She immediately looked away and focused on the neck of her guitar. As I watched her, I noticed an almost imperceptible movement of her eyes. *Bingo.*

"Excuse me," I said over and over as I moved along the wall to get a better look at where she had glanced. I reached a lamp post and scrambled around it. On the other side were a pair of bins. I stepped up onto them as best I could, using the lamp post as cover.

I scanned the faces in the area where I had seen Jessica look. I felt sure she had been looking at someone she knew. Perhaps I was mistaken, or perhaps it was a fan or friend she recognised. But perhaps not. My eyes picked out face after face, discarding each one that didn't fit the profile of Fischer or Moon.

A woman in a wide-brimmed hat caught my attention. Behind her, a short, stocky man with a shaved head and chest-length beard, wearing a black leather biker's jacket, was complaining to his companion. From what I could tell, he was annoyed that he couldn't see Jessica because of the hat. I watched as he tapped the woman in the hat on the shoulder. She looked around, and the bearded man gestured towards the hat. She answered him and looked back towards Jessica. Whatever the woman in the hat had said immediately shut him up. Beard Man looked at his companion, frustrated and open-mouthed. Together, they pushed through the crowd to find a better position, but not before grabbing the hat from behind and launching it, like a frisbee, into the mass of music fans.

Shocked, the woman twisted around looking for her hat. As she briefly faced my way, I recognised Faye Moon. I examined the faces nearby. Fischer wouldn't be far away.

"Cotton, this is Hardy," I said into my radio. "Faye Moon is at your two o'clock. She's wearing a red t-shirt, a silver-grey scarf and a denim jacket. Her hair is shoulder length, dark brown. Do not arrest her. I do not have eyes on Fischer. Repeat. Do not arrest her until we have Fischer."

"I see her," said Cotton. "She's wrapping the scarf around her head." I watched as Cotton moved calmly through the crowd to get within touching distance of Moon.

"That's her. You got it. Cotton is staying on Faye Moon," I said to everyone on the team. "Fischer is not far away. He's here somewhere. Let's sweep through the crowd and flush him out. If we don't get him now, he could be gone forever. Let's find him."

CHAPTER SEVENTY-TWO

As Jessica started her last song, I found myself in a stream of people moving past the stage. I sidestepped a couple of times to move back into the audience. As I turned around to push back towards the centre of the crowd, I spotted a plain-clothed officer from the team, Detective Sergeant King, in an altercation with a young man. "DS King?" I said into my radio. "DS King, what's going on?" King was silent. "King? DS King?" I looked over again, but I'd lost sight of him.

"Pickpocket, sir," said King, finally. "Right under my nose."

"Forget that," I said. "That's not why we're here. Focus on the job in hand."

"Yes, sir," said King.

Jessica's last song came to an end. She stood up on stage, waved and bowed. The crowd went wild with applause and cheers. She put down her guitar and took the microphone from the stand to address the audience. "It's a few minutes to midnight and the end of my set." The crowd booed. "Thank you, thank you. The end of my set also marks the end of today's music festival." The crowd booed again. "I know, but there will be more amazing live music tomorrow." Jessica threw her arms up in the air and the crowd cheered. She checked her watch. "In less than a minute there will be fireworks to celebrate all of today's incredible music and to thank you all for turning out to make this event such a fantastic success." The crowd cheered again. Jessica laughed. "I love you guys. See you all back here again tomorrow!" The crowd roared. "Here we go – let's all count down together: ten, nine, eight…" The crowd joined her and the chant became almost deafening. "…five, four, three, two, one!"

A shower of colour burst into the sky as firework after firework exploded and crackled overhead. I watched the rapt faces of the audience, bathed in light as they *oohed* and *aahed*.

As the pyrotechnics continued, people began to move slowly away from the stage area and closer to the water's edge to get a better look. Jessica took her chance to step off the stage, and as she did, I saw a look of surprise and then delight cross her face as a man wearing a panama hat took her hand and helped her down. He kept his head down and I couldn't see his face. *It must be him,* I thought. I had to wait to get visual confirmation. They embraced, and as they did, his hat pushed back slightly, revealing his face. "It's Fischer," I said into the mic. "Fischer is at the back of the stage with Jessica."

Cotton didn't waste any time. She and one of the plain-clothed officers moved in on Faye Moon. Cotton stepped up close behind her, grabbed her arms and cuffed her. Moon's face was full of desperation and panic as she called out for Fischer and fought Cotton to get away.

One down, one to go, I thought as Cotton led her away.

As I ploughed my way through the throng of people, I

watched Jessica urge her father to leave. *She's warning him*, I thought. I watched as she spoke into his ear and pointed behind him. He turned to see Moon being escorted away, and his expression turned to surprise, then distress and rage. He then looked my way and saw me fighting to get to him. For a moment we locked eyes. He turned and gave Jessica a kiss and a firm hug before melting into the crowd.

The last of the fireworks splashed their dazzling colour across the night sky, and the crowd started to disperse. If I didn't do something fast, I was going to lose him. I got back on the radio. "All officers. Make yourselves visible to the suspect. He is wearing a panama hat, a light-blue shirt and a dark-coloured waistcoat. Make it clear you're looking for him. Be obvious and loud. Engage any uniformed officers you can. We need everyone's assistance to drive Fischer towards the water. Create a perimeter and corral him towards the water. I want him left with nowhere to go."

I moved to the edge of the quay and hoped my plan would work, that Fischer wouldn't be able to slip away amongst the thinning crowd. I paced up and down, my head flicking from left to right as I frantically watched the number of music fans dwindle. *Where was he?* I wondered. *Had he somehow vanished?*

I watched as two female uniformed officers dealt with a group of drunken lads. A young woman, equally drunk, yelled and bawled into the face of one the officers. Behind them, Fischer stepped out from behind a gazebo that was being dismantled. He hadn't seen me. He kept his hat pulled low and his face turned away from the two female officers. He moved briskly, keeping close to the front of the shops and pubs and cafés. I was about to get back on the radio when, suddenly, he froze. He was looking at a man leaning against a wall at the entrance to an alley. The man straightened as Fischer approached, and they stood still, facing each other in some sort of standoff.

I started walking towards them. My view of the second man was obscured, but I could make out he had black hair and wore a tan suede jacket and blue jeans. He looked to be well built and tall. He opened his jacket slightly and revealed something to Fischer that I couldn't see. Whatever it was, it was enough to make Fischer turn and run. Dodging through the crowd, Fischer first went left up the pedestrianised road, then, seeing police officers, he turned and looked wildly around. He took a step and then froze again as he spotted the officers who had been dealing with the rowdy group and were now walking towards him. Hoping that he would run my way and towards the water's edge, I stepped back out of view behind a van that had been selling Mexican burritos.

A sound beside me made me turn. A man with white hair and beard, wearing an Aran jumper, was walking down the steps to the jetty below. He glanced at me, shook his head, and continued towards the boats.

I turned back and saw Fischer. I pressed myself against the van. He was directly in front of me now, about thirty metres away, and coming my way. I melted into the shadows. As I did, the van's engine started and it began slowly moving away.

The sound of the van's engine caught Fischer's attention. He looked over and saw me. As soon as he did, he turned on his heels and ran. I had no choice but to go after him. I spoke into my radio. "I'm in pursuit of the suspect. Fischer is headed along the quayside towards the bridge."

He had a good head start, but I was catching up. Coming towards us from the opposite direction I saw Cotton; she was moving fast. Fischer saw her too. He looked towards her and then towards me. Realising the net was closing on him, he turned to face the water. He grabbed his hat and tossed it aside.

At first, I thought he was preparing to jump in and attempt to swim to the other side, where he could potentially disappear amongst the buildings of the shipyard. I prayed he wouldn't: the water would be icy, and I really didn't want to go in after him.

But as I closed in on him, I realised he was watching a boat. He took one step back then three strides forward and leapt off the quay into a passing rigid inflatable boat. The boat rocked violently, and Fischer almost went straight over the side as he landed. He threw himself flat in the boat, then quickly got to his feet and looked back at me with a smile and a salute. The shocked boat owner jumped up and was about to protest when Fischer grabbed him by the arm and shoved him out of the boat. The man, who looked to be in his fifties, hit the water hard. I heard him gasp as the icy water shocked his body. Cursing with every stroke, he swam to the safety of the quayside as his boat, piloted by Fischer, turned and sped away towards the open waters of the shipping channel and Brownsea Island.

Cotton stood beside me now. Panting heavily, she said, "We almost had him."

"This isn't over yet," I said. "Not by a long chalk. Fischer might head for the island." To my left, I saw a sports cruiser pulling away from the marina. "I'll go on ahead," I told her. "You make sure he doesn't double back."

I ran towards the sports cruiser, waving my arms and yelling, "Police! Stop!" To my relief, the boat turned and headed my way. As it approached, I recognised the skipper as the white-haired man who had passed me earlier. He now wore an unzipped waterproof jacket over his Aran jumper.

He pulled the boat up in front of me and I climbed aboard. I explained the situation as briefly as I could.

"Peter Tullock," said the skipper, scratching his white beard. "Welcome aboard the *Lady Margaret*. As a former naval officer, it'd be an honour for me to assist an officer of the law in carrying out his duties. Sit tight, son. Next stop, Brownsea Island."

CHAPTER SEVENTY-THREE

Brownsea Island is around two miles long and a mile wide; it's a major tourist attraction for the area. The island is a nature reserve with oak and pine woodland, heathland and salt marsh. In 1907, it was the location of an experimental camp that, a year later, led to what became the Scout movement.

Situated on the island is Brownsea Castle, originally constructed by Henry VIII to protect England from the French during the final years of his reign. The island is a short distance from the mainland, and the *Lady Margaret* made the journey in just a few minutes.

The island's small dock was lit by a row of low lights. I climbed from the boat onto the dock and thanked Tullock.

"You're going to need this, son," said Tullock, as he passed me a torch. "Are you sure you don't need backup? I could help – I boxed for the navy as a younger man. I was pretty handy; had a mean right hook." The old man swung his fist. "They called me Peter 'T-bone' Tullock." He grinned and flexed his bicep.

"I'll be fine, but I'd appreciate it if you could wait

here," I said as I switched on the torch and checked my weapon. I ran along the pier then climbed a few steps leading to the path that ran towards the castle. Arriving at a spot in the path where it split in three, I continued straight and rounded a corner, where I brushed past a row of large hedges. Ahead, I could see the house.

I called Cotton on my phone. "I followed Fischer to the island. My best guess is he's holed up in the castle."

"I'm on my way," said Cotton. "Wait for me. We'll go in together." I could hear insistence in her voice.

"If I don't stay on his tail he could vanish for good," I said. I climbed half a dozen steps and walked around the house. I shone my torch along the side of the castle. There were no obvious signs of forced entry until I reached a glass-panelled side door. It swung gently back and forth in the breeze. "I've got to go," I said. "For Jenny's sake, I can't lose him."

I took out my pistol and pushed open the door with my foot. I shone my torch and peered inside. I called out, "Edward Fischer! Armed police. This is Detective Chief Inspector James Hardy. I know you're here. Come out."

Holding my pistol and the torch out in front, I moved cautiously from room to room. Entering the dining room, I could see large paintings hanging on the wainscoted walls. I moved past a long wooden dining table with two large silver candleholders displayed at either end. At the end of the room, a door stood open. I eased my way towards it. "Edward Fischer! Armed police," I repeated.

I stepped to the right side of the door and looked in the room. It looked like a small library with dark wooden floor-to-ceiling bookshelves. Either side of an unlit fireplace were two high-backed armchairs. Over the fireplace, mounted on the wall, rested a single sword; its twin was missing.

I pushed back the door and stepped gingerly into the room, shining the torch into the corners. I took another step. As I did, the lights in the room suddenly came on; the abrupt change from dark to light dazzled me. I felt a kick from behind and stumbled forward. Dropping the torch, I sprawled onto the floor. I rolled onto my back and looked up.

Coming at me was Edward Fischer, brandishing the missing sword. He stopped over me and pointed it at my chest. I raised my hands and Fischer froze as his eyes focused on the gun I still held.

"Drop the sword," I said. I fired wide. Fischer jumped but kept the sword pressed to my chest. "Put the sword down," I repeated.

"If I do that, you'll kill me," said Fischer.

"If you don't put the sword down, I'll be forced to shoot. Next time I won't fire wide."

Fischer thought about it for a nanosecond longer, then tossed the sword aside. It clattered to the floor. He looked at me suspiciously. "I see you came alone. I guess you don't want any witnesses."

"What are you talking about?" I said. I got to my feet, keeping the pistol trained on him the whole time.

"Don't play the innocent, Hardy. I know Kelly Lyle sent you. If there's anyone in this world she'd choose to kill me, besides doing it herself that is, it's you."

"Would you blame me? You ordered my wife's murder. It was your man who killed Helena."

"I didn't. The man I sent was meant to scare her so you'd back off investigating me. It was meant to be nothing more than a warning message. I swear, your wife was never meant to be harmed. I'm not a killer. I don't hire killers. Lyle set me up, just like she's set you up now. Whatever it is she has over you, it must be powerful. I can't imagine you can be bought, so she's not offering you money. Does she have something that'll end your career?"

I said nothing.

Fischer slowly reached round into his pocket and, with my permission, took out his cigarettes and lighter. He lit a cigarette and smoked it as though it were his last. "Something more personal? Your girlfriend? Your kids? She's made a threat against your family. I heard she took one kid. She could do it again easily enough." He took another drag on his cigarette. "You better get on with it." He pressed a finger to his forehead. "Shoot me then, if you've got the balls."

"Shut up," I snapped. "Do you have any idea, any idea at all of the hurt you've caused?" Memories were flooding my mind, threatening to swamp me. All the years of anguish surged through my body and hit me like a truck. I pictured holding Helena, my soulmate, in my arms, blood-soaked, hopelessly fighting for life. I remembered the heartache of looking into the faces of our daughters and telling them their mummy wouldn't be coming home, that she was in heaven. I recollected the nights my daughters and I had held each other, cried together and prayed for their mummy and told her how much we missed her. I recalled the birthdays and Christmases that felt empty without her and that were now seared into my heart. All that pain that had changed the course of all our lives, that had led along a winding path and resulted in my deal with Lyle to get Alice back – and Lyle's revelation that this man in front of me now was responsible for it all.

I stepped forward and pressed the gun into his face. "You deserve to die. You do. I should end you here."

Fischer swallowed hard. "She made a threat against your family, didn't she?" he said, his voice barely audible.

I said nothing. I was fighting with everything I held dear not to pull the trigger.

"I can see she has you in a corner. You've got no choice. Lyle will keep her word," said Fischer. "Do it." He looked around. "Admit it. That's why you're here alone, without backup. No witnesses."

"I'm here to arrest you," I insisted.

"If that were true, I'd already be face down on the floor in cuffs."

"Put your hands behind your head. Get down on your knees."

He didn't move. "Kill me," said Fischer. "At least if you shoot me now, it'll be quick. If you don't and Lyle gets hold of me, it'll be a slow, painful death. Do it. Shoot me."

Still holding the gun against his face, I hesitated. There were so many reasons I should kill Fischer. Besides my own need for vengeance and the fact that he'd put Jenny in the hospital with life-changing burns, he was also a convicted serial killer. "I suppose you'd tell me you're not a serial killer and I caught the wrong man all those years ago," I said. "You've managed to convince your daughter of that fact."

"There's no doubt the DNA evidence pointed to me, but that was all planted by Lyle. She set me up."

"Why?"

"I was in her house when her lover was killed. I was in the wrong place at the wrong time. I was there to rob the place. The guys whose job it was needed a third man at short notice. I was filling in. Again, nobody was supposed to get hurt. I'm starting to sound like a broken record, but it's the truth. I swear. I'm a thief. A damn good thief. Nothing more. Somehow, my life spiralled out of control. Looking at you now, Detective Chief Inspector, pointing that gun at me the way you are, with all the venom and hate in your eyes, I'd say yours has too."

Something inside me sagged in defeat. Fischer was right. The conflict in my head was causing it to spin. "Turn around. Put your hands behind your head," I repeated. "Now, get down on your knees."

He dropped the cigarette butt, ground it out, turned and reluctantly knelt in front of me. "Do it," said Fischer again. "I know you want to. You have to. It's okay. My prints are on the sword. You can claim self-defence."

I got out my handcuffs. "Edward Fischer, I am arresting you for—"

Suddenly a shot rang out, and there was the sound of shattering glass. Then another shot. I lurched backward and as I fell, hitting the floor hard, I saw Fischer's body jolt, then twist sideways. I crawled into the corner of the room and pointed my gun. I had no cover and was vulnerable if the gunman continued shooting. With the lights on and darkness outside, he could see in, but I couldn't see out. I pointed my gun in all directions, trying to get a fix on the killer. Outside I heard voices. Then more gunshots. Seconds later Cotton was outside the room.

"Don't shoot. Hardy, it's me, Cotton. Are you okay? For God's sake, don't shoot. I'm coming in."

Cotton stepped into the room and looked between Fischer and me. She checked Fischer for a pulse and then shook her head.

CHAPTER SEVENTY-FOUR

Fischer was dead. A shot to the head and one to the body.

"I nearly ran straight into the gunman," said Cotton. "He was heading away from the house. He must have followed you to the island. I didn't get a good look at him. It was too dark."

I thought back to Fischer's brief standoff with the tall, black-haired man in the tan suede jacket back at the festival grounds. I hadn't thought much of it at the time, but Fischer had seemed to recognise him, and whoever it was had scared him. "Let's notify the harbour police," I said, getting to my feet. "Let's go. He can't have got far."

"Where to?" asked Cotton. "We'll be like headless chickens running around in the dark."

"He'd have been forced to make a beach landing. If I was him, I'd have landed the boat close to the jetty but far enough away to avoid detection. Let's get down to the beach." I grabbed my torch and headed out the door, closely followed by Cotton.

"This is where we ran into each other," said Cotton as

we reached steps leading down to a lower path that ran down to the jetty.

"The path splits into three," I said as we paused under one of the lights illuminating the pathways.

"I'll take the right path; you take the left. If we find nothing, we'll meet back at the jetty." Cotton took out her radio. "Let's stay in contact."

I adjusted my radio, which had been set to radio silence. "Stay safe. No heroics," I said.

"I didn't know you cared," said Cotton with a smile.

"I'm just worried about all the paperwork if you get hurt," I quipped back.

"In that case, I'll make an extra effort to not get shot, and you do the same."

"You've got a deal," I said.

We took a few steps before we both stopped in our tracks. Through the still of the night we heard a boat's motor starting up. "That's him – it's got to be," I said. "Change of plan. Let's go straight down to the jetty. How did you get onto the island?"

"Harbour police dropped me off."

"Are they at the jetty, waiting?"

"No. They didn't stop. Their orders are to patrol the waters."

The path down to the jetty seemed longer than I remembered. Eventually we got to the dock, where Tullock was waiting in his boat with the engine idling. He'd seen us coming and had already cast off. Cotton radioed for backup, notified officers about Fischer's body in the house, and alerted the harbour police to the vessel we were now in pursuit of.

"Mr Tullock, I can no longer ask you to be involved in the pursuit," I said. "We're going to need to commandeer your boat."

"Not on your life, son. *Lady Margaret* doesn't take kindly to being handled by strangers. After all, she's a lady. Hold on, you two. She might not look like much, but she can really move when she wants to." He turned the wheel and shifted the throttle. "Grab that searchlight, son, and start searching for your boat. He won't have got far. I caught a glimpse as the boat passed, and I can tell you one thing: the skipper is inexperienced on the water."

I grabbed the searchlight and scanned the waves.

"Point it straight ahead, son," Tullock said, "Try over that way. My ears are attuned to the sounds of the water."

Sweeping the searchlight around, I caught a glimmer of light reflecting off the boat ahead. "There he is," I shouted. As I called out, the moon disappeared behind clouds and we fell into darkness.

There was a series of sharp cracks as shots rang out, one coming dangerously close to Tullock. He stroked his white beard and gritted his teeth. "The bastard," he growled, pointing to a shattered side window. "He shot *Lady Margaret*." With that, Tullock turned out all the boat lights, effectively making us invisible as we bounced over the waves. "Sit yourselves down, you two. I'm going to show this bastard what happens when he messes with *Lady M*."

Cotton and I grabbed the handrails and braced ourselves as Tullock threw the small boat around. As our speed increased, I could feel the cold sea spray splash my face and taste the salty sea water on my lips.

Suddenly we veered violently right, and both Cotton and I were thrown forward. There was a deafening crunch and the sound of splintering wood as *Lady Margaret* collided with the small pleasure boat we'd been pursuing. Tullock, who was laughing like a man possessed, hit the lights and lit up the boat we'd hit. He yelled, "That's what you get when mess with milady, y' picaroon."

I staggered to my feet, climbed up on the side deck of *Lady Margaret*, and looked back at Cotton. "Are you okay?"

"I'm fine," said Cotton. She'd hit her head and was wiping blood from her eye. "It's nothing."

"You go get him, son," said Tullock, putting out a meaty hand to help Cotton to her feet. "We're both dandy. The lass is as tough as they come."

I pulled out my pistol and moved to the foredeck of *Lady Margaret*. I peered into the vessel we'd hit. It was a lightweight pleasure boat with no cabin, just a canopy, which had been damaged and was now drooping into the water.

"The boat's empty," I shouted over my shoulder. "He must be in the water."

Cotton climbed up on the side deck and grabbed the searchlight. She panned it over the water. In the darkness, the beam of light picked out the bright white face of Fischer's killer. His arms flapped up and down as he struggled in the icy black water.

"Hold tight," called Tullock. He reversed and brought the boat around. Cotton stepped down, removed the boat's life ring and climbed back up on the side deck. As we approached, she tossed it into the water.

Coughing and spluttering and arms flailing, the killer grabbed the life ring and held on for dear life. I kept my gun trained on him while Tullock kept the searchlight on him and Cotton reeled him in.

Once the killer was hauled up on deck and handcuffed, we wrapped him in a blanket. He was still dressed in the tan jacket he'd been wearing when I'd seen him earlier on the quay, and, even soaking wet, he looked just like Mrs

Montgomery had described the man posing as a private investigator.

"What are you, some sort of cowboy?" asked Tullock, referring to the killer's clothes. "You might think you're Clint Eastwood, and those might be fancy boots where you come from, son, but they don't belong aboard a seafaring vessel."

Tullock radioed the harbour police and we slowly headed back to shore, towing the damaged boat we'd been pursuing.

I noticed the suspect eyeing me. Cotton noticed it too. "You look like you want to say something. Why don't you start by giving us your name?" said Cotton.

"Barton."

"Barton what?" asked Cotton.

"Just Barton."

Barton stared at me, and for the first time I noticed the different colours of his eyes. This was without a doubt the man Mrs Montgomery had described. *Where was his partner?* I wondered.

"Fine, Barton," said Cotton. "How about you tell us why you killed Edward Fischer."

"He knows," said Barton, nodding towards me.

"What do you mean?" said Cotton. She looked between Barton and me.

"I was there in case he didn't fulfil his end of the deal. Which he didn't. I'd say he's in a world of bother now. Where I'm going will seem like a holiday camp compared to what's in store for Detective Chief Inspector James Hardy."

Cotton now stared openly at me, her brow furrowed in puzzlement. I couldn't tell her about Lyle's deal, and even if I could, this wasn't the right time or place. Kelly Lyle would be coming for me and my family. Maybe not today, maybe not tomorrow, but I knew she'd come, and when she did I would be ready. I had to be.

"We've got company," said Tullock.

The harbour police came into view; the lights on their boat and the uniformed officers were a welcome sight. The *Lady Margaret* matched their speed, and we were escorted to the quayside, where Barton was taken away by waiting officers.

"Well, son, that was more excitement than I've had in quite some time," said Tullock. He put out his hand and we shook. "That cowboy fella seemed pretty insistent that you have some stormy seas ahead of you. Are you going to be okay?"

"I hope so," I said. "I had a choice to make, and I made it. Often the correct choice doesn't look that way at the time." I watched Cotton getting the cut on her head checked by a waiting paramedic. She winced as the wound was being cleaned.

"If I can ever be of service, just holler. A word of advice, though, if I may." Tullock put a friendly hand on my shoulder then stroked his thick white beard before speaking. "As skipper, you'll inevitably encounter treacherous storms at sea. These storms can come out of nowhere. Your duty as captain will be to decide a course of action. You need to consider which way to navigate. It's important to understand that there are some storms you simply can't sail through or outrun. Your job will be to find safe passage around them. Just remember that when you plot your course, the voyage will be scary as hell and you'll need to pitch and roll with the waves. Be ready to brace yourself for all sorts of surprises. If you ever feel like all is lost, you need to fasten the hatches and redouble your efforts. Always remember, your primary concern is the welfare of your shipmates. Remember that, and you'll be fine, son." Tullock patted my shoulder, and I watched as he left me and walked over to Cotton. I chuckled to myself as I saw her face light up at his approach.

CHAPTER SEVENTY-FIVE

It was early and just before official visiting hours at the hospital. My heart was in my mouth as I came onto the hospital ward. I made my way to Jenny's room, and there by her side, like a royal guard protecting his queen, was Rayner. I took a deep breath and entered the room.

As I approached, Rayner turned and looked at me. His face lit up. Without a word, he jumped up and put his huge arms around me and hugged me. I looked over his shoulder and could see Jenny propped up in bed. Her eyes were open and filled with emotion as she watched us.

Rayner cleared his throat. He had a big, broad grin on his face as he released me.

"She's going to be okay. So is the baby. Jen opened her eyes early this morning. We've been talking for hours. She's been asking after you and Monica ever since. I spoke to Monica a while ago. Is she with you?" I couldn't believe my eyes. I leaned over the bed and held Jenny and kissed her. "I came straight here," I told Rayner. "I haven't been home yet."

"You don't know how great..." I started. My own

emotions took over and I had to choke back the tears. "I'm sorry, Jenny. This is my fault. I'm so sorry."

Jenny put her bandaged hand on my cheek and wiped away my tears. She looked me in the eye. "Nonsense," she said, her voice a whisper. "Rayner explained everything. You're not to blame. You were never to blame."

"But your injuries…" I said.

"It'll take a while, but I'll get back on my feet. Just you watch me." Jenny gave me one of her beautiful smiles, as though her injuries were nothing more than an inconvenience.

"I have no doubt," I said.

"Here's your better half," said Rayner, turning towards the door. He was practically dancing with excitement.

I stepped aside and let Monica and Jenny see each other. There were more tears as the two embraced. Monica couldn't contain her joy. "As soon as you're ready, we need to go shopping for baby clothes. You know the way I like to shop, so it'll mean plenty of stops for tea and cake. You hear me?"

"That's my kind of shopping," said Jenny. She looked around Monica. "Are Alice and Faith with you?"

"I didn't think you'd be ready for those two just yet," said Monica. "You can imagine the type of questions you'll get from Faith. I also suspect Alice will be studying the doctor's approach to your care. They will want to nurse you back to health themselves."

"I wouldn't want it any other way," said Jenny. She put out her hand, and Rayner sprang into action and passed her a glass of water. She sipped slowly.

"We'll let you get some rest," said Monica. "We'll pop back this afternoon or this evening, if that's okay?"

Jenny shook her head. "Will you stay for a bit, Mon? The boys can take a break."

Rayner looked concerned, but Jenny was insistent. "You listen to me, Gabriel Rayner. I'm going to be fine. You're my rock, and watching over me the way you have been is amazing, and I love you for it with all my heart, but right now I want you to take a break. I want you to look after yourself. Go with James and get something to eat before you waste away. Get a change of scenery. I want to talk to my girlfriend for a while. Go on, shoo!"

The big man looked forlorn, but he did as he was told.

"Come on, mate," I said. "I'll buy you some breakfast."

"I'm not leaving the hospital."

"That's okay. Hospital canteen will do just fine." I opened the door and led the way.

CHAPTER SEVENTY-SIX

The hospital canteen was busy. The staff were working flat out and only just keeping up with orders. I put the tray down in the middle of the table and passed Rayner a large full English, a pot of tea and an orange juice. I put my decaf black coffee and full English down in front of me, then set the tray to one side.

Rayner stabbed the Lincolnshire sausage with his fork and practically swallowed it whole. He looked at me as he chewed. "You look like shit."

"You can talk," I replied. I dabbed my egg with a corner of the toast.

"Not much of a holiday. I think I'll book Disney next time," quipped Rayner.

"Yeah. I'm sorry, mate." I could see he was trying his best to lighten the mood, so I added, "I didn't even get a chance to do a barbecue and give you food poisoning."

"Maybe next time?" Rayner shovelled beans and bacon into his mouth then washed them down with tea.

"Who says I'm inviting you back?"

"Who says I'd come back? Anyway, from what I hear,

the accommodation will need more than a lick of paint before it can accept more guests." Rayner cut up the mushrooms and scooped them into his mouth with some fried tomato.

"He's dead," I said. "Fischer's dead."

Rayner paused for a moment, then buttered more toast and ate it. "Good," he said. "You're not in any trouble?"

"No. Kelly Lyle wanted him dead. She sent two guys to make sure it happened. One of them is in custody; the other was discovered dead in a hotel room. It seems the pair argued over money. A large sum of cash has been recovered from their rental vehicle."

Rayner nodded. He was quiet for a while as he finished his breakfast and drank his tea. He topped up the teapot with hot water. "I wanted him dead," he said at length, "but now that he is, I feel empty. I'd rather he was alive and suffering in prison. Suffering the way Jen is and the way she will be for months and years to come. It's like he got off lightly."

I nodded. "I know what you mean." We finished breakfast, and I bought Rayner some more toast and jam along with more tea. There was something else I needed to talk to him about, and I wanted to get it out of the way.

"I'm meeting Chief Webster tomorrow," I said.

"You are?" Rayner leaned back in his chair and crossed his arms. "Why would that be?" He grinned knowingly.

"Let's just say retirement hasn't worked out the way I'd planned."

"You can say that again."

"It seems I have too much unfinished business."

"Does Monica know?"

"Yep. She's one hundred percent behind the decision."

"How's it going to work with you down here in Dorset and the Met in London?"

"I spoke to Webster briefly on the phone. He wasn't at all surprised at my decision to return. I guess I was the only one who thought I really would retire. He thinks he might have a solution that would mean I wouldn't need to relocate. I'd hate to leave Dorset. Alice and Faith are settled into their new schools and have made friends, and we love living by the coast."

"Well, it's good to have you back." Rayner smiled briefly. "I say that, yet I'm going to have to decide what I do next myself. Jen's going to need care for a while to come. I can't just up and leave her. I also don't want her transferred to another hospital, at least not yet. This hospital understands her condition, and the treatment and facilities here are first class."

"Depending on what happens in the meeting with Webster, perhaps we can figure something out."

Rayner spread jam on his fourth slice of toast, which he washed down with tea. When he'd finished, he got to his feet. "It's time I got back to Jen. It's been good to talk, James. Made me feel like I'm back in the land of the living, at least for a little while."

CHAPTER SEVENTY-SEVEN

Louise dabbed her eyes and blew her nose on a tissue as Cotton entered the interview room and took a seat opposite her. "Thank you for coming," said Louise. She clenched her hands on the table and sat forward.

Cotton placed a clear plastic cup of water on the table and pushed it towards her. "I must remind you, Louise, you remain under caution," Cotton said. "You're facing very serious charges. You have the right to have your solicitor present."

Louise nodded. "Yes, I understand. I don't need my solicitor. I just want to talk to you."

"Go ahead. I'm listening." Cotton sat back in her chair and folded her arms. She thought about how, if the knife used on Alex had been a few inches either way, Louise would be facing a murder charge.

Louise cleared her throat and tried to control her wavering voice. "It isn't how it looks. I didn't hurt Alex."

"You didn't stab him in the stomach?"

"No."

"The stab wound, and the stitches required, would

suggest otherwise. Are you telling me that when the lab's finished analysing the blood on your clothes, it won't match Alex's? What about your bloody prints on the knife? I suppose Alex is lying – is that what you're saying?"

"He came to my house. He threatened me. Told me he'd kill me if I spoke to you again."

"So, you stabbed him?"

"No," said Louise. She looked down at the table.

"That doesn't sound very convincing to me."

"I'm exhausted," said Louise.

"What I don't understand is if Alex is as bad as you say he is, and you're frightened of him, then why let him into your home in the first place? I mean, you told me I should stay away from him. That I was in danger. Yet, he comes to your home and you let him in. Why?"

"I… I… I…" stammered Louise. She looked down at the table again.

"This whole routine of yours is getting very tiresome, Louise. I know you were charged with assaulting Alex in the past. I've seen the report. Those charges were subsequently dropped when Alex refused to press charges. You've got away with assault once; it won't happen a second time, I can promise you that."

"You're not listening to me," said Louise.

"I'm looking at the facts."

"No, you're not."

"Are you telling me how to do my job?"

"You're not doing your job. You're listening to *him*."

"It seems everyone else is to blame except you, Louise."

Louise smashed her clenched fists down hard on the table. It shook and her voice boomed. "For fuck's sake, why won't you listen? I'm the victim." Her eyes were wide with frustration.

Cotton sat back and stared at Louise. She let the

outburst hang in the air for a moment. "There it is. It seems you've found your voice, Louise. That's quite a temper you have."

Louise gathered her thoughts. "The truth is," said Louise, softly now, "I love Alex. I can't help myself. I forgive him. Then I hate myself when the monster inside him returns." Louise started picking at the table, her nail clawing at a chip in the surface. "You see, I love the good, kind Alex. The attentive, gentle, tender Alex. That's who came to my house. He's the one I let into my home. I won't lie. A part of me is jealous. I wonder if he really has changed. I'd hate to think he's changed, and it's you that gets him and not me. You don't know the good Alex like I know him."

"Why don't you tell me what happened? The truth."

Louise stopped scratching at the table and wiped it over with her hand. She looked up at Cotton and sighed plaintively.

"Alex told me I was to stay away from the two of you. That he wanted to keep you. That you were special. That you were his and nobody would come between you. If anyone tried, they'd regret it. I could see he meant it. The way he said it scared me. Like you were his possession."

Louise tucked her hair behind her ear, tilted her head and looked Cotton in the eye. "That's when he took the knife out of the drawer. I thought he was going to kill me, but he turned the knife on himself. He held the tip of the blade to his shirt, and then he pressed the blade hard and pushed it in. He looked at me the whole time. I swear, I didn't touch him."

"Your bloody prints are on the knife," said Cotton.

"I must have moved the knife with blood on my hands. I don't remember; I was trying to stop his bleeding. I took a tea towel and pressed it to the wound."

"You realise that doesn't make any sense. Why would he stab himself? He might have bled to death."

"Don't you see? He wants it to look like I'm the crazy one. He doesn't want anyone to believe me. But you must believe me."

Cotton shook her head. "Alex claims he was at the house to ask you to move on. To give him his life back. That you didn't want to talk about it on the doorstep. That you insisted he come inside to talk. And that once he was inside, you became abusive. Screamed at him in a jealous rage. He says he tried to leave and you then came at him with the knife. That you stabbed him. Then, shocked by what you'd done, you made him swear to say he'd accidently stabbed himself. That you'd only call an ambulance once he agreed." Cotton watched Louise's reaction closely. "Does that version of events ring any bells?"

"Christ almighty, he's got you wrapped around his finger. It doesn't matter what I say, does it? You've fallen for him, and you're so focused on your happy-ever-after that you can't see the truth."

"What I see is someone who manipulates and bullies to get what she wants, and when she doesn't get it, she lashes out. I only wish this was my case, but it's not. If it were, I'd be pushing for attempted murder. I'm going to be making sure Alex is free of you once and for all. He won't get scared this time, and he won't withdraw the charges. I'll give him all the support he needs. He deserves his life back; he deserves to be happy. And as for you… Alex is going to make sure everyone sees you for who you really are. He's going to expose your lies."

Cotton got up and walked out without looking back.

Louise thumped the table with her fists then swiped the clear plastic cup of water off it. The water splashed across the floor and up the wall. She yelled after Cotton. "You have no idea what's coming. No idea at all."

CHAPTER SEVENTY-EIGHT

I returned to the quayside and looked out across the water to Brownsea Island. It was early evening and the sun was still strong, warming my body as I watched boats queuing before the bridge was raised.

Behind me, a row of impressive gleaming motorcycles belonging to an enthusiasts' club lined the street. Passers-by stopped and pointed. The owners lined the low wall while enjoying refreshments and chatting.

The scene looked different to when I had been here last, when the music festival had been in full swing. I thought about Jessica, who only days before had performed to an audience that for the first and only time had included her father. I thought about Fischer and the choices he had made, which had finally led to his being murdered by Barton. Barton himself had now been charged with the murders of both his partner, Donny Dodd, and Fischer. Investigations were ongoing into all the murders committed by Barton and Dodd, including those of Timothy Spicer, Judy Primmer, a PC and a witness to the crime.

I thought about Moon during her interviews; she had appeared genuinely grief-stricken by Fischer's death. She hadn't seemed to care that she would be charged with aiding and abetting his escape.

"Penny for your thoughts." I turned to find Lyle eating an ice cream. She took out the chocolate flake, scooped ice cream onto the end of it and bit it off. She was a brunette this time, and her hair was wavy. She wore a tweed jacket and blue jeans. "I'm leaving for a while. A celebration, if you will. Cuba has been calling me. Sienna has never been, and I want to show her the romance of the country. Also, the mojitos and daiquiris are to die for." She tossed her ice cream into the sea and wiped her hands on a tissue. "We'll send you a postcard."

Seeing her shocked me, and I had only one thought on my mind. "Are we good? I mean, is the threat against my family over?" I sank my hands into my jacket pockets, where I felt a canister of pepper spray and zip-ties.

"You didn't fulfil your end of the bargain, did you, James?"

"I was never going to kill him, you know that." My grip tightened on the pepper spray. "Answer the question."

"James, my love, how could I ever harm your family? I'd hate to see that handsome face of yours sad." She reached over and stroked my cheek. "Your family are safe. In fact, Sienna and I are looking forward to meeting Baby Hardy. Sienna is particularly excited; she's getting more than a little broody herself."

I sighed inwardly with relief and eased off the pepper spray.

"I know you want to arrest me, James. Put me in a cell, throw away the key, blah, blah, blah. I'm sure you're considering it this very second. I will admit, I have been naughty in the past, but now, thanks to you, that's all behind me. Arresting me would be pointless. Not only will it ruin our burgeoning friendship, which I hope will one day become romantic – a girl has to dream – but I have friends in very powerful places. I say 'friends,' but their influence is mostly bought with blackmail, threats or bribes. Let's gloss over that, shall we? So, you see, it's better we keep the status quo."

"We can't meet like this anymore. You know that, don't you?"

Lyle looked taken aback. "If you feel that way, you won't want to hear my proposal. Sienna will be deeply disappointed. She's giddy at the idea."

"I really don't want to hear it."

Lyle smiled and tossed her hair. "Yes, you do."

"No, I don't," I insisted.

"Yes, you do. I can see it in your eyes. They twinkle when you're excited. You do, James. I'll be quick. Just don't say anything now. Think about it." Lyle prepared herself before continuing. She wanted to contain the smile on her face before going on but was finding it hard. "Okay, here goes. When it comes time to choosing godparents, I want it to be known that Sienna and I wouldn't be opposed to the idea. I hope you'll consider it and don't reject the idea out of hand. There's a lot to be said for having a wealthy godmother like me."

Before I could respond, Faith came bounding up behind Lyle. She clung to me and stared at the stranger I was talking to. I looked past Lyle and could see Monica, Mum and Alice heading our way.

Lyle smiled at Faith and said in a Scottish accent, "Aren't you bonnie? I was just asking your daddy here for directions to the town centre. I seem to have gotten myself a wee bit lost. Perhaps you know the way, lassie?"

Faith stood up straight and pointed down the road

towards the roundabout. "It's that way," she said. "There are signs down on the corner."

"You're a clever little thing, aren't you? That way, is it? Very good. Thank you." She looked at me and said, "Please think on it, James." Without looking back, Lyle headed off in the direction of the town centre.

Faith looked at me quizzically. "What did she mean, Daddy? Think about what?"

"Nothing. She was saying how beautiful Scotland is and how we should visit," I lied.

"Found yourself a girlfriend, have you?" said Monica, coming up beside me.

"Hardly. She was a tourist, looking for directions," I said.

"She was Scottish," said Faith. "She sounded funny."

"We'd sound funny to them if we were in Scotland," said Alice.

"Who'd like a fish and chip supper?" said Mum. "I'm buying."

"Yes, please, Nana!" Alice and Faith each grabbed one of Mum's hands and started telling her what they'd like. I held Monica's hand, and we all walked towards our favourite chip shop near the lifting bridge. For the first time in a long time, the knot in my chest had gone. I felt as though ghosts from the past had left me and unanswered questions had been resolved.

I squeezed Monica's hand and kissed her.

"How's my man?" asked Monica.

"Happy. How's my woman?"

"Happy." She stroked the baby bump. "Getting bigger by the day."

"More of you to love."

"You can say that again."

I went to say it again and she stopped me by putting

her hand over my mouth. "It's okay; you don't need to repeat it. I know I'm big. I wasn't trying to encourage you."

"I was going to say I love you."

"Yeah, sure you were."

"I was."

"Okay. You can say that. I like hearing that."

I put my arm around Monica and squeezed her to me. "I love you," I said. Then added, "Especially now there's so much more of you to love."

"You cheeky…" Monica took a playful swipe at me, and I had to move quickly to duck.

CHAPTER SEVENTY-NINE

Cotton tucked away her phone and took her ice cream. "Thank you."

"You'd better be quick. These are melting already," said Alex. He handed her a napkin, which she wrapped around the cone.

"Mmm, that's nice. Didn't they have mint choc chip?"

"Yes, but I was having butterscotch and I thought you might prefer it. It's good, isn't it?"

"Very good." Cotton licked around the cone to catch the drips. "Where shall we go next? The primates are that way and the reptiles are that way." She pointed.

"I don't mind. Primates?"

"Primates it is. How's your side holding up? If you need a rest, we can stop for a while."

"Sore, but okay. Let's take a break after we've seen the monkeys. Perhaps get a bite to eat?" Alex opened the map of the zoo. "It looks like there's a restaurant over by the monkeys. I'll buy you lunch." Alex pointed to a sign beside the path, and they began walking towards the primate house.

Cotton chuckled and gave Alex a sideways glance.

"What?" asked Alex with a chuckle. "What are you smiling about?"

"You. You're going all out. It's nice. I'm having a great time; I like being spoiled. Thank you."

"You're welcome, Miss Emma Cotton. I've been looking forward to today. I want today to be memorable."

"Me too. It's nice to take a break and find time to clear my mind. Think about things other than work."

"Is that who was on the phone? I noticed you on the phone when I was getting the ice cream."

"Spying on me, were you?" teased Cotton.

"No," said Alex, sharply. He stopped walking, his eyes fixed on Cotton's.

"I was just pulling your leg," said Cotton. "It was Hardy, the detective chief inspector I told you about. He's a nice guy. You'll like him. He had a couple of questions about the case we were on."

"I see," said Alex. He forced a smile.

"You'll get used to it. It's what we detectives do. Long unsocial hours, never a dull moment. Apart from the paperwork, that is. That's a chore."

Alex finished his ice cream, wiped his mouth and hands on his napkin and dropped it in a bin. "Ever thought of doing something different? Something nine-to-five?"

"God, no. It's all I ever wanted, since I was young. I'm doing my dream job. Yeah, it's crap sometimes, but the highs… There's nothing like it."

"Married, is he, Hardy?"

"Was. He has two daughters. He's in a relationship. They're expecting."

"You and him? You know. Any history I should know about?"

"What do you mean? No. I mean, he's... no. We're colleagues and friends, nothing more. He's not like that. You'll understand when you meet him."

Alex and Cotton reached an enclosure where an orangutan sat behind the glass watching them. Cotton waved and the orangutan placed its hand flat on the glass. "Sad to see them in there. I know they're safe and fed and warm and all that, but it would be nice to think they could just live in their own habitat and do whatever it is orangutans like to do."

"I'm sure they're happy," said Alex. "They don't need to go searching for food, and they get way more leisure time here than in the wild. Pretty cushy life."

Cotton and Alex moved along to some small golden monkeys that sat in the corner holding each other, their heads twisting and turning at every sound.

Cotton's phone started ringing.

"Leave it," said Alex. "It's your day off."

"I can't," said Cotton. She took out her phone.

Alex took the phone out of Cotton's hand and turned it off. "Yes, you can."

"What the hell are you doing? That might be important."

"It also might not be. Today is also important. You and I are spending time together. It's better if it's just the two of us. Without interruption. Don't you agree?"

Cotton took her phone back and turned it on. "In an ideal world, perhaps. But I'm a detective inspector in the serious crimes unit. It's vital I can be reached. Don't ever do that again."

"I'll tell you what. You make your call. I'll meet you in the restaurant." Alex turned and walked away.

Cotton felt herself go hot all over and her ears tingle. *What just happened?* For a fraction of a second, she wondered whether she was being selfish. "Alex?" she called. She watched him reach the restaurant and go inside. She looked at her phone. The missed call was from Hardy. The phone vibrated as a text message came through: *Sorry to call. All sorted. Enjoy the zoo. Never smile at a crocodile. Will leave you in peace. H*

Too late for that, thought Cotton. She tucked the phone in her pocket and headed to the restaurant to try to salvage the day.

CHAPTER EIGHTY

It was a surreal feeling to sign in as a visitor at New Scotland Yard. It was a place where, for too many years, I'd spent more time than at my own family home. Yet, here I was, ready to ask to return to the life I thought I'd left behind.

I was escorted through familiar hallways. There were new faces I didn't recognise, as well as the familiar faces of friends and colleagues. I passed the old offices, hearing sounds and smelling odours that awoke dormant memories. During my absence, the Metropolitan Police Service had continued unabated without me.

"Come in, come in," said Chief Webster. My old boss looked tired and older, his hair more receding and greyer than I remembered. We shook hands and Webster returned to his desk, easing himself into his well-worn leather chair. A patch of stuffing in the arm hung out, a small detail I'd forgotten. We'd seen each other a few weeks ago at my father's funeral, but we continued the small talk as though we hadn't. "You're looking well, considering. How are the family? Are they coping okay after the fire?"

"They're doing fine, thank you, sir. We're all staying at my mother's home at the moment. Naturally, Mum's spoiling them, so for the time being it's all a great adventure for them. There's talk of making it a permanent arrangement. Only time will tell."

"How does Monica feel about that?"

"With the baby on the way, I get the feeling she welcomes the idea. Many hands making light work and all that."

"Good, good." He picked at the chair's stuffing. "I've spoken to Rayner; he seems more optimistic. Of course, I told him to take as much time as he needs. His wife has to be his first concern right now."

I nodded. "He hit rock bottom. He thought he was going to lose Jenny. It was touch and go for a while, but she's getting stronger. So is he. I can see the big man returning."

Webster eyes appraised me. "What's this all about, Hardy, truthfully? I know what you told me on the phone – you're missing the job and all that. If that's all it is, then let me offer some friendly advice. Give it another six months. If you still feel the same way, we'll talk again."

"Nice try, sir." I could see he didn't mean a word of it. "My mind's made up, sir. I took a leave of absence, and now I need to find a way to get back to case work."

"It was a little more than a leave of absence, James. You as good as retired. Early retirement, you called it."

"What can I say? Like a champion boxer, I'm ready to come out of retirement and get back in the ring."

"I have cases I could hand you today, but I'm worried you're not ready. I just don't want you back for the wrong reasons. After Fischer, the house fire, and what happened to Rayner and Jenny, how can I be sure your head is in the right place? Give it more time. Go home. Finish writing that bloody book on psychological profiling you keep promising to finish."

"I didn't see it at the time, but all I needed was distance," I insisted. "I didn't take enough time after Helena's death. I never dealt with my grief. I just worked, and when that wasn't enough to blot out the pain, I worked more and harder. I've now had time to grieve, and that's given me perspective. I'm a different man to the one I was back then. A lot has changed. I'm a different man," I said again. "It's time I got back to what I do best, sir. Give me a case that needs looking into. I can stop killers. I can save lives."

"From what I gathered during our phone call, you want your old job back without the upheaval of moving the family back to London; is that what you're telling me?" Webster tugged at his earlobe and looked at me out of the corner of his eye. "You're sure this is what you want?"

"Yes, sir. Definitely, sir."

"Luckily, I'm owed a few favours. Do this job long enough and everyone and their dog wants something from you, which leaves you with credit for times like these."

"There's one other thing, sir."

"You've got to be kidding," said Webster, his bushy eyebrows raised so high they almost touched his hairline. "You're not kidding, are you?"

I smiled at his dramatic exasperation. "It's Rayner. He's going to be in Dorset indefinitely while Jenny gets her treatment. I'd like him to be reassigned, when he's ready. We make a great team. I'd also like to request that Heidi Hamilton, our forensic pathologist, be able to consult on my cases. She's the best; just don't tell her I said that. It'll mean a bit more travel for her, but I know she likes to get out of the lab."

"Anything else?" asked Webster with a touch of

humour in his voice. "A chauffeur, maybe? Front-row seats at Wimbledon?"

"No, sir," I said. "It's a generous offer, but not right now. Just access to Hamilton and for Rayner to join me."

"I thought you'd request Rayner. When Rayner's ready, he'll report to you. Hamilton shouldn't be a problem, as far as I'm concerned. Though she has a busy workload, so I'll leave you to discuss the finer points with her." Webster took a file from a tray on his desk and slid it in front of me. "The way I see this working is that I cherry-pick the cases. For the time being at least, they'll be cold cases or investigations that have lost momentum or come to a dead end."

I opened the file. Crime scene photos of a murdered family.

Webster made a list on a piece of paper. "I'll get copies of everything else we have on this case forwarded to wherever you want them sent."

"Thank you, sir."

Webster tapped the end of his pen on the note pad. "What you have in front of you is a file from the case Rayner was working on. Some sick bastard is murdering families with twin children; the twins are of the identical type. Maybe the pair of you, working together, will have a breakthrough. I'll expect to be kept updated no differently to when you had an office down the hall. I'm sticking my neck out for you here, James, and I expect results. It's only a two-hour drive from here to Dorset, so if I need to, I'll drive down and kick your bloody arse. Understood?"

"Understood. Thank you, sir."

"Good. Now push off, before I regret it."

I got up, we shook hands, and I headed for the door before Webster changed his mind.

"Detective Chief Inspector," said Webster.

I reached the door and turned. "Yes, sir?"

"It's good to have you back."

"It's great to be back. Thank you, sir."

CHAPTER EIGHTY-ONE

It had been nearly two weeks since my quayside conversation with Lyle. If she wanted me dead, she'd have attempted it by now. Life began to adjust to a rhythm as close to normal as my life ever gets.

I'd spent the morning at the hospital visiting Jenny. Both she and Rayner were in good spirits. Privately, Rayner had told me that, though tearful at times, she was coming to terms with her injuries. Both she and Rayner were open about the challenges that lay ahead and were ready to face them together. Whenever I saw Jenny, I had a nagging sense of guilt that I knew would never leave me. Through her smiles and laughter, I sensed a deep sadness in her eyes, and it cut me to the quick.

In the afternoon, I started looking at the case involving the murders of the families with identical twins; little by little, Rayner had been getting more involved. I was working out of the garage at Mum's when he visited, and I closed my laptop and stood up to take a break when he arrived.

Nana Hardy, as Rayner fondly called my mum, was

like a second mother to him. It had been that way since we were kids, and she spoke to him in a way only a mother could, dishing out tough love to ensure he looked after himself, behaved responsibly and showed respect where it was due.

We went into the house together, and she shooed the two of us into the kitchen and handed Rayner a heaping plate of food left over from our family lunch earlier.

"You eat that, Gabriel. There's more if you want it. Once you've finished that, I want you to shower, wash your hair and shave. You look a mess. I bought you some new clothes; they're on the chair there." She pointed across the room where a bag from High and Mighty sat on an armchair. "You need to start taking care of yourself. If you can't take care of yourself, then how are you going to be there for Jenny and the baby when it arrives? Hmm? I know it's hard." She reached up and squeezed his shoulder. "I can only imagine what you and Jenny are going through, but you need to be strong. You need to be thinking about the future, and that means getting back to work too. It'll be good for your mind to be thinking about other things. Have you called Chief Webster lately?"

Rayner shook his head.

"Well, you need to do that. He needs to be kept up to date. Do it today, after you've showered."

"I will," said Rayner. He scooped sausage and onion gravy and mash into his mouth. The man mountain towered over my mother.

"Please sit down at the table while you're eating, Gabriel. Otherwise, you might get indigestion." I watched the big man do as he was asked. I secretly winked at him and he grinned.

After eating, he showered, changed and called the chief as instructed. He and I then spent a couple of hours going over the twins' murder investigation. We analysed the case file Webster had given me, and Rayner brought me up to speed with the investigation as he saw it. It was good to see the old Rayner back for a while as we tossed theories back and forth. But Jenny was never far from his mind, and I could see he was soon itching to get back to the hospital.

"Give her our love, won't you?" I said.

Alice and Faith were playing outside as I walked Rayner to his car.

"Sure thing," said Rayner. He knelt beside the girls. "Which one of you can give me the biggest, strongest, squeeziest, most monster hug?"

"Me," said the girls in unison.

They both grabbed him and ferociously threw their arms around him, crushing him as tightly as they could. Their laughter turned to squeals of excitement as, with one tucked under each arm, he got to his feet and began running around in circles.

"I love you two," said Rayner, as he finally set them down again and looked at them properly. I could see he was getting emotional as he let his guard down for a moment. "Come here, you rascals," he said, "and let me give you a proper hug. Now, can I have a second one from each of you to take back to Jenny?" The girls leaned in, beaming, and squashed him again.

"Are you coming back tomorrow?" asked Alice. "I'm making an apple crumble with Nana."

"Apple crumble? That's my favourite. How could I resist?"

Faith was uncharacteristically quiet.

"Are you all right, Faithy?" said Rayner.

Faith nodded glumly. "My drawings for the baby got burned in the house fire. I wanted to give them to Jenny when the baby was born."

"Oh, sweetheart," said Rayner, his voice breaking a little. He reached out and pulled her close. "I'll tell you what. How about tomorrow you and I work on some new drawings together. I'm pretty good with a crayon, but I bet you could teach me a thing or two."

Faith beamed. "I'll get everything ready." She wrapped her arms around Rayner's neck, squeezed and kissed him, then ran into the house to start setting things up.

Alice and I watched Rayner drive away. She held onto me as we both waved him off. "He's different, somehow," said Alice. "Still Rayner, but not. Does that make sense?"

Alice's insight and empathy never ceased to amaze me. "You're right," I said. "Life changes us all. Just when you think you understand how it all works, something comes along and you have to rethink it. But he'll be fine. We all will, sweetheart."

I put my arm around my daughter and kissed the top of her head as we walked back to the house.

DCI Hardy will return soon.

If you've enjoyed this book, please help spread the word by leaving a review on Amazon. Your review can be as short or as long as you like. Reviews help bring the Hardy novels to the attention of other readers who may not have heard of DCI James Hardy – or me!

If you've never left a book review before, it's easy: simply write whatever is true for you – for example, your experiences as you were reading, your impressions of the characters, what you thought of the writing itself, and who else the story might appeal to. Your words will be a beacon of sorts for others like us, who love thrillers.

Many thanks,

Jay Gill

ALSO BY JAY GILL

Knife & Death

The body of a young college student is discovered in the River Thames, and DCI James Hardy is horrified to learn that the murdered woman was a family friend.

As he begins to investigate, he discovers that Anya, the victim's flatmate, is missing, seemingly on the run for her life. Realising that she could be the key to catching the killer, Hardy races against time to track down Anya before the killer does.

As the ugly truth behind the investigation unfolds, Hardy's own family come under threat. With two young daughters to protect and an investigation that twists and turns, frustrating him at every step, Hardy finds himself pushed to the limit.

Can he protect his family? Will Hardy be in time to save Anya? With his every move under scrutiny, how will Hardy handle the pressure and solve the investigation?

Walk in the Park
Short Thriller

When a close friend of DCI James Hardy is murdered, the detective questions whether taking the law into his own hands could ever be justified.

Detective James Hardy is enjoying a rare day out with his two young daughters when he makes the mistake of answering his phone. It's his boss.

A young mother, out walking her baby, has been murdered in broad daylight. The attack is followed quickly by a second terrifying, vicious assault on a young woman who is a dear friend of Hardy and his daughters.

Shaken and heartbroken, Hardy agrees to assist the team leading the investigation into a ruthless murderer dubbed *The Regent's Park Ripper*.

Knowing that in all likelihood the killer will soon strike again, the investigating team must put aside their differences, and work day and night to prevent more senseless deaths.

Over the course of the harrowing investigation, Hardy must constantly challenge his own very personal need for revenge. But all of that may change when he unexpectedly finds himself face-to-face with the suspect in a deadly confrontation that may change Hardy's life, and those of his loved ones, forever.

Angels

After the brutal murder of his wife by a crazed drug-seeker, Detective Inspector James Hardy walks away from his career as a Scotland Yard homicide detective. He has found love again, and, together with his two young daughters, he's making a fresh start in a small seaside town.

With his new career as a consultant taking off and the demons of the past behind him, Hardy's life couldn't be better.

But the peace is about to be shattered.

When a series of shocking murders take place in the seaside town, Hardy is contacted by local detective inspector Emma Cotton for advice. As Cotton investigates the killings, Hardy learns the disturbing crimes have all the hallmarks of a serial killer linked to his past.

The notorious Kelly Lyle, known as The Mentor, has surfaced again, and has Hardy and his family in her sights. As she embarks on her latest bloody campaign of murder and revenge, she rips apart the detective's new life – and reveals a dark secret that shatters everything Hardy believed to be true about his wife's death.

Hardy balks at being forced out of early retirement, but whether he likes it or not, the killer appears determined to draw him back into a world he wants to leave behind.

Knowing it will take something monumental to catch his attention, the killer raises the stakes and abducts someone Hardy loves more than life itself.

Is Hardy about to lose everything he's fought so hard to keep?

Hardy's only choice is to work with DI Emma Cotton

to discover the hard truth behind the killer's motives. If they play the killer's game, they might be in time to stop a tragedy beyond comprehension.

Hard Truth

DCI James Hardy's new-found peace is rocked when Kelly Lyle 'the Mentor' returns.

During her bloody campaign of murder, she rips apart the detective's new life and reveals a secret that shatters everything Hardy believed to be true about his wife's death.

James Hardy has walked away from his career as a Scotland Yard homicide detective. He has found love again, and, together with his two young daughters, he's making a fresh start in a small seaside town.

With his new career as a consultant taking off and the demons of the past behind him, Hardy's life couldn't be better.

But the peace is about to be shattered.

When a series of shocking murders take place in the seaside town, Hardy is contacted by local detective inspector Emma Cotton for advice. Hardy learns the disturbing crimes have all the hallmarks of a serial killer linked to his past.

Hardy balks at being forced out of early retirement, but whether he likes it or not, the killer appears determined to draw him back into a world he wants to leave behind.

Knowing it will take something monumental to catch his attention, the killer raises the stakes and abducts someone Hardy loves more than life itself.

Is Hardy about to lose everything he's fought so hard to keep?

Hardy's only choice is to work with DI Emma Cotton to discover the hard truth behind the killer's motives. If they play the killer's game, they might be in time to stop a tragedy beyond comprehension.

All Jay's books are available on Amazon.

ABOUT THE AUTHOR

Born in Dorset, southern England, Jay Gill moved to Buckinghamshire where he worked in the printing industry, primarily producing leaflets and packaging for the pharmaceutical industry. After several years of the London commute, and with his first child about to start school, he realised it was high time for a change and moved back to the south coast of England. This change freed up time for him to write the detective stories he dreamed of one day publishing.

Safe to say, he's caught the writing bug in earnest now. With three Hardy novels and a novella under his belt, a growing "family" of characters both good and heinous, and a host of exciting new ideas bouncing around in his head, Jay busily juggles his writing and family life and is hard at work on the next instalment in the DCI James Hardy series of thrillers.

Want to hear what he's working on, and enjoy DCI Hardy bonus material?

I *occasionally* send newsletters, usually once a quarter. I talk about what I'm working on, new releases and other bits of news relating to the DCI James Hardy series.

It's easy to join my mailing list, and you won't get spammed (I promise):

1. Receive news, announcements and updates on new releases before anyone else.
2. Read a profile of DCI James Hardy called: Who is James Hardy? *(Exclusive to my mailing list, you can't get this anywhere else.)*
3. Access to bonus scenes from *every* book in the Hardy series: For example, you'll find out what happens to the nasty piece of work, Melvin Barclay - featured in Hard Truth - when Kelly Lyle catches up with him again. *It isn't pretty!* There is also a scene from INFERNO which has been described as taut and nerve-shredding. *(Exclusive to my mailing list, you can't get it anywhere else.)*

Sign up for updates at www.jaygill.net/newsletter

Printed in Great Britain
by Amazon